BRIDE
by ritual

THE
Underworld

MAGGIE COLE

PULSE PRESS INC

To all my Romance
Addicts who've
thought they wanted
power but only needed
a love that could
survive blood and fire,
this one's for you.

XOXO—

Maggie

Mafia Wars universe

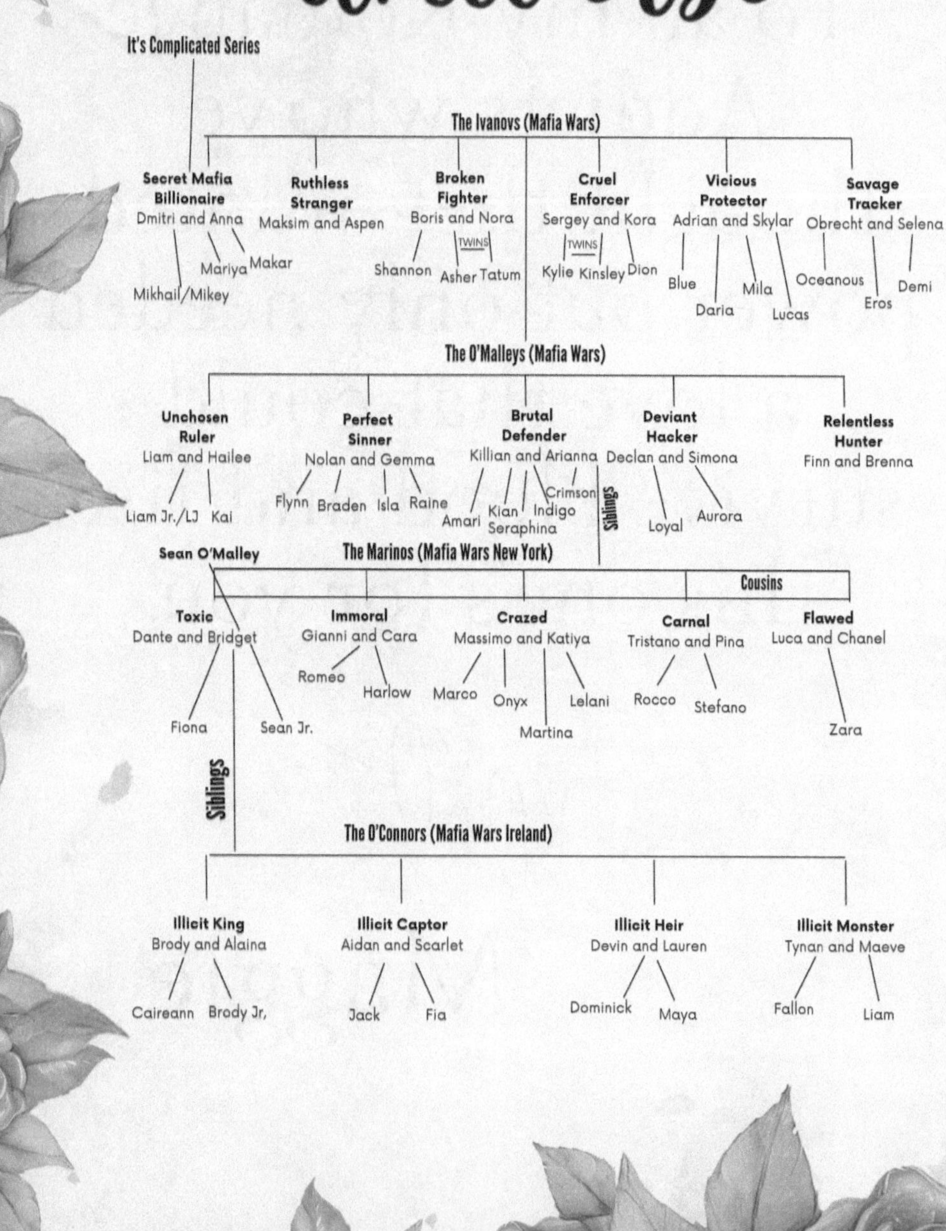

THE
Underworld

Bride by Initiation
Zara and Sean Jr.

Siblings

Bride by Coronation
Fiona and Kirill

Bride by Ritual
Valentina and Brax

TWINS

Willow   River

Zavier

Brax O'Malley

Prologue

A father is supposed to be a compass, but I grew up learning how to navigate without one. There were only a handful of times he wasn't in prison. When he would get out, he spent his time inebriated with my mother, high on whatever they could get their hands on.

By the time I was eight, I had learned how to be a master of the streets, relying only on myself and taking calculated risks.

Then everything changed. One day, a mint-condition, black 1985 Camaro IROC-Z sports car pulled up to the curb. A bald man, built like a brick house, oozed authority like I'd never seen. From several storefronts away, I could hear the chill in his Irish accent.

A new challenge emerged when I was fifteen. My gut screamed to stay back, but my ego wouldn't let me. I made the error of pickpocketing him, and soon found myself shoved in his car, my wrists zip-tied, and racing through Chicago.

Finn O'Malley turned out to be more than my captor. He became the father figure I'd never had. And joining the O'Malley clan was the first luxury I ever wanted in my life. He showed me what family meant, why loyalty was important, and how hard work wasn't enough.

Then he took it a step further. Before I even was initiated into the clan, he vouched for me and told me I was an O'Malley so I might as well legally change my name.

Brenna insisted I get a private teacher, even though I never sat a day in school. She made me learn to read and write, practice proper hygiene, and taught me how to cook and do laundry.

Finn took me to the O'Malley gym, showed me how to put on muscle, and put me in the ring. He patiently taught me how to work on cars and fix things around the house. And he shielded me from the family business until I begged so much that he finally caved.

His biggest lesson revolved around his number one rule. You had to be smarter than those around you at all times. The minute you didn't use your brain was the moment your enemy would use it to circle and pounce.

Over the years, I lived by those rules. Life was better than I ever dreamed. But then I broke the rule. I didn't use my head, and now, I'm inside a twisted secret world. My best friend Sean and his sister Fiona are there as well. And while the cult tries to convince you it's your choice to join, it's not. When life or death is the only option, survival wins.

Every step inside the Underworld has consequences. And just like my initiation, I've been roped into marrying Valentina. She wants a seat at the table, and her only chance is to marry me.

So I'll play along. For the time being, I'll have fun with my little Minx. But once I take my seat, I'll figure out how to destroy the Underworld. I'll save Sean and Fiona.

Everyone else can be dammed, including Valentina.

Valentina Abruzzo

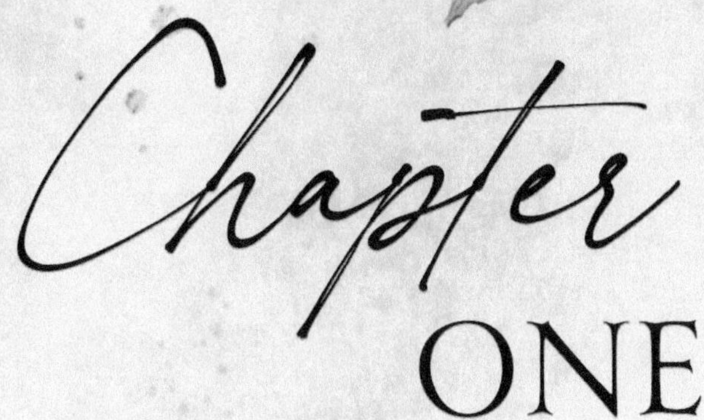

Chapter ONE

Voices roar, fusing into a single sound bouncing off the concrete floor and straight up my spine. Thick air is trapped between my lungs and buzzing ribs. A high, relentless whistle pulses between my eardrums, pressing behind my eyes and stealing the space where thoughts should be.

Thirteen men no longer breathe. Sean O'Malley barely stands. He's fighting for air, bloody and swollen beyond recognition.

I turn to leave when three long beeps cause the hairs on my arms to rise, along with panic and curiosity. I grab my cell phone out of my purse.

Security: Code Red.

My lungs scream for fresh air as the atmosphere turns more stifling. I peer over the crowd and watch the security team of four drag a tall, broad-shouldered man into the ring. He attempts to fight them, and for a moment, I think he might overpower them, until a knife gets placed next to his throat. The back of his body goes taut.

John breaks the deafening silence. His Irish accent booms, "You were told not to bring anyone here."

"I didn't bring him," Sean claims.

"Then how did he get here?"

Sean stays silent.

"You weren't careful," John accuses.

Sean stands taller.

John takes a pocket knife out of his jeans and opens it. He holds it in front of Sean's face. "You do the honors."

"The honors of what?" Sean questions, his expression hardening.

John orders, "If you didn't bring him, and you don't want him here, then get rid of him. Slit his throat."

Sean lifts his beaten body even higher. He roars, "No. I vouch for this man."

A chilling gasp fills the crowd.

John sarcastically chuckles, "You vouch for him?"

"Yeah. I vouch for him," Sean repeats.

Tension mounts.

I hold my breath, unsure what should happen in this case. No one staring in the face of death has ever vouched for anyone. Especially not anyone as important to the Underworld as Sean O'Malley Sr.'s offspring.

Byrne interjects in a stern but respectful voice, "He hit thirteen. He won the bid."

John snaps his head toward him. "He didn't follow directions."

"I did," Sean argues.

John jabs him in the chest. "You were careless."

"He still hit thirteen," Byrne insists.

The crowd takes over, chanting in a deafening tone, "Thirteen! Thirteen! Thirteen!"

Another alarm sounds. This time, it rings for five full seconds.

Crap!

Another hush falls over the crowd. I hand my clutch to my assistant, Cassian. I angrily push through the membership, debating over what route to take.

Someone's going to pay, and it better not be me.

Sacred rules exist in the Underworld. Everyone has a job, and if you fail at your duties, people get hurt. Often they die. So there will be consequences for whoever is responsible for this security breach and possibly for me.

This was my event to manage and control.

The Omni, trust me, I tell myself in order to calm my flipping stomach, but it's a lie. Until you get a seat at the table, your every move is watched and judged.

The crowd parts. I touch my ruby-encrusted red mask over my eyes and nose to ensure it's secure. I lift my chin and saunter through the small path and stop in front of Sean. I grab his chin and remark, "You're the spitting image of him."

A brief flick of emotion erupts on his face. It's gone so fast I barely caught it. He asks, "You knew him?"

I shake my head, replying, "No. It was before our time. But my parents did, and I've seen photos."

"Who are your parents?" he questions.

Amused, I almost break out in a smile, then harshly reprimand, "That's not a question for you to ask."

"What question should I ask?" he fires back.

I stare at him for a moment, taking in every characteristic I can see through the swelling and blood. I offer, "They said you have your father's humor. I guess they were right."

He blurts out, "Some say I do."

I nod. "I suppose you do."

I study him further, then step closer. I curl my finger, lean closer, and whisper in his ear, "Do you think your father's position allows you to not abide by the rules?"

He retreats and, in an apologetic but firm voice, answers, "No. I do not. I was careless coming here. I admit it. I was thinking about making it on time, and I apologize. It will never happen again. But I can assure you, I can vouch for this man."

He vouches.

Again.

What to do.

My heart races faster.

I should kill them both.

He's Sean Sr.'s offspring.

He's the Chosen One.

I ask, "Why do you have so much loyalty for him?"

Sean reaffirms, "I vouch for him."

I step back and glance toward the intruder.

Holy shit.

The back of his body, from afar, doesn't tell the whole story. He's got the kind of build forged from real labor, not vanity. His light brown hair is unruly, begging to be tamed. Dark, steady eyes with arrogance stare back at me, even though he's about to get sliced to pieces. And his challenging expression can't hide dimples that have no business existing on a jaw so sharp.

My gaze travels down his body, taking in his thick thighs and large bulge against his gray sweatpants. But the kicker lies in his hands.

They're enormous. There's no doubt they can break, lift, hold, ruin.

A small spark flickers in my chest. I'm unsure if it's a desire or a curious interest. There's one thing I know for sure.

A man like this is either a danger, a tool, or a problem masquerading as the opposite of what you want from him.

He doesn't flinch. To my surprise, his expression turns to a predatory stare.

I turn to Sean and blurt out, "Granted, he's sexy in a rough way, but so are others. Why are you vouching for him?"

Jesus. Why did I say that?

He doesn't hesitate, claiming, "I know who he is."

Naive little offspring.

Amused, I raise my brow. "You know who he is?"

"Yes."

"Ah. You're a foolish one."

"Why is that?"

I steal a quick glance at the intruder, already knowing he still has his provocative expression pinned on me, as if he doesn't care about the predicament he's in or the knife against his throat.

Ignoring the pulsing between my thighs, I turn back to Sean, warning, "You think you know people, but I can assure you, you do not."

The flicker reappears.

Adrenaline spikes, but I can't fully hide the sadness laced in my tone. "Ah. I see. I've spoken a truth, and you're unable to deny it."

He stands straighter, asserting, "I can vouch for this man, and I will not kill him. If you must, take my head and let him go."

Gasps fill the crowd.

I peer closer. *Who is this man to him that he's so loyal?*

I question, "You would rather be killed than kill him?"

Sean affirms, "I would rather you attempt to kill me."

My lips twitch. "Attempt?"

"Do you believe I'd go out without a fight?" he challenges.

He killed thirteen men and earned his spot.

It's his fault this stranger is here.

It's also a security breach.

Sean led him here.

Why do I not know who this intruder is if he's so important that Sean would die for him?

I finally make a decision. I smile and warn, "Those who vouch for the uninvited choose a different path."

Sean blurts out, "I don't understand what that means."

I can't help but take another look at the intruder. He's got the same consuming expression pinned on me. I curse myself for looking at him and turn my attention back to Sean, challenging, "Are you sure you want a different path, Sean O'Malley Jr.?"

He nods and shouts with conviction, "I vouch for this man."

The crowd gasps.

Good choice. It would be a waste to kill a man who looks like this.

It's not just his looks. It's how he holds himself up in the line of fire.

What am I saying?

The path will now change.

What will the Omni say?

Will I be blamed?

What's done is done.

I snap my fingers toward the stranger.

The men release him and push him toward Sean.

I take my time and give him another once-over. Unable to stop myself, I praise, "At least you vouch for a man who seems to have..." I tilt my head, letting my eyes wander, and continue, "Shall we say, benefits for the ladies?"

Sean reiterates, "I vouch for him."

Who is this man to him?

I step back. "Then he's your responsibility. Go home, Sean O'Malley Jr. Heal. Your bid is secure. But remember, you've selected another path."

I spin toward the crowd and shout, "He will now compete for an initiation with rings."

The crowd erupts, and the pitch oozes down my spine once more. I strut through the membership, toss daggers at the security team, and push through the exit.

My driver, Vito, stands next to the rear door. He opens it. "Ma'am."

I slide inside, not saying anything.

Cassian hands me my clutch and shuts the door. He opens the passenger door and gets in.

I demand, "Who was he?"

Cassian turns. His dark eyes fill with as much anger as I feel. "I don't know."

"It's your job to know, so I know," I seethe, right as Vito slams the driver's door shut.

"I'll find out," Cassian assures.

I hit the button for the divider window and pick up my phone. It rings once.

Kirill's heavy Russian accent fills the line. "Valentina."

"Did you see it?" I ask, my nerves filling with more fire.

"Yes."

I lick my lips, but my mouth is dry. "Why wasn't I given intel on him?"

"I can't answer that," Kirill states.

"You're the king," I remind him.

The line turns silent.

The SUV makes a sharp turn and accelerates. I close my eyes, asking again, "Why wasn't I informed?"

"You know the answer to that," Kirill answers.

I take several deep breaths to calm my insides, but new worries fill me. When I trust my voice, I declare, "It was another test from the Omni."

Kirill stays silent.

I swallow hard. "Did I pass?"

"Are you seated in your SUV heading home?" he questions, but it's not really one.

I release an anxious breath. "Yes."

"There's your answer."

I close my eyes again, leaning my head against the rest, allowing myself to feel the sense of relief for a moment.

Kirill interjects, "The path has now changed."

More anxiety hits me. "I know."

Several moments of deep silence pass.

I blurt out, "Maybe I should have had him killed?"

"That would have eliminated the Chosen One."

My heart thumps harder against my rib cage. "What is the new path?"

Kirill sighs. "Don't ask questions you know I can't answer. But when the time comes, you will be tested again."

I freeze.

The SUV swerves in and out of traffic.

"This is your cross to carry now, Valentina. The security leak, Sean's lack of following orders, the man you know nothing about..."

"Sean's disobedience shouldn't be on me. It's Byrne's job to make sure he obeys orders," I remind.

Kirill grunts.

"What does that mean?" I snap.

He scoffs. "Think about what you just said, Valentina. You're a smart woman. Put two and two together. What do you want?"

I dig my nails into my thigh, muttering, "A seat at the table."

"So who's responsible for everything?"

I try to clear my dry throat, but it doesn't help. My voice cracks, "I am."

He asserts, "That's right. If you want the seat, you have to prove you can handle every obstacle that comes your way. Now I've asked you before, but I'll ask you one last time. Are you sure you want a seat?"

"Yes," I say without hesitating.

"There are consequences to failing. This isn't a task I would want. I will allow you to back out, but you must do it right now," he offers.

I stay quiet.

He cautions, "There won't be another chance. Back out and be happy where you are, or go forward. You'll either gain a seat at the table or die trying."

Part of me screams to step back and be happy with my current level inside the Underworld. But I know myself. Until I earn the seat my parents held, I'll never rest. And what is happiness anyway? It's just an emotion for weak-minded people who don't want to see what's really going on in front of them.

I sit taller in my seat, declaring, "I want my seat, Kirill."

"Then your choice is made," he says in a sad voice.

"Don't get all excited for me," I snap. Kirill may be the king, but I'm his only friend. And he's the only person in the world I trust.

Still, that won't get me any passes. I have to earn my seat or I'll die. And I wouldn't put it past the Omni to make Kirill be the one to see to it I never take another breath.

"Like I said, you've made your choice," he repeats.

The SUV veers right and stops.

I glance out the window and hit the button for the divider window. "Why did we stop?"

Vito glances at me through the rearview mirror. "Orders, ma'am."

"Cassian?" I question.

He turns his head, his eyes full of questions. "I'm not allowed inside."

My gut drops. "Kirill?"

"Penthouse. Your handprint will work. You've got six hours," Kirill states and hangs up.

Six hours for what?

Vito opens my door. He reaches for my hand to help me out. "Ma'am."

I harden my gaze, take his hand, and get out of the SUV. I push through the gust of wind coming off Lake Michigan.

A young bellman opens the front door. "Ma'am." He nods and stares at me like he knows who I am.

Of course he does. I'm sure he's in the Underworld.

I don't give him another thought, ignore the security at the desk, and head toward the elevator. I push the button.

The doors open, I step inside, and press my palm against the screen. The sound of the metal shutting hits my ears, and the box smoothly rises.

The elevator opens, and I step into a large foyer, then past the front door. A beautiful great room boasts the Chicago skyline, black leather furniture, red accents, and freshly baked cookie scents.

Roaring flames fill the fireplace. I glance around, but no one is in the room. "Hello?" I call out, stepping toward the wall. I turn the button, but the fire doesn't get smaller.

Great.

"Hello? Anyone here?" I try again, strolling down the hallway and looking in rooms. It takes a while to get through the luxury penthouse, but I finally decide no one is here.

I return to the main room and take the bottle of champagne out of the ice bucket. It's melted into mostly water, due to the blazing fire. I pick up a flute and fill it. I drink most of it, trying to cool off, but it only makes me hotter. Still, I top it off and stand next to the glass, staring at the glow of the buildings, wishing I could open a window, but it's one solid piece of thick glass.

What am I doing here?

Six hours.

No answers come. I pace the family room, replaying the evening's events, getting angry all over again.

I studied everything the Omni gave me about Sean Jr. I memorized it until I could recite any fact in my sleep. It was over 100 pages, including supporting photos and other assets, and they only gave me 10 hours to review it. Still, I memorized it all.

Did I miss something?

I do a quick run-through in my head.

No, I didn't. I would have remembered.

A bead of sweat trickles down my face. I realize I'm still wearing my mask.

I pull it over my head, toss it on the table, and lean back, tousling my hair and trying to get the sweaty pieces not to stick to my neck.

A low whistle startles me.

I jump and spin.

The stranger from the fight stands in the doorway, his arms crossed, biceps straining against his T-shirt. An arrogant gaze wrapped in obsenity and promise slips down my body, turning the already-hot room into an uncomfortable inferno.

My heart beats wildly, beads of sweat trickle on my thighs, and every second he spends taking me in intensifies all of it.

He finally pins his dark eyes on me, taunting, "So the mask comes off."

I hold my breath.

His mouth curves, and one eyebrow arches.

Snap out of it, I scold myself.

I lift my chin and square my shoulders. "What's your name?"

Surprise fills his expression. "You don't know?"

A trembling rush coils behind my ribs, competing with the warm flutter rising low and sharp in my belly.

He adds, "You—"

"When I ask a question you'll answer," I warn, but I've lost my authoritative demeanor.

He grunts, shuts the door, and moves forward.

I stand frozen, unsure where to go.

"What happens if I disobey you?" he baits.

I study him for a moment, then reply, "There are consequences."

He closes the gap between us and leans over me. He takes one finger, moves my chin upward, and slowly breathes in and out.

What's he doing?

His eyes drift to my lips.

He stares so long my insides tremble, and my mouth waters.

"Why is it so hot in here?" he asks in a distracted tone, then brushes a bead of sweat off my cheek.

Sparks percolate under his touch.

He drags his finger over my jaw, then my collarbone, and leans into my ear, murmuring, "Did you bring me here for business or pleasure?"

Brax

The heat hits first, and the brunt of it isn't from the roaring fire. The same woman who decided whether I lived or died stares at me unmasked, her skin glistening in the thick, hot air.

I should be angry, calculating the exact words that'll level this woman and whatever she's involved in. I only caught a small glimpse of the secret organization she represents. And I already decided I don't like it. So I shouldn't even contemplate what I want to do with her.

Yet she stands spine straight, chin up, and with the audacity of a queen, hazel eyes pinned to mine, showing no fear. Her legs are longer than I expected, and the red strapless minidress showcases her heart-shaped ass. Her posture screams she's prepared to kill me, then fix her lipstick. And the word FINZIA is inked in red right under her collarbone.

Is it a stamp?

Brand?

Is she owned?

It's hard to tell. But her dark and wild hair isn't helping matters. It's a riot of curls, full of chaos she controls, and something tells me it's always like this.

My uncontrollable pulse doesn't slow. A bead of sweat rolls over my Adam's apple, and her eyes slowly dart to it.

She hunts for the smallest weakness.

She thinks she found one.

I'm still waiting for her to tell me if she brought me here for pleasure or business, but I warn, "It's just from the heat, so don't read into it."

Her lips part as she peers closer. The same Italian accent that gave me a hard-on when a knife was to my throat earlier murmurs, "You're calmer than most men in your position would be."

"What position is that?" I ask, leaning an inch closer. I shouldn't. I should be cautious of her. I'm smart enough to know she's a trap wearing perfume.

So why does my blood feel like it's fizzing in my veins? It's like someone poured gasoline through my bloodstream and handed her the match.

Her breath drags in then out, hitting mine.

Something primal sparks, creating an infuriating pull. She's danger-ous, and I need to get out of her world, not step farther into it. But it's like all the lessons the O'Malleys taught me about discipline simmer in the heat.

End this before it begins, I order myself.

The fire flickers in her eyes, turning the hazel molten.

Any remaining sense disappears. I blurt out, "You look at me like you already own me."

She replies in a low voice, "And you look at me like you want to."

My wet T-shirt suddenly feels like it's part of my skin. The fizzling in my veins turns to full-on explosions, and every warning bell blares between my ears.

Silence stretches, and the suffocating air wraps around my ribs and throat while her gaze remains steady but turns more curious. It's the same way she studied me in front of the crowd.

It only makes her more dangerous.

She breaks the silence. "What should I call you?"

"I would think you already know my name," I admit.

Her jaw twitches.

"Ah. So you're not the head honcho of whatever sadistic cesspool I stepped into?" I taunt.

Her eyes turn to slits. She advises, "I suggest you change your tone to one of respect regarding the Underworld."

The Underworld?

I drag the bead of sweat over her FINZIA tattoo, letting my finger linger on the top of her cleavage. "Or what?"

She gives me a look that sends a chill down my spine.

I step back, needing fresh air, but there is none. It wouldn't surprise me if I were actually in the real Devil's den. I wait another moment, then inform, "Brax. And you?"

"Short for Braxton?" she asks.

"No. Just Brax."

"What kind of name is Brax?"

I cross my arms over my chest, wishing my shirt wasn't drenched. I demand, "And your name is?"

She waits, as if she's contemplating whether telling me will get her killed or let her live.

I scoff. "Seriously?"

"Valentina," rolls off her tongue.

I step so close that her curls brush my forearm, and her perfume swirls between us. I lower my voice. "You run things?"

Her tongue slowly licks her lips. She answers, "I manage what I'm instructed to control."

I grunt. "So you're in charge until the boss is ready to step back in and play?"

She softly laughs.

"What's so funny?" I question.

"You're so naive."

"Then why don't you fill me in?" I ask, glancing at her lips.

She steps back, picks up the champagne bottle, and fills a flute. She drinks most of it, then tilts her head. "You snuck into the underground fight uninvited. Sean may have vouched for you, but you have no idea what you've gotten yourself into."

She's right.

"Why don't you fill me in?" I order.

She walks toward the kitchen, rinses out the flute, then refills it with water. She drinks all of it, then sets the glass in the sink and spins. "First, you answer my questions."

Sweat rolls over my eyelid and stings my right eye. I blink hard.

Jesus, it's hot in here.

I peel the bottom of my T-shirt and wipe my face, but it's pointless. "Fuck it," I mutter, and tug it over my head, then reply, "And if I don't?"

Valentina's eyes drag over my torso.

My dick pushes against my zipper harder with every second her stare lingers on me. I tease, "You still didn't tell me if I'm here for pleasure or business."

Her eyes meet mine. "If you don't answer my questions honestly, there will be consequences. There are always consequences, as I'm sure you learned tonight."

"Consequences where men are beaten to death for probably no reason?" I ask.

Her stare hardens. "There's always a reason, even if you don't know it."

"Is that so?"

"Yes."

"You answer like no part of you questions anything," I state.

Her gaze turns cold. "I don't question the Underworld, and neither should you."

"The Underworld?" I ask.

"Yes. That is what our society is called."

I hold back what I think about that name and push, "So you blindly do what they say?"

Valentina stays quiet, but her expression gives off a warning.

I shouldn't be scared, but something about it tells me to take her threats seriously.

"Ah. Good boy. You do have some smarts in that brain of yours," she declares. Her lips curve, taunting me further.

I grin. "I'm more than muscle, little Minx."

She opens her mouth, then shuts it. She turns back to the sink, refills the glass with water, and then sits on the couch. Sweat shimmers on her bare legs, and she slowly crosses them. The red satin moves dangerously high.

Sweet Jesus.

My blood fizzles again.

"Sit," she orders, pointing to the chair.

I don't see the point of arguing, so I obey, but it makes my predicament worse. The front angle is more torturous than the side.

"Should I just uncross my legs and let you examine me closer?" she reprimands.

I don't miss a beat. "If that's what you want. I'll oblige."

"I'm sure you would."

I shrug. "Don't put a dog bowl in front of a dog."

Valentina arches her eyebrows, half amused, half insulted. "So I'm a dog bowl?"

The flick of the match burns inside me. I don't hesitate. "If you want, I'll show you how a dog eats."

A flush erupts on her cheeks.

"Back to the original question. Am I here for pleasure or business?" I repeat, wishing she'd say pleasure and let me get on with what I'm sure would be an unforgettable night.

"You're here to learn." She shifts on the couch, uncrossing and recrossing her legs.

I point at her. "The only thing that's going to do is make me want to study every inch of your thighs."

She tilts her head and smirks. "You wish."

"Pretty sure you do."

Her red fingers snap. "Pay attention, Brax. There's less than six hours, and time's ticking. Every second you waste could be what causes your demise."

I grunt. "Less than six hours for what?"

"To learn."

"Learn what?"

"Rules. Procedures. The trajectory of your life now that you've stepped into the Underworld," she discloses.

I roll my eyes. "Spare me the drama. And do you mind if we turn off the fire? It's hotter than shit in here."

Her voice turns to anger. She hurls, "*Ma sei proprio un cretino!*"

"I'm not an idiot," I declare.

Her eyes widen. "You know Italian?"

Arrogance fills me. I cross my arms, sit back, and grin.

"How?" she asks.

I jump off the couch and walk toward the front door. "None of your business. Now, this little visit has been nice, but I'm sweating my balls off. You're welcome to join me for some fresh air if you're tired of this inferno." I reach for the door handle, but it's locked.

"It's locked."

"No shit," I say, but then my gut drops. There's only a keyhole and no way to unlock it. Alarms ring in my ears. I spin. "What's going on here?"

Valentina rises. "I told you that we have less than six hours. My suggestion is that you take this seriously."

The hairs on my neck rise. "Or what?"

Her face falls. She sighs. "You entered the Underworld. No one enters and leaves unless through death. Do I need to spell it out?"

My gut sinks further. I ask, "What about Sean?"

"What about him?"

"How did he get involved in your cult?"

"It's not a cult," she snaps.

"No? Sure seems like it has similar characteristics. I mean—"

"Last warning. Do not speak disrespectfully of the Underworld. I cannot protect you from the consequences," she threatens in a firm voice.

I open my mouth but don't speak. Her eyes have a warning I haven't seen before, and it sends a chill down my spine.

She lowers her voice. "The Underworld is always watching and listening. Choose your actions and words wisely."

My heart thumps harder. As soon as Valentina left, men pulled me away from Sean and brought me here, so I couldn't even talk to him. I don't know what I've stepped into, but I don't like it.

She runs her fingers over her tattoo. "Make a choice, Brax. Take this seriously, or it'll be the last choice you make."

"Because you'll kill me?" I ask in a teasing voice. I'm sure Valentina can hold her own, but I also think I could overpower her. I've never killed a woman, but if I had to choose between her and me, I'd choose myself.

She smirks, "You don't think I could?"

"You don't think I'd kill you?" I threaten, locking my gaze into hers.

Her smile widens. "While I'd love the opportunity to show you what I'm capable of, that isn't my role tonight. But if you do not use this time wisely, others are waiting. And trust me, there will be no option to fight if they come through this door."

My chest tightens. The room suffocates me further. I don't move.

She softens her tone. "If you die, I will too."

"Aw. You love me already, Juliet?" I tease.

Her expression hardens. "This isn't a game, Brax!"

I put my hands in the air. "Fine. Lighten up, though. It's hot enough in here without you breathing fire at me."

She tilts her head.

I glance back at the keyhole on the door and decide I'd better take this seriously. I saw how they made Sean kill all those men. So I grumble, "Fine. Do your thing. But is there any ice in here?" I step in front of the fridge and push the lever on the door.

It grinds, but no ice comes out.

I mutter, "You sure they don't want to kill us from heat stroke?"

"It's our punishment."

I spin. "Our?"

She stares at me.

"Go on. I can handle it. Why would we both get punished?" I ask.

She shakes her head. "Don't ask questions."

"Why?"

"Do you ever listen?"

I nod. "All the time."

"Then use those skills now. We have..." She glances at her watch and her voice drops. "Less than five hours."

"In this sweat lodge?"

"Yep."

"Fuck." I shake my head in annoyance, then step into the hallway.

"Where are you going?" she frets, close on my heels.

"To find the shower. You can join me," I offer, and swing open the first door.

"Brax, this isn't a game," she warns.

"Yep. I get that. But I need to cool off," I state, and find the bathroom. I open the glass door, turn the knob, and water rushes out. "Thank you, Jesus."

I drop my sweats.

"Really?" she whines.

I turn my head and wiggle my eyebrows. "I'll unzip your dress if you want."

"You're not taking this seriously!"

"Valentina, chill out. I need a quick shower to cool off, then I promise I'll do what you want," I vow, and stick my hand in the water. "Fuck!" I shout, pulling my hand back.

"There's no cold water in the bathroom. Only the kitchen faucet," Valentina says.

I turn the knob, but the steam grows.

"You're only making it hotter," she claims.

"Dammit!" I turn off the water and spin. "This is absurd!"

Her eyes widen. She looks at my cock and swallows hard.

"Don't worry. It gets bigger," I flaunt.

She slowly lifts her gaze to mine.

I grin.

Valentina jabs my chest. "Get your clothes on and stop messing around. I'm not dying or losing my spot at the table due to your stupidity!"

"Seat at the table?" I question.

"Get your clothes on," she repeats, spins, and leaves.

I glance at my wet sweatpants and boxers. There's no way I'm putting those on. I open the linen closet and grab a towel, wrap it around me, and go directly to the kitchen sink.

"I said to put your clothes on," Valentina calls out.

"Not wearing wet pants, sexy Minx." I turn on the water, lean down, and splash cold water on my face.

She snarls, "Can you please take this seriously?"

I turn. "Fine. Is there any food in here?" I yank open the fridge.

She groans.

"These people are sadistic," I mutter at the empty fridge and reach for the pantry.

"You won't find anything. Drink some water if you must," she orders.

"Not a huge fan of water unless I'm fighting," I admit, then jump up on the counter.

She keeps her darts aimed at me.

I put my hands in the air. "Well? Go on."

She scrubs her hand over her face and groans. "You're impossible."

"More like amazing. So do your thing. Teach me, oh wise one," I taunt.

She pulls out the barstool and sits. "The first thing you have to memorize is the Underworld Inscriptions."

"Inscriptions?"

"Yes."

I grunt. "And you don't call this a cult?"

Anger fills her expression. "Say it again and it'll be the end for both of us."

"So dramatic."

"Brax—"

"Fine. I won't call it a cult."

She stares at me, her chest rising and falling slowly.

I jump off the counter and take the stool next to her. "Underworld Inscriptions. You were saying?"

She turns. "Number one. Blood remembers. No oath is forgotten. No betrayal fades. The body pays for what the soul declares."

I glance at her crossed thighs. "I'm ok if you want your soul to declare to make my body pay."

She swats me. "Time to pay attention, Brax. Take this seriously."

I groan. "Fine."

"So repeat it," she orders.

I state, "Blood remembers. No oath is forgotten. No betrayal fades. The body pays for what the soul declares."

She asks, "And do you understand what that means?"

I run my index finger over her tattoo. "Sure do, little Minx."

She pushes it off her. "Then tell me."

I whine, "You're no fun."

"You said you'd take this seriously! This isn't a joke! You're going to get me killed!" she cries out, fear erupting on her expression for the first time.

It stops me in my tracks.

She blinks hard and turns her head.

I cave. "Okay. Sorry. I get it. I'll be serious."

She looks at me. "Then tell me what it means?"

I don't hesitate. I'm not new to the world of loyalty. "I assume it means that once you're part of the Underworld, there's no getting out. Anyone who dares be disloyal pays by death."

She nods and smiles. "Good."

"Told you I had a brain," I tease.

She cracks a smile. "The next one will be harder for you to comprehend."

"Why is that?" I ask.

Valentina relays, "Speak little. See everything. A silent tongue lives longer. A careless tongue feeds the grave."

"You're wrong. I know all about taking secrets to the grave," I boast.

"Why do I find that hard to believe?" she questions.

"I'm not a rat," I hurl.

She holds her hands in the air. "I didn't say that."

"Didn't you?"

"No. I just meant you talk a lot."

"Joking around has nothing to do with knowing when to keep your mouth shut. I'm not a rat now and never will be. And I know how to observe others," I insist.

She sits straighter. "Okay. Good."

I glare at her.

She clears her throat. "Number three. Repeat after me. A life taken is a debt paid. But a life spared is a chain placed. Mercy binds the hand that offers it."

I recite, "A life taken is a debt paid. But a life spared is a chain placed. Mercy binds the hand that offers it."

She presses, "And what does it mean?"

"It means—" I freeze, except for my stomach flipping.

Valentina insists, "Tell me what it means, Brax."

The chill resumes in my spine. I meet her eye. "It means I just placed a chain around Sean, and the Underworld isn't going to show him any mercy."

She gives me a knowing look. "That's right. So now do you understand why this isn't a joke?"

I say nothing, feeling a dread pour over me like nothing I've ever felt before.

Valentina

Chapter
THREE

Three hours have passed since we got trapped in this inferno, and it's wearing on me. Every breath feels like the air could have been scraped from the sun itself. The fireplace hasn't dimmed once. If anything, the flames blaze hotter, even showing blue at times.

Sweat owns my skin. My stained, silk dress clings to me. I already know there's no dry cleaner who could ever return it to its previous state, which pisses me off. I paid a fortune for this dress. And my inner gut tells me that whatever Omni decided to put me here, they knew I'd be wearing this.

Brax sprawls across the sofa like heat doesn't bother him, but his towel is soaked, his chest slowly rises and falls with what I've quickly come to learn is irritation. Every few minutes, he glances at me with his infuriating smirk, which makes me believe he's surviving only to torment me.

He teases, "Still memorizing your sacred inscriptions, Minx?"

"You should be thankful that I'm double-checking what I'm teaching you so you know every intricate detail," I inform. I scan the lines I scrawled across the back of a napkin again. The letters blur from the humidity in the room.

He chuckles. "You're cooking yourself alive in that thing."

I look up, arching an eyebrow at him.

He grins, twirling his finger at me. "That dress is just added torture."

I toss the napkin on the floor. "Your point?"

He prods, "How do you stay in it?"

"It's called discipline."

"It's called stupidity." He sits up. "You know what I'd kill for right now?"

"An air conditioner?"

"And..."

I shrug. "A beer."

His face lights up. "Steak. Medium rare. Grilled over an open flame, with a side of whiskey."

My lips twitch. "That's primal of you. But not sure how you can think about anything having to do with flames right now."

He slides on the floor and pins his face next to mine. "Since there's no steak, I'll take you without that dress."

My butterflies flip. "Yeah?"

Hope flares in his expression. "Yeah."

"Try the sink. That will fill you up."

"Tried it. Tastes like metal."

A laugh flies out of me.

His eyes cut to my chest. "Take it off, Valentina. For the love of God, take it off before it melts into your perfect skin."

I crumble the napkin and toss it next to the rest of the wet paper I've accumulated over the last few hours. I glare at him. "Do you have a death wish?"

"Probably." He murmurs in my ear, "You're drenched. It's distracting."

The heat of his breath teases my lips. "So close your eyes."

"Not a chance."

I don't move.

He jumps off the floor, stretches, and every muscle shifts under his glistening skin. The towel hangs low on his hips, ready to slip off.

My pulse jerks. I force my gaze to the fire.

He whines, "This is torture. Whoever thought to put us here is sadistic."

"I'm sure you've done worse to your enemies," I comment, rising off the floor.

He pins his blues on me, confirming my suspicion. I still know nothing about him other than his name is Brax O'Malley. That last name confirms he's part of the clan, but time hasn't allowed me to drill him about other things.

My pulse ticks up. I clear my throat. "Focus on your rules."

He moves closer, and a new ripple of heat hits my body. "Three hours of rules. I think I get it."

"Enlighten me."

He chants, "Blood remembers. Betrayal kills. Keep your mouth shut. Don't piss off the queen."

I cross my arms. "We don't have a queen yet."

He gives me a funny look, half amusement and half suspicion. "Why not?"

My loyalty to Kirill and the real truth fight.

"Cat got your tongue?" Brax pushes.

I lock the truth in my mental vault and lift my chin. "Because the king hasn't chosen her yet."

Sarcasm curls on his tongue. "Such a responsibility."

"It is," I snap.

"Don't have to get all touchy about it," he says.

I point at him. "You're disrespectful, and that's going to get you killed."

A crooked smile appears. He lifts his brows.

I shake my head. "You should take this seriously, Brax."

He groans. "I am. But you have to admit this is a lot for any normal man to take in. Kings. Queens. Next, you're going to tell me there are knights in shining armor, too."

I stare at him.

"You've got to be kidding me," he mutters.

I offer, "Look, I know this is a lot to absorb, but your mouth is going to get you in trouble."

He laughs softly. "Good. Let it. Take the dress off, Valentina."

A shot of lava flows through my veins. "No."

"Scared?"

"Of what?"

"Of wanting me."

I roll my eyes, but the tremor in my core grows. I accuse, "You're delusional."

He prowls closer until his breath brushes my temple. He grabs my wrist and plants his thumb on it. "You keep saying no, but your pulse says otherwise."

I pull my hand away. "Ha ha funny."

He leaves the room and returns with a fresh towel. He takes it to the kitchen, runs water over it, then wrings it out. "At least cool off before you pass out." He tosses it to me.

It lands against my chest, damp and cold, but the relief only lasts a few seconds. I sigh. "That was nice but short-lived."

"Admit it felt good for a brief moment," he demands.

"I just did. Do your ears not work?" I tease.

His grin turns wicked. "Imagine if you could feel the relief longer."

I don't move. I'm pretty sure if I take my clothes off, it's only going to get hotter. I don't trust him or me if we're both naked.

He lowers his voice and firmly commands, "Valentina, take that dress off before you faint."

I remind him, "You don't get to order me around."

He shrugs. "Then think of it as a suggestion."

"Keep suggesting, and I'll—"

"What?" he challenges.

"I'll make sure your next breath hurts," I warn.

His smile deepens. "You're beautiful when you threaten me, Minx."

Minx.

Every time he calls me his little pet name, I don't correct him. I should, but I can't seem to tell him to stop.

The clock chimes for the top of the hour. A new crackle fills the air.

Brax moves toward the thermostat and spouts, "God dammit!"

"What?"

"It's at 103 now."

More sweat pops out on my forehead. It's not new. Every hour it's risen.

"For the love of God, take off that dress," he demands.

"Fine," I hiss, unable to stand the material any longer. "You want a show? Here."

I reach behind my neck and tug at the zipper, but it's stuck.

"Let me get that," Brax offers, sliding behind me before I can object. His fingers glide down my bare spine.

I gasp, then try to pull it together. I spin. "I'll get it."

"I already unzipped you," he claims.

I reach behind and confirm.

He adds, "You'll have to peel that nasty material off you."

"It's not nasty," I declare.

"Maybe not at the start of the night. But now? Ew." He wrinkles his nose.

I laugh.

"Off," he orders.

He's watching me.

So? It's not the first time a man's watched me.

Flashbacks of all the things I've done in the Underworld pummel me at once.

Pretend it's just another ritual.

I tug at the material. It falls to the floor, and a moment of relief fills me. I sigh, then my self-consciousness comes back.

I'm not naked. I'm in my thong and bra. But I feel naked.

For a heartbeat, he doesn't move. Then his eyes drag over every inch of me before he challenges, "Take the rest off, Valentina."

"I'm good."

He points to my panties. "Is that because I've been exciting you all night?"

I glance at the soaked lace, then slap the back of my hand against his arm. "Funny."

He tosses his own towel aside. "Don't be shy. I refuse to get heat stroke."

My breath catches, and I freeze.

The bar of silver gleams against the light. I saw the flash of metal earlier when he dropped his sweats, but the same coil in my gut reoccurs.

He smirks. "Like?"

I swallow. "You're ridiculous."

"Not what you were going to say."

I turn away, pretending to adjust my towel. "I always wondered why a guy would pierce himself there?"

He laughs under his breath. "Ever heard of the Kama Sutra?"

I force myself not to look at his dick again, affirming, "I'm familiar with it."

Cockiness erupts on his expression. "Then you know it's not just about positions. It's about precision."

"So you're worried you won't get your cock in the hole?" I tease.

He chuckles. "Never had a problem with that."

I stare at him, my heart racing.

He continues, "Centuries ago, men wore metal to honor the gods of pleasure. They believed it gave control. Power. Connection."

"So you're superstitious or religious?" I ask.

"Neither." He drags a fingertip down my damp shoulder. "Some things survive because they work."

My throat goes dry. "So Brax O'Malley is a scholar of ancient love rituals?"

He grins. "I'm a man who appreciates history. And results."

"You did it for results?"

"Let's say motivation." He circles me until we're face-to-face again. "You see pain. I see promise. Some men mark victories with ink. Others with iron."

I glance at the ink running down his arm. "You have both."

He grins cockily. "I cover all my bases."

I look back at the barbell on the head of his penis. "Doesn't it hurt?"

He lifts my chin, answering, "It did. Now it just reminds me that pleasure and pain share the same nerve endings."

My pulse hammers so hard it drowns the crackle of the fire. I want to scoff, to tell him he's disgusting, but my tongue won't obey. The image of his body, the glint of metal, the idea of ancient hands forging it in the name of pleasure...it all lodges under my skin.

"So what are you thinking?" he asks.

"Nothing."

"Liar."

I open my mouth, but he closes the space between us.

He demands, "Say it."

"Say what?"

"That you're curious."

"I'm not."

"You are."

"I'm not," I insist, though the air between us vibrates with the truth.

He reaches up, pushing a sweat-laden lock of hair off my cheek. "You keep fighting every instinct you have."

"Instincts get people killed."

"Or they keep them alive."

"Not in the Underworld. Rules and structure keep you breathing," I insist.

He smiles faintly. "Then maybe it's time someone rewrote the rules."

For a heartbeat, the world shrinks to the space between our mouths. The blue flames grow more prominent. Sweat beads at my hairline, and my skin tingles from the nearness of his. My heart pounds with new force.

My voice comes out raw. "You have to stop making jokes about the rules."

He intensifies his gaze on me. "Who said I was joking?"

Our lips don't meet, but everything in me strains toward him. The heat in the fireplace bends as if it's alive, watching and waiting for God only knows what.

A loud metallic click shatters the moment. The front lock disengages with a heavy thud.

Brax's jaw tightens. He spins and steps in front of me, pushing me behind him.

I peek around him.

The door swings open, flooding the room with a rush of cool air and the silhouette of a man in all black, wearing a matching ski mask.

"Time's up," he says, his voice carrying the weight of the Underworld's authority.

Brax doesn't move.

Panic hits me. There's more to teach Brax and I don't want to be held accountable for not doing the job that was assigned to me. So I argue, "It hasn't been six hours."

The man's gaze flicks between us, then lingers on the scattered towels and the faint steam rising from the floor. "I don't make the decisions."

"Of course you don't," Brax sneers.

The man tosses a duffel bag on the floor. "The king is waiting for you."

"Me? Or Brax?" I question, with more anxiety brewing.

"Both of you. Get dressed." He grabs our clothes off the floor and puts them in a trash bag.

"What are you doing with my stuff?" Brax barks.

"Orders," he says, then disappears through the door.

Brax turns, annoyed. "Guess class is over."

I nod, saying, "For now," but wondering if I failed the test. I pick up the duffel bag and unzip it. I pull out two pairs of sandals, shorts, T-shirts, and zip-up hoodies. I hand the men's to Brax. I step into my shorts.

He slides into the sandals, drops the clothes, walks to the doorway, and steps into the foyer area. He holds his arms out and spreads his legs.

I stare at his ripped shoulders that V to his muscular ass and thighs, asking, "What are you doing?"

"Cooling off. Not sure how you can put those on right now."

I pull the T-shirt over my head, put on the flip-flops, grab his clothes and my hoodie, and walk over to him. I hold out his shorts. "The king is waiting. Get dressed."

"I need a minute."

My voice rises. "You don't get a minute. Let me teach you another lesson you should never forget. When the king is waiting, you drop everything and go."

He sarcastically taunts, "Why? Is he going to behead me?"

I stare at him, my chest tightening.

His eyes widen. "You've got to be fucking kidding me."

I wiggle his shorts in front of him. "Get dressed. Stop messing around."

He shakes his head and releases a frustrated breath. He slides into the shorts and pushes the elevator button.

"Aren't you going to put on your shirt?" I ask.

"Nope."

"Fine."

The metal opens, and more cool air hits me. We step into the elevator, but the burn beneath my skin doesn't fade. The ghost of his voice, lecturing about ancient promises and metal forged for pleasure, haunts me as we make our way through the lobby.

Outside, it's a cloudy morning. There's a harsh chill in the air, and the gusts of wind turn my sweat cold.

Vito stands outside my SUV. He sees me, opens the back door, then pins his scowl on Brax.

"Ma'am," he says as I slide inside next to a blanket.

"Morning, Vito," I reply, and grab the throw, smiling. Leave it to Kirill to know I'd be too hot to put on more clothes inside, but colder once I got out here.

Brax moves next to me, still shirtless. "You can't tell me you're putting that on?"

I unfold it and place it over my legs, then slide into the hoodie. I drag my eyes over his glistening pecs. "Put your shirt on."

"No. I'm still hot."

Vito growls, "Ms. Valentina said to put it on." He eyes Brax through the rearview mirror.

Brax grunts. "She's not my boss."

Vito spins, and Brax lunges forward, grabbing his throat.

"Brax!" I cry out.

Vito's face turns red. He gasps.

"Let him go!" I order, tugging on his arm.

Brax turns toward me. "No one is going to threaten me. Understand?"

"Let him go!" I demand again.

He stares Vito in the eyes for a few more seconds, then says, "I'm going to release you now. Don't ever try to come at me again." He releases him.

Vito chokes, sputtering for air.

"Jesus, Brax!" I scold.

"You should get a driver who can protect you," Brax states.

"He can," I seethe.

Brax sits back in the seat and puts his ankle over his knee. "He just put you in a compromising position if I wanted to hurt you."

I gape at him.

Is he right?

Brax directs, "Drive. The king is waiting for us."

Vito stares at him through the mirror.

Brax puts the divider glass up. "Seriously, Minx. You need a better driver if he's supposed to also be security."

The SUV veers onto the road.

"Put on your shirt so you don't disrespect the king," I order then stare at my hands, replaying what just happened.

The ride to Kirill's is quiet and short. The SUV pulls to the curb in front of the glass tower, black and gleaming against the gray morning.

Brax is already halfway out the door before Vito can get out. He glances up the building with a suspicious squint, making me believe he's cataloging every window, camera, and any possible way out.

I step beside him. "Don't stare too long. It makes them nervous."

He meets my eye. "Maybe they should be."

"Don't be stupid." I push past him. The sliding doors part, and warm air scented with polished wood and espresso wraps around me. Two men in suits straighten and nod.

"Ms. Abruzzo," the taller one says, pressing a hand to his earpiece.

The other motions for me to go ahead. "Mr. Petrov is expecting you."

"Of course he is," I mumble.

"Abruzzo?" Brax snarls.

I glance up at him. I had forgotten that outside the Underworld, my family is his family's enemy.

"Petrov?" he says with just as much disgust.

I curse myself for not warning him. The last thing I need is a scene in the lobby. The security may be Underworld members, but the rest of the building knows nothing about our secret reality. So I beg in a whisper, "Please don't make a scene. I'll explain later."

Brax stays planted.

"You look cold, Ms. Abruzzo. Can I get you a coffee?" Bruno at the front desk asks.

Brax glances at him then jeers, "You've got fans."

I smirk, "Jealous after only a few hours with me?"

He grunts.

I stride across the marble lobby, relieved when he follows me. I flash my hand at the security checkpoint, and the scanner flashes green. Another set of guards steps aside. Brax follows, his expression full of distrust, but I'm unsure if it's of the men being around me or for what's ahead.

The elevator is open when we reach it. I ask the guard, "Is this fixed yet, Jasper?"

"No, ma'am," he relays.

I roll my eyes and step inside. For the last few months, it's been slow. Kirill's been all over the building maintenance to get it fixed, but nothing has improved.

Inside, Brax leans against the mirrored wall, arms folded. "So you've been here before?"

"Too many times to count."

The doors shut, and the box moves at a snail's pace. "What's this Petrov's deal? Couldn't become Mafia royalty so he took on the role of corporate cult leader?"

"Enough of the cult talk," I reprimand. "And the king is smarter than anyone you've ever met. Don't test him."

He smirks. "I'll try to keep my mouth shut. No promises."

The elevator stops at every floor, even though no one is waiting to go up.

On the fourth floor, Brax rumbles a curse under his breath.

I taunt, "Don't get frustrated now. We only have a dozen more stops before we get to the penthouse."

His eyes grow wide. "You've got to be kidding me."

"Unfortunately, not."

Ten minutes later, the elevator dings softly, opening into the penthouse foyer.

"About fucking time," Brax mutters.

"Mind your manners," I remind him. Then I open the door and call out, "We're here."

Kirill stands by the wall of glass, his reflection stretching across the skyline. He turns and the knotted, diagonal scar across his face is just as brooding as always.

I barely notice it anymore but I'm always conscious of it whenever anyone new is in front of him.

He welcomes, "Valentina." He assesses Brax with a scowl.

I stop a few paces in and curtsey. "Your Majesty." I sneak a glance at Brax to make sure he's showing respect.

He wrinkles his face, then it hardens.

My gut flips. I want to slap him, but it's a typical reaction when anyone sees Kirill for the first time.

At least he tried to hide his reaction quickly.

I nudge him.

He pins his eyebrows together. "What?"

"Bow," I say through gritted teeth.

"Seriously?"

I glare at him, my heart racing so fast I think I might pass out.

Brax groans, then faces Kirill. He bows his head and says with an attitude, "Your Majesty."

"Relax," Kirill orders. Then his gaze and voice turn as cold as frost on water. "You made it through the trial."

Brax's jaw ticks. "If you call a sweat lodge and starvation a trial, sure."

Kirill's scowl intensifies. "You're here because you survived, not because you understood."

"He did," I insist, worried I'm going to be in trouble.

Kirill's voice softens. "You did your part, Valentina. However, it's clear the importance of the Underworld hasn't sunk in for Brax yet. That's why I've appointed you as his mentor."

He's going to fast-track Brax?

I glance up, confused. "Mentor?"

His gaze cuts to me. "Yes. You, Valentina. You'll oversee his training."

I argue, "That's not protocol. Mentorship is for lower levels. I've already—"

"The Omni has made its decision," he interjects.

My stomach drops. It's not the first time I've seen someone get fast-tracked into higher positions within the Underworld. Sean made sense since he's the Chosen One. But Brax? Why is he so special? And why is it only men I've seen get fast-tracked? I've been working for years, and it's not fair. So I insist, "He's not ready. He doesn't even—"

Kirill raises a hand, silencing me. "Then make him ready."

Brax laughs under his breath. "You've got the wrong guy. I'm not interested in joining your underground empire."

Kirill walks closer, the room shrinking with every step. "You misunderstand. This isn't an invitation."

Brax

Chapter FOUR

Petrov stands in front of me, and I just bowed my head like he's actually royalty.

That detail sits in my gut like a stone, heavy and obnoxious. Petrov is the kind of name you learn to hate before you learn to speak. And I knew Valentina was trouble the moment I laid eyes on her. I never considered she could be an Abruzzo, but I should have with that Italian accent and killer look in her gaze.

It makes everything about this entire predicament worse. Petrovs and Abruzzos don't dine with O'Malleys. In my world, they either cross the street on opposite sides or end up in the ground. Standing in front of two of them, without any backup, isn't smart. So I wonder again how Sean's father ever created this demented secret world I've been forced to entertain.

Kirill's scar twitches over his jaw. It's the worst imperfection I've ever seen on a man's face.

How did he get it?

He thinks he's going to threaten me?

He's got another thing coming.

My laugh comes out hotter than I want. "You think you're the first to try and recruit me? Don't flatter yourself."

"I know all about the gangs on the street who wanted the homeless boy who refused to join them," he replies in a flat tone.

My gut coils. How does he know anything about me? Valentina didn't seem to, so how does he?

Kirill threatens, "Don't confuse choice with illusion. You can't run from the Underworld."

I snarl, "Don't dress your threats in velvet."

"Brax," Valentina warns through gritted teeth.

I don't look at her, and now I'm glad I didn't fuck her.

She's an Abruzzo.

Kirill moves closer. "You misunderstand power."

"You don't own me now. Nor will you in the future," I declare, standing taller.

Sympathy appears on his expression. He lowers his tone. "The Omni have given their orders. You fall in line or fall in blood. Take your pick."

"You think you scare me?" I fume, stepping closer.

Valentina jumps between us. She puts her hand on my chest and sparks burst under her touch, making me loathe myself. She asserts, "You're acting rash."

I scoff, "Rash? Nah. I'm the only sane one in the room."

Worry fills her hazel gaze. I want to kiss her and push her away.

She's the enemy.

Kirill interjects, "I'm giving you a 24-hour pass so you can get your senses back. Valentina will mentor you."

My eyes dart between him and her.

Valentina's jaw tightens. She opens her mouth, but Kirill speaks first.

"You will train him. He will learn. You will live," he finishes, pointing at me.

Chaos fills my chest, reminding me of how hard it was to breathe in the other penthouse. I ask, "Do you know what happens when you force someone to be your project?"

No one speaks.

I don't take my eyes off Kirill's and add, "You end up regretting it."

His lips twitch. "We'll see about that. Like I said. I'll give you 24 hours to choose your role in the Underworld or death. It'll be up to you."

The same alarm I felt when I got caught watching Sean fight seeps into my bones. I sniff hard and ask, "Anything else you need to tell me?"

Kirill peers closer, then shakes his head. He steps back. "You're free to go."

"Great. Where's my shit?"

He points to a black bag on the table. "In there. But you don't get it back yet."

I vibrate with anger. "You're not keeping my wallet and shoes."

Arrogance washes over Kirill. "You will get them back when you take this seriously. Now leave on your own, or my guards will escort you out." He points past me.

I spin.

Four men with deadly scowls and built like brick houses stare at me.

I decide it's best to go quietly and not look back. I pass the guards, get on the elevator, and curse as it stops at every floor.

When I get outside, the cold gusts of wind nearly knock me over. I instantly regret not taking the hoodie out of the SUV, but luckily for me, my anger keeps me moving. Plus, it's not the first time I've walked in cold weather with barely anything on.

The déjà vu of my childhood comes roaring back. All the hustling, days of no food, nights spent in rain and snow, and every gangster face who wanted me as theirs are memories clawing through me.

I push past pedestrians, stomp around the corner, and the smell of rot in the alley makes me nauseous.

Two blocks down, a man wearing a thick coat and a gold chain yells, "Kid, come over here."

A scrawny boy about twelve cautiously approaches him.

When I get closer, I warn, "Careful, kid. You're his cheap labor or bait."

He pins tough, wide eyes on me.

"Mind your own business," the man threatens.

"Go to hell," I snarl, and keep moving.

It's all the same playground, just different predators. And I refused to be owned then, and I won't be now.

Then why do I feel cornered?

I didn't survive hell to kneel in another man's kingdom.

Sean's building appears before I realize I was heading toward it. I slip into the lobby when a group exits, and take the stairs, two at a time.

When I get to his apartment, I don't knock. The door's unlocked, and when I step inside, another round of rage hits me. "Jesus Christ."

Sean moves his head off the sofa pillow and winces.

I shut the door and assess him. One eye is swollen shut. The other has a small slit. Both are purple and yellow. A blanket is half over him, and the rest of his body displays similar bruises and swelling.

He sighs in relief. "Thank God you're alive."

"You got a lot of talking to do," I state.

"You shouldn't have followed me," he asserts.

"Little late for that now," I point out, then add, "You look like shit."

A broken chuckle escapes him. He winces again.

I lift the blanket, asking, "Your ribs broke?"

"Don't think so."

"You sure?"

"Nope."

"I don't know how you kept going, to be honest," I admit.

"How much did you see?" he asks.

"The last nine."

"Should have seen the first four when I had all my energy," he jokes.

I chuckle, and it feels good.

Sean's voice drops. "Seriously, Brax. You shouldn't have followed me. Now you're in this mess, too."

I drop into the chair across from him. "You should have told me what was going on."

He shakes his head slowly. "You don't get it, Brax. I couldn't talk then, and I can't now. You stepped into something that doesn't forgive curiosity."

I stare at him. "Don't play that game with me. I was there. I spent the rest of the night into the early morning learning about laws and rules of whatever it is your father started. How the hell did you get involved in this?"

His swollen face barely moves. "Doesn't matter how."

"The fuck it doesn't," I snap.

"Listen to me, Brax. Stop asking questions and take whatever they say seriously," he asserts.

I hurl, "You dragged me into a blood circus."

"I didn't drag you anywhere. You put your nose where it didn't belong!"

"To protect you because you're like my goddamn brother!"

"I don't need protecting!"

"You sure about that?" I challenge.

Tense silence builds.

Sean's voice comes out way too calm for my nerves. "You don't talk about it. Not here, not anywhere."

My pulse spikes. "You're protecting them! They own you, don't they?"

His eyes flick toward the ceiling, then back at me. "I'm protecting you, idiot. Just because you know about things doesn't mean you can discuss them."

"Easy for you to say. You don't have a Petrov and an Abruzzo trying to secure a leash on you like you're their new pet project," I burst out.

His face pales even with the bruises. "What... No. Don't say anything else. It's dangerous."

It hits like a punch. For a second, I forget to breathe. Then I erupt. "You better start talking, Sean!"

"Brax, you didn't trust me before when I told you to mind your own business. I'm telling you again, but this time, you need to listen and adhere to my words," Sean warns.

Fury curls in my chest. "Are you telling me you joined something that wants to own us like property and you're okay with it?"

He slams his hand on the table. A crack ripples through the room. The wince on his face is unforgettable. He seethes, "Shut up! I'm not going to tell you again."

I scowl at him, and it hits me. Sean O'Malley doesn't buckle for anyone. Not our uncles. Not the cops. Not God himself. I accuse, "You're scared of them."

He takes a painful breath, then declares, "All I'll say is this. I don't know what we're involved in. But I've been warned about keeping my mouth shut. And these people aren't playing games, Brax. So do me a favor and don't get yourself killed."

"Fine. Keep your secrets to yourself." I rise, grab my spare key out of his kitchen drawer, and move toward the exit.

"Brax!" he calls out.

I stop but don't turn back.

"You're my brother. That's not changed. If I could talk to you, I would," he claims.

"Sure. Get better," I spit out, slam the door, and leave the same way I entered.

A new level of anger hits me, and the cold welcomes me like a punishment. I keep my head down, ignoring anyone I pass, the sting in my feet, and the burn of rage under my ribs.

When I finally get to my apartment, I take a shower, put on fresh clothes, and make two ham-and-cheese sandwiches. I scarf them down, then go into my home office.

There are six computer screens on the wall. Sean's uncles, Declan and Nolan, also took me under their wing. At an early age, they taught me how to hack, access the dark web, and find things others never will.

I turn on the power and mutter, "You want to hide your secrets? Then I'll come find them."

I crack my knuckles and start typing.

Kirill Petrov.

I hit enter, then go out to the kitchen and grab a beer from the fridge. The cold feels good sliding down my throat. I take it to my office and sit down, watching the green letters move too fast to read.

The dark net isn't accessible to most. It's not monitored like Google or social media. It's a network of backdoor trails, half-deleted files, government warnings, blacked-out dossiers, and encrypted data nodes labeled "Redacted."

I finish my beer, and the letters stop moving. A long list pops up on the screen. I click one link and direct it to screen one. Images of Kirill standing beside a coffin draped in a Russian flag appear. He wears a hardened expression, and his scar is still red. The caption reads: *K. Petrov — classified operations, Eastern Bloc, 2004.*

I peer closer. "What the hell were you, Scarface?"

I scroll further, but every link leads to a dead end of deleted accounts and disappeared witnesses to crimes. The only constant is the scar on his face, turning paler as he ages. And it's always the same angle with the same dead eyes staring at whoever took the photo.

I read through situations and crimes the government decided to hide for who knows what reason. However, that isn't uncommon in my world either. Crime families know how to make things disappear.

Nothing seems abnormal for a criminal in a mob family.

Why hadn't I heard of him before?

I read dozens of files, start to get bored, then type in my next victim.

Valentina Abruzzo.

The results are worse. Nothing but art auctions, fake modeling profiles, and coded references to "FINZIA", the same word tattooed under her collarbone. I click on a thread labeled *FINZIA PROJECT – Milan Archive.*

The page flickers before I can read more than a few words, then the words bloodline, inheritance, and seat-at-the-table flash before it's gone.

"Dammit!" I slam my hand on the desk.

They're like ghosts wrapped in gold.

They have their claws in Sean.

And me.

No, they don't.

They'll kill me.

Not the first person who wanted me dead.

This is different.

A sinking reality hits my gut. I stare at the blinking cursor before I start another search.

The Underworld.

For a moment, the screen stays blank. Then one by one, words crawl across the monitor. Then everything flashes fast.

Access Denied.

You shouldn't be here.

Leave now.

The system freezes. My cursor won't move. The fans inside my computer whir louder until the sound rises into a whine. Lines of red code flood the screen, looping phrases I can't decipher fast enough.

Then everything goes black.

A chill sweeps through me. I shiver, mumbling, "What the fuck?" and clicking the power button, but nothing happens.

"What the fuck!" I fume louder, then shove my chair back, and rise.

My pulse hammers between my ears. The black monitor never flickers to life, and I stare at my reflection with new dread.

Whoever wrote that line of code, "you shouldn't be here," wasn't bluffing. Now, someone knows I was looking.

I shove the chair away and press my palms to my temples, fighting a headache. The silence in my apartment gnaws at me. I contemplate trying to sleep, but my phone buzzes on the desk.

> Finn: Dinner. Pub. 7 p.m. Brenna and I haven't seen you in days.

I'm about to reply when another one comes in.

> Finn: Don't make me send her to drag you to dinner.

I crack a smile. The best thing that ever happened to me was when Finn and Brenna took me in as their own. They're the most important people in my life and the only people I consider my parents.

> Me: On my way.

I slide my arms into a jacket, my feet into sneakers, and make my way out of the building. Even though the pavement is wet, there are plenty of people walking around. It takes ten minutes to get to O'Malley's.

It's warm inside, and the familiarity is comforting. Beer, fish and chips, and burgers fill the air. I inhale deeply and glance past the long wooden bar that always gets restored whenever Nora decides to remodel.

Several booths in, I spot Finn and Brenna. I push past mostly people I know, nodding as I go.

Finn teases, "Look who remembered to come eat with us."

"Sorry. Been busy," I claim and slide into the booth across from them.

Brenna pats my hand and beams, "Don't let him guilt you. I keep telling him you have a life outside of us. What's new?"

I hung out with an Abruzzo I wanted to fuck last night, and then I had a Petrov give me orders.

I try to ignore my guilt. "Just normal stuff?"

Finn signals the bartender, and within seconds, three pints hit the table. He says, "Tell him about the rooster."

"Rooster?" I ask, taking a large swig.

She rolls her eyes and leans closer. "The neighbor behind us decided to get a rooster. I was out for my walk yesterday, and it attacked me."

Worry builds. I close one fist. "What? Are you okay?"

She waves her hand in front of her face. "Yeah. It's fine."

"No, it's not," Finn insists.

I arch my eyebrows, keeping my fist tight.

He seethes, "She has peck marks all over her calves."

"Oh shit!" I blurt out.

Brenna insists, "I'm okay. But the poor rooster."

I lock eyes with Finn. "You break its neck?"

"Of course I did."

I nod. "Good."

Brenna's lips twitch. "That was a little extreme."

"No, it wasn't. The neighbors are lucky I didn't break theirs," Finn declares.

"Too right," I offer, and hold out my mug.

Finn clinks it, and we both drink.

Brenna groans.

The server, Jessica, comes over. "Are you ready to order?"

Finn states, "We both want fish and chips. Not sure about Brax."

"Same," I answer.

"Another round?" she asks.

"Please," I say.

She nods and leaves.

Finn's tone shifts. He tries to act casual, but it's not. I know when he's prying, but trying not to pry. It's something I respect about him. He understands that a man deserves independence and privacy. But when he suspects something is off, he'll step in.

He comments, "So I knew Sean was hiding out, but what's your excuse?"

My throat tightens. "We're both around."

"He's missed workouts. Killian's losing his damn mind, not sparring with him every morning. And now both of you didn't show up this morning," Finn points out.

My heart races. I quickly state, "Sean's just been tired."

"Since when does Sean O'Malley get tired?" Finn pushes.

Brenna sighs. "Finn—"

He lifts a hand, eyes still on me. "And what's your excuse? I waited an hour at the gym. Kept thinking you'd return my calls or texts."

Guilt expands, but I force a smirk. "Sorry. I was sleeping. We had a late one."

He doesn't blink. "Late one?"

"Yeah." I lean back, trying to relax. "Sean and I went out. Blew off some steam. You know how it is...beer, cards, bad decisions."

Brenna laughs lightly. "Boys' night, huh? No wonder you look like you haven't slept in days."

"Do I?"

She winces and puts her two fingers together. "Little bit."

I laugh, hoping it sounds natural.

Finn isn't amused, and he isn't buying it. He studies me with his weathered green eyes that saw straight through every lie I ever tried to sneak past him.

I drink more beer.

"Where did you go?" he asks.

"The new club downtown. After that it gets a little blurry," I fib.

He scoffs. "That makes sense for last night, but where has Sean been all the other days?"

As upset as I am that Sean won't tell me everything he knows about the Underworld, my loyalty toward him will never fade. So I lie further, "Like I said. He's been busy."

Brenna interjects, "Hopefully, things will calm down for him soon."

Finn doesn't move. He pins his stare on me. "If he's mixed up in something, you can tell me. I'll help him figure out how to handle it."

His offer twists in my gut. I wish I could accept it, but he has no idea what "it" even is. Hell, neither do I, really. And if he knew about Kirill, or Valentina, he'd be livid. Plus, there's no way he could figure out how to get me out of the 24-hour problem I have.

It's less than 24 hours now.

My gut flips. I decide I have to give him something. "It's not a big deal. We got into a brawl, and we both spent the day recovering."

"Last night you got into a fight?" Brenna asks with worry all over her expression.

"We're fine," I assure her.

Finn exhales through his nose, unconvinced. "You're loyal to a fault, kid."

I keep my eyes locked on his. "Guess you taught me that."

"Yeah, but I also taught you when loyalty gets you killed."

The words hang there. I take another long drink, hoping the cold will wash away the lies coming out of my mouth.

Across the pub, someone shouts at the dartboard, and Brenna laughs. "There's Stacy from the vets. Haven't seen her in ages." She slides out of the booth. "Let the boys be boys. You were young and dumb once, too," she teases, patting him on his hand.

He grunts.

As soon as she's gone, Finn leans forward again, elbows on the table. "All right. No audience. Tell me what's really wrong."

"Nothing."

He gives a humorless laugh. "If you're lying to protect him, fine. But don't protect him from me."

He's right, and it makes the guilt worse. I should tell him. I should let someone else shoulder the weight before it crushes both Sean and me. But Sean's words echo like a warning bell.

Don't talk about it, not anywhere.

So I deceive him again. "It's just been a wild week. We'll get our shit together."

Brenna returns, smiling. She slides next to him. "Leave the boy alone, Finn."

He grumbles but leans back, arm around her shoulders.

I smile, but it feels wrong. They deserve only the truth from me. Instead, I hide behind another sip and stare at the green glow of the O'Malley's sign reflecting in the window.

Family's family.

And there's no way I'm betraying mine for whatever this cult is that Sean's father created.

Valentina

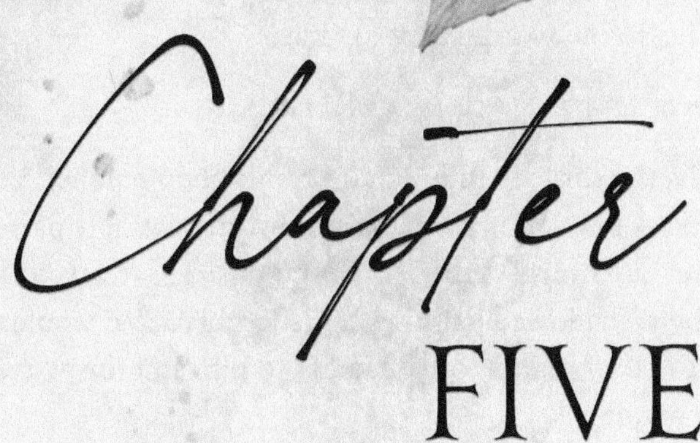

FIVE

Soft morning light slips between the half-closed blinds. It lands across Brax's bare chest, showcasing every ridge of sculpted muscle and his green O'Malley tattoo.

It's ironic. He sleeps like death isn't hovering inches from his throat, calm, worriless.

Reckless man.

Reckless men usually die young.

Is he going to cooperate?

The fear I won't just lose my seat at the table but my life, sparks in my gut. I inhale slowly, matching his breath, wondering how he can be so damn calm.

I study him with my arms crossed, waiting for him to rise with his fists clenched, ready to take me out. But his chest rises with steady, unapologetic breaths that belong to a baby, not a man in a life-or-death situation.

It's time.

The Underworld sent its last reminder two hours ago, and nothing about its merciless, cold words surprises me.

Deadline expires at dawn. Fall in line or fall in blood.

He rolls slightly, the shift revealing more of his abdomen beneath the sheet. Heat flickers low in my stomach at how infuriatingly perfect he looks when he's unaware of his surroundings. His relaxed, broad shoulders, stubble-shadowed jaw, and lips slightly parted would make it easy for me to take him out, or slide next to him and throw responsibility out the window.

Don't get distracted.

My seat at the table hangs by a thread, and here I am fighting the urge to trace the path of sunlight across his skin.

Pathetic.

I loudly clear my throat.

His lashes twitch before his eyes open slowly, hazy for a moment, then sharply aware. His gaze locks on me with a mixture of confusion and irritation that quickly morphs into something smug.

"Morning, Minx," he murmurs, voice still rough with sleep. "Didn't expect a wake-up call from you." He stretches in a long, lazy motion that sends every muscle in his torso flexing.

My pulse misbehaves. I school my expression into ice. "Glad you could join the living world. You owe the Underworld a choice."

"A choice," he repeats, scrubbing a hand along his jaw. "Right. The live-or-die one."

The sheet shifts lower as he sits up. He doesn't bother adjusting it or hiding half of his morning wood.

My eyes drift, but I pull them back up to his, noting, "You're surprisingly calm for someone on a clock."

His arrogance mixes with a lewd expression. "I don't panic before breakfast. And you standing in my bedroom… Well, I can't lie. It's a decent way to start the day."

"Get out of bed," I order, fighting a smile.

"Maybe I'll negotiate from here."

"You lost the right to negotiate the moment you refused to listen yesterday."

He smirks, like he enjoys provoking the sharpness in my tone. "You came to kill me, sweetheart? Or to stare at me while I sleep?"

I step closer, glaring harder. "I'm here because you're out of time. You can choose obedience or prepare for the consequence."

His smirk fades. "So you think you can kill me?"

I don't flinch. "If needed."

His expression turns into calculation. A muscle jumps in his jaw. He studies me in a slower, deeper way.

"Don't underestimate me," I warn.

"You're cold, Minx."

"You think this is easy for me?" My voice stays calm, but truth edges through. "If you fail, the blame lands at my feet."

Brax's expression shifts a fraction. It's enough to tell me he finally understands the cost to him and me, even though he has no idea about my future seat at the table.

"Go ahead, then. Do what you need to do." He rises, naked as a jaybird, and struts into the bathroom.

I gape at him.

Pull it together!

The sound of water hits my ears. I lunge into the bathroom. "What are you doing?"

He turns his head, smirks, and taunts, "Taking a shower. Want to join before you kill me?"

"This isn't a game!"

"So you've said, Minx." He steps behind the glass, and water drips over his silhouette.

My heart thumps hard against my chest cavity. I debated taking him out in the shower for too long.

He turns the water off, glides the door open, and reaches for a towel.

I swallow hard, keeping my eyes on his.

He challenges, "Well? Why haven't you done it yet? It would have been nice and clean in the shower."

I glare at him harder.

He wiggles his eyebrows and adds, "Ah. So you want me to live."

I lie. "No. I want you to decide."

A slow, maddening smile erupts across his lips. "You're looking at me like you're hoping I'll choose yes."

I lift my chin. "Say the words, Brax."

He lunges across the bathroom, slides an arm around my backside, and lifts my chin. "You think you have power over me?"

My core turns to fire. I declare, "You're seconds from losing your life. Stop testing my patience."

He searches my face with an irritating cockiness pinned on me.

Heat coils low in my stomach.

He softly chuckles, then releases me. He walks out of the bathroom and into his closet. He calls out, "Fine, Minx. Have it your way. I choose to live today."

A rush of relief slams through my ribs. I step into the doorway. "Good decision. Get dressed and we'll begin."

Brax tugs a T-shirt over his face, still naked from the waist down, his morning wood at full mast. He meets my gaze. "You don't smile."

It flusters me. "Yes, I do."

"Do you?"

"When it's warranted."

He steps into a pair of gray sweats, then positions himself in front of me. "Maybe this cult stuff has made you lose your happiness."

I freeze.

Has it?

No.

"Stop trying to play with my head. It won't work."

"You can play with my head." He wiggles his eyebrows.

"You wish," I sing, smile big, then step back to regain control. "You'll be tested today. I suggest you take it seriously and cooperate when needed. It's mandatory."

He keeps his gaze defiant and hungry. "If you want cooperation, Minx..." He lazily slithers his gaze over my body, then returns to mine. "You'll have to earn it."

My pulse stutters. My ambition claws upward in warning. I firmly state, "I've already earned it."

"Earned what?"

"My place."

"Your place?"

"In the Underworld...my level," I clarify.

"And what's at the top? Eternal salvation?"

A laugh escapes me.

"Ah. She laughs."

I slowly inhale and exhale, then offer, "A seat at the table of the Omnipotent, or Omni, is the highest honor you can get."

"Shouldn't you aspire to be queen or something?" he asks.

"Good question."

"Well?" He arches his eyebrows.

I shake my head. "I'm not destined to be queen. But my blood right is a seat at the table."

He prods, "Then why do you have to earn it?"

"Because Sean's father didn't believe in handouts. Every position, every privilege, every breath you take has to be earned," I relay.

"It all sounds stupid," he comments.

"It's not. And you'll come to understand it all," I assure him.

He rolls his eyes. "If you say so, Minx."

I fold my arms. "You may think the Underworld is stupid, but it doesn't care what you think. It only cares that you fall in line."

A dark, disobedient expression falls over him. He grinds his molars, looking at me like he wants to kill me.

"It is what it is," I say in a softer tone.

He looks at the ceiling, then back at me. "Then start teaching me. Isn't that your job?"

I stay silent.

He leans against the doorframe, crossing his arms over that maddening chest. "What's lesson one? Bowing? Saluting? Or chanting some creepy Omni hymn?"

"You use humor to cover your fear."

"I'm not afraid of you."

"You should be."

He raises a brow, unfazed. "Show me why."

Hot blood flows through my veins. I turn sharply and walk out of his room.

He follows me, close on my heels. "Scared to show me?"

I go directly to the place I prepared last night. It's a space no one should ever be comfortable entering.

I step into his laundry room and open a newly installed panel.

"What the fuck?" he mutters.

I punch in a code. A near-invisible vertical seam in the wall opens.

Brax steps next to me. His tone is more curious than angry. "What the hell is this?"

"Your mentorship."

I step inside first.

He hesitates for all of two seconds, then comes after me.

The door seals shut with a hydraulic hiss behind him, cutting off the outside world.

The space is small, windowless, and cold. The concrete walls echo. The rubber floors only have a single steel chair bolted to the ground. And one lightbulb hangs overhead, barely bright enough to see.

He scans it all slowly. "You put a torture room inside my house?"

"It's a training room."

"Same thing."

I shrug, smiling. "Call it what you want. But it helps to think of it as a training room."

"Gee. Thanks for the insider information," he chides.

"Sit," I command.

He squints and crosses his arms. "Why?"

"Because if you don't, lesson one becomes a lesson in pain instead of discipline."

He doesn't flinch.

"They're watching. Always. So take your pick, Brax," I order.

He glances to the corner wall where a tiny camera's planted. It's so small you have to look for it. He clenches his jaw.

"Last chance to decide," I warn.

He scowls, then plops down in the chair. The chains rattle faintly as he adjusts his broad frame. He quietly states, "Glad you're enjoying this."

"Who said that?" I question.

"You are," he insists.

I lean down, reach for the steel cuff attached to the armrest, and secure it around his wrist. I whisper in his ear, "This is the only path to see the sun rise tomorrow."

The pulse in his neck jumps.

I add, "If you insult me again, I'll tighten the cuff so it breaks your bones."

He tests it with a subtle tug. It doesn't move. He slowly pins his defiant, pissed eyes on mine. In a neutral tone, he declares, "Don't confuse me for a pussy, Minx. What's next?"

Butterflies dance in my stomach. I keep my breath on his neck. "Lesson one is control."

"Control of what?"

"Your impulses. Your reactions. Your pain. Your tongue. Everything that makes you you," I inform.

"If you wanted my tongue, you could have asked," he says, turning his face so his mouth is next to mine.

A hot, dizzy swirl tightens low in my stomach, flooding me with a pulse I shouldn't feel.

His eyes narrow. He says with certainty, "So you want to break me."

My lips graze his ear. "I'm going to take the edges off you until the Omni can figure out how to best use you."

He lets out a frustrated, angry breath. Pissed eyes meet mine. "What do I get out of it besides seeing tomorrow?"

Without hesitating, I answer, "Power."

We stare at each other until the air turns too heavy. I force myself to go to the wall and turn the dial on.

The chair vibrates beneath him, barely at first. Then it intensifies while a low hum fills the room.

His back goes rigid. "What the—" He clenches his teeth as the microcurrent hits his muscles.

I stand over him, asserting, "A member of the Underworld must exhibit composure. How quickly will you lose yours, Brax O'Malley?"

He groans under his breath. His jaw locks. His biceps flex against the restraints. His legs tense, toes curl, and then his determined blues fixate on me.

I don't move, fighting sensations that shouldn't be attacking me in this moment. But I've quickly learned Brax isn't like other men I've met. Something is different with him. I just can't put my finger on it yet.

A bead of sweat slides from his temple down to his jaw.

"Breathe," I instruct. "If you resist the current, you'll make it worse."

He ignores me. Of course.

Another surge hits him, and he sucks in a sharp breath.

His body jerks in small movements, enough to indicate he's reaching his limit.

"Had enough?" I smirk.

He doesn't answer.

I go to the wall and turn the dial up one notch.

A raw, primal, and infuriatingly arousing growl comes out of him, echoing against the concrete.

I lower my voice. "Say. It."

His chest heaves, and his hands clench into fists so tight his knuckles turn white. Finally, he breaks, snapping, "Enough!"

I turn the dial off.

The room drops into silence except for Brax's ragged breaths. His muscles twitch as the current dissipates.

I approach slowly and unlock the cuff.

His arm drops to his thigh, heavy, almost limp. His voice shakes. "What...was that?"

"Lesson one."

"Of how many?"

"Three."

His laugh comes out dark. "You enjoyed that."

"No, I didn't."

He lifts his head, eyes locking onto mine with heat that could scorch the walls. "You like seeing me suffer."

"I like seeing you survive."

He stands slowly, muscles still trembling. He's bigger than me, stronger than me, and could squeeze the life out of me.

If I'm not careful, he might.

His hand slides between my thighs.

I gasp.

His voice drops low, dangerous. "I knew your panties just got wet."

My heart's never raced so fast. I can't move, and I should.

He strokes his finger over my pants. "What's lesson two, Minx?"

The red light blinks in the corner for the first time since we got into the room.

They're watching and calculating what to do with him.

And me.

I push away from him and clear my throat. "Loyalty. And that one is much harder."

"Loyalty. Let me guess. I kneel. Swear my soul. Kiss a ring?" He glances at my lips.

I snap back into control and walk toward the door. "Follow me."

He obeys.

The panel automatically opens into the laundry room with another hiss.

"Well, abracadabra," he mutters.

I bite on my smile and go into his kitchen. I gesture to the table. "Sit."

He taunts, "You keep ordering me around. I think you like it."

I select the seat across from him and repeat, "Sit."

He turns the chair backward and drops into it. He asks, "You said loyalty is harder than letting you electrocute me? Is it harder than watching you pretend you don't want to climb me?"

Heat flares in my chest. "Stop testing my boundaries."

"Stop pretending you don't like it when I do," he provokes.

My cheeks heat. I reprimand myself and start, "Loyalty means you give the Underworld something that matters."

"Money? Information? Blood?"

"Truth."

He laughs like he can't help it. "Minx, I don't know who taught you how to interrogate men, but truth is the last thing you'll ever get out of me."

"You think so?"

He nods, leaning forward, elbows on the table. "People like me survive by lying."

I lean forward. "People like you die by lying."

Amusement crosses his expression.

I tilt my head, widen my eyes, and coyly ask, "Tell me why you broke into restricted files?"

His face hardens.

I add, "Why did you run a search on me?"

It's not the question I have to get an answer to, but I can't help asking. When I found out he searched for me, it kept me up at night.

He goes still. Something sharp shutters behind his gaze. His knee nudges mine under the table. "Why do you think I looked for you?"

"You tell me."

"What was I supposed to do? Get stuck in a sweat lodge with a woman who drills me for hours and not find out who she is?" he relays.

I arch an eyebrow. "And what did you find?"

His voice drops to gravel. "You're fake online. They don't have anything on the real you."

My thighs clench. Damn him.

A hidden red light for a camera installed near his top cabinet blinks.

They want results.

I exhale and sit back. "The Underworld requires more than wordplay. More than flirting. More than defiance."

His jaw ticks. "Then tell me what the hell loyalty means in the Underworld because I sure as hell know what it means in the real world."

I smile. "It means you give me something you don't want to give."

He tilts his head. "Like what?"

"Your weapons," I reply.

He laughs. Loudly. "Oh, sweetheart. I'll give you my tongue before I hand over my weapons."

"You'll give me both if I want them." My pulse skyrockets.

Shit. Why did I say that?

He stares at me with a look that says he's torn between throwing me against a wall and throwing me out of his house.

"Why?" he demands. "Why do you need my weapons?"

"Because you're unpredictable. Dangerous. And not in a good way."

He grunts, "There's a good way to be dangerous?"

"Yes."

Something dark flashes in his eyes. Slowly, like each movement costs him, Brax reaches down his side and pulls a knife from the waistband of his sweats. He places it on the table between us.

Damnit! He could have killed me!

"Good boy. Now go get the rest," I order.

He glares. "You've got to be kidding me."

"No. And if you leave anything out, they'll know and tomorrow will never come," I warn, pointing at the red light.

He slowly turns his head and mutters, "Fuck."

"All of it," I reiterate.

He scowls, but gets up. One by one, he piles weapons on the table from all over his house. Every time he acts like that's it, I give him a look and he grumbles, then brings more.

Finally, he reaches behind him, pulls a gun from the chair cushion, and slams it down.

My brows rise. "Done?"

"No."

He stands, opens a cabinet, and retrieves a crowbar.

"Brax—"

"Not done," he snipes, then yanks open a drawer. A smaller gun. A set of lock picks. Another knife. He dumps a six-inch gun, a set of brass knuckles, and another knife on the table.

I fold my hands, trying not to seem shocked, but we're running out of table room. I had no idea Brax had an entire arsenal. I ask, "Is that all?"

"No," he growls.

He stomps to the bedroom, returns with a bat, and tosses it on top.

He fumes, "Assume you want that, too?"

I rise and stare at the camera.

The light turns blue.

I spin. "Go ahead and put your weapons back."

He scrunches his face. "I'm confused. I thought you were taking them?"

"Nah. Good to know where you keep everything. I'll see you later," I nonchalantly state, wink, and exit before he can say anything else.

Brax
Several Months Later

Chapter SIX

It's been months since the Underworld touched my life. I started wondering if Valentina actually showed up at my house or if my brain just made her up during a stress-induced blackout. Nobody's killed me or contacted me, yet I can't shake the feeling they're watching, even though the camera is no longer in the kitchen. And I searched all over my house, but I couldn't find anything.

One day, I returned home after a three-day O'Malley shift and went to do a load of laundry. The keypad they'd installed was no longer there.

It fucked with my head more than anything. I'd gotten used to punching in the code Valentina entered to open the wall, yet it never worked. And the thin door line I'd run my finger over to make sure was still there was also gone. The new drywall is perfectly matched to the rest of the house, and even the microtexture is spot-on.

One night, Finn and Sean's uncles grilled me for hours at the pub about what Sean's involved in, and I had to lie to all of them. I came home with so much angry energy that I tore apart half the wall and found nothing. No wiring. No residual cuts. No studs out of place. Just an empty apartment ready to be rented.

It was like the room never existed.

Like *she* never existed.

But I can't even ask Sean about any of it. The minute I bring up anything, he shuts down completely.

The biggest kicker came when he and Zara went off and secretly got married. They came home with their dad's skull branded on their bodies. It was still a fresh wound when we all found out, and the shit hit the fan in both families.

Tension's thick for everyone, but I miss my best friend and am sick of covering for him by lying to Finn. So I'm stuck in the middle of the chaos, pretending I'm not waiting for the next Underworld punch to land, but I am.

And where did Valentina go? As much as I hate her since she's an Abruzzo, I can't stop thinking about the sexy little Minx.

A week ago, I decided the Underworld figured I was no use to them and forgot about me. Then Byrne barged into my garage like a bulldozer, slammed the door open, pointed at me, and said, "You're planning Sean's bachelor party and you're going to convince Fiona to plan a bachelorette party for Zara."

I reminded him that Sean was already married.

He didn't care.

So that's how I ended up at a strip club packed wall-to-wall with neon lights, bass-thumping speakers, and bodies grinding like the world isn't on fire.

Yet for the first time in months, I let myself breathe. Sean's not getting any lap dances, but it feels good to be out with him. And our cousins and I are taking full advantage of the attention the ladies are splashing on us.

The stage lights flash pink, then blue, then something that looks like melted gold as dancers twist around the pole, hair swinging, heels glinting. The air is thick with perfume, whiskey, heat, and sweat. Music pounds through me, loud enough to drown out my worries but not my thoughts. The damn ghost of Valentina refuses to stop stalking the back of my mind. Every stripper that comes over, I compare to her.

Our cousins have taken over the VIP booth like they're kings of Chicago.

A redhead with long legs and a wicked smile straddles L.J.'s lap. Kian's buried beneath a brunette who keeps whispering things that make him cackle like an idiot. Two blondes fight for Romeo's attention, and he's loving every second of it.

For the first time in a long time, nothing feels wrong. Everything feels simple. It's almost as if life hasn't twisted into something I can't control.

Sean sits beside me, split between boredom and irritation. Every dancer who gets near him gets waved off immediately.

"Not a fun bachelor," one mutters, sashaying away.

I shake my head. "You could at least fake enthusiasm."

"I'm happily married," he claims.

"Not that I got to stand by you on your big day," I remind him, still bitter that he got married without me being his best man.

He winces. "I've said sorry a thousand times."

"Yeah, so I've heard." I finish my whiskey, and another one magically appears.

Hours blur together with more dancers, shots, and my cousin's giddiness over everything the strip club has to offer. The months of knotted tension in my stomach slowly unwinds.

An Irish-accented voice booms, "Looks like you're passing the test, lad."

All the hairs on my arms stand on end. I turn, my pulse rising.

Byrne drops into the seat beside Sean like he's been here the whole time. His red beard catches the stage lights, making him look like some aged Celtic god who walked out of a battlefield. He clinks his whiskey glass against the table. "Looks like your boys are celebrating something."

I force a nod. "Aye. Except Sean isn't having any fun."

Sean throws me a glare. "I'm already married."

I glance at the cousins. None of them even notices Byrne's arrival. They're lost in women, drinks, and bad decisions.

Sean asks, "What tests are you talking about?"

Byrne takes a long drink, then leans forward. "Loyalty to your wife."

Sean stiffens beside me. "I'm always loyal to her. And I always will be."

Byrne nods slowly. "That's right. So you pass the test."

Sean scowls at me and accuses, "You set me up."

I raise both hands, palms out. "Sorry, mate. He made me."

"Brax," Byrne says, turning toward me like he's about to hand out divine judgment, "go get a private dance."

I blink. "Now?"

"Yeah, now."

I stand, smirking. "Excuse me, ladies. I need to share the love."

They whine, pouting as I gently move them aside.

I glance around and find two dancers with long legs, big smiles, and glittering eyes. I curl a finger at them, and they bounce over, linking arms with me before leading me toward one of the private rooms where the music is softer and the lights are dimmer.

For several hours, I try to stop comparing the girls to Valentina. But deep down, under the music and the laughter, something sharp twists in my gut.

"I've gotta get out of here," I mutter, pushing DD-cup titties out of my face.

"What's wrong?" the brunette chirps.

I toss money at her. "Nothing. You're great." I hightail it out of the VIP room and look for Sean, but he's nowhere.

Great. Another night of wondering if he's coming back alive.

I stumble my way to the exit. The moment I step out of the strip club, cold air cuts through the heat still clinging to my skin. The neon sign above the door flickers, buzzing like it's trying to warn me. The muffled music fades deeper as I move across the parking lot.

The limo SUV pulls next to me. The driver rolls down the window. "Mr. O'Malley?"

"I'm going to walk."

"Not the best neighborhood," he warns.

I snort. "Not worried. Take care of the rest of the boys." I walk farther into the dark, away from the chaos, trying to blow off steam I shouldn't have.

Why can't I get her out of my damn head?

I stagger through the neighborhood I grew up in, on streets I used to hustle, passing buildings boarded up. The same alleys I used to dumpster dive for food reek of the same rot.

My stomach flips, and I wonder how I ever did it.

I turn a corner and a couple stumbles out of a bar and into a rideshare. More guests stand outside smoking, drunk in conversation and spirits.

The cloud of smoke is thick. I push through it and walk several more blocks. The hairs on my neck rise, and I freeze.

The city feels off. It's too quiet and still. Even the breeze seems to hold its breath, but it's like my instincts snap awake, one by one.

Someone's watching me.

I scan my surroundings, but the street's vacant. I tap my pocket knife and step into the alley's shadows.

A shadow peels itself off the brick wall, and my chest locks.

I'm seeing things.

Valentina steps into the faint strip of streetlight like she owns it. Her head's high, shoulders are relaxed, and she wears a red-diamond-encrusted eye mask. She fixes her gaze on me with a look that makes it hard to breathe.

She shouldn't be here, not in this neighborhood, and especially not alone, or in this dark alley. Yet here she is, as if she's waiting for me.

How did she know I'd be here?

Her black coat hugs her body. Her pinned hair exposes the deadly line of her throat. Her boots barely click on the pavement as she takes two steps toward me.

For a second, I forget how to swallow.

"Brax." Her Italian accent gives me a hard-on even though she says my name like she's snapping a chain around my neck.

Every emotion I've shoved down for months erupts at once. It's anger, heat, relief, and frustration. I clench my fists, unsure if it's so I don't reach for her or push her away.

I mutter, "You're not real. I'm drunk. Or hallucinating."

She tilts her head, eyes flicking down my chest like she's checking whether I've improved since she last dissected me. She teases, "I can assure you I'm real. Not sure if you're drunk though?"

I take a step back on instinct.

She takes a step forward on purpose.

"Where have you been?" I demand, too raw, too fast.

Her hand lands on the front of my shirt, stopping me cold.

She smooths one small wrinkle between her fingers in a slow, deliberate, and possessive way.

Heat shoots down my spine. My pulse slams so loudly I know she hears it.

"Don't ask questions you're not ready to have answered," she threatens.

I snap, grabbing her wrist. "Like hell I'm not."

A slow smile curves her mouth, so damn beautiful it makes my stomach drop.

"Good." She pulls her wrist free. "Then follow instructions."

Before I can respond, she fists my shirt near my collar and yanks me into the alley. Then she spins.

My back hits the brick wall hard.

Her body presses close enough to warm the chill seeping through my shirt.

I swear my heart stops entirely. I growl, "What are you doing?"

"Assessing." Her tone is smooth, calm. "You look intact. I wouldn't claim you're drunk. That's...useful."

Her hand slithers down my chest. Her fingers caress each muscle as if I'm her property. Her lips hover near my jaw. She murmurs, "You're late."

"For what?" I grit out.

Her fingertip drags slowly down the center of my sternum, and every coherent thought fragments.

She breathes, "Your summons. The Underworld is ready to see you."

The words hit like ice water dumped over my head.

My voice comes out rougher than I intend. "What the hell does that mean? You disappear for months and suddenly—"

Her fingers trace up my throat, silencing me.

My pulse jumps beneath her touch, traitorous and loud.

She caresses it. Her eyes darken. She murmurs, "Brax, you were never forgotten. The Underworld has been waiting."

A cold shiver cuts through me. Anger and desire twist together in my chest until they're indistinguishable. "Where's Sean?" I demand, stepping forward so she has to either retreat or let me close the gap.

She doesn't retreat.

"Safe. For now." She smirks.

I snarl, "For now? What does that mean?"

Her hand slides from my throat to my jaw, her thumb brushing the corner of my mouth with maddening precision. "Ask fewer questions. Walk with me."

I shove her hand away, but she catches my wrist mid-motion, twisting my arm behind my back with humiliating ease. She presses me against the wall, her breath warm at my ear.

"Don't make me drag you. Unless you want me to?" she softly warns.

My entire body reacts. I close my eyes, hating the sound of my own heartbeat, hating her for hearing it.

I'm drunk.

Why am I letting her do this to me?

I grind out, "You think you can just show up and expect me to fall in line?"

Her lips graze my ear. "I don't expect it. I require it."

My cock pulses against the brick. My skin tightens to the point of suffocation. I turn my head an inch, contemplating if I should push my mouth against hers.

She pins her challenging gaze on me, egging me on to do it.

Don't!

I threaten, "You're two seconds away from—"

"The Underworld is ready for you. Walk," she commands.

"And if I don't?" I challenge, breath still uneven.

Her smile deepens, wicked and intimate. "Like I said. I'll drag you."

Too curious to leave, I shrug. "Fine."

Valentina leads me to the back of the alley, and we pass through an unmarked door. "You first," she offers, pointing at a staircase and smirking.

The space between my ears pounds. I move down five flights of stairs with her on my heels. I finally step out into a candlelit corridor.

She moves in front of me, leads me down it, and reaches for a red skull mask on the wall. It's the same as Sean and Zara's branding mark. She orders, "Put this on."

"Prefer not to."

"Do it. Or we can't go in," she adds.

I stare at it.

She shakes it in her hands. "Nothing to be afraid of. It's just a mask."

"Fine." I yank it from her and slip it over my face.

Her lips twitch. She tilts her head.

"Happy?" I ask.

She doesn't answer and opens the door.

Black stone walls rise high into shadows that swallow the ceiling. Hundreds of candles flicker in waves, casting warm light across masked faces.

The crowd stands shoulder to shoulder. A long stone platform dominates the far side. Behind it, six men in matching silver-skull masks and robes sit with gravels.

"Judges?" I mutter.

Valentina puts two fingers over my mouth and gives me a warning look.

A gong fills the room, vibrating between us. The wall in front of the men's table lowers to the floor, revealing a stage.

It has three elevated stone pedestals, each occupied by a woman who looks like she stepped out of some forgotten mythology. One glows under the light, her white-blonde hair braided to her hips, her skin almost luminescent. Another stands draped in gold fabric that clings to her figure and shines against her deep-bronze skin. The last has violently red hair and a leather dress, hewn so tightly to her curves it looks painted on her. Their arms are in the air, tied by a thick rope attached to the vaulted ceiling.

Valentina's pace falters.

It's slight, but I catch it.

"What's wrong?" I murmur.

She swallows hard and lifts her chin. "Nothing." She grabs my hand and leads me to the edge of the crowd.

What the fuck is this?

The center judge lifts a hand, silencing the room so thoroughly that the air feels like it cracks.

A yellow-masked man steps onto the stage, wearing nothing.

One of the judges speaks first. "Candidate One. You are assigned the Rite of the Whispered Path."

A murmur rolls through the crowd behind me, thick with unease and curiosity.

The man bows his head. A woman wearing nothing but chains and a black-skull mask leads him through a doorway on the left side of the stage.

A dark-haired naked man wearing a blue-skull steps forward.

Another judge states, "Candidate Two. You will undergo the Rite of Demonic Gods."

The crowd cheers.

Another chain-wearing woman leads him away.

A third candidate approaches.

"Candidate Three. You are to complete the Rite of the Shrouded Mirror."

The crowd gasps, then chatter arises.

A judge bangs a gavel. He shouts, "Silence!"

The crowd obeys, and a woman leads the man out of the room.

The crowd shifts with nervous energy. The center judge gestures again. "Next."

My gut tightens.

Valentina grips my forearm. She doesn't look at me and steps forward, her posture perfect, chin lifted, an icy expression on her face. She reaches the stage and says, "Take your clothes off."

"What?"

She locks her gaze on mine. "Do it. Then get on stage. You're up."

I don't move.

Her voice turns panicky. "Please."

I grind my molars.

"Brax," she quietly begs with fear in her eyes.

It tugs at my heart. So I drop my pants, unbutton my shirt, and take my place on stage.

The judge points directly to her. "Stand beside him."

Valentina's head jerks backward.

A ripple of whispers cascades through the room.

The judge bangs the gavel and waits.

Valentina releases a slow breath, then stands next to me.

"What's going on?" I ask.

"Quiet!" another judge shouts, banging his gavel.

I wait for her to give me some indication, but she looks forward at the judges, not blinking.

One of the judges leans forward slightly. "Guardian Valentina Abruzzo. Initiate Brax O'Malley."

Our names echo through the chamber, ricocheting off stone and flame.

Valentina stiffens.

My heart slams hard, and a drop of sweat forms under the skull mask.

He continues, "You will complete the Ritual of the Scarlet Hour."

Gasps, sharp breaths, and people stepping forward as if they're trying to get a better view create chaos in the crowd. Even the women on the pedestals tilt their heads, their expressions sharpening with interest.

Valentina takes a step forward, unable to contain her fury. "No," she says, her voice cutting through the air like steel striking stone. "I've not had any marks against me to partake in that ritual."

Marks?

So fucking cryptic.

The judge in the center rises to his feet, and the entire room drops into complete silence. His voice cuts low and deadly. "Did your security fail and this man is now before us due to your lack of oversight?"

Valentina's eyes widen. Her jaw locks.

"Well?"

She answers, "I was not given the proper intel."

"You didn't look for it, did you?" he prods.

"Hey, it's my fault I followed Sean. Not hers," I interject.

"Silence!" the judge shouts, banging the gavel. Then he adds, "And your mentee can't seem to keep his mouth shut."

Shit.

Valentina swallows hard.

The judge declares, "The ritual stands."

Her voice turns desperate. "This violates tier protocol. He is not marked or trained. He cannot comply or compete. He—"

"You may either proceed or you may offer your seat to another," he calmly insists.

Her body goes rigid except for her lower lip. It shakes with anger while her fingers curl tight at her sides.

What the fuck is going on?

The room trembles with tension.

Her eyes close behind her mask. She draws in a slow, painfully controlled breath, like she's trying to hold herself together. When she opens her eyes, nothing in her gaze resembles the woman who pulled me into the tunnel with confidence.

Valentina

Chapter
SEVEN

Everything inside me lurches sideways, crashing into itself from a wave I never saw coming. My breath backs up into my throat, sharp and thick, and the roar from the crowd ignites hotter.

The chanting starts slowly at first, a few voices pulsing together, low and guttural. Then more join. Soon, the entire room vibrates with a single thundering sound. It's a deep and primal vibration that shakes through the soles of my boots and climbs up my spine.

"Oooommmm. Oooommmm."

Each beat lands against my sternum, squeezing my lungs as the air inside burns. My heart claws viciously against it as if trying to break free.

This can't be happening.

Not the Ritual of the Scarlet Hour.

Not with Brax.

Not when I've done everything right.

I didn't. He should never have been inside.

I didn't know.

It was my responsibility.

My insides twist into a violent knot. I taste iron on my tongue, like the air itself is bleeding. My fingers twitch at my sides, wanting to reach for Brax, shove him off the platform, and scream that they made a mistake.

But I don't.

Because they didn't.

This is a deliberate, calculated move. A punishment crafted specifically for me, and I assume it was before the night of the fight.

They set me up.

The realization slams into me so hard my knees almost buckle. I swallow the panic, but it scratches its way up my throat mimicking broken glass.

For years, there have been Omnis waiting for me to fail and prove I'm unworthy of the seat my parents died for. I didn't until now. Yet I gave them the opportunity with Brax O'Malley.

I should have found the intel they withheld. I could have dug deeper until every path was exhausted.

Could I?

There wasn't any time.

There are no excuses.

Brax turns his head toward me, the red-skull mask unable to hide the question in his posture. His chest expands like he's about to speak, but I cut him a sharp glare. If he opens his mouth, he'll feed the fire, licking eagerly at the edges of this ritual.

The chanting swells louder, shaking the torches mounted on the walls. The flames turn into creatures, swaying violently with the shadows.

The judges stare down at us, still as stone.

A sharp clang of the gong echoes as a door behind the stage bursts open.

Stay calm. You're trained for this, I remind myself, fighting the nausea rolling in my belly.

Three figures emerge. Men almost as tall as Brax, shirtless, with bodies carved from ritualistic brutality. Their masks are white. Something red, resembling blood, is splattered over their masks and skin.

The crowd inhales as one organism, resembling a predator scenting fresh carnage. Then the deep-toned male groans mix into the *oooommms.*

My throat closes. This isn't what they told me Brax's initiation would be.

The men take positions flanking the stage, their breathing slow and synchronized. Their splattered red barely covers the slashes, burns, and marks of previous rites endured and survived.

Behind them, another figure appears. A naked woman, except for a chain around her waist and cuffed wrists, gracefully floats across the stage on her toes. It's an effortless illusion that defies the laws of the human body. She keeps her head bowed. Her long black hair cascades over her shoulders.

In her hands, she carries a thick, stiff, scarlet leather V. Gold chains hang from its ends, clinking rhythmically as she steps across the platform.

The sight of it turns my stomach. My skin prickles with cold terror despite the room's heat.

The Scarlet Letter.

I've never seen one, only heard the whispered rumors.

V is for me.

I'll forever be marked.

I swallow bile rising up my chest.

The Ritual of the Scarlet Hour is used only as a punishment. It's to test, break, and stain you for life.

Brax stiffens beside me. He growls under his breath, "What the fuck is going on?"

My hand snaps out before I can think, fingers pressing against his thigh, warning him to stay silent. I softly hiss, "Shut up."

Another loud groan vibrates beneath us. The stone floor shifts. A fourth pedestal rises from the center of the stage, polished in a black mirror with similar red splatters over it.

The judges lift their gavels and strike them in perfect unison.

The crowd explodes with more energy, their chants more frantic.

The judge who sentenced me orders Brax, "Step upon your pedestal."

Brax blurts out, "Like hell I'm—"

I move in front of him before he finishes. I press my hand hard against his chest.

His heart slams against my palm, a violent rhythm matching my own. He leers down at me.

I plead, "Please. Do it. If you want us to see tomorrow, just do it."

His chest rises again. His breath comes out as harsh as his words. "You have to be kidding me?"

My voice cracks. "I'm not. Please."

Something flickers behind his eyes. He shakes his head. "This is insane."

"It will be worse if you resist," I beg, pushing him gently. "Just step onto the pedestal."

His breath shudders. Then he mutters a curse and caves, taking his place.

Men circle him the second his bare feet meet the black stone. Thick ropes lower from the vaulted ceiling, swaying slightly in the heated air.

Brax glares at them. He bites, "Seriously? You all need hobbies."

They ignore him and seize his wrists.

He tries to fight, but there are too many of them. They hold his arms straight out.

A judge bangs his gavel. "Silence!"

The room quiets.

He demands, "You will relax and allow the ritual to take place. If you fight, it means you are not choosing this. There will be no ritual."

He grunts, his defiance growing as his fists clench.

The judge commands, "Declare your acceptance of the ritual. Or this will end now!"

Brax says nothing.

"Say 'I choose this ritual!'" the judge orders.

Before he can answer, I urge, "Say it!"

He jerks his head toward me. Fire explodes in his expression.

"Say it," I repeat, trying to sound confident, but it comes out in a shaky beg.

He stares at me a moment, mutters, "Fucking hell, Valentina," then purses his lips, looks at the judge, and roars, "I choose this ritual!"

There's a gasp, then the crowd resumes chanting louder than before. The men secure the cuffs around Brax's wrists, and the slack gets eliminated. His muscles flex against the pull, broad shoulders stretching, chest rising.

The gong sounds again. The ropes lose their tension, and the women on the other pedestals lower their arms. Men unlock the cuffs from their wrists. They step off the pedestals and kneel around Brax, settling into their new positions. Their masks glitter from the torches, and they tilt their heads back.

Sweat beads at the base of my spine. My heartbeat thunders, and the woman with the scarlet V steps forward. She leads me several feet directly in front of Brax, demanding, "Strip!"

Brax's eyes turn to slits through his mask.

Every heartbeat is a punch to my ribs. I fight to keep my hands from shaking and remove all my clothing until I'm wearing nothing but my mask.

Brax's jaw clenches.

I keep my gaze locked on his, surprised he doesn't take his off mine.

The three empty pedestals vanish into the floor with a grinding rumble. Another mechanism groans overhead. A thick rope unspools, lowering a black leather swing directly in front of Brax.

The leather glistens under the flickering flames, its surface scarred with cracks and darkened red splotches that look uncomfortably like dried blood. The iron attachments creak as it descends, steady and ominous, stopping just a few feet from his chest.

Brax's gaze snaps to it, then to me. Agitation radiates off him in waves. His breath turns shallow. Every muscle in his restrained arms pulses with new force.

Everything between us is about to shift into a place neither of us will forget.

No one will forget.

I'll always be the one.

The woman with the scarlet V lifts it and presses the cold leather against the center of my chest.

A tremor races up my spine. My stomach rolls.

She drags her fingers over the gold chains and moves behind my back, fastening them with slow precision. When the clasp snaps shut, the room fills with whispers. Condemn her, brand her, execute her are just some of the phrases.

Heat rushes to my cheeks and travels down my neck. The weight of the V settles between my breasts in a heavy, suffocating, and permanent way.

Somewhere above, a spotlight clicks on with a sharp crackle of electricity. Dust rises around us. Shadows leap. And then a grand piano ascends from the dark floor just left of center stage.

A woman, draped in a red sequin gown that clings to her curves and wearing a mask identical to mine, sits in front of the keys. Her fingers hover for barely a second before she presses the first seductive note.

A languid melody slides into the room and curls around me. The chanting falters, but not completely, their voices blending with the music, humming in perfect, erotic harmony.

My throat tightens again.

This is really happening.

There's no way out.

I glance at Brax, and my mistake nearly destroys me.

His gaze drills through the skull mask, burning through my defenses, my training, everything I've built to survive this place. The women around him run their hands slowly up and down his thighs, their fingertips tracing the lines of muscle with reverence. He doesn't flinch, doesn't react, doesn't even look at them. His eyes stay locked on mine with questions that slice through my skin.

But there's also his darkness. It screams he's ready to kill, and I'm afraid he might as soon as he's released.

I mouth, "It's okay."

His breath only gets harsher.

Something inside my rib cage twists so sharply I nearly step backward. And I wish he'd stop looking at me. I wish he'd look away and just let everyone else witness this test that the Omni hopes I fail.

The music swells, reaching a haunting crescendo. The chanting turns melodic. It rises and falls, truly a dark prayer whispered directly into my bones.

When the final note breaks, the judge who sentenced us rises slowly. The room falls silent, and he asks the question. "What do you choose, Valentina?"

The question slams through me like a blade.

My stomach curls so tight it cramps. A violent wave of dizziness rolls through me. I clutch the chains holding the scarlet V to the point my knuckles hurt. My vision blurs at the edges. Every instinct I have screams at me to run, to refuse, to demand another punishment, another rite, anything but this.

There is only one choice. I survive, or I die. I complete the ritual, or I easily get replaced. And I can protect Brax, or watch him bleed for my failure.

I remind myself, *I've been trained by the best.*

It's just humiliation. There are worse things.

I lift my chin.

The scarlet V shifts with the movement. Its gold chains tighten across my ribs.

The room leans toward me, hungry for my answer.

My knees tremble, but I force my voice to rise.

"I choose—"

The words catch. Emotion hits me harder than I ever thought it could.

Brax's eyes widen through his mask. The faintest shake of his head pleads with me to stop. But there is no reconsidering. There never was and never will be in the Underworld.

I seize what remains of my strength, bite into the wavering fear in my throat, and scream the words the Omni have demanded from me,

"I choose the Ritual of the Scarlet Hour!"

The crowd erupts. It's not in applause but a guttural roar that shakes the entire chamber. The pianist's fingers return to the keys.

Heat sweeps over my skin. The floor vibrates under my feet. The three blood-masked men step forward in unison, and everything inside me fractures.

It's not because of what the next hour holds but because Brax is still staring at me. And I wish I didn't care. I'd give anything for the entire Underworld to see me but not him.

A gold clock lowers from the ceiling behind Brax. It's close to the hour, and every tick of the second hand is loud, competing with the music and chants.

The men lift me, almost reverently, onto the leather swing. Two leather straps get lowered several feet in front of me. They each have cuffs attached and get secured to my ankles, so I'm spread open on display for Brax.

His eyes dart around, taking me in.

I look away.

"Valentina," he barks.

I blink hard and meet a dark, unhinged, heated gaze.

"There you are," he says in a calm voice.

It soothes me. I don't know why.

The clock rings three times, signaling the start of the ritual.

It's sixty minutes of my life.

A man steps forward. Another moves behind me. A third positions himself next to me.

The girls do the same to Brax, dragging their hands all over him and pressing their lips to his skin.

His jaw twitches.

A cart gets rolled next to me. It's full of gadgets. Each man grabs one.

The chants turn to long erotic ohs.

Fifteen minutes of fingers drag over our bodies. Lips touch everywhere but mouths and genitals, teasing, but not going further. Then it's game on.

The white-blonde woman skims her body down Brax's and kneels again. She takes a red-nailed finger and strokes his cock, then gets fixated with the metal. She caresses it over and over.

His erection grows. A flush rolls through his skin.

Nipple rings get placed on my chest. I zone out, focusing only on Brax's determined gaze, right as the man to the side of me pulls it, and sensation shoots right to my core.

I barely register my whimper through the music, chants, and place I'm trying to get to.

The man behind me slides his arm around my neck, bending it like a choke hold, but doesn't squeeze. His fingers grip the gold chain holding the V, reminding me of the lifetime of shame I'll now carry. His lips graze my lobe as his hand grips my ass cheek.

The one in front of me drags his finger through my pussy and then shoves two fingers inside me, pumping while circling my clit with his thumb.

I breathe through my nose, trying to quiet the sensations I don't want to feel.

Brax's expression changes.

I break his gaze, dropping mine down his taunt torso.

The redhead kisses his nipples. The one in the gold dress is bent behind him, doing something to his ass. And the white-blonde is circling her tongue around the tip of his dick.

I cringe, hating the sight of them touching him. Yet the same heat appears as when I learned about his piercing.

"Valentina!" he roars through gritted teeth.

I lift my gaze to his.

He breathes hard.

Several things get pushed into my pussy, then pulled out. The man in front of me holds glistening beads in the air and hands them to the one behind me.

Relax, I remind myself.

"Jesus, you're fucking hot," Brax mutters. His jaw twitches.

"Don't cum," I blurt out.

His hot breath comes out like fire, chest heaving.

"Please. When this is over you can cum in me," I add.

His eyes singe behind his mask.

The beads slide inside my ass as I glance at the clock.

Twenty-three minutes.

A new challenge roots itself deep inside me.

The Underworld isn't getting him tonight.

I am.

No cumming for twenty-three minutes," I tell him, even though he's allowed to orgasm. I'm the one with the scarlet letter being punished, not him. But everything within me wants him to wait for me. I've waited for months for the Underworld to direct me to go to him. There hasn't been a day my mind hasn't wandered, thinking about his cocky ass.

His eyes widen, but then his determination comes roaring back. He sniffs hard and grits out, "Twenty-three minutes, Minx."

I nod.

A tongue circles my nipples, playing with the clamps just like the woman played with Brax's piercing. I don't look down, trying not to give it any attention. And then everything gets taken up a notch.

The man behind me lowers his mouth, tonguing the bead near my entrance and gripping the chain tighter near my spine.

A vibrator gets inserted inside me. The motor's at a low speed, but I know it's only going to go up, and the sensations are already hitting me. The man thrusts it in rhythm to the music.

"She's so fucking wet," the man in front of me claims, then takes his other hand and traces the V on my chest.

"Don't you dare cum, Valentina," Brax growls.

The woman giving Brax a blow job moans loudly. "Your pre-cum tastes so good. Give me more."

My eyes dart to his cock. She's moaning feverishly and massaging his balls. Sweat drips down his torso in long streaks.

"Don't!" I warn, then gasp for breath as someone's tongue begins to work my clit.

Brax's gaze drops. Jealousy flares in his eyes.

My core heats like a match to dry wood. I blink hard. My breath turns ragged.

He warns, "If you fucking cum, I'll kill you myself, Minx!"

I try to focus on him.

"Fucking hell," he grits.

I glance at the girl going to town on him and the others.

They aren't fucking him. I am, I tell myself with renewed determination.

"How-how much time?" Brax asks.

I glance behind him. "Four and a half minutes."

He nods and clenches his jaw, staring at me.

Everything gets turned up a notch. The man eats my ass like it's his last meal. The other one licks and sucks my pussy to the point I can barely breathe. And the man in front of me puts the vibrator on full power.

I count seconds, not taking my eyes off Brax. My arousal drips down my legs, and the scent flares around us.

When the clock strikes four, the gavels get slammed against the table. The vibrator gets removed. Two men step back, along with the women. There's a grinding noise as the swing gets lowered a few feet, then another sound rips through the room.

The man behind me pushes the swing forward.

The tension on the rope gets reduced. Brax's arms lower, and he immediately reaches for me. He grabs my waist, pulls my head toward his mouth, then sinks his cock deep into me.

A feral groan escapes him. "Jesus Christ, Minx," he murmurs near my ear.

I clutch my arms around him, rocking back and forth over him, so pent up I can't last very long.

He moves my face to his as I break. His tongue slides into my mouth, muffling my cries, and my body collapses into a violent spasm.

He grunts, thrusting into me with a powerful force, and holding me against him with kisses consuming all my breath.

The adrenaline doesn't stop. It overflows into every nerve I have, creating a chaos I've never experienced before.

"Mine, Minx," he cries out in a guttural tone again, then tugs at the anal beads.

Another sensation attacks me.

His cock hardens further, then he groans. He stretches me further, battling my orgasm with his own. He tightens his hold around me, murmuring with his gaze locked on me, "Mine."

Brax

Chapter
EIGHT

Valentina trembles against me, our breaths still tangled, her pulse beating wild under my palms. Every small after-shock that ripples through her travels straight into me, turning my muscles to liquid and concrete at the same time.

Spasms fade further, but I don't let her go, keeping her pressed against my chest like my body alone is enough to shield her from whatever the hell this place decides to do next.

She lifts her damp lashes and pins her hazed gaze on me.

I've never come that hard in my life.

Not in a bed.

Not in a bar bathroom.

Not in the backseat of a car or in a locker room or anywhere else.

Our sweat and her perfume dance between us. It's just as intoxicating as the look she gives me.

I kiss her again, addicted to the way her tongue sweeps mine. She kisses me back, and it's just her and me.

Then a deep gong explodes through the chamber.

The vibration slams through my chest and rattles my teeth, yanking us out of whatever world we just created and slamming us back into this sadistic one in front of us.

Valentina flinches, fingernails digging into my shoulders. Her body tenses, and her expression changes. She shutters back behind a neutral, hardened wall.

The crowd erupts. Their voices meld into something that doesn't sound like any language I know. It rolls through the chamber like a living force.

"Korr-velash...korr-velash...korr-velash..."

The chant grows louder with every repetition. The floor under my feet vibrates in a slow, steady thrum that climbs my legs, then my spine. It settles inside my rib cage.

Torches shake on the walls. The air thickens with tension.

"Korr-velash...korr-velash..."

Valentina's breath hitches. Her haunted eyes grow wider through the edges of her mask. Then her gaze dims, replaced with a cold, sharp composure that makes my skin crawl and my dick twitch at the same time.

I don't loosen my grip. I keep her flush against me, her twitching thighs still wrapped around my hips, my arms banded around her waist. I'm staking a claim I don't understand and probably don't have the right to, and it's not smart. She's still an Abruzzo and I'm an O'Malley.

The thought slams into me over and over again as the chant grows more frenzied.

What the hell did they just make us do?

What did they make her do?

I've had sex more times than I can count. I've had the pleasure of women out of anger, recklessness, boredom. The things I've done would be considered scandalous to most. But this...this wasn't crossing a line. This was obliterating it. There's no world where I'm supposed to be buried inside Valentina Abruzzo while standing on a pedestal, with hundreds of masked lunatics chanting for our souls.

Yet my body is still clinging to hers like it never wants to leave. And I'm still restrained, or I'd find a way to get her out of here.

The judges bang their gavels. The sharp cracks slice through the chant. The echoes dissolve into an eerie quiet.

"Release her," one of the silver skulls orders.

My eyes snap to the table. My fingers grip her hips harder.

The three blood-masked men step toward us. They circle Valentina like she's theirs to take.

"Don't touch her," I growl.

My voice doesn't carry as well as the judge's, but it's enough. They hesitate for a breath, shifting their attention to me.

"It's fine," Valentina says quickly, her hand pressing my chest to release my grasp over her.

One of the men reaches for her.

I tug her back into me and push my shoulder forward.

Valentina firmly states, "Brax. Let me go."

I glance at the men, then her.

"It's okay," she reiterates.

I cave, release her, and they unlock the cuffs around her ankles. They lift her out of the swing. She takes a minute to find her balance, then stands tall.

The white-blonde woman steps in front of her and smooths out the leather scarlet V.

Shame shadows Valentina's face.

It pisses me off further.

A man releases my cuffs, and I jump off the pedestal and tug Valentina to my side. I turn toward the judges and hold up my hand.

The crowd quiets.

I announce, "It's been fun. Thanks for the laughs. We're leaving now."

A low rumble erupts behind us.

I turn my head.

The floor at the far edge of the stage splits open, stone grinding against stone. Harsh, dry heat washes over the stage. A small circular table you'd find at a bar to stand at, along with a red-hot cauldron, rises from the depths with two metal rods. Flames lick the sides, hungry and wild, casting an angry glow across the dark room.

Inside the cauldron, I see them.

"What the fuck?" I blurt.

Valentina's body stiffens against mine, but she doesn't pull away. She murmurs, "You made it."

I glance down at her. "Great. Let's get out of here."

Her eyes meet mine for half a second, tangled full of relief, grief, and guilt.

The center judge rises to his feet. "Initiate Brax O'Malley."

Every gaze in the room swivels toward me.

I freeze.

"Profess your loyalty to The Underworld," the judge orders.

I snort softly, humorless.

Loyalty.

These bastards wouldn't recognize real loyalty if it wrapped itself in chains and bled on their floor.

I've been loyal my entire life. First to myself. Then to Finn, to Sean, to the entire O'Malley clan. I've taken punches and thrown them, kept secrets, stepped into fights I had no business stepping into, all because that's what you do when you belong to a family like ours.

I already pledged my loyalty for life. It's carved into my bones. And it sure as hell isn't to this cult.

I'm about to tell Valentina we're leaving, but when I look at her, a chill runs down my spine. She offers a tight smile and nods.

Her expression tells me the only chance to live is to do what they want.

These people are crazy. I put nothing past them. If I have to play along to get us out of here in one piece, then that's what I'm going to do.

"Step forward," the judge orders.

I reluctantly slide my arm off Valentina, my fingers dragging down her arm until they have to let go. I step toward the cauldron's glow.

Someone presses a piece of wood into my hand.

"It's to bite down on," Valentina says quietly behind me.

I arch my eyebrows.

She adds, "Trust me. Curl your fist, then put it on the table, thumb-side up."

My pulse hammers between my ears.

A man in a red cloak, mask like the one I'm wearing, comes out of nowhere. He wears a thick, red glove that runs to his elbow. He lifts one of the rods out of the cauldron. Sean's father's skull glows hot.

So this is how Sean and Zara got their marks.

"Step forward," the judge orders.

I don't see any way out. I curl my fist and put it on the table.

Two men hold my arm.

"Repeat after me," another judge orders, then begins reciting, "By the power of my blood and the oath of my name, I pledge my loyalty to The Underworld."

I don't want to say it. Every syllable tastes like betrayal.

Sean is somewhere in this madness.

He'll have my back if it comes down to it.

One thing Finn taught me is that life is a chessboard. Sometimes, to win, you move a piece you hate.

I spit the words, "By the power of my blood and the oath of my name, I pledge my loyalty to The Underworld."

Lies.

The judge continues, "From this moment, I stand as brother, soldier, and weapon."

Fuck you. I'll stand next to you and slit your throat someday, brother.

I repeat, "From this moment, I stand as brother, soldier, and weapon."

He continues, "I obey the Omni. I guard the table. I honor the skull."

I repeat it all. Every word. Crafting in my head what I'll do to all these people.

No matter what they burn into me, my loyalty belongs to Sean, to Finn, to the people who raised me and bled with me. These vows are noise. A sick, theatrical ceremony that means nothing.

They think this means they own me?

They don't.

When the last line leaves my mouth, the judge nods. "So it is vowed."

The crowd holds its breath.

Valentina directs, "Bite on the wood."

I put it in my mouth.

The blazing orange-red skull moves toward me, ready to claim my flesh.

My stomach flips. I clamp my teeth on the wood.

Valentina wraps her hand around my forearm, tight and steady.

I stare at her, then feel the heat approach me.

"This mark binds you to your vows. You will carry it until death," the judge declares.

I turn in time to see the skull pressed into my hand. Steam lifts into the air, my skin sizzles, and a burnt flesh odor turns my stomach. My muscles coil, my heart slams, my vision narrows.

Valentina squeezes my arm. "Breathe through your nose."

I drag in one deep breath through my nose. The wood presses so tightly between my teeth that my jaw aches. I lock my gaze on the flames beyond the cauldron as pain detonates up my arm, white-hot and blinding.

The skull gets pressed harder.

My muffled roar bursts past the wood. My knees threaten to buckle. My vision explodes into black-and-red spots. Nothing exists except heat and pressure and the knowledge that a piece of metal is carving a dead man's legacy into my body.

"Good job," Valentina praises, and I realize the pressure lifted.

Cold rushes over the brand a second later as someone smears an ointment or salve across it, trying to temper the damage.

It doesn't help much.

My hand throbs with a deep, pulsing pain that syncs with my heartbeat. Every ache is a reminder.

You're theirs now.

Marked as part of their cult.

There was no choice.

That's a lie.

I spit the wood out of my mouth and bend slightly, sucking in air. Sweat drips down my temples and neck. I force myself to straighten, to look at what they did.

Through the clear, glistening ointment, the skin on the side of my hand is angry, charred, and already blistering. Yet, the skull image is clear.

"*Zaii'venar...zaii'venar...zaii'venar...*" the crowd chants.

The hair on my arms rises.

Valentina shifts next to me with a small tremor in her bottom lip. The scarlet V still gleams on her chest, with the gold chains lying heavy on her shoulders. She stares at the judges.

"What now?" I ask.

She doesn't look at me.

A new realization makes my toes curl.

The Omni just got what they wanted from me.

Now they're coming for her.

"Take your place," the judge orders.

Valentina steps forward.

"What are you doing?" I ask.

She continues not to look at me.

The woman wearing the chains appears again. She unhooks the gold links and lifts the leather V away from Valentina's chest.

"About time. Let's go," I order, grabbing Valentina's hand.

She squeezes her eyes shut and releases a heavy breath, shoulders rising and falling in a slow, resigned rhythm.

"Step away from her," a judge orders.

My chest tightens. I spin. "We're leaving."

The judge points to the group of men. They lurch at me, grabbing my arms.

"Get off me," I bark, fighting, but they pin my arms so I can't move them.

"Stop fighting, Brax. You're making this worse," Valentina orders.

I freeze, my heart beating a mile a minute.

What is she talking about?

A man steps behind her. He restrains her so her arms are behind her back. Two kneel and hold her legs against their bodies.

My insides tremble with anger and confusion.

The judge asserts, "Blood remembers. The body pays for what the soul declares."

A man puts a piece of wood to her mouth.

She accepts it and bites down.

Heat from the cauldron intensifies. The man reaches in with his gloved hand and lifts the second metal rod. When he raises it, the tip catches the light, revealing a six-inch-long V that glows molten red.

Rage detonates inside me. I snarl, "Don't you touch her!" I try to fight again, but the men overpower me.

The room seems to hold its breath.

Valentina's lips shake, yet she stands taller, shoulders squared, spine straight.

I fight again for my freedom, and another man steps forward and grasps my throat. I choke, struggling to breathe.

The cauldron's flames flare, turning her skin to gold and shadows. Time slows.

Valentina swallows hard as the red-hot metal V comes toward her.

"*Zaii'venar...zaii'venar...zaii'venar...*" fills the chamber so fiercely that it vibrates against my rage.

Two men step forward. One pulls her breast to the left. The other moves her breast to the right. The metal V gets pressed to her torso, the top tips touching the side of her breasts and the bottom above her belly button.

Her body jerks violently. A muffled scream rips from her throat, trapped behind the wood. The smell of burning flesh rises again.

It's worse than before. It crawls up my nose and wedges itself behind my eyes, mixing with the memory of my own pain and the visual of her tears falling down her cheeks.

I fight again, and the fingers squeeze my neck so hard I almost black out. I miss the rod getting pulled away.

The crowd's chant turns to, "*Ohm. Ohm. Ohm.*"

Someone slathers ointment on her stomach, and they release her.

She trembles alone, tears falling down her cheeks, staring at the judges while trying to look brave. But she's branded and brilliant and broken open in a way I don't think anyone would ever know how to fix, including me.

My heart aches. Anger floods me to the point I can barely see.

The hand gets removed from my throat.

I choke.

"Easy. Don't want to die on your initiation night," the man warns, and steps back. "Release him."

They obey, and my arms fall to my side.

I rush over and reach for her.

"Don't touch me," she warns.

I freeze.

The judges rise in perfect, eerie unison, their long robes whispering against the stone. One raises a hand, and the room falls silent.

"Brax O'Malley," the center judge intones. "Your duties now lie with The Underworld."

My jaw clenches.

The Underworld can shove its duties—

"You are to speak of none of what transpired tonight," the judge continues, his voice slicing through my thoughts. "Not to your family, not to your friends, not to the woman beside you. Silence is your shield now. Break it, and your life is forfeited."

A cold pulse moves down my spine.

Valentina's breaths grow shallow.

More guilt eats me that I didn't stop them from harming her.

Another judge leans forward. "From this moment on, every step you take will either gain you power or strip it from you."

My chest tightens. The brand on my hand throbs, and my hatred grows stronger.

I didn't survive the streets to be owned by anyone.

I force myself to stand taller, even as my vision pulses from the pain radiating up my arm.

The judge warns, "Your path begins now. Choose wisely, initiate."

Yeah.

I'll choose.

And when the time comes, I'll choose against every one of you bastards.

Valentina stands perfectly still beside me, her tears drying from the heat of the fire still roaring beside us.

The Omni bang their gavels again, sealing whatever twisted ceremony they just conducted.

The chant starts back up, lower this time, almost reverent.

"Korr-velash... korr-velash..."

The sound vibrates through the brand on my hand and the fresh wound on her stomach, tying us together in pain and fire and vows that don't mean what these bastards think they do.

They think they own us.

They have no idea what they've just created.

Valentina turns. "It's time to go." She doesn't wait for me. She moves through the crowd with her head held high.

I follow.

We reach the exit, and someone hands us our clothes. We step into the hallway naked.

The door shuts, muffling the chants.

"Minx—"

She holds up her hand. "Silence is your shield, Brax. Now get dressed. A car is waiting outside to take you home."

Valentina

Sex Months Later

Chapter
NINE

Glass and steel reek of obscene money. Security cameras blink red in the corners, monitoring everyone and everything. Guards make their presence known. The scent of lilies and polished stone fills the space, clean and perfect.

It makes sense that Sean bought his penthouse here. The new Chicago building sold out almost instantly. It screams O'Malley arrogance and Marino power.

"Happy birthday to you!" a group sings, then clapping fills the air. I turn toward the coffee shop, and a millennial woman with blue hair and green eyes grins. She blows out candles on a cake.

Nausea rolls through me as soon as the flames go out and smoke swirls upward. Six months later, I still smell burning flesh when I close my eyes.

Mine.

His.

The V stained into my flesh still has faint pink remnants, unfaded against the parts that have turned white. Every time I look in the mirror, fresh shame floods me.

Time doesn't soften anything. I keep moving, hoping the memories will turn into muted ghosts I can peacefully live with, but it's only a wish that never comes true.

The doors open, and a gust of wind blows through the lobby. The faintest smell of blown-out candles tortures me. Another round of nausea hits, and I press my hand to my stomach.

The scar on my stomach pulls and throbs. I wince and move to the corner of the lobby, then lean against the window. I close my eyes, forcing myself not to leave.

The elevator bank glows at the far end, four sets of doors framed in brushed gold. My heart bangs against the V burned into my skin.

I came to see Zara. I brought a baby gift for her since I couldn't go to her shower.

Another ache tugs at my heart. I'd have given anything to get an invitation, even though I know it isn't possible.

It's not Zara's fault. Some things will never change, no matter how hard you try. So I remind myself it is what it is, and at least Zara doesn't hold the past against me. And that's the one good thing I have in the hell I'm surviving in.

Barely.

I shake off the pain in my torso, a flashback of the branding ceremony when the hot metal got pressed into my chest.

It wasn't the first time I got branded. I have the skull on the back of my neck, just like Zara does, only mine is red, as hers is pink.

I wanted that skull, I remind myself.

I blink hard and take deep breaths.

The gust of wind hits. I glance toward the doors and freeze.

Zara's father, Luca Marino, steps through the lobby doors like he owns the building, the city, hell, the whole damn world. His black coat flares around his legs as he takes one power step after another.

My pulse skyrockets. *Shit!*

The years have carved deeper lines into his face, silver threads through his dark hair at his temples, but I would know him anywhere.

Luca's my mother's brother and my uncle. He's the man I adored before I could talk. And I loved him. But that was before I knew what bloodshed and betrayal meant.

I shouldn't be here. Not right now. I duck behind a column, then study him, trying to push more emotions away.

He stops to greet the guards, then comes closer.

I pull deeper into the shadow. My lungs refuse to cooperate. He stands next to the elevator and exhales slowly like he's already tired of whatever fight waits upstairs.

The tiny scar on his cheek catches the chandelier's light. He didn't have that when I was little. Back then, his skin was smooth, his eyes mischievous, his smile warm and wide. My Luca brought pastries and candies and whispered stories in Italian that made me giggle under my blankets when I was supposed to be asleep.

Now, his mouth is a flat line. His eyes scan the lobby with the detached, lethal focus of a man who's ordered more hits than hugs.

I angle my face and press my nails into my palms.

Why can't you still love me?

The thought hits me with a punch. I blink harder, then wipe under my eye.

He adjusts the cuff of his shirt, revealing the edge of a watch that costs more than most people make in a year. Then he unbuttons his coat and makes small talk with another guard.

The elevator doors slide open, and he steps inside. The doors begin to close. Luca's shoulders straighten, his expression hardening as if he's bracing himself for impact.

The gold metal doors shut tight, and another flashback haunts me. It's the last time I saw him in person. I was four, maybe five, clutching a stuffed rabbit in an Italian villa while my parents screamed in the other room.

"You can't trust him, Valentina. He's using you. He's using all of us," my father declared.

Mom insisted, "He's family. He would never do that to us."

My phone vibrates. I pull it out of my pocket and read the text message.

> Cassian: Luca, alert! Do not go inside Zara's!

Anger spools, and I bang my fingers across the screen.

> Me: I should have known that ten minutes ago.

> Cassian: Apologies.

I stare at the screen, fuming. There should never be a time when I don't know if I'm in danger. Luca, seeing me, represents the highest threat.

I need to talk to Kirill about replacing Cassian. He's making too many dangerous mistakes.

I should have predicted Luca would come based on Zara's texts this morning.

> Zara: I think my father knows something is up. And Sean's uncles, too. We're both getting the nonstop questions on all sides.

I asked Cassian if I was in the clear.

Did he lie?

He's just incompetent.

Is he? For two years, he made no mistakes.

I press the back of my skull against the marble and stare at the elevator numbers as they tick upward.

Ten.

Eleven.

Twelve.

My throat burns.

When I was a child, Luca was my world. He smelled like espresso, expensive cologne, and the slightest hint of cigar smoke blended into Scotch. He taught me how to swim without fear, to hide so I wouldn't get caught, and how to keep my mouth shut when it was important.

He used to call me Stellina, meaning his little star.

Then the war between the Marinos and the Abruzzos went from simmering to volcanic, and everything caught fire.

My father was Abruzzo. My mother was Marino. They thought love would be enough, and my father even kept Luca's infiltration into the Abruzzo clan a secret, knowing how much my mother loved her brother.

It was my father's greatest hope that the wars would stop and children could grow up in both families without further bloodshed.

But it wasn't that easy. Luca had slipped into the Abruzzo world as a spy. My mother met my father by mistake, and Luca had to explain his role which didn't make my mother stop seeing my father. It was out of necessity that my mother lied to my father about who they really were.

But my father found out. Instead of turning them in to his family, he kept their secret. It was my love for my mother that made my father view the world and his family politics differently.

So Luca smiled at my father's table, drank his Scotch, and held me on his knee. All the while, he reported everything back to his own family.

My father knew it, yet he hoped things would change. When he realized how bad things were getting, how close the Marino fire was to swallowing us whole, he moved us to Italy.

We got a new house and a new set of rules. Instead of calling me Finzia, my parents insisted I use my middle name, Valentina. My father changed our last name, and no one was to know we were Marinos or Abruzzos.

I didn't understand then, but I do now.

Luca hated my father for "stealing" his sister. My father hated the Marinos for using Luca as a weapon. The only thing they agreed on was that the streets were eating all of us alive.

So my father joined the Underworld. He bought into the promise they sold him. He craved a neutral ground, shared power, and a table where Abruzzos and Marinos and every other rival name would sit side by side, sworn to work together. It was the only way I would survive since I had both blood in me.

So my parents earned their seats. They bled for them, vowed loyalty, and within a month, their plane "malfunctioned" and fell out of the sky.

They never determined whether it was engine failure, pilot error, or bad weather. You can pick whichever lie you want. It doesn't change that the only thing left of my parents came back in charred boxes and folded flags.

The only true question is whether it was the Abruzzos or the Marinos who orchestrated it.

My eyes sting. I blink hard and drag air into my lungs until my vision clears. That's why my seat at the table matters. It's why I've swallowed everything the Omni has fed me. I took their punishments without arguing and survived their tests. Once I claim what my parents died for, maybe I can finally drag these families into something that isn't constant bloodshed and retribution.

Seeing Luca makes everything raw. I'm a reminder of the Abruzzo man who "ruined" his sister's life. I'm the product of a marriage he never approved of, and I stepped into the Underworld, refusing to take the Marino side.

And Luca knows about the Underworld. My father gave him the chance to join them, but he wouldn't. Somehow, Luca escaped the wrath from the Omni no one else does. You don't learn of the Underworld and refuse to pledge without dying.

He preferred to keep the war. If he didn't, he would have chosen the Underworld. So he'll say I'm dangerous, unstable, manipulative. He'll tell Zara I'll hurt her.

I won't. Zara has become the sister I never had.

She curses too loudly, laughs too hard, and loves too fiercely. She'd throw herself in front of a bullet for Sean without thinking. But I know she'd also do the same thing for me.

So, I would die before letting anything happen to her.

But Luca won't ever choose to believe it. In his story, there are only Marinos and everyone else. So he'll continue to paint me as a threat Zara needs to cut out of her life if she wants to survive.

I push away from the column, keeping my shoulders low, head bowed, hair falling like a curtain around my face. Too much time passes, and I get antsy. Then my phone vibrates with two new messages.

> Zara: My father is here. He's being an ass.

> Zara: He won't shut up about you.

A third appears before I can move.

> Zara: I told him if he doesn't knock it off, I'll throw him off the balcony. You good with that?

I smile and hold back a laugh.

> Me: I'll see you another time. Have fun with him.

> Zara: I'm sorry. Call you later.

I exit the lobby, and the cold gust slices across my cheeks.

Vito springs out of the black SUV before I reach the curb.

Cassian steps out of the passenger seat, posture stiff, eyes scanning the area like he suddenly remembers what his job is.

Too late.

"Valentina," Cassian greets, voice even.

"Don't," I cut him off. Rage simmers under my skin, hotter than the winter wind.

Cassian flinches. "It won't happen again."

"It shouldn't have happened at all. Once is enough to get me killed. Don't make me repeat myself," I snap.

His jaw tightens, but he lowers his gaze. "Understood."

I slide into the backseat.

Vito shuts the door gently, then circles to the driver's side.

Cassian gets in front, saying nothing.

"Kirill's," I announce, then text.

Me: We need to talk. Are you home?

Kirill: Yes. Come over.

Vito starts the engine without looking back. The city lights smear against the windows as we cut through traffic.

I stare straight ahead, my pulse pounding in my ears. My thoughts spiral over Luca, Zara, my dead parents, and the Omni, who aren't making it easy for me to earn my seat. Then there's Vito and Cassian, who I'm no longer confident can keep me safe.

When we pull up to Kirill's building, Vito jumps out and opens my door.

I step onto the pavement and duck into the lobby. The guard nods at me. The elevator doors slide open immediately. I get on it and it smoothly lifts to the penthouse. When the doors part, I enter Kirill's.

He stands in front of the massive glass wall overlooking Lake Michigan. The evening clouds turned the endless water dark. City lights glitter along its edge. Snow flurries drift past the glass like ash.

"You're pacing," I say softly.

"I was," he replies, his voice distant. "Not anymore." He finally looks over his shoulder. He wears his unreadable expression, carved from stone and shadow. It's the kind of face that makes grown men confess their sins before he asks. But there's something softer in his eyes, too.

It's the look he always gives me now. It's the same expression I see on Brax whenever I have a task to complete with him.

Kirill asks, "Are you okay?"

I ignore answering what he's really asking and step closer. "No. Cassian didn't know Luca was going to Zara's. He didn't alert me until Luca was already in the elevator. He missed the signs about Brax. He missed other things, too. He's losing focus, and I can't afford that."

Kirill peers closer. "You want him replaced?"

I shake my head. "No. I need him replaced. If he can't anticipate basic threats, he's a liability. I need someone better."

He clenches his jaw.

I continue, "Why is Vito still driving me? I requested a new driver months ago."

His jaw tics. "The Omni denied your request."

My stomach drops. "Why?"

He stares at me.

My pulse stammers. My bitter and hollow laugh echoes around us. "Of course they did. Why support the girl they branded in the Scarlet Hour? Why give her competent guards?"

Kirill shifts. The floor vibrates under his weight. "Valentina—"

"No. Don't use that voice," I sharply reprimand.

"What voice?" he asks quietly.

"That one. The one filled with pity."

His eyes soften even more. "It's not pity. It's understanding."

"And pity," I insist.

We stare at each other across the room, an entire history of friendship and scarred skin.

He shakes his head slowly. "You walked in shaking."

"I'm not shaking."

"You're pale."

"I'm cold."

"You're lying."

The words lash through me. I lift my chin. "I'm fine."

He studies me, unblinking. "Are you?"

The question hits me in a place I avoid at all costs. My throat tightens. "I don't need you to worry. I need you to trust I'm fine."

He replies, "I'm allowed to check on the people I care about."

"Don't say it like that," I breathe.

"Like what?"

"Like I'm breakable."

The room goes still.

"You survived the Scarlet Hour." His voice drops, low and reverent in a way that makes my skin crawl. "You aren't breakable. But you're hurting."

My stomach knots. My voice cracks. "Just stop."

A long, heavy silence settles between us. It's thick enough to choke on.

I pull myself upright, drawing every shard of dignity back into place.

"I need a new driver and assistant. Competent people, not liabilities."

Kirill straightens, jaw tightening. "I will put in another request with my highest recommendation."

"Sometimes I wonder what being king is for if you can't make these decisions," I blurt out.

His face darkens. He mumbles, "Agree."

I glare at him a moment, then announce, "I'll see you later." I turn to leave.

"Valentina—"

"I said I'm fine," I snap, turning back.

He exhales long and slow, like he's trying to decide whether to chase after me or let me self-destruct for a night. But he doesn't move to stop me when I turn toward the door.

As soon as the elevator closes behind me, the weight of his concern crushes my lungs. The ride down stops at each floor, even though most are empty. Every second stretches thin, feeling more suffocating each time the gold doors open.

When I step outside, Vito is already holding the door open. Cassian sits in the front seat.

I slide into the backseat, and for the first time in a very long time, I don't know whether the car I'm sitting in belongs to allies or enemies.

"Home," I order.

Vito pulls into traffic. The Chicago skyline blurs past us. We turn onto Lakeshore Drive, headlights illuminating the dark water beside us. I rest a hand on my lap, and my rings graze my stomach. The dull sensation is a fresh reminder of my shame.

I get home, step inside my condo, and freeze.

Brax stands in the middle of my living room, hands in his pockets, shoulders tense. He pins the same eyes Kirill has on me.

My heart pounds harder.

Silence stretches between us like a wound.

I break it. "What are you doing here?"

He holds an envelope out. His sarcasm-laced voice states, "I'm supposed to give you this. Apparently, the Omni thinks I'm their personal errand boy."

"What's in it?" I ask.

He shrugs, jaw flexing. "No idea. They don't trust me with anything more complicated than door-to-door delivery."

"You have to earn trust," I remind him.

He grunts. New anger settles into his scowl.

"It'll get better," I offer in a softer tone.

Shock fills his expression. "How can you say that after all they did to you?"

My breath catches. I harden my expression. "Is there any other reason why you're still standing here?"

He studies me a moment, and my insides quiver. Then he shakes his head. "Nah. Don't worry, Minx. I'll get out of your way." He brushes past me.

"Brax—"

"I was there, too," he hisses, spinning back toward me.

I blink hard, taking short breaths. It doesn't calm me, so I close my eyes. My voice trembles. "We aren't talking about this."

He sighs.

I keep my eyes shut until I hear the door click, then slowly open them. I regain my composure and stare at the blank envelope.

What is this?

I get my letter opener, slide it across the seal, then pull out dozens of photos.

Every single one has Luca and me. I'm a child with missing teeth, wild curls, and sunburned cheeks. My first tooth came in, and I'm wearing pigtails and a tutu. It's my birthday, and I'm sitting on Uncle Luca's lap and blowing out the candles.

Who sent these?

My breath shatters. Each image breaks me, and the first sob hits before I can stop it.

Brax

Several Months Later

Chapter TEN

By the time I reach Sean's penthouse, I've worked myself into a mood that could crack stone. It's been a shit few months with endless duties. As soon as I finish my O'Malley work, the Underworld gives orders delivered without explanation.

I've been to countless meetings where masks say more than the people wearing them. They give me tasks I don't understand, assignments I can't question, and a brand on my hand that throbs every time one of those silver-skull bastards looks at me for more than a second.

Tonight marks twelve days since I've slept for more than three hours. The last order was two days ago. As soon as I turned my phone on, I saw all the missed messages about where I've been. And Finn sent multiple demands to know why I missed the twins' arrival party.

It all made my frustration worse. It's just like when Zara went into labor. I should have been waiting outside the delivery room with cold coffee, cigars, and stupid jokes. Instead, the Omni had me digging holes in the ground. So I missed the twins' birth and a full-blown interrogation occurred after.

So, even though I'm beyond tired, I get home, shower, and grab the present I'd bought a few weeks ago.

They're already two months old and I haven't even seen them.

I step into Sean's lobby and stop in front of the tree with all the cherry blossoms. I inhale it deeply, then walk into the main room, calling out, "Where are these babies?"

My stomach knots as the world stops. My pulse jerks painfully, like someone grabbed my heart and squeezed.

Valentina sits on the huge corner couch like she belongs there, draped in a short black dress that clings to her curves in a way that should be illegal, hair pinned up, one diamond stud catching the light. But it isn't the dress or the heels or the way her legs cross that hits me.

She has the twins tucked into her arms, tiny heads resting on her chest, while she laughs at something Zara just said.

It's nice. I haven't seen her smile or heard her laugh in months, minus a brief incident at Kirill's penthouse where she gave me shit and I gave it back just as good. But then I had to get lectured by Kirill on "growing up" and "getting to know Valentina."

"Brax," Zara beams.

Valentina pins her gaze on me. Her laugh dies instantly, her spine snapping straight.

My entire bloodstream turns into a shaken can of soda, overflowing everywhere.

"Where've you been?" Sean demands, stepping into view.

I drag my gaze away from Valentina, force my heartbeat down, and shrug off the question. "You know I'm not answering that."

Sean's face turns to guilt and concern. "You alright?"

It's the same thing he always asks.

I assert, "Of course I am."

I drop the gift bag on the sofa table and move to the couch. I dive headfirst into bubbling tension neither Valentina nor I have dealt with since the night everything changed.

Her body goes rigid the moment I sit down beside her. Our thighs brush for a split second. Tension snaps something low in my stomach before she subtly shifts an inch away.

I follow her, leaning closer to the babies, then mutter, "Holy hell."

I've never seen anyone so small. Or so terrifying.

The one on Valentina's left arm sleeps with her fist curled up near her cheek, lips parted in a soft O. The one on her right wiggles, nose scrunching like he's about to make his displeasure known.

Zara beams from across the couch. "Meet Willow and River."

I clear my throat and grin. "Thank God they look like you."

Zara throws her head back and laughs. "Everyone keeps saying that."

"That's the truth," Sean agrees, smiling just as wide.

I run a finger down Willow's cheek, pretending this moment is normal and nothing's fractured between the woman holding the babies and me.

"They're precious, aren't they?" Valentina asks in a soft tone, looking at them lovingly and holding them as if she were built to protect them.

Something unfamiliar twists in me. It's not the sharp, unwanted pull I've felt around her since before the Underworld ripped the ground out from under us. Nor is it guilt or anger. It's something soft I don't want to acknowledge, and as much as I need to remember she's an Abruzzo, everything's changed since that damn ritual.

I smile at her, enjoying seeing her without her guard up, but it's brief.

Zara chirps, "Do you want to hold one?"

Sean stiffens. "He hasn't washed his hands."

"I'm not filthy," I grumble.

"Go wash them. It's worth the inconvenience," Valentina offers.

I nod and rise. I head to the kitchen sink, scrubbing like I'm preparing for surgery.

I sit back next to Valentina and reach for River.

Sean hovers like I'm holding a bomb, warning, "You have to hold the back of his head."

I cradle River and remind him, "It's not the first baby I've held."

"You've always been good with babies," Zara acknowledges.

"Thanks," I say, then coo, "You're a good-looking O'Malley, aren't you, little guy?"

He stretches slightly in my arms, tiny mouth puckering.

Zara informs, "He's been screaming at everyone else. Looks like he likes you."

We stay in that strange bubble for a while, talking about feedings and diapers and how Sean nearly passed out in the delivery room. Nothing deep. Nothing dangerous. Just small talk that feels like a borrowed piece of history with Valentina and me sneaking glances at each other between new topics.

Zara eventually stands. "Valentina, come help me put the babies down?"

She nods, rises from the couch with River, her dress sliding over her thighs in a way I try not to track.

Zara takes Willow from me and leads them into the babies' bedroom.

"How's it feel?" I ask him.

He arches his eyebrows. "Being a father?"

"Yeah."

"It's scary as fuck," he admits.

I chuckle. "I can imagine."

Sean exhales and rubs his face. "You know what would make it less scary? If I could figure out how to change the Omnis' minds about Fiona."

My gut drops. "I can't believe they're going to make her marry Kirill."

He shakes his head, eyes tight. "Zara and I have tried everything. They won't budge. They want my sister as queen and tied to Kirill."

Kirill's scarred face appears. I wrinkle my nose. "He's not her type at all."

Sean paces a few steps, his jaw clenched. "If I push any harder, they'll think I'm questioning the table. I can't afford that now that the babies are here."

I lean forward, forearms on my knees, adding, "Imagine how Fiona's going to feel when she finds out you promised her to him."

He stops dead, then snaps, "Don't say it like that."

"How else am I supposed to say it? You agreed to it," I remind him.

His nostrils flare. "I didn't have a choice, Brax. They were going to kill Zara. What the fuck was I supposed to do?"

"Yeah, yeah," I mutter, cracking a knuckle. "I know. Doesn't change the fact Fiona's going to lose her mind when she finds out."

He grimaces. "That's why I need your help keeping her calm."

I grunt. "I don't know how to do that."

"Do what?" Zara asks, and the women appear without the babies.

"Help Fiona stay calm," Sean states, with fresh guilt on his expression.

Zara's quickly matches his. She pins her eyebrows together, biting her lip.

Valentina's phone twists on the table, rattling against the wood. She grabs it. Her happy expression disappears.

"What's wrong?" I ask.

"Time to go," she informs.

I groan. "I just got back in town."

She shrugs. "I don't make the agenda."

"So I'm told," I mutter, and head toward the door, calling back, "You two make beautiful babies."

"Thanks," Zara says.

"Stay safe," Sean adds in a warning tone.

I glance back. "Later."

Valentina and I step into the hallway. Brutal silence forms, but it's nothing new. It's been months of silencing, distancing, and avoiding anything that breaks open the cracks between us.

She keeps her gaze fixed ahead. Her heels click softly on the marble.

I shove my hands in my pockets, my pulse hammering harder than it should. There's so much to say, but I don't know how to bring any of it up without her shutting down. And as much as she wants to pretend things are fine, I know they aren't.

They can't be. I was there, witnessing the punishment they were too eager to bestow upon her.

The elevator doors slide shut behind us, sealing in a silence that's thicker than concrete. Valentina stares forward, pretending like she hasn't been ripped open and stitched back together by people who think pain is devotion.

The elevator hums, descending to the ground. The doors open in the lobby, and we exit the building.

Vito waits by the passenger door. He scowls at me.

I return the expression and slide next to Valentina. I ask, "Want to tell me where we're going?"

She shrugs. "Like I know."

I dramatically sigh, then sit back in the car. Ten minutes later, we're at the private airport. The SUV pulls up to the staircase attached to a black jet. We say nothing and board.

Inside the plane, dim lights glow. There's a stewardess who doesn't look at us. The sealed captain's chamber provides no indication of whether the pilot is inside.

Valentina sits by the window, pulls her seat belt tight, and angles her body away.

"Message received, Minx," I mumble and take the seat across from her, then lean my head back. "It would be nice to know if it's something dangerous we're walking into."

She snaps her gaze toward me, then just as quickly diverts it. "It's always dangerous."

The engines roar. The staircase moves away from the jet and the cabin vibrates.

I try again. "Val—"

"Don't," she warns quietly in a defeated voice.

So I shut up.

Eventually, exhaustion wins, and I drift off, lulled into a shallow, uneasy sleep filled with flashes of her muffled screams as they branded her. I wake with my jaw clenched so hard my teeth ache, and the wheels hitting the ground.

Valentina unbuckles her belt and rises.

I follow.

We step off the plane and into a narrow hallway lined with sconce lights flickering orange. The air smells like earth, soot, old stone, and something colder.

She leads us down it, passing several unmarked doors. The passage twists so many times that I get disoriented.

"What is this place?" I finally ask.

"Stop asking questions, Brax. And don't forget, they're always listening and watching," she warns.

A chill digs into my bones. I adhere to her warning, looking for recording devices, but I don't see any.

She stops in front of a heavy metal door with two wooden hinges bolted into the wall beside it. On one hanger, a crimson thong with a matching red satin eye mask dangles. On the other hangs a black tuxedo jacket, crisp white shirt, black pants, and a red, gleaming skull mask.

Every muscle in my body goes rigid. I step in front of her, blocking the door. "What the hell are we walking into?"

She pushes past me and grabs the thong off the hanger. "I don't know."

"Then how do you know where to go?"

"I said I don't know, Brax." Her voice cracks just slightly. She swallows, avoiding my eyes. "This wasn't on the agenda. I was summoned. Same as you."

Summoned.

Because they own me.

They don't.

Before I can say another word, she reaches under her dress. She pulls off her black panties and steps into the red thong, then shimmies into it.

"What are you waiting for? Get dressed," she orders.

I shake my head but turn and pull the shirt off the hanger. I remove my clothing, get into the tux, then spin.

My mouth salivates.

Her dress pools at her feet. The curve of her waist dips beautifully, displaying a thin satin strip between her ass cheeks. She reaches behind her, unclasps her bra, and drops it next to her dress.

She spins confidently, head held high, yet the sconce light shows the flicker of vulnerability.

My eyes drop to the white V across her torso and chest.

She stiffens.

I drag my eyes to hers. "You're still beautiful, Minx."

Shame washes across her face in a way that guts me. She puts on her eye mask and orders, "Put your mask on."

I glance at the skull mask, wondering what Sean's father was thinking when he created the hollow, soulless, twisted empire it represents.

"Please put it on," she begs.

I clench my jaw and slide it over my face.

"Ready?" she asks.

"No," I answer honestly.

"Sorry. The Underworld doesn't wait." She opens the metal door.

A deep, vibrating, "Oooooooohhhhhmmmmmm," rattles my bones. It echoes off stone pillars and swells into the warm night air. Stars fill the sky, there's a full moon, and I glance around in awe.

It's a massive outdoor arena. Thousands of masked figures stand around the perimeter in tuxedos, holding lit torches. Women wear long, red dresses and fancy eye masks, mirroring Valentina's.

The chanting grows louder.

"Oooooohhhhhmmmmm. Oooooohhhhhmmmmm."

A huge stage sits in the middle. The only things on them are two steel tables. One's flat, meant for lying down. The other table is a two-top. Two tattoo artists in black leather aprons and masks like mine sit waiting, machines gleaming, needles already loaded. The one at the two-top has an empty chair across from him.

A man in a black robe with a black-skull mask steps forward. His voice booms, "Welcome to the Ceremony of the Scarlet Seal."

My blood runs ice cold.

What the hell are they going to do to us now?

Valentina flinches so slightly that no one else would notice, but I do.

I put my arm around her waist and tug her into me.

She glances up at me in surprise.

The man in the black robe steps closer.

"Don't touch her," I snarl.

He orders, "Take your position, Valentina. Brax, sit in the chair."

"What's going on?" I ask her.

She forces a smile. "You're moving up a level. Your skull gets its color. It's fine. Go sit down."

It sounds innocent, but I know nothing in the Underworld is as it seems. So I blurt out, "And you?"

She lifts her head. Her voice sounds brave. "I get color, too. Sit, Brax." She steps next to the bigger table and lies down on it.

It hits me.

"You're coloring her mark? That's going to be excruciatingly painful for her!"

"Brax, it's fine. Sit down. Please," she begs again.

The war inside me rages hard.

"Don't cause any trouble," she pleads.

I sit. Not because I want to but because I'm afraid of what they may do to her if I don't.

The tattoo artist snaps on gloves. He grabs my hand and positions it, stating, "Keep it still." The machine buzzes to life and red ink stamps the skull.

Pain ripples through my arm. I grit my teeth, used to the feeling since it's not my first tattoo. But then I pin my gaze on Valentina.

She lies on the steel table, gripping the edges so hard her knuckles turn white. Her breathing quickens, and she cringes under her eye mask, while scarlet ink gets stained over the V.

"Let her go," I growl, trying to stand.

Hands shove me back down. A masked man warns, "Don't move again." A knife slides next to my neck. Another man holds one next to hers.

Shit.

The entire time they shade my skull, I watch the needle color her knotted skin.

They strip every layer of her open, ink burning into the most intimate part of her body while she lies there, exposed to hundreds of masked strangers. Her entire body stays rigid, her fingers clamped on the edge of the table. She bites her lip so hard she draws blood. Silent tears slide down her temples into her hairline.

When they finish mine, I'm told not to move out of my seat.

Hours pass. Red ink slowly blooms across her body, filling every curve, every hollow, until the scarlet color is bright, violent, and public for all to see.

The chanting never stops, intensifying at times and slowing at others.

Valentina endures every second of pain, never uttering a sound.

My vision tunnels. My pulse pounds so hard I feel it in my gums. Raw fury claws up my throat. By the time the machines go quiet, I'm drenched in sweat, chest heaving.

Her tattoo artist puts his needle down. The man who held the knife to her throat pulls her into a sitting position, then helps her off the table.

She tries to stand, but her legs buckle.

I surge forward, catching her before she hits the floor.

Her head drops against my shoulder, breath trembling. "Don't...say anything."

I clench my jaw and wrap an arm around her waist, shielding as much of her bare skin as I can.

"Step back, Brax!" the black robe man orders.

I hurl, "It's complete. Let us go."

"The ceremony is not complete," he announces.

The hairs on my arms rise. I grit through teeth, "What else do you want from us?"

"From you? Nothing. Valentina, go stand on the X," he directs.

I glance at the X in the middle of the stage floor.

Valentina squeezes her eyes shut, then takes a deep breath, squares her shoulders, and lifts her head. She steps onto the X.

The robed man lifts his hands. "The Scarlett Seal is completed. Renew the bond of blood and loyalty!"

Silence fills the arena so quickly, a chill runs down my spine. It lasts about a minute, then frantic whispers break out. They get so loud they vibrate through my chest.

Valentina stands, her hands shaking, staring straight at the crowd.

I rush over to her and grab her hand.

She looks up at me.

I squeeze her hand and stare straight ahead.

The whispers don't let up, and it goes on and on, until one thing is clear. It gets sealed deep inside me.

I will burn this entire fucking Underworld to the ground.

Valentina

Chapter
ELEVEN

The whispers don't stop. They crawl across my skin, acting as fresh kindling for the shame I can't escape.

I knew this day was coming. It was only a matter of time until they'd color my scarred flesh scarlet, solidifying the mark that will never be hidden. And I'll see it every day in my reflection. No matter what I wear to hide it, the members of the Underworld will never forget it. It'll shine bright in the eyes of all who look at me.

My parents would be so disappointed.

Brax's mumble is full of fresh rage. "I'll burn this entire fucking Underworld to the ground."

I want to tell him to be quiet. They're always listening, and every ripple in the air has ears. But my mouth won't open. The pain inside me is greater than the hours I spent under a needle, and if I speak, I might not survive the night.

The world blurs at the edges, and the next thing I know, someone pushes us toward the tunnels. The arena fades behind us. The torches disappear. The chanting dies.

Everything inside me is numb. I'm moving, but I don't feel my feet. I only stay upright because Brax keeps his arm around my waist, leading me away from the predators.

We reach the hallway, and something closes in my chest. Brax helps me into my dress, then puts on his clothes. He tries to guide me, but my knees give out.

Before I fall, he catches me, then picks me up. I put my face against his chest, wishing I could hide.

I'll never be able to.

The blur of the sconces dances through the side of my wet gaze, twisting with us through the tunnels.

Brax speaks, but I can't comprehend it.

The next conscious moment is the familiar scent of air freshener. Then the gentle press of leather against my legs as I lower into the seat.

I blink.

Once.

Twice.

Everything is muffled, distorted like I'm underwater and the world's above the surface. Even the vibration humming under me seems strange.

I stare at the window, but it's covered with a mirror. My reflection is blurred. All I see is the bright, scarlet V loudly staining my chest, burning through my dress to mock me.

Brax shifts next to me and strokes my cheek. "Valentina."

I turn and stare at him. Fresh tears glide down my face. My pulse races to the point of dizziness.

He wipes the tears off my jaw and states, "We're home."

"Home?" I ask.

He nods. "Back in Chicago."

I don't move.

"Come on," he gently says, then helps me to my feet. He guides me off the plane.

The cold night air slaps me in the face when I exit the plane. It only pulls me out of my trance for a moment. As soon as I get back into the SUV, I stare out the glass and succumb to new numbness.

"So this is where you live," Brax says quietly.

I blink, realizing I'm in my home. I glance around my living room, but all I see are the red accents.

Just like the V.

My hand flies to my stomach. I used to be so proud of my skull being shaded red. It's only for members of the Underworld that the Omni feel are dangerous in ways rules can't contain. Now, I'm as far from that as possible.

"Nice place. Very classy," Brax offers.

The words tug something inside me. Something sharp and painful. Before I can stop myself, I grab my favorite red vase and hurl it at the wall. It shatters into pieces, flying across the room.

"Whoa!" Brax blurts out.

My voice barely comes out. "You can go now."

"No."

I force myself to meet his gaze. My hand trembles as I point at the door. "Go."

He shakes his head. "Like hell."

I swallow. "Brax..."

"No. I'm staying, Minx." He crosses his arms.

"Suit yourself," I whisper, exhausted, not able to find any fight left inside me. I brush past him and go into my bedroom, then freeze, staring at my pillows.

Why did I put red all over my house?

"Go to bed," Brax murmurs behind me.

"I didn't invite you inside my house," I remind him.

"I never invited you into mine either, Minx." He moves toward the bed, pulls back the comforter, revealing scarlet silk sheets. He wiggles his eyebrows. "Come on. Slide in."

I step closer, my voice wavering. "Please go home."

He reaches behind me, unzips my dress, and pushes it to the floor. He repeats, "Get in bed."

I glance down at the red ink all over my chest. New tears form, so I dive under the covers and push my face into the pillow.

For a moment, it feels safe. Then the mattress dips, and my breath catches.

Brax slides beside me. His chest presses against my back. One arm wraps around my waist. The other tucks beneath my pillow as he curls his entire body around mine.

My voice trembles out, "What are you doing?"

"Sleeping," he whispers in my ear, his breath brushing my neck.

"Brax—"

"Shhh. Just close your eyes." He brushes hair off my cheek.

Something inside me cracks. It's a hairline fracture that's been there for months, finally shattering under pressure. A sob punches out of my chest before I can stop it. Then another. Suddenly I'm shaking, crying so hard my ribs ache. My hands fly to my face, but I can't stop anything. It's pouring out, uncontrollable and ugly.

I choke out, "I'm scarred. I'm—" My throat closes. "I'm so ugly now."

His arms clamp tighter around me. "Not true."

"It's true. Everyone saw. They all saw—"

"Enough." His voice is rough, commanding, but tender. "You're not ugly. Not scarred in any way that changes who you are."

"You don't know what I look like anymore," I whisper into the sheets.

He grunts. "Sure, I do. I saw every inch of you tonight."

My stomach twists.

He murmurs against my neck, "And you're still the most beautiful damn woman I've ever seen."

I cry harder.

He shifts, turning me gently until I'm facing him. His hand cups my cheek, thumb brushing away tears that keep falling faster than he can wipe.

He leans closer, his forehead touching mine, and demands, "Look at me, Minx."

I can't. I sniffle hard.

He urges again, softer. "Look at me."

I force my eyes open. His gaze burns through the shadows, fierce and warm and agonized all at once.

"You're beautiful, strong, and beyond brave. None of what they did changes that. They don't get the power to define you."

Another tear drops.

He catches it with his thumb. He adds, "Think of it as your superhero symbol."

"What?"

He grins. "All superheroes have a symbol. It's like Wonder Woman's. And everyone knows she's the hottest creature they ever created."

I pin my eyebrows together.

He adds, "Lord knows you're just as hot as Wonder Woman."

A tiny giggle escapes my lips.

His lips twitch. "Ok. Maybe even a tad hotter."

I take a shaky breath.

His eyes search mine like he's trying to stitch me back together with nothing but his gaze. He asks, "You know what I keep thinking?"

I swallow hard. "What?"

"That I've never seen anyone walk through that much hell and still look like they could boss the world around with one raised eyebrow." His mouth tugs up at one corner.

I bite on my lip, gaining better control of my breath.

He declares, "You terrify them, Minx. So they can try to take you down, but they never will."

Warmth wraps around my ribs from the inside. I blurt out, "They can eliminate me at any time."

His thumb makes lazy circles near my ear. "Nah. You're too valuable to them."

"Why would you say that?" I question.

He leans in, his nose brushing mine. His breath becomes a ghost over my lips, hot and steady. He answers, "You've survived their torture. Most others wouldn't have."

My pulse thumps hard in my neck.

His gaze drops to my mouth. He murmurs, "Wonder Woman was always my favorite hero."

My heart trips. "Brax—"

He closes the distance, stealing my breath.

The first press of his lips is careful, almost reverent. It's a question, not a demand, testing if he should or shouldn't continue.

Sparks fly down my spine. My fingers curl into the silk between us.

He tilts his head, kissing me again, slow and unhurried, like he has all morning and he's going to use every second.

I sigh into him, my body betraying me, melting into his chest. He pulls me closer, anchoring me to him. His other hand slides from my cheek to the back of my neck, fingers threading into my hair.

I whimper.

He deepens the kiss. His tongue teases the seam of my lips, a gentle flick that sends a pulse pounding between my legs. I part them without thinking.

He groans, low and rough, and the sound vibrates straight through me as his tongue slides against mine.

Heat explodes under my skin. I clutch at his shirt, needing to hold onto something as he coaxes me into the rhythm he sets. Every slow, intoxicating stroke makes my toes curl under the sheets. Each flick glides deliberately. There's nothing rushed or greedy.

It's the opposite of the night we fucked on stage. He kisses me like I'm precious, like he's ready to wreck me but willing to do it one piece at a time.

My thighs press together, an ache building, sharp and insistent.

His chest rises and falls faster against mine.

I press closer, desperate for more, lifting onto my knees, angling to get nearer.

His shirt brushes my scarred skin.

A new tenderness erupts. It runs right to my core. I gasp in his mouth.

His hand slides down my spine, stopping at the small of my back, splaying wide as he holds me in place. He murmurs, "Easy," though he doesn't stop kissing me.

I slide my fingers through his hair, gripping it tight.

His stubble faintly scrapes along my chin. His teeth nip my lower lip in a quick, wicked tug. Then he soothes the sting with a slow lick.

I moan.

He swallows the sound, kissing me harder for a few seconds. His hand slides along my side, his thumb brushing the outer curve of my breast.

My nipples tighten instantly. A needy little sound escapes me, humiliatingly desperate.

His breath stutters.

For a heartbeat, his grip at my waist tightens, his hips press forward, and his tongue thrusts into my mouth with a raw hunger that steals all my thoughts. Sparks race down my spine. I arch against him, chasing friction, wanting more.

He tears his mouth from mine. His breath comes out hot and hard.

I blink, dizzy, lips swollen and tingling. The room spins in slow, lazy circles around us. I furrow my brows.

His forehead rests against mine as he drags in a deep breath. Then another. His chest heaves. He mutters, "Fuck. You're dangerous."

The word should sting. It doesn't. It coils inside me with something like pride. Still, I try to capture his lips again, but he leans back, just far enough that I miss.

His fingers tighten at my waist, as if he's holding himself in place by force. He reaches up, brushing his thumb over my bottom lip, his gaze glued to it. Then his expression shifts, hardening with resolve. "You need to rest, Minx."

Heat crashes into cold so fast it stuns me. I repeat, "Rest?"

"You've been through enough for ten lifetimes tonight. Get some sleep so your body can heal," he orders.

My mind seizes on the word, twisting it.

Heal.

The red V throbs on my chest, as if it heard him and agrees. I'm broken, ruined, not fit to be touched. At least not the way I want him to touch me. Nor the way he just did.

I swallow, my throat aching. "You don't have to…pity me."

His jaw flexes. "That's what you think this is?"

I can't meet his eyes. I glance down instead, tugging the silk higher, even though I'm fully covered. The fabric drags over tender, seared flesh, and a sharp sting radiates out as a brutal reminder.

I'm stained.

No man wants a woman who carries the Underworld's graffiti carved into her skin. Men like Brax fuck perfection. They don't claim damaged goods.

Shame turns into a tidal wave, thick and suffocating. I swallow it back and turn, curling onto my side, away from him.

It's a small mercy. He doesn't have to pretend to find me attractive when the ugliest part of me is in full view.

The scarlet letter burns in my chest. I stare at the wall, eyes burning, heart pounding loud enough I'm sure he can hear it. The buzzing in my ears starts again, the echo of the crowd, the chanting, the roar of the arena. Then the whispers take over.

Slut.

Whore.

Marked.

My fingers dig into the pillow. I bite the inside of my cheek to keep the tears from spilling again.

The mattress shifts behind me.

I go still, bracing for distance along with the drag of the sheets and the creak of the bed as he gets up and leaves.

Instead, the heat of his body crowds my back again. His chest molds to my spine; his arm slides around my waist. He tugs me flush against him like he's determined to erase even a millimeter of space.

"Brax—" I start, my voice hoarse, then freeze.

His cock pushes firmly against the curve of my ass, thick and pulsing.

Heat flares under my skin, scorching every insecurity trying to claw its way up my throat.

His mouth finds the shell of my ear. He demands, "Stop thinking things that aren't true."

The words punch right through my defenses. My lungs seize, then finally expand. My vision blurs, but this time the tears don't spill. The knot in my chest loosens an inch.

His hand spreads over my stomach, fingers splayed wide but not touching my sensitive skin. He holds me to him like he's claiming me in the only way he can right now. His face buries in my hair, his stubble scraping my neck as he breathes me in.

"I'm not going anywhere," he mutters, half into my hair, half into my skin. "Sleep, Valentina."

My muscles slowly unclench. I let my weight sink back into him, giving in to the steady press of his body.

The arena fades. Whispers get silenced. The only sounds left are his heartbeat thudding against my spine and his breathing evening out, deep and heavy.

I match my inhales to his, letting the rhythm lull me. For the first time since the ritual, my body doesn't feel like an enemy.

Sleep pulls me under before I can fight it. When my eyes blink open again, the room is gray-blue with early morning light seeping through the sides of my curtains.

I turn and stare at the empty, cold sheets.

He left.

Disappointment slams into me so fast it steals my breath. The hollow space where his body should be gapes like a fresh wound. It's stupid. I knew he wouldn't stay forever. Men like him don't linger.

But some pathetic, traitorous part of me thought he'd still be here. Instead, it's just me and my scarlet decor.

A curse slips out under my breath in Italian. I throw the covers off and swing my legs over the edge. I force myself to my feet and shuffle to the bathroom. I flick on the light.

Brightness floods the space, bouncing off marble and mirrors. I squint for a moment, then stare at the red V.

Angry, swollen skin surrounds the mark, the edges still slightly raised and tender. The color is so vivid it almost glows, a searing, violent crimson that refuses to be ignored.

Ugly, my mind hisses.

I step closer to the mirror, fingers lifting before I can stop them. I hover a centimeter away, afraid to touch, but incapable of looking anywhere else.

This is what they wanted.

To put me in my place.

Every morning and every night, I'll be reminded that no matter how powerful I become in the Underworld, no matter how composed I appear in rituals or other tasks, underneath the couture and diamonds, I'm tarnished.

My vision burns.

I need to get over this.

I blink hard, refusing to let the tears fall. I mutter to my reflection. "You don't get to win."

The V doesn't care. It just sits there, carved into me, a permanent reminder. My jaw tightens. I finally let my fingertips brush the edge of it. The touch sends a sharp sting through my skin, but I don't pull back. I trace the angle slowly, forcing myself to feel every centimeter.

If this is my reality now, I have to own it even if it kills me.

"Hotter than Wonder Woman," Brax's deep voice rumbles from the doorway.

I jump, jerking my hand away from my chest as my gaze snaps to his reflection behind me. "What are you doing here?"

His lips twitch. His eyes drift over my body. His voice grows lower. "Trying to decide if I like your ass or your tits better."

A laugh flies out of me.

He steps forward, kisses my forehead, and states, "I made breakfast. I don't know about you, but I'm starving. Let's go eat, Minx."

Brax

Chapter
TWELVE

Pancakes are my favorite breakfast food. Anytime they're in front of me, I gobble them up so I can eat more. But today, I barely taste them.

Valentina's sitting in her red silk robe, legs crossed, and her hair pulled into a messy knot. Worse, every time I tell her a stupid joke, she laughs. Her face lights up, and the old her comes roaring back.

It's torture.

I should be dragging her back into bed, kissing and holding her until every trace of last night fades out of her muscles and her mind.

So here I am, forcing myself to keep the mood light while she takes dainty bites of pancakes like the world didn't try to break her hours ago.

She takes a bite and groans. "Who knew pancakes could taste so good?"

"Me," I boast, puffing my chest out.

Her lips twitch. She pokes the stack of leftovers on the serving plate. "You made too many."

I stab another forkful. "Nah. You can never have enough pancakes."

She smirks. "You've eaten six."

"Are you counting my cakes?"

"Yep."

"Watching every bite that goes into my mouth?" I pin a heated look on her.

She blushes. Her gaze drops to my lips, but she catches herself. She sits straighter and shoves another forkful into her mouth. "Mmm."

I wait until she swallows, then I tug on her chair, pulling her closer to me.

"Whoa!" she laughs.

I hold a fork to her mouth. "This has the proper amount of butter and syrup." I lean into her ear. "It's like you. Sweet and creamy."

She takes a deep breath, pinning a hazy gaze on me.

I wiggle the fork in front of her, softly ordering, "Try it."

She opens her mouth.

A sharp knock erupts.

Valentina jumps. Her eyes widen. "Who is it?"

I shake my head and rise. I go to the door and open it.

Zara pushes past me with sharp eyes and fierce energy. She rushes toward Valentina. "Are you okay?"

Shame pops back into her expression. "Word travels fast."

Zara pins her gaze on me and firmly announces, "Sean's waiting for you at the gym."

My jaw tightens. "Now?"

"Yes. Don't drag your feet. Get moving," she orders.

I hesitate. I don't want to leave Valentina. Not today. Not when invisible stitches hold her smile together.

She places her fork down. Her voice is too calm. "Go."

"Valentina—"

"Go," Zara reorders.

I keep my eyes on Valentina. "I'll come check on you later."

Zara's blues dart between us.

Valentina shifts in her chair. She puts on a fake smile. "Brax, I'm fine. Thanks for everything."

Thanks for everything?

I scowl.

Zara pushes my chest. "Go on. Sean's waiting."

I cave, take the stairs two at a time, appreciating the sting in my calves. I exit the stairwell into a gust of wind, find my footing, and break into a jog.

Fresh bread wafts from the bakery. The corner newsstand has a line of buyers, and a group of commuters clutches their coffees like life preservers. Chicago grinds awake around me like everything is normal.

It's not.

By the time the gym comes into view, my lungs burn, and my pulse is a heavy drumbeat in my ears. I lunge up the stairs and pop out into the gym.

The smell of sweat and metal slaps me in the face. Metal weight clunks on machines. Groans, chatter, and dense, meaty thuds vibrate from the boxing bags.

Killian and Finn are already arguing by the ring, their gestures dramatic enough to knock over a grown man.

Finn spots me first. "Well, well. Look who decided to join the land of the living."

Killian crosses his arms. "Thought you died. Or finally got yourself arrested. Or joined a fucking monastery."

I give them a flat look. "Nice to see you too."

Sean jumps toward the ropes, already taped and warmed up. His eyes give me one quick, assessing sweep. He doesn't waste a single second. "Get in the ring."

I duck between the ropes and climb next to him.

Sean peers closer. He mutters, "All good?"

"Yep." I slide my hand into my glove, internally wincing when it hits my skull.

Finn helps me lace my gloves. "Let's see if you remember how to fight."

"Hopefully he's not too out of shape," Killian adds.

"Shut up, you two," I mutter, not in the mood for their interrogation or side comments.

Killian leans over the ropes. "Sean, don't be nice. He's been MIA. Make him work for it." He dings the bell.

Sean's a controlled hurricane. He comes at me fast with a jab, a hook, then a body shot.

I block, dodge, and give it right back to him.

Finn shouts, "Move your feet, Brax! You're not a statue!"

Killian yells, "Sean, he's slow on his left! Crush him there!"

Sean catches my ribs.

I grunt and counter with a hit to his jaw.

He smirks like a bastard who enjoys the pain.

We fight hard. Sweat drips into my eyes. My lungs feel like fire. My fists sting. Sean presses harder. I swing faster. Finn and Killian argue like two coaches who hate each other.

"Break his stance!" Killian shouts.

"No! Break his face!" Finn orders.

The chaos is exactly what I need. Every punch I land sends a jolt through the skull branded on my hand. By the time they call the match, Sean and I are drenched and gasping. We retreat to our corners, grabbing water bottles.

Killian and Finn pounce toward me.

Finn wipes sweat off his forehead. "Where the hell have you been, Brax?"

Killian adds, "And don't give us some generic 'busy' crap. You vanished."

Sean snarls, "Jeez. You two act like Brax is a ten-year-old instead of a thirty-year-old man."

Killian snaps, "So you do know where he's been. Fill us in."

Sean grunts. "I don't know. But if I did, I'm not a rat."

Finn glares at Sean.

He holds his hands in the air. "I don't know anything, but let the guy have some privacy."

Killian tilts his head. He points between us. "You're both liars."

I take a long drink of water. "Look, you're worrying over—"

"What the fuck is that?" Finn growls.

I freeze, bottle midair. A muscle in my jaw ticks as I glance at my hand. I immediately lower it.

Tension crackles between us.

Finn explodes first. "I asked you what the fuck that is."

I sniff hard, lifting my chest. "You know what it is so don't ask stupid questions."

Killian's face turns beet red. "Not you, too!"

Sean's face hardens.

Killian roars at Sean, "What did you get him into?"

"He didn't get me into anything," I declare.

Finn jabs my chest. He snarls, "What have you done?"

I push away from them. I'm tired, sick of the entire fucked-up situation I'm in, and don't need this right now. I walk away, stating, "I'm done here."

Finn calls after me, "Brax! Get back here!"

For the first time since I was a homeless, skinny, thieving kid, I don't listen to him. I jog down the stairs, exit the gym, and run back toward home.

I knew this day was coming. I'd hidden the skull brand better than Sean did when he first got his. With everything going on with Valentina, I had forgotten about it.

I knew they'd lose their shit.

Horns blare as I cut across traffic. I work my lungs and legs hard, but it doesn't matter. I can't push away Finn's outrage, Killian's questions, Sean's stare, and the skull on my hand that's still pulsing like it owns me.

I run past an alley and the stench of rotting fried food flares. My stomach pitches. I turn the block, but it stays with me, suffocating me as mercilessly as the Underworld.

By the time I reach my building and drag myself up the stairs, sweat chills on my skin. I push my apartment door open, toss my keys on the table, and go into my living room. I freeze and bark, "What in God's name are you doing here?"

Blue Ivanov coos from my couch. "Oh, good! You're alive."

How the hell did she get inside again?

There have been at least three incidents in the last few months where I come home and she's in my house. I've changed my locks and spoken with security, but somehow she always finds a way inside.

Her turquoise miniskirt barely exists. It matches her bright hair and falls in a straight sheet to her jaw. A low-cut tank top fights for dominance with a denim cropped jacket, and bright orange, six-inch booties dangle off her toes as she stretches one leg across the cushions.

I shut the door hard. "I told you to stop sneaking into my house."

She lifts a shoulder. "You should be thanking me. I brighten up the place, don't you think?"

"Stop playing games. How did you get in this time?"

"Magic."

My jaw tightens. I go over to the couch and grab her arm, pulling her to her feet. "You can't keep doing this."

"Then you shouldn't ignore my texts." Her perfume wafts between us. She puts her hand on my arm.

I shrug out of it and wrinkle my nose. "I've been busy."

She arches a brow. "Too busy to answer me at all? Brax, it's been days. I texted last night. And this morning." She crosses her arms under her chest, pushing up cleavage like punctuation. "You can't pretend I don't exist."

I scrub a hand over my face. "Blue, we're not a thing. We're never going to be a thing. I'm not interested. I've told you that."

Hurt flickers in her eyes, fast, but she masks it. "You don't have to be an asshole."

"Apparently, I do because nothing else works."

She steps closer, so close her breath brushes my throat. "Maybe you're just scared to want me."

I step backward. "No. I've told you before this isn't happening."

Her mouth trembles before she forces a smirk. "Because I'm younger? Because my dad would rip your head off?"

I snap, "Yes! All the above! And because I'm telling you, I'm not interested. That should be enough."

She scans my face, searching for cracks. "I don't believe you."

"Not my problem," I deadpan.

Her tone sharpens. "You know, most guys would be honored I broke into their apartment."

"I'm not most guys."

"They'd be impressed at my skills," she adds.

I stare at her.

She bats her eyelashes and lowers her voice. "I have other skills."

I cross my arms over my chest and hold her gaze. "Blue, go home. Before someone sees you here and your father thinks I'm doing something I'm not."

Her eyes flare, wounded. Then she moves. Fast.

She presses herself against me, flings her arms around my neck, and rises on her tiptoes. She whispers, "Just admit to me that you think about us."

I grab her wrists behind my head, lower them, and firmly warn, "You need to listen. It's never happening between us."

She jerks back, eyes flashing. "You're unbelievable."

"Good. Then you're finally listening." I point at the door. "You're leaving."

"You can't kick me out."

"I can. Keep watching, kid."

"I'm not a kid! I'm old enough to drink!"

"You are, and your immaturity is showing at this very minute," I scold.

She pouts, but her eyes turn to glass.

I sigh. "Listen closely, Blue. You're a great-looking young woman. There are tons of guys who would love to date you. But it's never going to happen between us. Don't take it personally."

She clenches her jaw, glaring at me. Then she mutters, "One day you're going to regret not giving me a chance."

I shake my head. "I regret a lot of things. This won't be one of them."

She glares. "You're just terrified of my father."

"I'm fully aware your father could end me for sneezing in your direction, yes."

"So you *are* scared."

"You should listen better. I just rattled off all the reasons it's never happening, and your father is only a small part of the equation." I open the door. "Move."

She stomps past me into the hallway, heels clacking like gunshots. I follow, shutting and locking the door behind us, even though none of it keeps her out.

We walk the corridor together, and I silently beg for no neighbors to appear. I steer her toward the stairwell.

She turns. "If my father asks where I was, I'm telling him I came here."

That's all I need.

"If he asks, I'll tell him how you've been stalking me and breaking into my apartment. Then I'll file a restraining order to keep you away," I threaten.

She gasps dramatically. "You wouldn't."

"Want to test me?"

A reluctant smirk tugs at her lips. "I hate you."

"Great. Make it permanent."

We descend the stairs in silence. Her heels stab each step. At the bottom, she pauses at the exit, pinning her sad expression on me.

Some of my attitude melts. Her expression reminds me of the little girl I've always known as Adrian and Skylar's daughter before she became fixated on me.

I soften my tone. "Go home, Blue. Don't break into my apartment again, or I will have a discussion with your father."

Her throat bobs. Then she straightens, flipping her hair back into place. "You're going to regret this someday."

"So be it," I reply, then push her out the door.

When she disappears into the crowd, I exhale and return to my apartment, still flabbergasted that she broke in again.

I need to know how she's getting in.

I mentally catalog all the ways I can grill the super without mentioning Adrian's daughter is a pint-sized stalker. Blue is annoying, but the Ivanovs are family. It's still Adrian and Skylar's daughter, and I don't want her reputation tarnished.

I get to my unit and unlock the door. I step into the family room and once again freeze.

This time, the intruder isn't one I'll push out.

Valentina stands in the middle of the room like she stepped off the cover of a magazine. Red minidress hugging every curve, high stilettos making her already-long legs look endless, dark hair curled and spilling down her back. Her lips are painted the same dangerous, sinful shade as the dress.

My brain short-circuits, and my dick goes painfully hard.

She doesn't smile. Her cool gaze flickers over my damp shirt. She taunts, "Rough day?"

My heart pounds harder. "You tell me. You're the one breaking into my apartment."

Her eyebrows arch. "Well, I had to wait for your other...guest to leave."

"Is that a question or an accusation?" I retort.

She purses her lips in disapproval.

I step closer.

Her eyes flash. "She's cute. Your little turquoise shadow."

"Blue's her name, and she's just a kid," I clarify.

Valentina's mouth twists. "Is that what we're calling her now? A color palette? Because from where I was standing in that hallway, she looked pretty comfortable in your space. Again."

My shoulders go tight. "Well, if you were eavesdropping, then you should have heard me tell her I don't want her."

She lifts a shoulder, the movement making a curl slide against her collarbone, right next to her Finzia tattoo. "She seems determined to have you."

I step closer, cockily asserting, "And that bugs you?"

Her brows shoot higher. "Clearly, I interrupted a very romantic moment."

"Jesus, Valentina." I drag a hand through my hair. "We're nothing. She's nothing. She's had a crush on me since high school. That's it."

Valentina's gaze narrows. "Funny. She doesn't look like a high school girl anymore."

I groan, "She's not. But she *was* when it started. And she's Adrian's daughter. I've told her no a thousand times."

Valentina's lips press together. "It sure seems like there's more to it."

I step forward, and Valentina steps back until she's up against the wall. I growl, "What's that supposed to mean?"

"She was in your apartment, Brax." Her voice cracks around the words she's trying to keep sharp. "Again. Dressed like that. Hanging off you. And you didn't look like you hated it."

"I *did* hate it."

She questions, "Did you? Because she looked pretty sure of herself."

Anger fills me. "I've never touched her and never kissed her. Not once have I even thought about it. I'm not into her. I told you—"

"Right." She nods, eyes going flat. "You're not into her. But yet she breaks into your apartment and throws herself at you."

I exhale hard. "Why do you care so much?"

The question hangs between us, heavier than any punch Sean landed today.

Her chin jerks back a fraction. "I don't."

"Bullshit."

Her tone sharpens. "I just think it's reckless. And stupid. And if Adrian finds out, he's going to—"

"Don't make this about Adrian! This is about you standing in my apartment in a dress you know is killing me, picking a fight about a girl I've been actively trying to keep away from me for years."

Color spills into her cheeks, but she doesn't back down. "You're imagining things."

"Am I?" I lean closer, an inch from her mouth.

She presses her palms against my chest. "Yes."

"I think you're jealous."

Valentina softly laughs. "I don't get jealous."

I slide my finger down her cheek, then grip her jaw, stating, "You are. Otherwise, you wouldn't still be here."

Her mouth curves into a dare. "And if I am, Brax? What exactly do you want to do about it?"

A beat of silence passes. The air thickens, charged, crackling between us.

That coil inside me snaps. I press my mouth to hers and tug her dress to her waist.

Her arms reach for my pants, shoving them down.

I lift her bottom, and her legs wrap around me. My cock slides inside her in one thrust.

She whimpers, trembling slightly.

"This is what I'm going to do about it, Minx," I warn, pinning her even closer to the wall and thrusting with all the months of longing I've had to be inside her again.

She flicks her tongue inside my mouth, grips my hair, tugging it slightly. Her hips rise and fall, grinding over me.

I groan, lower my lips to her neck, and nibble on her collarbone.

"*Gesù, aiutami,*" she mutters in Italian.

"God's not helping you, Minx," I reply, gripping her hip tighter, happy Brenna made me learn Italian.

She shifts over me, her lips near my ear. "Like that. Oh shit. Just...oh!"

My mouth catches hers again. Our tongues turn to fire, dancing around each other.

She grips me tighter, kisses my jaw to my ear, then starts rattling off Italian I don't know while riding me harder.

I move my hands to her ass, gripping each cheek and pushing harder. Sweat pops up, adding to my already-drenched shirt. Fire flows through my veins, and my eyesight turns blurry.

Her pussy clenches my cock. She moans more Italian.

I warn, "Keep talking like that and I won't let you walk tomorrow."

Her laugh catches in her throat, turning into something incoherent. Her body spasms over mine, and she cries out, "Brax!"

I squeeze my eyes shut.

Don't cum yet.

I thrust slower, not wanting it to stop.

"Oh fuck! Oh fuck! Oh fuck!" she screams, and her body violently trembles.

"Say my name again, Minx," I order, speeding up my thrusts.

"Brax!" she calls out in a shaky breath.

I lose it. Every ounce of pent-up desire spools out of me. I push as deep as I can into her, and a high hits me so hard I see stars.

My breath hits her neck, and my vision evens out. I lift my face, and she pushes out of my grasp. She yanks her dress down. "See you later."

"What? Where you going?" I ask, following her to the foyer.

"I need to go."

"That's not an answer."

She finally meets my eyes. "You know better than to ask questions."

"Then I'm coming with you," I say, my protectiveness in full force.

She puts her hands on my chest. "You know you can't."

"Listen, Minx—"

Her fingers push my lips.

I stare at her, my pulse racing.

"Everything is fine. I'll see you later." She spins and opens the door. Then she looks back, says, "But it was fun. Keep Blue out of here," and winks.

I watch her saunter down the hall, get on the elevator, and wonder what the hell just happened.

Valentina
A Few Weeks Later

Chapter
THIRTEEN

Flashbacks of the tattoo artist inking my chest keep popping up. I breathe through it, relieved that Fiona's coronation is over. The Underworld filters out of the aisles, disappearing through stone corridors in waves, while the chanting fades.

When it's time to exit, Brax puts his hand on the back of my waist. I lean into it, then shake it off.

It's been a few weeks since the night I went to his apartment and let him push me against the wall. Too many days have passed since his knuckles scraped down my thighs and his mouth brushed my jaw. And every night, I replay how I allowed my carefully constructed control to shatter in his hands.

But I was reckless and can't go down that road again. I'm his mentor, and I'm fighting an uphill battle for my seat at the table. I'm not naive. Hundreds of others will kill for the spot. So I have to stay focused. Otherwise, the scar on my chest was all for nothing. So I don't allow myself to climb back into the danger zone and forget the only thing that matters, which is my seat.

Plus, I'm pissed at Brax. Sean, too, but Brax is the one I'm in charge of, and he could have allowed the entire coronation to go up in flames.

What was he thinking?

He splays his hand on my back again, but there are too many people around us for me to get away from it. We turn down the main corridor. The flames flicker gold against the wall. Small, almost-invisible crowns carved into the corners of each block serve as a reminder that this corridor belongs to royalty.

The crowd turns a corner, but I turn the opposite way, then shake off his grasp and speed up.

"Slow down," Brax mutters behind me.

"Try harder to keep up," I snap.

"Try walking like a human and not like you're racing to murder someone," he fires back.

I am racing to murder someone. He just doesn't realize he's first on the list.

The massive, royal skull on Fiona's chamber door comes into view. I push it open, and as soon as Brax steps inside, I shut it. The heavy wood slams with a hollow thud, shaking the sconces.

Brax removes his skull mask, then slinks toward me with his brows shot up. "If you wanted me alone this badly, you could have just asked."

Tingles race down my spine, and anger churns hot under my ribs. "How could you let Kirill and Sean fight before the wedding?"

He blinks, then gives me a slow once-over as if we're having a different conversation entirely. His gaze trails over my throat, the exposed line of my shoulders, the hem of my dress, then back to my face. It's the same heated focus from his apartment. It burns there, infuriatingly unbothered.

He carelessly shrugs. "The king wanted to box. You stand in front of him and tell him no next time. I'll watch. Could be fun."

I stare at him, disbelief warring with the urge to strangle him. "This isn't about fun. You could have ruined the entire coronation!"

He leans back against the nearest column, arms crossing over his broad chest, smirk deepening. "You sure? Looked pretty fun to me. Two guys working out their issues with gloves instead of knives. Seemed like the upgrade option in your world."

"You think this is a joke?" I step closer, the fury I've held in since I interrupted their brawl unravels.

His jaw ticks. "He asked who wanted to fight. Sean jumped in before I could."

I hurl, "He's the king. You don't let him do anything that puts him at risk. That's your job. If you fail, do you know who they'll punish?"

"Let them punish me," he arrogantly asserts.

My voice rises. "You idiot! They'll punish me too!" Tears well in my eyes, and I turn, blinking hard and hating how emotional I get ever since they branded me.

His voice softens. "Shit. I'm sorry."

I get control back and glare at him. "You're sorry? You almost cost me my seat. Everything I've clawed my way toward for years could have gone up in smoke because you decided to play gym coach while the king traded punches with the queen's brother!"

He pushes off the column and closes the distance between us in three long strides. His height and bulk crowd my space. The heat of his body hits me like a wall.

"Yeah. I'm sorry. But you don't get to act like you're the only one with something to lose. Everything in my life has been ripped apart since I got pulled into this little secret society circus."

"Shh," I warn.

He moves closer so his mouth's an inch from mine. He adds, "I'm still here, doing what I'm told, keeping my mouth shut. So don't stand in front of me and tell me I'm not taking it seriously because I let the king throw a few punches to clear his head."

My heart races faster. His breath hits mine, taunting me to break the vow I made not to touch him again.

He lifts my mask, letting it rest on my head, then drags his finger over my jaw.

I don't breathe.

He continues in a firm tone, "All you think about is your seat at the table. Maybe you should try remembering I had to give up my life to be ruled by it."

"Lower your voice," I whisper.

His gaze flickers down to my mouth, then back up, challenging just as loudly, "Make me."

My pulse slams against my neck.

He slides his hand down and grips my neck, lifting my chin. He studies me closer, the gold flecks in his irises flickering from the wall torches.

I manage to get out, "I am not losing my seat because you aren't making smart decisions. You want to be angry about your life? Fine. Join the club. But you don't get to turn that rage into stupid decisions that put the king at risk. Next time he says he wants to box before a ceremony, either redirect him or find me, and I'll do it. Understand?"

Brax murmurs, "That's the thing about kings. They don't care about anyone's seat but their own."

My temper spikes so high it makes me dizzy. "For someone who walked in here from the outside, you certainly have a lot of opinions about how this world works."

"For someone who was born in it, you're shockingly blind to how much it costs the rest of us," he states.

"It's a privilege to be here," I remind him.

"It is? From where I stand—" His gaze cuts toward the door.

Sharp, muffled voices get louder.

The hairs on the back of my neck rise. My fingers curl around Brax's wrist, and I drag him across the chamber. I dive into the cedar wardrobe and pull him next to me. I shut the door so there's only a crack.

Silk gowns and ceremonial cloaks swing gently on brass hangers.

Brax's hand automatically finds my waist in the tight space, steadying me.

I slap my palm over his mouth before he can speak. His body goes rigid from the surprise, muscles tensing against mine, but he doesn't push me away.

The door creaks open. Two men stride into Fiona's chamber wearing the same masks Brax did.

Why are they here?

We shouldn't be here either.

It's Brax's fault. He makes me lose my mind.

The queen's quarters are sacred. Unless you're invited, you shouldn't be here.

I know damn well these men weren't.

My breath tightens, and I lean toward the crack in the wardrobe doors, careful not to shift too much of my weight against Brax's body.

His chest rises and falls behind me, tense and controlled.

A low, male Russian accent announces, "The fifty thousand came through. When they return from the honeymoon, we will have twenty-four hours to kill her."

I know that voice.

A sharp, icy tremor slices down the length of my spine. I don't breathe as my pulse stutters, then slams into my ribs. I tilt my head just enough to look up at Brax while trying to figure out where I've heard that voice before.

His pupils tighten, shrinking to sharp pinpoints inside the darkness. The skin around his eyes pulls taut, and his shoulders angle forward as if he's preparing for war.

The second man answers. His voice is American with no hint of an accent. Yet it's smooth with a slightly nasal ring, which is just as familiar. "Where's my deposit?"

"It's coming," the Russian replies with irritation.

"I don't work without it."

Brax steps closer to me, but I push him back against the wall. His fists curl at my waist.

"Don't," I mouth silently.

His jaw flexes with hatred, but he doesn't push past me.

The Russian insists, "Don't worry. It's coming any moment."

The American scoffs. "I'll believe it when I see it."

"It's coming."

A moment of tension mounts.

The American asks, "When do we get the other four-hundred-fifty-thousand?"

"When we send her head to them," the Russian answers without hesitation.

My blood freezes.

Them?

Brax's fury radiates around us.

My own rage rises, pressing hard against my sternum, threatening to burst. Someone inside the Underworld who has enough access to be in the royal hallway is plotting Fiona's execution. The treachery is enough to wipe out entire bloodlines.

A soft electronic ding slices through the room. There's another pause, then the American's tone shifts. In a satisfied voice, he declares, "Money's in my account. I'm in."

The Russian jeers, "No shit. Stop doubting me."

A dark chuckle escapes the American. "Let's go sharpen our knives."

Footsteps scrape across the stone. The chamber door clicks. Silence follows.

I keep still for ten long seconds. Only when I'm certain they're gone do I ease my hand off Brax's mouth and push the wardrobe door open a fraction.

It's empty. Still, I step out cautiously, scanning every inch of the chamber.

Brax storms past me, heading toward the exit.

I grab his arm. "Stop!"

He halts with violent restraint, turning back toward me with a glare that matches the rage vibrating under his skin. "We could have taken them both out by now."

"And gotten killed since we have no weapons."

"I could have strangled both of them," he sneers.

I add, "We need to get out of here. If anyone finds out we're in the queen's chamber, there will be consequences."

"We need to go after them! The longer we wait, the farther they'll get, and we won't be able to tell who they are with all the other masked men!" he declares.

"Shut up so I can think," I push, pacing toward the center of the room and gripping the edge of the table.

He stalks after me. "Why?"

"Because I've heard those voices before," I admit, raking a hand through my hair, trying to sift through the memories.

"Who are they?"

"Let me think!" I demand.

Brax shuts his mouth with his scowl deepening.

I begin to pace.

"You're wasting time," Brax argues.

"Shut up," I bite out again.

He releases heavy breaths through his nose.

My brain races through faces, accents, meetings, family alliances, bloodlines, and rivalries. It takes a few minutes, but then the pieces click. I stop pacing. I turn toward Brax. "I know who it is."

Brax's eyes narrow. "Who?"

My tone fills with disgust. "Lev and Igor Petrov."

His jaw drops. Then his expression twists in the same revulsion I feel. "This is exactly why the Underworld will never work. You can't put rival families under the same roof and expect loyalty. Kirill's own bloodline wants his wife dead."

I rub my hands over my face. "The Petrovs hate Kirill."

"Why?"

The question lands harder than he realizes. I stiffen. "It's none of your business."

"Valentina—"

I cut him off sharply. "We need to go. Now." I stride toward the chamber door, forcing my thoughts into ruthless order.

Fiona is marked. The Petrovs are planning a coup. And the Omni allowed this test to happen inside the queen's own chambers.

Everything is shifting under my feet, accelerating at a speed I can't control. And Brax is a firecracker waiting to explode.

He falls into step behind me as we slip into the corridor with the assassination clock ticking, and the only ones who know anything about it.

And it has to stay that way. I don't know who I can trust with this information. Lev and Igor were too comfortable inside Fiona's chambers, which made my gut sink further. Someone at the top hired this hit. They have money and hatred for both Kirill and Fiona.

Brax stalks beside me toward the jet, every step radiating fury that only grows stronger the farther we get from the queen's corridor. We both sneak glances behind us, checking shadows, corners, and blind spots for enemies.

I miss the days when I considered everyone in the Underworld as friends. Ever since Sean O'Malley arrived on the scene, there have been few members I still trust. Everything has turned upside down, and there's nothing I can predict.

Brax motions for me to go first. I step into the jet, take a seat, and he follows. I murmur, "Not a single word."

Brax's jaw twitches.

The doors close, the plane moves onto the runway, and is soon in the air. I ask the flight attendant for a notepad and a pen.

She brings it back. "Can I get you anything else?"

"No," Brax replies roughly.

She forces a smile and scurries to her area.

I write, *Don't talk. Cameras everywhere.*

He stares at the note, then grabs the pen, and scribbles underneath with short, angry strokes. *Where do they live?*

I jot back, *Chicago. South Side. Petrov territory.*

He scratches his next question. *Do you have their numbers?*

My pulse jumps. I answer, *Yes.*

He takes deep breaths, grinding his molars.

I write a question mark on the paper.

He takes the pen. *We need to set them up. More people are involved in this, and we need to know who they are.*

I write, *Agree.*

He writes down an address in Gary, Indiana. It's on the outskirts of Chicago and not a place people like to spend any time in since the run-down city's full of crime.

I arch a brow at him.

He orders, *Text them with a meeting time.*

I pull out my phone and type a new message thread. I add Lev and Igor. At the last second, I add Brax so they aren't shocked when they see him.

He puts his hand over my cell.

I look at him in question.

He writes, *Do it when we land so they don't have any time to think about it.*

It's a good call. I nod, put my phone away, fold the note into a tiny piece, and stuff it into my bra.

Brax glances at my cleavage.

My face heats.

Don't get any ideas.

I turn toward the window, and my mind races the entire flight. It takes forever for the wheels to lower and the jet to taxi toward the hangar.

As soon as we're in my SUV, I pull out my phone and text the group.

> Me: New job. Meet in one hour.

I add the address.

> Igor: My flight hasn't landed.

> Lev: I'm on the runway, but there are two planes in front of mine. It's going to be a bit before I'm allowed off.

> Igor: The captain just said to prepare for landing.

> Me: Get there as soon as you can.

Brax rolls the divider glass down an inch and tells Vito, "Take me to my place."

I ask, "What are you doing?"

"We're taking my car," he snarls, scowling at Vito.

He glares at Brax in the rearview mirror.

I don't argue. Vito shouldn't even be my driver after I made my requests, yet the Omni won't give me another.

The SUV weaves through traffic and stops in front of Brax's building. We get out, and he leads me through the parking garage to his rebuilt 1980s Mustang. He cocks a grin and opens the passenger door. "Get in, Minx."

A sharp, warm flutter runs through my core. I obey, and he shuts the door, then races to the driver's side.

The engine snarls to life. Brax hits the accelerator and peels out of the garage. Streetlights smear past the windshield in streaks of amber as he slices through traffic.

He grabs his phone, swipes it, then holds it to his ear. A moment passes, and he orders, "There's a plan to assassinate Fiona."

Sean's roar comes through the phone. "What the fuck are you talking about?"

"Hack into Lev and Igor Petrov's data. We need to find out who else is involved. Valentina and I are taking care of them now," he states.

Sean's muffled voice fills the car.

Brax shakes his head and makes a sharp turn. "No. I'll take care of them. I need you hacking." He hangs up.

"We need to tell Kirill," I say, then dial him, but it doesn't even ring. I groan, then text his head of security, Draco.

Me: 911

His reply comes seconds later.

Draco: Contact the Yacht.

The Mustang roars louder as Brax overpowers a semi. He veers off the ramp.

I dial another number.

Sergio answers, "Hello, Valentina. How may I help you?"

"911. I need to speak to him immediately."

His voice turns to worry. "One mom—" The line goes dead.

"Fuck!" I attempt to call again, but it won't go through.

"What's wrong?" Brax asks.

"They're probably in international waters. Sometimes the phone doesn't work when it's moving to another satellite."

"That's convenient," he mutters.

I try eight more times, but the line never rings.

Several minutes go by as we pass huge buildings with shattered glass, loading bays with crooked doors that can't shut properly, and bare steel flanks.

Brax turns into a dark, empty parking lot and kills the headlights. He gets out, as do I.

We scurry through the shadows and get in front of the entrance.

He stops me, warning, "Be careful, Minx."

"Not the first abandoned building I've been in," I remind him.

"Just be careful. I'm going first," he declares and slides past the warped door.

I follow him and glance around the abandoned machinery, dangling chains, and deep pockets of shadows. I mutter, "This place is perfect."

Brax nods, steps behind a stack of metal crates, then pulls out industrial-grade zip cables and a Glock. He holds it toward me. "Take it."

I don't hesitate.

He points. "Go hide behind that wall. When they come in, shoot them both in the kneecap. They can't die until we get more information from them."

"Agree," I say, and take my position in the darkness.

My heart beats wild, waiting. Then the low growl of an engine crawls up the drive. Two silhouettes approach the building.

Igor steps in first, his Russian accent thick, demanding, "Where's Valentina?"

"Who knows. I just get summoned," Brax states in his normal sarcastic tone.

"I'm here," I announce, step out of the shadows, and shoot two quick shots at them both.

Blood bursts everywhere. They both go down screaming.

Brax pounces over them, holding a gun, warning, "Don't move or I'm blowing your head off."

"What the fuck," Lev grits through his teeth.

"Arms over your head and get on your stomachs," Brax shouts, then shoots a bullet next to Igor's face.

Dust flies in the air. He pisses his pants. "Don't kill me!"

"Okay! Okay!" Lev agrees, putting his hands over his head and rolling onto his stomach.

I reach down and grab his gun from his waist and toss it across the room. Then I do the same with Igor's.

"Tie them up, Minx," Brax orders.

I grab a zip tie and secure their feet and wrists.

Brax hands me the gun. "Keep it on them."

I point it at them.

He drags them one at a time several feet, then lowers a rope and ties it to their ankles. He hits a button on a wall, and the rope loses its slack until they're hanging upside down like butchered animals.

Lev spits blood. "You—"

Brax backhands him hard across the mouth. "Shut up! Now I want to know who else is involved in your assassination plot."

Igor grunts, swinging around in a circle from trying to pry himself loose. "Go to hell."

Brax reaches into his pocket, then presses the flat of the blade to Igor's throat. "You misunderstand me. I didn't come for Hell. I came for answers."

Lev snarls something in Russian.

My pulse skips a beat, and I translate, "He said you're too late."

Brax drags the edge of the knife slowly across Igor's ribs, not cutting, just enough pressure to draw a howl. "Who else is involved?"

Igor jerks wildly as the blade presses deeper into his skin. "Stop! Stop —please—just stop—"

Brax doesn't move. "Names! I want names! Who hired you?"

The warehouse amplifies Igor's ragged breath. His voice breaks into a scream. "Gavin O'Malley!"

Every drop of blood drains from my body.

Brax freezes. The knife lowers. His jaw clenches hard enough that a visible tremor cuts through the muscle. He spits on Lev's face, the gesture dripping with a hatred I've never witnessed from him.

I pull out my phone and dial the yacht.

The call connects on the third ring.

"Sergio," I say sharply.

"Valentina? What's going on?"

"No time. 911!"

"I'll get the king now," he says.

Brax's head snaps toward me. He strides over in three steps and snatches the phone. "Let me talk to him." He paces.

Please don't let them be right.

Don't let it be too late.

Brax growls into the receiver. "There's a plot to assassinate Fiona."

Brax

Chapter
FOURTEEN

It's all happening too fast. Valentina's still shaken from the confessions, indicting Ulrich and his wife Jytte as the culprits behind Fiona's assassination attempts.

I offer, "I never liked either of them, nor did I trust them."

"They're members of the Royal Council," she reminds me.

"So what? They're snakes, and you trust too easily," I declare, then add, "They need to die."

"We better get there in time," she frets.

My stomach flips. As soon as we discovered that Ulrich and Jytte were behind everything, we got text messages telling us to head to the arena. We were only on the plane for an hour when Sergio texted Valentina that they had taken Kirill. And then Sean called to say they kidnapped Fiona, too.

Time drags until the wheels of the jet finally descend. The wheels hit the ground and we both jump out of our seats.

"Move," I bark at the flight attendant who stands in the aisle. I grab Valentina's wrist and pull her toward the door.

We hit the corridor at a full sprint. The light flickers in the wall sconces, and muffled chants vibrate through the walls.

We turn the final corner. The massive arena doors loom a few hundred yards away. Valentina stays a half step ahead, her red dress ripped at the slit, curls flying behind her like a furious banner snapping through a storm.

By the time we reach them, my lungs burn.

She slams the door open, and it crashes against the wall.

The world on the other side punches me in the chest so hard I can't breathe. Torches slam in unison against the stone floor, a heavy, punishing thud that vibrates straight into my ribs. Hundreds of voices chant in a dark, guttural rhythm, each syllable rolling through the air like an ancient curse. Fire lunges upward from bonfires surrounding the stage, smoke spiraling toward the massive ceiling of the underground arena.

Two guillotines sit at the center of it all. Kirill and Fiona are locked into them, naked from the waist up, throats pressed into carved wooden grooves. The polished blades hang over their heads, catching firelight as they wait to drop. Knights flank them with swords held high. The crowd hisses and moans, hungry for royal blood.

Ulrich raises his arm, mid-sentence, voice booming like he's about to deliver holy judgment. "By the power vested in me by the Omni—"

"Stop!" Valentina's voice tears through the noise.

My body snaps into fight mode. I roar over her, "We have proof!"

Torches freeze mid-strike. The pounding stops. The chanting collapses into a shock-filled silence that buzzes inside my brain.

Hundreds of skull-masked faces whip toward us.

Kirill jerks his head as far as the wood allows him. Fiona's terrified eyes lock onto Valentina. Tears streak her cheeks. Her hair tangles around her tiara. They're both seconds from death, and explosions of rage detonate through my chest.

I take the stairs two at a time, leaping onto the stage. Knights shift at the edges, but I ignore them. Heat from the bonfires slams up at me, thick with smoke, sweat, and panic.

"Stand back or you will be next!" Ulrich bellows.

"We have proof," I snarl, cutting across the sacrificial deck. I slam my shoulder into the executioner near Fiona and shove him off the platform.

He staggers, catches himself on his hands, and stares at me through his mask.

Across the stage, another executioner reaches for the release by Kirill, but he never touches it. Sean appears like a weapon unleashed and crashes into him, knocking the guy across the blood-splattered boards. He snaps, "Get the fuck away from the king."

The crowd explodes in hissing and shrieks. Firelight twists over skull masks and white satin gowns, turning the arena into a fever dream filled with demons.

Zara's voice cuts through the chaos, sharp and regal. "I declare an Act of Betrayal! Jytte and Ulrich Koch, you are hereby condemned!"

Every head swings toward her.

Jytte chokes on her breath. "You can't do that!"

Zara marches toward the stage with lethal precision. "I am the successor queen. I can, and I will."

Ulrich jabs a finger at Sean. "They're lying to protect his sister!"

"We're not. We have proof," Valentina insists, moving toward Devika, an Indian woman on the Royal Council.

Ulrich snaps his chin at the executioners. "Get in position!"

I place myself in front of Fiona's neck, blocking the guillotine's drop point. My voice lowers into the threat I only use when I mean to end someone. "Step closer, and I'll choke the air out of you."

Sean growls across the stage, "Same."

"Knights, get into position. We have an act of hostility upon us!" Jytte commands.

Swords rise. Boots shuffle. The heat at my back intensifies as the bonfires swell, flames licking at the air.

Devika says in an impossibly calm tone, "No one moves."

"We have confessions that these two plotted to overthrow Kirill and Fiona. It's all here," Valentina says, pulling out her phone and clicking on a video.

Devika takes the phone. She hits play.

Screams blast across the arena.

My voice demands, "Tell me who paid you to kill the queen!"

More screams, wet gurgles, and crackling sobs echo the arena.

Valentina's voice follows, lethal and steady. "Speak, or I'm taking another finger."

The video goes on and on.

Devika turns it off.

"There's more on there. You're missing the best part," I point out.

She shoots me a death glare.

Valentina faces the Omni. "There are two other men on video. They all say the same thing."

Phones begin dinging everywhere. A cascade of chimes echoes through the arena.

Sean lifts his. "That's everyone's inbox. Brax and I hacked into Ulrich and Jytte's private chats. Everything is documented."

"He's lying!" Jytte shrieks.

A roar rises from the audience. "Free our Majesties! Free our Majesties!"

The knights circle Ulrich and Jytte.

Sean moves first, kicking bolts loose on Kirill's guillotine. I reach down, unlatch Fiona's, and yank the heavy wood up. It resists me for half a second before the mechanism snaps open.

Fiona gasps and jerks backward, hands flying to her throat. I grip her shoulder, grounding her. "You're okay. I've got you."

Sean frees Kirill, who immediately yanks Fiona to him, shielding her body with his. His eyes burn with a fury that could level kingdoms. He orders, "Bring the queen her royal robe! Now!"

An Omni scrambles with folded fabric. I step back as Kirill wraps Fiona in her robe with trembling hands. He dons his own and plants himself between his wife and every threat in the arena.

He points at Ulrich and Jytte. They're pale, sweating, and surrounded by knights who now understand exactly where their loyalty belongs. Kirill roars, "The only ritual we complete tonight is the Black Veil."

A collective gasp surges through the crowd.

Metal poles roll out. Nooses swing above flames. A bridal gown and tuxedo appear.

"Get dressed," Kirill commands.

Jytte buckles. Ulrich spits excuses. No one listens.

Zara pins a rose on Ulrich. Valentina shoves a blood-red bouquet into Jytte's trembling hands and orders her to hold it. When the thorns dig into her palms, she screams, and Valentina binds her fingers with wire until blood runs down the stems.

My cock hardens.

That's my Minx.

Sean and I place the nooses around their necks. Ropes get secured under their armpits.

Valentina adds a veil to Jytte's head.

"This is a mistake!" Ulrich howls again.

"Yeah. A deadly one. Raise them into the air," Kirill orders.

The pulleys crank and the ropes strain. The couple rises into the air, their robes swaying above the firepits.

A new chant erupts. Torches strike in unison. The arena turns into an inferno.

I stare up at Ulrich and Jytte and think of Fiona's head locked in wood and Kirill's neck exposed to a falling blade. I've never wanted to snap a neck more in my entire life.

Kirill looks at Fiona. "Last chance. Do you want me to show them any mercy?"

She trembles. Then shakes her head. "No."

"Move them over the fire," Kirill shouts.

Hell opens up. Deafening screams fill the arena as lace and roses explode into flames. Fabric curls and blackens while threads of rope burn. Their bodies drop farther as the metal wire bites into their necks.

Fiona gags behind her hand.

Kirill pulls her away.

Sean steps up to handle the sentencing as they leave the stage.

The taste of smoke and vengeance thickens on my tongue. I glance back at the guillotines, my stomach twisting.

Valentina steps beside me, grabs my hand, and urges, "Come with me. This is our chance."

"Huh?"

She tugs at me, and I follow her, darting through the arena toward Fiona and Kirill.

The hallway swallows us in cooler air the second we step into it. Torches line the walls in a softer rhythm, their flames swaying instead of attacking the ground like they did inside.

Fiona leans heavily into Kirill, robe clutched tight, her legs unsteady.

He hovers around her with lethal protectiveness, checking every shadow as if another knife could come flying out at any second.

Valentina and I close the distance fast. She shouts, "Wait!"

Fiona and Kirill turn.

"What's wrong?" Kirill asks with alarm.

She frets, "Are Sean and Zara okay?"

I tease, "They're fine. Living it up with the hanging corpses and declaring a national chastisement for trying to overthrow you."

Fiona blurts out, "Thank you for saving us! Both of you."

I puff my chest out, boasting, "Piece of cake."

"Then why did my wife almost get beheaded?" Kirill seethes, holding Fiona tighter.

Valentina slaps the back of her hand into my stomach so hard I breathe out through my teeth.

Fiona offers a soft correction to her husband. "He's being funny."

"There's nothing funny about it," Kirill repeats, still glaring at me.

Fiona tries again. "Kirill—"

"He's right. It's horrendous, and we need to weed out the rest of the traitors. And that's why you must give us their seats," Valentina announces.

Us?

I'm not joining their cultic table.

Kirill and Fiona freeze, staring at her.

"Please," she adds, voice cracking with urgency.

Kirill exhales, jaw grinding, and closes his eyes like he's bracing for a blow. He opens them slowly.

"Of course you can have them," Fiona offers.

Hope flashes across Valentina's face. Then it dies.

Kirill states, "No. Unfortunately, you can't give them the open seats."

Valentina's body stiffens beside me. "Why not?" she demands.

"They saved us," Fiona cries out, looking genuinely confused and hurt.

Sympathy softens Kirill's features for only a moment. He turns to Valentina. "There has to be a cleansing ritual. You know this, Valentina."

Fiona scrunches her face. "What does that mean?"

"It was one of the missing sections in your Royal Doctrine. It's Amendment 666," he informs her.

I stare at him, trying not to snort.

Amendment 666.

Of course it is.

Fiona scoffs. "The same amendment that almost got us beheaded?"

"Yes."

"And what is so special about this amendment?" she asks.

Kirill glances between us, then pins his attention on Fiona, answering, "Seats must be refilled with the same status as those who left."

"Meaning?" Fiona pushes.

"If an individual dies unmarried, another unmarried individual takes the seat. But if a couple dies, then another couple replaces them," Kirill asserts.

Fiona wrinkles her nose. "That's stupid."

"Agreed," I mutter.

Kirill snaps his attention to me. "Don't belittle the rules Fiona's father created. They are to keep balance."

Fiona folds her arms. "So they should get married."

I jerk my head backward and grunt.

Sure, Fiona. And fairies exist, too.

Kirill shakes his head. "No. The amendment states that the evil needs to be cleansed from the seats during a purity ritual."

She admits, "I'm still lost."

"The couple can't be together due to an arranged marriage or a predetermined selection. It has to be a couple who is truly in love and has chosen to marry without outside forces. The seats must go through a rebirth period, and only love can change the energy from negative to positive," he explains.

Valentina blurts out, "We're in love and getting married!"

I whip my head toward her, only to witness her expression dead serious.

You've got to be kidding me.

"We are!" she insists, grabbing my hand. She looks up at me, lashes narrowed, silently promising she'll stab me in the kidney if I don't play along. "Aren't we?"

Every muscle in my body tightens.

Marriage?

Kirill waits, arms crossed.

Valentina continues, "We check all the boxes. We'll take the seats."

I clench my jaw.

The little Minx is going to get it when we're alone.

Kirill chuckles and points at me. "I see. You're joking again. The look on your face is priceless. Well played."

"We're not joking," Valentina insists, tugging my arm. "Tell them the truth so we don't lose the chance to take our seats."

I glance at her, my chest tight, ready to tell her no.

She pleads with her eyes, and my dick turns harder.

Fucking hell, Valentina.

I slowly slide my arm around her, tug her closer, and stand taller. I grin, pinning my gaze on Kirill and declaring, "We're in love, and I asked her to marry me."

Kirill points to her hand. "Where's her ring?"

Valentina interjects, "Getting sized. Brax thought my finger was a seven, and it's a seven and a half."

Seven and a half.

This is getting good.

I affirm, "My bad. The jeweler is fixing it."

Kirill studies us for a moment, shakes his head, then looks at Fiona.

She bites on her smile, trying not to laugh, but she doesn't call us out.

Valentina begs, "We meet the criteria. Please! Let us take our seats!"

Kirill sighs, then gives her an apologetic look. He lowers his voice. "Amendment 666 is important. Sean created it for the sole purpose—"

"Of restoring light to the table and safety to The Underworld," Fiona interjects.

Pride fills Kirill's expression. He praises, "Yes, my queen. You're exactly right. How did you know that when the amendment wasn't in your Royal Doctrine?"

"It's part of Act 7. Balance is essential for safety, and light must always shine upon the table," she recites.

She always was a bookworm.

Kirill puffs his chest, gushing, "I have the smartest wife."

I mutter, "Don't fill her head."

Valentina elbows me hard again.

"Ouch," I grumble.

Kirill scowls.

Fiona adds, "Which is why Valentina and Brax can take their seats as long as they get married on the next full moon."

I swallow hard.

I need to stop this before it goes any further.

Shock fills Kirill's expression. "You aren't buying this?"

Her lips twitch. "Oh, Brax has always wanted to get married, haven't you?"

I clench my jaw.

"Answer the queen," Kirill instructs.

"Yeah. All day long, it's all I think about," I state.

Fiona motions between us. "It's clear they're madly in love."

Really, Fiona?

Way to have my back when I just saved you from getting beheaded!

"It is?" Kirill retorts, furrowing his forehead.

"Of course," she lies.

He continues to look at her like she's insane.

"We are. We'll have our wedding on the next full moon," Valentina declares.

"On the..." I scrunch my face, then blurt out, "That's in three weeks!"

"Yes. Is there a problem?" Fiona sternly questions.

Valentina squeezes my bicep and offers, "No. No problem at all. Brax told me this morning he's dying to marry me sooner rather than later, didn't you?"

I lock eyes with her, then slowly lower my gaze over her.

You're going to pay me with your body every second of every day for going along with this charade.

I meet her gaze and reply, "I sure did, my sexy little Minx."

A flush crawls up Valentina's cheeks, and I almost cum in my pants.

Fiona beams, "Sounds like our problem is solved. I'm tired and want to go home. Congratulations on your engagement and future seats at the table and on the Royal Council." She steps forward and hugs Valentina.

Valentina hugs her back. "Thank you."

Fiona repeats, "Thank you for saving us."

Valentina smiles. "Anytime."

Fiona steps in front of me.

I glare at her.

She teases, "Give me a hug to celebrate."

My jaw tics, but I go through the motions. I'll deal with this problem at a later date.

She steps back. "Thank you as well."

I nod. "Happy to be of service."

"Can't wait for your wedding," she adds, winking.

My face hardens again.

She spins toward Kirill. "Ready?"

His gaze darts between Valentina and me, then he looks at Fiona like he can't believe she's his wife.

Can't say I blame him. I still can't believe it either.

She repeats, "I'm tired. I want to go home."

With a sigh, Kirill hugs Valentina and shakes my hand. "We'll discuss this in more detail back in Chicago."

"What's to discuss?" Valentina frets.

"Nothing," Fiona assures her, then squeezes Kirill's hand.

He glances at her

"Correct?" she asks.

Something passes in his expression.

"Kirill?" Valentina asks in a low voice.

Fiona winks at him.

He takes a deep breath, then points at them. "The Omni will insist on proof your love is real, and you must marry on the next full moon. If there is any doubt, you know the consequences."

Jesus Christ. What the hell is Valentina setting us up for now?

Valentina affirms, "Yes. We understand. There won't be any issues. We'll prove how in love we are, won't we?" She pins a naughty grin on me.

I stay quiet.

Kirill peers closer at me. "And what about you? Will there be any issues? The last thing I want is Valentina dead, so tell me now before this goes any further."

Valentina's anxiety wafts between us.

Fiona interjects, "Nah. He'll make sure it goes smoothly. Won't you, Brax?" Her lips twitch.

I gaze at her.

She arches her eyebrows.

"I'm waiting for an answer," Kirill warns.

I smack my palm against Valentina's ass.

She jumps with a gasp.

I grin at her. "No issues. Can't wait to be tied to this little Minx for eternity."

"See. All good," Fiona chirps, then pulls on Kirill's arm. "Let's go home."

He studies us for another moment, and then his lips curve. "Then I guess congratulations are in order." He kisses the top of Fiona's head. "Let's go home."

She flicks her fingers in a wave, smirking. "Bye-bye, lovebirds. Can't wait to have a double date with our soon-to-be-married besties."

I scowl.

Kirill chuckles and steers her onto the plane.

Once the doors shut, I turn toward my bride-to-be and question, "What the hell did you just get us into?"

Valentina

Chapter
FIFTEEN

Brax's sharp scowl could scrape across bone. He breathes through his nose, his shoulders tight, dark eyes pinned on me.

My pulse misfires from my reckless declaration, but when there's an opportunity in the Underworld, you take it. And it's not just a normal Omni seat. It's one on the Royal Council. All the years of waiting to take my rightful spot will be worth it. I'll skip right to my final destination without any more tests.

I'm marrying Brax.

He crosses his arms, demanding through gritted teeth, "I'm waiting."

I can't blame him for being angry. I locked us into something irreversible. But I also won't apologize. He's going to get all the benefits of being on the Royal Council.

I step closer, rise on my tiptoes, and whisper in his ear, "We'll talk about this in private." I take a step back.

He grabs me by the ass, tugs me back into him, and slides his hand through my hair. He holds me to his body, knocking the wind out of my lungs, and murmurs, "We sure will, Minx."

A shiver runs down my spine. I draw a steady breath and force myself to stay calm. "We need to return to the arena."

He seems to want to argue, holds me for another moment, then finally releases me. He forges ahead through the corridor and then opens the door.

Heat and the foul odor swell. It's still burning, the bonfire crackles viciously beneath the blackened, suspended forms of Jytte and Ulrich. Smoke drifts upward in thick, ghostly spirals, distributing ash. Many members of the Underworld cough or hold their mouths. Some adjust their masks, while others stand tall, not moving an inch.

Brax guides a hand to my lower back as we push through the crowd. His palm stays anchored, steady and warm, a silent tether in the chaos.

Sean and Zara stand at the center stage, full of authority and framed by smoke and flames.

Zara's voice carries across the membership. "Anyone involved in the attempt on the king and queen will face consequences equal to the ones hanging above you."

Gasps erupt from the crowd.

Sean lifts his chin, roaring, "No one is permitted to leave. Not until the bones incinerate to ash. Interrogations begin immediately."

Zara points to the Omni and warns, "Your cooperation isn't optional. Each one of you will answer to your role in this charade."

Some of them shift on their feet. Others stay planted. A few members choke or mutter under their breath.

Sean's arm slips around Zara's waist. He orders, "Valentina. Brax. With us." He doesn't wait for a reply. He leads Zara offstage, passes us, and moves toward the tunnel.

Brax keeps his hand planted on my back. He guides me out of the arena, through the corridor, and onto Sean's jet.

He orders, "Get this thing off the ground," and steers Zara to the back.

The door closes before we get halfway through the cabin. We take seats on the couch across from Sean and Zara.

They're still pissed. Sean's jaw tics. He spouts, "I'm going to kill anyone who was involved!"

Zara puts her hand on his thigh.

He looks at her, shaking his head in anger. Then he glances at the ceiling, his eyes darting around it.

"You think they put cameras in here again?" she frets.

He pins his eyes back on her, asserting, "We're getting another sweep when we're back. No one is to be trusted at this point."

Zara releases an anxious breath, nods, and tense silence grows between them. She breaks her gaze and turns it on us, asking, "Where did you two go?"

My breath catches. My thoughts scramble again. I glance at Brax, suddenly tongue-tied.

He shifts back into his seat with deliberate slowness. He acts like he's lounging on a yacht instead of sitting inside an aircraft that possibly has surveillance on us even though it shouldn't. His lips press together in a line that mirrors amusement and warning all at once.

I try to concoct a structured explanation and open my mouth, but Brax stops me in my tracks. His hand slides onto my inner thigh, firm and claiming.

His signature sarcasm drips through every syllable. "Oh, we were telling Kirill and Fiona we're getting married."

Zara blinks.

Sean's brows rise toward the roof.

Neither of them speaks.

My heart pounds hard against my rib cage.

Brax continues to brush his thumb against my thigh in a slow, deliberate stroke, igniting a fire inside my core. He adds, "My little Minx is just chomping at the bit to marry me. Aren't you?"

He pins a heated, accusing gaze on me.

I clear my throat and smile, leaning closer to him. "That's right."

Sean snorts.

Zara cuts off a short laugh.

"What's so funny?" Brax questions.

Zara's lips twitch, a quick flash she tries to bury. Her gaze wanders to Brax's unapologetic grip on my leg.

I place my hand over Brax's to steady myself. "Kirill and Fiona agreed we could take Ulrich and Jytte's seats on the Royal Council!"

"I need a drink," Sean mumbles, and reaches for the cantor of whiskey. He takes the cap off, pours two fingers in a crystal tumbler, then downs all of it. He fills another one and hands it to Brax, offering, "Assume you need this."

Brax downs it faster than Sean drank his.

I sit straighter.

"And the timeline?" Zara asks, tone neutral, words slow and measured.

Brax blurts out, "The next full moon. You know how the Underworld loves its deadlines."

Sean refills his glass and Brax's. They swallow all of it again.

Zara exhales through her nose. It's almost a laugh but she suppresses it.

Sean puts his tumbler back on the table and leans back. "Big commitment."

"Love demands it," Brax replies smoothly, sliding his hand higher on my thigh. "You of all people should know."

Zara's mouth twitches so fiercely she puts her hand over it, her eyes beaming bright.

Sean's face hardens. He wags his finger between us. "They're going to push the limits to make sure this is real."

"Oh, it's real," Brax says, his thumb shifting higher.

I force myself not to shift in my seat, and lift my chin, grounding the story. "We're prepared. We'll pass their tests."

Sean's eyes sharpen. He warns, "Make sure you do."

Brax's grip tightens around my thigh. "We will."

Zara hits the buzzer.

The flight attendant appears. "Can I get you something, Mrs. O'Malley?"

"Champagne. The good one, please."

"Yes, ma'am." The attendant rushes off.

She redirects her gaze to Brax's hand on my thigh, then adds, "Never thought I'd see you getting married." She smirks at him.

He slings an arm around me and tugs me against him. "What can I say? Can't keep my hands off my little Minx." He turns his arrogant daggers on me.

Heat rushes through my bloodstream.

The attendant returns with a silver bucket containing an open, chilled bottle. She pours generous glasses, the bubbles rising in a stream. She hands one to Zara and me, then starts to pour another.

"We'll stick to whiskey," Sean interjects.

She puts it back into the bucket. "Very well. Can I get you anything else?"

"That will be all. Thank you," he states.

She disappears, and he pours two more glasses, then hands one to Brax.

Zara raises her flute. "To the upcoming union between Valentina and Brax. May the next full moon bring love, stability, and an eternity of happiness." Her lips twitch with a barely contained laugh.

Eternity.

Brax stiffens next to me.

Sean huffs under his breath, but he lifts his glass. "To the two of you. And to the fact that my heart didn't stop six different times tonight. *Sláinte!*"

"*Sláinte!*" Brax mutters and downs his whiskey.

"*Salute!*" I offer.

"*Santé!*" Zara adds in French.

I take a slow sip. The crisp champagne adds more heat in my stomach.

Brax drags the backs of his knuckles along my shoulder with unhurried strokes, spreading tingling sparks through every nerve in my body.

I shift slightly.

He pulls me fully against him as if the two inches between us are unacceptable. His low voice comes out playful but feels like a warning. "No escaping me now, Valentina."

I swallow, but my throat tightens too much to respond.

The conversation shifts. Sean and Zara talk quietly about the arena, the Omni, and more possible traitors. The words drift around me in a faint blur. Every inch of my awareness narrows to Brax's hands, his heat, and his earthy, masculine scent, edged with smoke from the fires we just left behind.

It all makes me ache with something so needy I feel like I might explode.

He brings his arm back to my thigh. His thumb makes a slow arc on my skin.

My entire body coils tighter with every pass.

He leans back casually, as if all he's doing is lounging through the eight-hour flight instead of systematically dismantling my self-control. Whenever I shift, he pulls me closer with firm and intimate pressure.

Zara observes us between sips. Her mouth curves every time Brax asserts another inch of possession, as if she's watching a show she wasn't expecting but refuses to look away from.

By the third hour, there are two empty champagne bottles and a torturous hum in my veins. Heat builds inside me, pouring through my limbs with a pulse that steals the air from my lungs.

Brax never takes his hands off me. His thumb strokes upward in a slow, coaxing motion, getting closer and closer to the danger zone.

Five hours in, he drops a kiss just below my ear. It's a quick graze, done while Sean and Zara discuss security protocols, but my entire body tightens in response. He pretends nothing happened, his eyes fixed innocently ahead, but the faint curve of his mouth betrays him.

By the seventh hour, I'm so wound up that the fabric of my dress clings to the heat rising off me. The air moves too slowly. My pulse flutters too fast. The press of Brax's palm against my thigh becomes its own gravity, dragging every thought toward the promise simmering beneath his calm exterior.

Whenever turbulence hits, he uses it as an excuse to anchor me harder against him, his fingertips tracing the same small, confident patterns.

I'll lean an inch away, and his lips brush my temple. Then he'll reposition his hand on me, controlling every sensation I have.

By the time the wheels touch down, my chest rises and falls too quickly, and every muscle in my body is strung tight with hypersensitive awareness.

The moment the door opens, a rush of cold Chicago air fills my lungs. I step into it gratefully, trying to recenter my mind.

Sean's driver waits beside the SUV, holding the door open. Sean and Zara slide in first, muttering about immediate calls they need to make.

When the car stops at my building minutes later, I reach for the door handle. "I'll see you tomorrow," I announce, needing distance from Brax's relentless heat.

I step out.

Brax steps out right behind me.

I turn sharply. "What are you doing?"

He shuts the door with his forearm, gives me a look dripping with sarcasm. "Funny, Minx." Before I can argue, he takes my hand and leads me through the glass doors of my building as if I'm not perfectly capable of entering without assistance.

The elevator opens with a soft ding, and he pulls me inside. We ascend in charged silence, the tension thick enough to compress the small space.

The second my door clicks shut behind us, Brax's hands grasp my hips. My back hits the wall, and he cages his body against mine, crowding every inch of air between us. His face hovers so close his breath taunts my lips. "I don't think you realized what you've gotten yourself into, Minx."

I press my palm against his chest, the steady rise and fall under my hand warning that he's seconds from losing whatever restraint he boarded the plane with. "Don't be mad."

The sound he releases is a low, dangerous grumble. "Don't be mad?" His palm slides higher on my hip, and his chest expands beneath my touch. "You decide to get engaged to me in front of the king and queen, lock us into a full-moon wedding, and you tell me not to be mad?"

I draw in a careful breath. "We're getting seats on the Royal Council."

His nostrils flare. He asks a sharp, dynamite-laced question. "This is what you want?" His eyes search mine with an urgency that steals the next breath straight out of my lungs.

My stomach tightens. I meekly insist, "Yes, I want my seat."

He steps in closer, the hard planes of his torso pressing me deeper into the wall. "I'm not talking about that, Minx, and you know it."

My pulse jumps under my skin. I swallow, repeating, "I want my rightful seat."

He shakes his head, jaw tight, eyes locked on mine with relentless precision. "At least state the truth."

I shift under him, caught between instinct and desire, power and surrender. His gaze sharpens even more, the kind of focus that warns he won't back off until he drags the truth from me.

My voice thins. "Don't twist things."

He brings his hand to my jaw and tilts my face up toward him. His thumb presses against my chin, steady and commanding. "Admit you want me."

Heat tumbles through my body in a rush that forces my spine to arc against the wall. My breath stutters, and my hand tightens against his chest.

His eyes narrow. "Say it, Minx."

My voice cracks. "I want you."

His mouth consumes mine with a hunger sharpened by hours of denial. His fingers dig into my hips, then slide lower, lifting me effortlessly until my legs wrap around his waist. He moves me through my apartment, his kiss dragging deeper, rougher, and stealing every bit of air inside my lungs.

A low sound vibrates in his chest, reverberating through my own, and his hand grips my head, holding me so I can't retreat from his mouth.

Not that I would.

He pushes open my bedroom door with his shoulder. His hand moves from my head to my zipper and tugs. He drops me onto the mattress and yanks my dress and panties off my body.

His gaze sweeps over me with a promise. He removes his clothes and kisses his way up my legs, teasing my pussy, then continuing upward till his lips are against my knotted skin.

I grip his hair to pull his face to mine, but he won't bypass the scar.

His lips and tongue coax it, exploring the V as if it's something to be cherished instead of hated.

"Brax," I mumble.

His mouth moves to my nipple, and he nips at it.

I sharply inhale.

He tastes each one, then moves to my collarbone, continuing his journey until his forehead presses against mine. He pins me beneath his body, taunts my clit with his cock, and asserts in a warning, "Eternity's a long time, Valentina Abruzzo."

My ragged breath shakes with my lip. I keep my gaze locked on his, spreading my legs open.

He shifts his hips, teasing me further. Through clenched teeth, he adds, "I should leave you here wet and hungry for me." He shifts faster.

I whimper, mouth open.

He tilts his head slightly, narrowing his gaze.

I grip my nails into his shoulder blades and roll my hips with his, daring, "You won't."

"No?" he asks, eyebrows arched, face reddening.

I reach for his ass, lift my hips, and push him inside me. "No," I get out before I moan.

A loud, guttural sound escapes him. He holds still, deep inside me, his gaze turning to dark fire. He grits out, "From here on out, I call the shots."

I hold my breath, my pulse racing for new reasons.

He thrusts slowly, his lips curling, and adds, "Still want to marry me?"

His warm skin stirs every lodged-up sensation I tried to kill over the plane flight home.

My eyes flutter open and shut.

"Answer me," he orders, keeping the same excruciating pace.

"Yes," I choke out, gripping his ass cheek tighter.

"Who's in charge in this marriage?" he demands.

I stay silent, trying to get him to thrust faster.

"Who!" he barks, not giving in to my wishes.

"Please," I get out.

"Tell me!" He thrusts fast several times.

My vision turns white.

He slows it down.

I dig my nails into his ass, warning, "Don't!"

"If you want any more of me, you're going to tell me who's in charge, Valentina!" He pulls back with the tip of his cock brushing my entrance.

I push on his ass, but he doesn't move any closer.

"Tell me. If you want me to vow my life to you, then you tell me, Minx," he orders.

My chest thumps harder. The tension crackles against my skin. I cave. "You're in charge!"

"Fucking right I am," he says, then slides back inside me. He grits his teeth and thrusts hard, pinning his dark gaze on me.

Everything explodes into chaotic relief. I convulse against him, arching my back, gripping him tighter.

He lowers his mouth to my ear, warning, "You want me, well, you're going to get me. All of me, Minx."

"Yes," I breathe, with adrenaline intensifying.

He thrusts harder. His sweat trickles against my cheek. A low groan rumbles in his chest, and his cock swells, then a fresh wave of warmth fills me.

He doesn't let up. He pushes through it, his body vibrating against mine, until there's nothing left. Then he collapses over me, his breath on the curve of my neck and the weight of his body pressing over me.

It takes forever until my tremors slow. I finally unclutch my arms from around him.

He lifts his face inches from mine. Darkness swirls in his expression. He reiterates, "I mean it, Minx. From here on out, I'm in charge."

I swallow hard, trying to squash the fear rising in me. No one's ever been in charge of me. I take care of myself.

As if he can read my mind, he brushes a lock of hair off my cheek. He asserts, "Don't worry. You'll get used to it." He rolls over, tugs me into him, and kisses the top of my head.

Part of me wants to shove him away and reclaim the space he swallowed so easily. But the deeper part, the one I've never acknowledged, stirs under the quiet dominance in his voice.

His arm tightens around me, anchoring me in a way I don't know how to process. The steady beat of his heart thrums against my ear, a silent command I didn't realize I was already obeying.

Then it hits me why I'm not fighting him. It doesn't have anything to do with his agreement to marry me so I can get my seat.

Brax feels like protection.

It's everything I'm not used to but suddenly don't want to end.

Brax

Three Weeks Later

Chapter

SIXTEEN

In two days, I'm supposed to stand in front of the Underworld and declare my love and devotion for Valentina in some fucked-up cleansing ritual. No matter how many times I ask her or Sean what's involved, they won't tell me, claiming they can't. So a million different twisted things have popped into my mind about what it entails.

Everything I can think of makes me more determined to take down the Underworld and everyone but those closest to me. I don't know all the details about how Sean and Zara got into this mess, but I've seen enough of how the secret cult works. And I'm fully aware of how Fiona had to marry Kirill to save the twins from being orphaned.

Nothing the Underworld does is good. Its entire proclamation rests on bringing crime families together to stop the wars, but from my experience, it's just a bunch of con artists plotting to take the others down.

All I see is destruction. They branded Valentina's chest to make her feel eternal shame. Sean had to promise his sister to Kirill to save Zara from death, and even Kirill didn't want that for Fiona. Then Fiona and Kirill almost got beheaded.

There are other things I've witnessed through all their twisted rituals. I often feel sorry for the poor bastard who's going through it, but that isn't my problem. Most people want to join the cesspool. I'm sure Sean only got in because his father created it, which is another thing I don't understand.

What the fuck was his father thinking?

Regardless, the only people my loyalty lies with are those whom I've known before I ever heard of the Underworld. But for now, the only option is to move forward with this charade and make sure I don't get killed.

Hence why I'm standing outside Valentina's apartment door with an elevated heartbeat and a plan burning a hole in my pocket.

It's now or never.

I wipe my forehead and pound three times on the door.

She opens it, her hazel eyes wide with an unusual unease, hair tumbling down her shoulders in a dark cascade, and an oversized tan sweatshirt swallowing her body.

The sight of her punches something deep in my chest. My palms turn sweaty.

She steps back, arms folding, voice tight. "Brax. What are you doing here?"

"There's something I need to do."

Her shoulders tense. "Are you bailing on me?"

I grunt and brush past her into the living room.

She shuts the door with a soft click that carries more tension than it should.

The lamps cast a warm glow over her neatly arranged furniture.

Everything sits precisely where it belongs, the opposite of the storm swirling under her skin.

She demands, "Answer my question."

I chuckle. "You need to calm down, Minx. What's got your panties in a twist tonight?"

She furrows her eyebrows, then looks away.

My stomach curls. I step closer and move her chin so she can't ignore me. "What's going on, Valentina?"

She asks, "Why are you so calm?"

I tease, "I'm always calm."

"No, you aren't."

I grunt. "Sure, I am."

She throws her hands up and steps backward. "Brax, don't do this."

"Do what?"

"Pretend everything is fine."

"Everything is fine."

She lets out an incredulous sound. "It's two days before our wedding!"

My chest tightens. I lean against her counter. "Are you bolting?"

Her head jerks back. "Excuse me?"

"You heard me."

Her jaw tightens. "You think I'm going to bail?"

"I'm not the one freaking out."

"I'm not... You're twisting things!"

"Am I?"

She paces once, twice, then spins to face me. "You think you're so perceptive."

"I think you're rattled."

"I'm not rattled." Her voice lifts a notch too high for that statement to hold any weight. "I'm realistic."

"About what?"

She asserts, "Your family is going to hate you."

My heart thumps hard against my chest cavity. I've thought about it a thousand times, and she's right. I have no idea how Finn will ever accept her or what will happen between us once I marry Valentina. But I snort and retort, "They'll get over it."

"Will they?"

"Yep. What else is wrong?" I ask.

She looks away.

"Dammit! Look at me and tell me," I demand.

She slowly faces me. She bites her lip and blinks hard. Then she claims, "You're going to hate me."

I stare at her, frozen mid-breath.

"Stop staring at me like that," she demands.

I order, "Say that again."

"You heard me."

"No. Say it again."

She grips the edge of her sweatshirt, tugging the fabric hard. "You're going to hate me for life."

My muscles lock one by one.

She unravels further, her words tumbling out with raw terror she doesn't try to hide. "You're going to hate me, Brax. Or you're going to bail. Those are the only outcomes. Either option ruins everything, and it's my own fault."

"Valentina, you're being a bit harsh toward yourself," I offer.

She shakes her head violently. "No, this is my fault. I announced we were in love and getting married. I set you up for a lifetime of resentment, and I know it. So don't stand there and pretend you're fine."

Her chest rises and falls in rapid, uneven breaths. Her hands tremble at her sides. The woman who commands an arena with a single look is no longer in the room.

Something tightens viciously in my stomach. I move toward her slowly. I softly command, "Stop spiraling."

"Don't tell me—"

I take her shoulders, anchoring her. "Valentina."

Her lips press together, tight and pale.

I mumble, "I've never seen you like this."

"I'm just being honest."

"You're being—" I stop myself before the wrong word fires this higher. "You're letting your mind run."

"It's not running. It's accurate."

I shake my head. "Minx. You're wrong."

"I'm not."

I insist, "You are."

"How? Tell me how I'm wrong, Brax."

"Well, I'm here, so I'm not bailing on you," I point out.

She blinks harder. Her eyes turn glassy. She argues, "Then you're just going to resent me for eternity."

Something in me snaps clean in half. Before I think it through or weigh the consequences, I drop to one knee right in front of her.

She stutters, "Wh-what are you doing?"

I slip my hand into my jacket pocket, pull out the velvet box, and open it. A massive square diamond sits in a platinum claw setting. It's cut so sharply it captures every glint of light. Rows of smaller diamonds surround it. The band is a seamless line of gems, shimmering like frost.

She doesn't move except for her hands trembling against her sides.

Before I can stop myself, a bold, unapologetic declaration comes out of my mouth. "Listen, Minx, I'm not going to hate you. You're the only woman who has ever challenged me, clawed at me, pushed me, and still pulled me in with the same breath."

Her eyes dart from the ring to my face.

I add, "You crashed into my life like a damn hurricane, and somehow everything makes more sense with you in it. So if I'm going to take a seat, then I want you next to me."

She swallows hard. Her breath comes out shallow.

A wave of nerves hit me hard. I try to tease, but it comes out sounding strange. "I guess this is where I ask you to marry me."

Silence crashes through the room. Tension builds to the point my skin crackles.

Her eyes move from me to the ring, back to me, and the unreadable expression on her face slams more anxiety straight through my ribs.

I start sweating under my T-shirt.

What the fuck did I just say?

Jesus. How reckless could I be?

This isn't what I planned to say or do before I got here.

Why the hell did I drop to my knee?

Valentina might as well be a statue. She doesn't move or blink. Then she narrows her eyes.

My heart slams once, brutal and loud. I school my face into something impassive, rise quickly, and shut the velvet box. I set it on her counter. "Forget I said anything. Here's your ring. See you at the wedding, Minx." I turn toward the door and take several steps.

"Brax! Wait!" she calls out, then grabs the back of my arm.

I stop, harden my expression further, and slowly turn.

She pulls me down into a kiss that strips the air right out of my lungs. When she breaks away, her lips brush mine as she whispers, "Thank you. For what you said. And for marrying me."

Relief hits me, but I don't move, still confused over what I said and did.

Her phone dings several times. She slowly pulls it out of her pocket, swipes the screen, then groans. She announces, "I have to meet Kirill."

Another round of relief hits me. I need air. This is all too much. But I still offer, "Want a ride?"

She shakes her head. "No. Vito will take me."

I scowl. "When we're married and on the council, you're getting a new driver."

She affirms, "You won't hear me complain."

Panic hits me. "Has he done something?"

She shakes her head. "No. But like you said, you could have killed him, so I need someone better, right?"

"Yes. For sure."

We stare at each other for a moment.

She walks to the counter, opens the box, and slides the ring on. She stares at it, then turns. "This is the most beautiful ring I've ever seen."

I softly grin, but puff my chest. "I'm glad you like it."

"I love it."

"Good."

Uncomfortable silence follows.

She clears her throat. "I really do need to go."

"Sure. I'll walk you out," I offer, escort her through the building, and scowl at Vito as we approach.

She goes to get into the vehicle, and I tug her back toward me.

She arches her eyebrows. "What's up?"

"Where's my kiss?" I wiggle my eyebrows.

A tiny laugh escapes her.

"Well? I'm waiting," I tease.

She slides her hands behind my head, pulls my face toward her, and kisses me so deeply that fire burns through my veins.

I kiss her back, holding her tighter to me.

She retreats, murmuring against my lips, "I have to go."

I pat her ass. "Okay, Minx." I peck her on the lips and release her.

She slides onto the backseat.

I warn Vito, "Nothing better happen to her on your watch."

He ignores me and gets into the driver's seat.

I text Kirill.

> Me: Valentina needs another driver.

> Kirill: I told you it'll happen once you're on the Royal Council. Until then, the Omni won't approve it.

> Me: Not good enough.

> Kirill: Two days. Deal with it.

The SUV turns the corner, and I make my way to the parking garage. I'm almost there when I stop dead in my tracks.

Blue barrels toward me like she's been waiting hours for her chance to strike. Even from a distance, her expression packs every emotion she refuses to hide. It's simmering and livid to the point her steps click sharply on the concrete. Her purple hair whips behind her, and her designer coat flares with each step.

I curl my fists at my side.

What is she doing here?

She stops inches from me. Her wounded, angry expression deepens. She hurls with a cracked voice, "What did you do?"

I cross my arms, already exhausted. "That's a bold question coming from you?"

Her eyes widen dangerously. "Don't play dumb with me."

"I'm not playing anything."

Her nostrils flare. "You don't think I saw it?"

"Well, you probably saw everything in my life since you seem not to understand that you're stalking me," I jab.

Her blue eyes turn to flames, hot enough to choke someone. More hurt fills her voice. "You gave her a diamond?"

My pulse pounds between my ears. No one is supposed to know about Valentina and me. Once we're married, I'll have to explain, but until then, no one should know but the Underworld. So I snarl, "You don't know what you're talking about, and you need to stay out of my business."

"And she's your business?" she accuses, her expression resembling a wounded puppy.

I stay quiet, not wanting to hurt her but tired of her obsession with me. And now, she's playing in dangerous territory.

Her breath stutters out in a furious rush. She rattles, "How could you be engaged to an Abruzzo? First, Fiona marries a Petrov and now... Now you're with an Abruzzo?"

In a firm tone, I warn, "Keep your nose out of my business, Blue. You don't know what you're talking about and need to get some therapy or something."

Rage emanates from her. She roars, "I need to get mental help while you're kissing an Abruzzo like you're in love with her!"

"I'm not in love with her."

"Aren't you?" she hurls.

"No," I affirm, my chest tightening.

Am I?

Blue doesn't know what she's talking about, I remind myself.

It's a fake marriage to secure power.

She steps closer. "Then tell me you didn't give her that massive ring she's flaunting!"

"She's not flaunting it," I scold.

"She is!"

"No, she's not!" I insist.

Stop fighting with her. She's off her rocker.

"Blue, you need to stop following me. My life has nothing to do with yours. Do you understand? Now go home and get over this crazy obsession you have with me," I order.

Her mouth drops open, dramatic and offended. I think she might leave, but she pins another bruised gaze on me, stating, "So that's who you've been sleeping with. I knew there had to be someone."

I release an exasperated breath. "There's nothing between us, Blue. I don't know how many times I have to tell you that there never has been and never will be. So stop standing here and acting like I cheated on you."

She lifts her chin. "So you're going to marry her?"

I step closer, warning, "I'm only telling you this one more time. Stay out of my business, Blue, or I'm having a long talk with your father."

She scoffs, and hostility pours out of her. "Will you tell him about Valentina Abruzzo?"

Hearing her say Valentina's full name sends a chill down my spine. I snap, "Say her name one more time and I swear to God, Blue—"

"Swear to God, what, Brax? Go on. Tell me what you'll do!" she challenges.

I squeeze my fists tighter.

She snarls, "You're walking straight into a trap! That woman burns everything and everyone until she gets what she wants."

My stomach tightens. "You don't know anything about her!"

"Don't I?" Blue shouts.

"That's it!" I grab her arm and pull her inside the parking garage. I move us into the shadows, trapping her in the corner.

Her lips tremble and her voice shakes, "I know all about her. And I can't believe you're stupid enough to fall for her little game. She's playing you!"

"She's not playing me!" I argue, even though I shouldn't.

Blue jabs her finger in my chest. "She's going to drag you down and stomp all over you."

"You don't know what you're talking about. Stay out of my business," I reiterate.

She swallows hard, then tears pop into her eyes. "So you choose her over everyone you've known forever?"

I don't flinch. "I'm choosing to live without you shadowing my every step."

She flinches.

Maybe I'm finally getting through to her?

I add, "You've crossed the line, Blue. You pop up in hallways and lurk near entrances. You follow me from a distance like I wouldn't notice, but I always do."

"No, you don't," she claims.

My pulse races faster.

Don't take her bait.

I declare, "It all ends tonight. Your parents didn't raise you to be a stalker, so go home, get a good night's rest, and wake up tomorrow being the normal woman they raised."

She lets out a humorless laugh. "Stalking you? Brax, you've lost your mind."

"Stop pretending this behavior is normal," I order.

"That woman you just kissed is the one who isn't normal!" she hurls.

"That's it. I'm done being the nice guy. I'm talking to your father."

She recoils like the name physically hit her. "You wouldn't."

I sarcastically chuckle. "I would. And I will. Adrian can help you get your shit together."

Her voice cracks behind the anger. "You're serious."

"Completely."

She shakes her head, eyes darting everywhere except my face. "I'm trying to protect you."

I scoff, "I don't need protection from you."

"Yes, you do! You've lost your standards! Hell, you've lost your damn head! The only place for Valentina is a coffin!" she threatens.

My entire body tightens in one swift surge. I step closer, put my hand under her chin, and push her head up. I lean over it and seethe, "Watch your mouth."

Blue laughs, sharp and furious.

"This isn't funny," I say through gritted teeth.

Her expression hardens. It reminds me of Adrian's when he's about to kill. She claims, "She's trash and there's only one thing to do with trash."

A chill digs into my bones. I have to stop myself from lowering my hand and squeezing her neck until her breath leaves her body. If she were a man, I wouldn't hesitate. But she's a young woman. A troubled, delusional one that needs help.

I release her and step backward, afraid that if I don't, I might hurt her.

"Last warning, Blue. And I advise you to take it seriously. You stay away from Valentina. If you come near her..."

"If I come near her, what?" she pushes, the corner of her mouth curling.

Before I can think, I blurt out, "She's mine. If anything happens to her, you'll see what I'm capable of."

Her breath catches.

Then I take a step toward her, forcing her backward, and putting any sympathy I've had in the past for her aside. "You want the truth? I'd pick Valentina over you every time."

It breaks something in her expression. For a moment, I think she might cry. She whispers, "Why?"

I don't hesitate. "Because she's not you."

Blue stares at me as if I just ripped the floor out from under her. Her anger fractures into something jagged, something bruised, something completely out of control.

She shakes her head quickly, trying to rebuild her armor. "You don't mean that."

"Oh, but I do."

"She cast her spell on you!" Blue states with new flames in her eyes.

"I'm done with this conversation. Don't take my warning lightly, or you will find out my wrath," I threaten, then spin and walk toward my car.

"She'll ruin you," she shouts.

I spin, grinning. I spread my arms high in the air and cry out, "I welcome it."

Blue's mouth hangs open.

My smile falls. In a firm tone, I warn again, "Stay away from Valentina."

I get to my car, get in, and start the engine. I rev it, pull out of the garage, and make a resolution.

As much as I dread it, Adrian and I are going to have a conversation. I thought I could handle her on my own, but she's gone too far. No one is going to make threats toward my wife. Not anyone in the Underworld, and definitely not Blue Ivanov.

Valentina

Two Days Later

Chapter
SEVENTEEN

Zara circles me with a concentration that borders on predatory artistry, her fingers adjusting the final fold of the obsidian bodice. Fiona stands behind me, anchoring a veil so it drapes down my back. Both women move around me with decisive precision, almost ceremonial, as though the three of us stepped into a different realm the moment they closed the dressing room doors.

It's freaking me out.

"Hold still," Zara murmurs, lowering to smooth one of the skirts' fiery layers. "If you shift again, it's going to fall wrong in the back."

"I'm not shifting," I counter, even though my hands have betrayed me at least a dozen times, drifting up, then down, then hovering uselessly at my ribs. Each breath coils tighter inside me, and the room gradually shrinks, pressing against my temples.

"You're vibrating," Fiona says lightly, though her words land with more weight than she probably intends.

I attempt humor but miss the mark. "This ritual isn't exactly tea and gossip."

She gives me a sympathetic glance in the mirror. Then she smiles wider. "If anyone can do it, you can."

Zara stands, dusts off her palms, then angles my shoulders so I face myself head-on. "Exactly. Now look. Eat your heart out, Brax O'Malley."

My butterflies have a field day in my gut.

The gown dominates every inch of the reflection. It clings to me as though it were poured onto my torso. The bodice is a sleek slab of obsidian, sculpted to my torso with an unforgiving grip. From the waist down, the skirt erupts into a molten cascade. Charcoal melts into deep ember red, blazing gold, then violent orange. The colors merge and clash with breathtaking drama, each fold shifting with the slightest movement, as though alive. The train behind me ripples across the floor, a fiery tide stretching outward like a living reminder that I'm walking into a ritual that will change everything.

Fiona takes my shoulders and turns me. "Look at the veil!"

It's a black sheet of sheer darkness, edged with painted flames that curl upward as if trying to lick the back of my neck.

"An elemental bride," Zara murmurs, watching me through the mirror.

"Brax is going to flip," Fiona comments.

My pulse picks up. I try to draw a slow breath. The attempt only intensifies the flutters in my stomach that surge up my throat. Panic hits, and I blurt out, "I don't think I can do this."

Fiona presses her hands around my wrists, grounding me. "You're allowed to be anxious, but you're not going to crumble. You're Finzia Valentina Abruzzo. I have witnessed you command the arena, be cut-throat in negotiations, and win in situations far more hostile than a cleansing ritual."

I mutter, "That is debatable."

Zara laughs under her breath. "It's not. You're a badass and you need to remember that."

My pulse kicks faster with each passing second. The air thickens as if warning me that once I walk out of this room, the Underworld will swallow me whole. The cleansing ritual has always been an imposing, half-mythical tradition from a distance. Standing on its threshold makes it something else entirely. It's more binding, permanent, and intimate than any vow I ever declared.

A brisk knock breaks through my spiraling thoughts. Fiona opens the door an inch, listens, then turns to me with a small nod. "It's time."

A cold prickle crawls up my spine. I close my eyes and take deep breaths.

Pull it together!

Zara takes my hands and squeezes them. "You're ready."

"You are! And soon you'll have your seat on the Royal Council," Fiona reminds me.

I slowly open my eyes. No part of me shares her confidence, yet the two of them flank me without hesitation, guiding me toward the hall. The guards posted outside dip their heads as if the dress alone demands reverence. The low hum of chanting bleeds through the stone walls. It vibrates through the air, the cadence steady and deep, almost ancient. The closer we get to the arena doors, the louder it becomes, expanding until the floor beneath my shoes thrums with the rhythm.

My breath grows shallow. I stop just before the entrance.

"Just...give me a second." I brace my palm against the cold stone, my gaze fixed on the thick wooden doors ahead of me. The chanting rises and falls in waves as raw, primal, and relentless as ever. It surges through my bones, rearranging the atmosphere around me until the corridor seems to pulse along with the crowd.

Fiona touches my elbow. "The longer you wait, the higher your nerves will spike. Walk in before your head starts inventing reasons not to."

She's right.

I swallow once, set my shoulders, and force myself forward.

A guard opens the doors, and a roar slams into me from thousands of voices chanting in unison, echoing into the moonlight. Women wear long white formal dresses and eye masks. Men are in tuxes and skull masks. Torches line every row, flickering enough to cast an eerie glow around the thousands of white lotuses, neatly placed in a huge circle. The heat mixes with the rhythmic shouting, gripping the edges of my lungs and tightening them.

People aren't simply watching. They're participating, feeding some invisible current that pulses through the air. It should be no different than any ritual or ceremony the Underworld conducts in the arena, but this time, everything feels exponentially extreme.

Zara and Fiona hug me one last time, then the chanting switches to low hums.

I pull away and walk through the crowd. A lifetime passes before I see Brax.

He stands near the edge of the ritual circle, a black tux framing the hard angles of his body with sinfully precise lines. The suit clings to his broad shoulders and powerful stance.

He's the only one not chanting. He's completely still, except for the slight rise of his chest and the dark, unblinking stare locked on me.

My pulse slams into my ribs. My insides shiver with anxiety.

His gaze drags over me, and the closer I get, the more I realize it's approval.

Everything is going to be fine, I tell myself.

I just have to get through this.

Heat rolls across my skin under the obsidian bodice.

He studies me with an intensity that coils through my stomach. It's a wordless promise threaded through his expression. A comfort that whatever this ritual demands, he intends to take control of the situation the moment it arises.

My steps carry me forward even as my heartbeat spikes. The skirt fans behind me in a fiery trail.

Brax tracks my movement, his jaw tightening, his mouth curving with a hunger that sends a sharp current between my ribs.

When I reach the steps leading to him, he takes a single step forward, and the air shifts.

The arena, the chanting, and the torches all blur around the edges.

His voice cuts through the noise, low and rough in a way that should be illegal. "Good to see you, Minx." His lips curl.

A shiver snakes down my spine. My anxiety dies a little.

His eyes sweep over me again, slower this time, taking in the dress, the veil, the fire curling along my hem.

My chest tightens with a rush that has nothing to do with nerves.

Brax offers his hand. The simple gesture shouldn't have the power to steady me, yet something beneath his composed expression anchors the scattered pieces rattling inside my rib cage.

A man in a skull mask steps forward from the shadows of the platform. His crimson robe sweeps along the ground, the gold embroidery catching in the firelight until he looks carved from the same flames swirling along my dress.

A woman wearing the same white dress as the women in the crowd, matching eye mask, and blonde hair moves beside him. Her expression shifts from regal calm to something suspiciously tender when her eyes meet mine. Her subtle nod encourages me forward.

"Stand before us." Kirill's Russian accent slices through the arena with an authority that reverberates from the lowest rows to the highest balcony.

Relief hits me.

Thank God the Omni let him lead the ritual.

It also gives me comfort knowing it's Fiona next to him behind the mask.

Brax's fingers tighten around mine as he guides us past the white lotuses and into the ritual circle. The torches surrounding it flare brighter, and the crowd's hum intensifies, becoming a living current pressing at our backs.

We stop at the center.

Kirill faces us, his posture straight, while Fiona takes her place slightly behind him, hands folded with a serene confidence.

Kirill begins, "Tonight, two alliances bind into one. Two bloodlines merge under oath. Let the vows be spoken so the Underworld may witness."

A knight steps forward. He bends and lights the edge of the lotuses. A ring of fire bursts around them.

Kirill holds up his hand for silence. Once it's quiet, he gestures to me. "Do you enter this marriage freely?"

"Y-yes," I say, then clear my throat.

Brax squeezes my hands.

I glance at him.

He gives me an arrogant look.

I try not to laugh, and more anxiety flies out of me.

His attention doesn't drift. Not once. He watches me like the arena doesn't exist, and it's only us and the vows we're about to state.

I inhale slowly, lifting my chin.

Kirill inquires, "What brings this marriage to the Underworld?"

Silence fills the arena.

I whisper, "You have to answer."

Brax grunts and looks at Kirill. "Love." He pins his gaze back on me.

The king orders, "If love brought you here, then speak your vows for all to hear."

Brax rubs his thumb over my hand and grins. Then he wiggles his eyebrows.

I can do this.

I rise taller and state, "Brax O'Malley, from this moment forward, I commit my heart, my loyalty, my blood, and my devotion to you. I stand with you, not only as your wife but as the woman who will protect our union, honor the path we walk, and submit myself to the duties required by the Underworld."

"And?" Kirill asks.

My chest tightens, but I push the vow out with absolute clarity. "I vow to obey when obedience is commanded, to support when strength is demanded, and to stand by your side through every shadow, every fire, every threat that rises against us."

A wave of whispers cuts through the crowd.

"Quiet!" Kirill shouts.

The arena obeys.

The king turns to Brax and arches his eyebrows.

Brax studies me with a growing intensity, like each word threads itself inside him. The hunger in his gaze sharpens, but behind it lies something more dangerous, almost reverent.

He shifts closer, his voice dropping into a dark, resonant rumble that curls under my skin. "Valentina Abruzzo, from this moment on, you are mine to protect, mine to defend, and mine to destroy anyone who attempts to harm." His eyes narrow around the arena, and he goes off script, adding, "And God help any of you who try. I will slit you to pieces before you know it's happening."

Gasps fill the crowd.

My heart warms into something I've never felt before.

"Silence!" Kirill demands.

Brax's eyes turn back on me. He asserts, "I vow to stand between you and any threat, whether it's seen or unseen. I vow to kill for you without hesitation, to guard your body, your honor, and your bloodline. No blade, no enemy, no man will ever reach you while breath remains in me."

The words cleave through the arena, more violent than anything I vowed, yet more intimate than if he'd whispered love into my ear.

He lifts my hand and presses his mouth to my knuckles, not tenderly but with a possessive certainty that sends a deep rush through my chest. He finishes, "I will command beside you. I will conquer beside you. And I will die before I ever allow harm to stain you."

A hushed inhale of breath falls across the arena. The torches crackle, and a cloud moves. The moon shines brighter.

Kirill's voice booms, "The vows have been spoken. The bloodlines bind." He holds out his hands toward us, palms up. "The Underworld bears witness. Your vows hold power, and power must be cleansed."

There's no, *you may kiss the bride*. I've studied cleansing rituals. I knew it would be like this, but the anticipation climbs through me, tightening, building, lifting the edges of the moment until something trembles inside my every cell.

Kirill's voice slices across the arena, sharp and electric. "Let the cleansing ritual begin!"

The crowd erupts. Torches blaze upward as though fed oxygen from the command. The chanting returns full force, and vibrations surge up the soles of my shoes and spread through my body, expanding until my lungs quiver with the sound.

Brax's head turns as the white lotuses go up in flames, turning to ash.

Two women step in front of me.

"Get away from her," he snarls, pushing me behind him.

"It's okay. They aren't going to hurt me," I assure him.

He keeps his scowl on them.

I tug on his arm.

He glances at me.

"It's okay," I repeat and offer a smile.

He slowly releases me.

One woman unzips my dress. The other pushes it off me. It falls at my feet in a huge ball of chiffon. They hold their hands out.

My heart pounds harder. I take their hands, step out of my dress, and shoes. The floor parts and a mirror rises in front of me, displaying my branded, naked body.

The gong bangs three times.

"Strip," Kirill orders Brax.

I watch in the mirror as he removes all his clothes.

"Take your bride," Kirill orders.

Brax obeys, stepping next to me, his expression locked on mine and full of questions.

My pulse explodes between my ears.

"*Offrila. Reclamala*," the crowd chants, pounding torches into the ground.

Offer her.

Claim her.

Brax's jaw clenches. He studies me in the mirror, his unblinking focus turning my skin hotter.

For a moment, I think he isn't going to figure it out. I worry he's not going to make a move, and we'll both be killed.

It wouldn't be his fault. He's never been told what his role in this ritual is or how he passes the test. As sweet as he is to me, he didn't marry me for love, and that's what the entire Underworld wants to see.

I shouldn't have put him in this situation.

Now they're going to kill us both.

The more he stares at my reflection, the closer I get to a full breakdown. I bite on my lip, blinking hard. I'm close to tears when he spins me, pushes me against the glass, then tilts my head. He leans over me, his breath hitting mine.

I inhale sharply.

He states through the chants, "You're mine, Minx."

I barely catch my breath when his lips hit mine, pulling me into a world where the Omni don't exist, seats aren't important, and he's the only person in my existence.

His hands grip my ass, pick me up, and pin me to the mirror. The cool glass hits my spine, and a shudder runs through me. He rubs his cock against my clit, taunting me, murmuring, "Mine," as his mouth roams my jaw, my neck, my collarbone.

Fire burns hotter around us as more lotuses fall from the ceiling onto the ring. Chants turn to, "*Domina la sua carne. Sottometti la sua anima.*"

Dominate her body.

Subdue her soul.

Brax's lips find mine. His tongue swipes around my mouth in a fury. He slides faster over me until adrenaline spikes out of control and I'm clutching him, crying out, "Oh *Dio!*"

"Mine, Minx," he says with more authority, and as I come down, he thrusts deep inside me.

"*Dio, aiutami,*" flies out of my mouth, and I arch my back into him.

His deep grunt rumbles against my chest. He presses his damp forehead to mine. "God's not helping you. Only me." He moves his hand and presses a finger into my ass.

I gasp in his mouth.

His mouth consumes me. He presses inside me until I can't tell if it's his finger or his cock working my insides.

"B-Brax," I stutter, closing my eyes and digging my nails into his shoulders.

"Say it," he orders, working my body like he knows just what it wants, then slowing down.

Another round of adrenaline spikes. It sits on the edge waiting to spill over.

"Say it," he repeats.

I open my eyes, unsure what he wants.

His eyes darken in a way that has nothing to do with anger. The brown I usually see collapses into something deeper, almost black, as if every unspoken emotion he carries gathers behind his pupils at once. They're heavy with possession, hunger, and a razor edge of vulnerability he'll never admit to.

It strips me bare, telling me my words have the power to steady him or shatter him, and he hates that almost as much as he needs it. The question fades, and the answer he wants rolls out of my mouth, "*Ti amo.*"

I just told him I loved him.

Before I can process it, he murmurs in my ear, "Mine," and thrusts hard, skillfully moving another finger inside me.

The next few minutes, I can barely breathe. Every time his cock goes in, his fingers come out. The entire time, his mouth consumes me like I'm his obsession.

The torches keep thudding, the women start moaning, and the men grunt.

It's all too much. I can barely hang onto Brax while convulsing between him and the mirror.

"Mine, Minx," he grits out.

"Yours," I agree, my eyes rolling and the fire turning to a blurry haze of orange and blue.

"Mine!" he growls one more time before his body erupts in a tidal wave so catastrophic that he presses me closer to the glass, and an incoherent sound flies out of his mouth.

For several moments, neither of us moves. The arena spins in a molten blur around us, a vortex of firelight, sweat, and the metallic tang of power hanging in the air. The torches slowly crackle back to life, illuminating the circle of ash and flames, and I realize there's only our breath and silence.

Brax slowly lowers me to my feet, his hands remaining at my waist as though his body hasn't accepted the idea of letting mine go. A sharp tremor runs through my legs, but his grip tightens before I can falter. When I manage to meet his eyes, the darkness inside them hasn't lifted. If anything, it's deepened into something fiercer, more territorial, more certain.

The ritual didn't cleanse us. If anything, it ignited something neither of us can extinguish.

He brushes a strand of hair from my cheek with knuckles still trembling, and the gesture lodges itself in the center of my chest.

The king steps forward, arms in the air, voice cracking through the arena like thunder. "The bond is witnessed. The Omni approves. The cleansing is complete."

The crowd answers with a roar that shakes the stone beneath my feet, but all I hear is Brax's uneven breath against my ear.

He leans in and warns, "It's done, Minx. You're mine, and the entire Underworld knows it." He threads his fingers through mine and turns toward the exit, pulling me with him through the smoke, the ash, and the consequences of our vows.

Brax

Chapter

EIGHTEEN

The gong slams through the arena three times, each strike rolling over my bones with enough weight to rattle the breath out of my lungs. The crowd reacts, their heads snapping up, and new whispers surging into a single shiver of sound. They're hawks, waiting for more prey, and Valentina and I are it.

I lock my hand over Valentina's waist and move her toward the exit. The dry heat and ash burn my throat. Sweat clings to the back of my neck. The chanting still rings in my ears. Every instinct I have demands I get her out of this place before the Underworld decides we haven't performed enough for them.

She stays rigid beside me, eyes fixed ahead. Her palm is damp. Her chest rises too fast.

"Keep walking," I mutter, pushing through more members.

Her heels skid. "Wait!"

My pulse spikes. "For what?"

She twists out of my grip and looks sharply over her shoulder toward the center platform. The torches lining the arena cast a restless glow over her glistening skin. Everywhere around us, the contrast of white and black dances from the flames.

I clench my jaw, ready to kill everyone in this room.

My bride was a force to be reckoned with and in a dress no other could pull off. Yet it only created more hatred for the Underworld.

They dressed her in black not to honor her strength but to shame her as if she carried a stain and was less. And yet she stood there with her head high enough to confront every person who tried to diminish her.

Despite the twisted meaning, she looked incredible. She was stunning in a way the Underworld doesn't deserve to witness. But she should have been in white, not these hypocritical members around us, screaming they were better than her.

It pissed me off the moment I saw it, and the anger spikes hotter now. My Minx was never less than anyone in this room. If anything, she's a hundred times better. Yet, I see the shame they've put in her head.

They're all going to pay.

"We have to go back," she whispers, voice punched with dread.

"What are you talking about? We're done. They announced it. We're leaving," I insist.

Her words tremble. "Three rings on the gong. You heard it and you know the rules."

I drag a harsh breath from my lungs. "What else do they want from us?"

Her expression tightens. It's not the usual storm of killer instinct and confidence. Her eyes widen in a slow stretch, her jaw tightens, and something raw creeps through the cracks of her composure. It isn't a weakness but a warning.

Her voice drops until it's just breath. "Brax, we have to go back."

And I hate it. Fear enters her expression, and that's not the woman I know her to be. No, my Minx will slit someone's throat if they look the wrong way, and I prefer it over her giving her power to these assholes.

Her hand lifts, fingers brushing the side of my face, her cool palm pressing against my cheek. "Brax…please."

I lean closer and murmur in her ear, "Don't let them intimidate you. You're Valentina Abruzzo O'Malley now." I pull back and lock my gaze into hers.

She takes a deep breath and nods.

I tug her into my chest, slide my arm around her waist, and turn us toward the chanting mass. I mumble, "Let's get this over with, Minx."

The crowd parts slowly, their voices scraping in a low hum. Torches return to hitting the ground, but unlike before, it's a soft touch instead of a violent beating.

I lead us up the steps and back onto the center stage toward the king and queen.

Kirill and Fiona stand side by side. He has a protective arm around her, and I can't say I blame him. The last time they were here, they almost got beheaded.

His heavy frame blocks one of the flames behind him, making the scar slicing across his cheek and peeking out from under his mask look darker.

I want to hate him, but I can't. Not for this moment. Not when relief hit me hard when I realized it was him stepping forward instead of one of those Omni bastards who enjoy turning simple instructions into brutal punishments. And deep down, I know he has to do what he has to do. He didn't make up these rituals. Sean and Fiona's father did.

I still don't understand why. So as much as I don't want to admit it, I trust him. He's a Petrov, and somehow, through all this craziness, I don't fear him. Valentina is his only friend, and I know he would never willingly harm her. But I still stare at him with caution. His job is to conduct the ritual, and who knows what else is in store for us.

I ask, "Why did you call us back?"

His voice booms, echoing against the stone columns, "You forgot something."

My gut knots hard. I tighten my hold on Valentina's waist until her breath shudders quietly against me. She doesn't pull away.

Kirill lifts a hand, ordering, "Bring them their robes."

Two members emerge through the shadows, each carrying a folded white robe across both arms. They're thick and luxurious.

Valentina tenses.

One of the robed members stands before her. I don't release her.

"It's okay. Let her put it on," Fiona quietly orders.

I look at her eyes through the mask.

She smiles and nods.

I reluctantly release Valentina.

"You too," Fiona states.

I help Valentina into hers first. Then I slide into mine, grinding my molars. This is just more symbolic theatrics. Every step into this world tightens something invisible around my throat. And I'll be damned if they hurt my wife any further.

My wife.

Jesus.

I'm married.

I tug Valentina back into me. "Thanks for the robes. Can we go now?"

Kirill's lips twitch. He angles his body toward the crowd and raises his voice again. "Tonight, they have proven themselves worthy."

The arena erupts, not in chaos but in a sick twist of reverence.

My spine stiffens. I don't trust it. I never will.

Kirill steps forward and announces, "Pay homage to those worthy of seats on the Royal Council!"

My head snaps toward Valentina.

I expect the arena's firelight to catch on her face, to brighten her eyes, to send some burst of triumph across her expression. She's chased this goal for years. She's bled for it. Sacrificed. Obeyed.

But her face shows nothing. There's no smile, excitement, or pride, just an eerie stillness that slices sharper than any blade I've seen tonight.

The arena shakes from the new chant, "*Revarum! Revarum! "Revarum!"*

I glance at Valentina, confused.

She got what she wanted. Why does she look like the ground beneath us shifted in a direction she didn't anticipate?

The chanting tapers into a low hum that crawls across the arena's curved walls. The members bow their heads. Torches dim. A hush settles over the space and prickles my skin.

Kirill steps forward, and the arena turns silent. His voice cracks through it. "The seat on the Royal Council requires more than perseverance. It requires vows that bind deeper than blood."

Here we go.

I tighten my hand on Valentina's waist.

She remains motionless beside me, her expression carved from marble without a single glimmer of anything reflecting what should be triumph.

It gnaws under my ribs, confusing me further. She should be shining. Instead, she stands distant, unreadable in a way that leaves my stomach tight.

"Repeat after me, together," Kirill commands.

A fresh knot twists inside me. All their vows and proclamations are another thing I hate. My loyalty will never be with the Underworld. I'm an O'Malley by choice, and I'll never choose this cult over my clan.

Kirill lifts both hands. "Through shadow and order, through silence and consequence, I pledge to the Royal Council."

I grind my jaw, but my voice matches Valentina's as the words roll out. "Through shadow and order, through silence and consequence, I pledge to the Royal Council."

Kirill continues. "My service is unbroken. My allegiance unshaken. My path intertwined with the Underworld. This is my true family."

We repeat it, and my stomach tightens enough to cramp.

My family is Finn and Brenna. That word is reserved for them and Sean, Fiona, Zara, and the rest of the O'Malleys.

Kirill's stare moves from Valentina to me. He drills it into my skull, as if he sees every internal objection without needing me to speak it aloud.

He continues, "I will guard the Underworld with my life. I will die in loyalty to the order that raised me anew."

My chest goes still.

Raised me anew?

The Underworld didn't raise me.

Finn and Brenna did.

He pulled me off the streets and taught me to swing a wrench. Brenna shoved books and vocabulary in my face so I could speak like someone who mattered. Declan and Nolan trained me to fight, hack, build, and repair. Sean became the closest thing to a brother I could ever have without sharing blood.

Those people raised me. This world didn't.

Beside me, Valentina repeats the words on command, her voice unshaken, unbroken, even as her face remains void of emotion.

I stare at her, heart thudding, trying to read anything in her eyes that might tell me she isn't willingly giving these people everything.

But she says the line again, steady, obedient, carved clean from every piece of control she's mastered over the years.

Kirill's gaze pins mine with something that borders on warning.

"Repeat it, Brax."

My jaw throbs. My breath grates at the edges of my lungs.

I can lie.

I can play along.

I can say the words.

But something inside me twists with the rebellion I grew up on. Men tried to own me my entire childhood. Gangs tried to drag me in. Dealers wanted me as a mule, an errand boy, or muscle. I never submitted. Not once. I stole, ran, fought, and survived alone until Finn saw something worth saving.

I owe loyalty to him until my last breath. Not to this masked ritual.

Fiona steps closer. She softly asks, "Do you need Kirill to repeat it?" Her eyes beg me not to rebel.

So I force the words out, each one scraping like broken glass as it passes my tongue. And the vow drops into the air with a weight that sickens my gut. "I will guard the Underworld with my life. I will die in loyalty to the order that raised me anew."

Kirill nods.

Fiona steps forward. Her hands lift and settle on Valentina and my shoulders. Her powerful voice fills the arena. "May you always have strength when needed, wisdom at all times, and clarity on every path set before you. We grant you protection by the order you now serve and weave safety around your lives so the Underworld does not lose what it has rightfully gained."

Did she feel safe and protected when her head was almost cut off three weeks ago?

Humming returns, echoing through the arena. Torches sway, shadows twist, and the air turns heavier.

Her hands remain steady as stone. "Stand as shadows that cannot be pierced. Stand as pillars that cannot be shaken. Stand as two who now rise together under the order's watch."

Valentina doesn't move. Her face stays stone, and it freaks me out.

What is she thinking?

Why isn't she happy? This is what she wanted.

Fiona releases us, smiling.

Kirill raises his palm again. "The pledges are sealed. You are bound. Rise as council-bound, and serve the Underworld with unyielding devotion."

The arena erupts into a new chant. It rumbles the floor beneath our feet. "*Onorath... Onorath... Onorath...*"

Valentina doesn't move. Her expression stays untouched by triumph or dread. There's no spark of victory, just an emptiness I wasn't expecting.

Where are you, Minx?

I lean down, my lips brushing the shell of her ear. "We're done. I'm getting us out of this hellhole."

She still doesn't speak or look at me.

The chant peaks, and my pulse hits the back of my throat. I pin my question on Kirill. "Can we go now?"

"You may."

I guide Valentina off the stage. The crowd parts, and I move us through the torchlight, ignoring the people. The second we clear the exit, I storm toward the plane.

It's waiting for us. I step on it, nod at the flight attendant, and say, "Evening. Please get us in the air," then steer Valentina into the back bedroom and shut the door.

Valentina doesn't move farther into the bedroom. She stands in her white robe, hands slack at her sides, gaze fixed on nothing. The over-head lights cast a muted glow across her face, and it hits me hard how young she looks without a mask, without torches, without a crowd demanding she perform.

She should be on fire right now. She should be drinking in victory. She should be grinning in my face and telling me she warned everyone she was unstoppable.

Instead, she looks hollowed out.

I yank the robe open, slide it off my shoulders, and toss it onto the chair like it burned me. "Talk to me."

She doesn't blink.

I take two steps closer. "Minx, what is going on? You got what you wanted. You have your seat on the Royal Council. You can make the whole damn Underworld get on its knees and chant your name. Why aren't you happy?"

Her head turns slowly toward me.

A broken woman appears, stunning me. Her eyes have that same dead-still distance I saw on the stage. Gone is the Valentina who walks into rooms like she owns every breath inside them, the one who doesn't flinch when blades glitter, the one who would rather bleed out than let someone see a tremor in her chin.

My chest tightens with something I don't want to name. I don't do helpless. I can't watch someone I care about drown while I stand there with my hands in my pockets.

I move to the bed, pull back the covers, then unrobe her. I order, "Get in bed."

She obeys.

I slide next to her, lean back against the pillows, and pull her to my side. Her head lies on my chest. I stroke her hair and kiss her on the head.

A warm tear trickles onto my chest.

Anger fills me. Not at her but about what they've done to her.

I slide my hand up her back in slow, steady strokes. I press another kiss to the top of her head. "Talk to me, Minx."

Her breath shudders in her throat. Not a sob, not a breakdown, just that first crack in a wall someone has held up too long. "I-I can't."

"I'm your husband, so you have to," I insist.

She slowly looks up at me.

I drag my knuckles over her cheek. "It's you and me, so fill me in. Why aren't you happy? You got everything you wanted."

She blinks hard, then her face crumbles. She squeezes her eyes shut, and more tears spill.

"Hey," I softly say, tugging her closer, my heart beating faster.

She sniffles. "I don't know. I-I just kept seeing my parents. I-I don't think they'd be proud of me. I always thought they would, but not like this. Not branded with a scarlet letter and forcing a man to marry me."

The words hit me like a blunt object. I inhale deeply and release it. "You're being too hard on yourself."

She shakes her head. "I'm not. They stripped me over and over, and for what? So I could trap you for life and still be the only one in the membership with a scarlet letter?"

My heart sinks. I tug her over my waist so she has to look at me. In a firm tone, I tell her, "You didn't trap me. I agreed to this. I could have said no, and I didn't."

"Because I put you in this position!"

"No. You could have killed me the night they discovered I snuck into the fight. You didn't. So I owe my life to you," I admit.

She stares at me with glossy, rimmed-red, hazel eyes.

I swipe my thumb over her cheekbone. "You are Valentina Abruzzo O'Malley. You walked into their arena in black and turned it into a damn crown. You survived their trials. You outsmarted their games. You won."

Her mouth trembles. "I don't think I did."

My brow knots. "Minx—"

"That seat doesn't change anything. My parents are still dead. The

Underworld didn't give me justice. It just took more of me to let me sit at their table and smile while they pretend they're righteous."

My throat locks.

She stares at me with that helpless honesty that makes my chest ache. "And now you hate me."

"I don't. How many times do I need to tell you that?" The words punch out of me before I can soften it.

Her gaze drops. "You're an O'Malley. I'm an Abruzzo. You said my name in that vow because you had to. Not because you wanted to. You were forced into this seat because of me. You resent me. I saw it."

There's a vicious coil in my gut. I cup the back of her head and force her eyes back to mine. My voice comes out rough, sharp enough to cut. "Stop. I don't hate you. Not even close. And I never want to hear you say that again."

Her lips part.

My words spill out with heat I can't throttle. "I don't care what your last name was when you walked into this. I don't care about any of that. I care about the woman in front of me. The one who survived an arena full of monsters and still had enough spine to look them in the eye. And that woman doesn't need anyone's permission to exist."

Her eyes flicker, just barely.

"Do you hear me?" I press.

She nods.

I drag a breath through my teeth, the anger settling into something steadier. "When was the last time you slept?"

Her eyelids flutter like the question has to travel miles to reach her brain. "I don't know."

"Try. What day was it?"

She swallows and shrugs. "Maybe three days ago. Maybe longer. Everything blends together."

Jesus. She's running on fumes.

I slide down in the bed, pulling her with me. I say, "You're exhausted."

She doesn't argue.

I kiss the top of her head again. "Go to sleep. Right now. When you wake up, things will be better."

Her breathing stutters. "What if they're not?"

I order, "Look at me."

She sniffles and obeys.

I wiggle my eyebrows. "You're married to me. It's only up from here."

A tiny smile plays on her mouth.

I kiss her on the lips. "Go to sleep, Minx. Everything is going to be okay. I promise."

Her body finally sags, the last fight draining out of her. Her lashes lower, then lift once, then lower again. In less than a minute, her breaths deepen, slow and even, the kind of sleep that comes only when someone is past the edge.

I stay still so I don't wake her.

The cabin hum wraps around us. The jet's engines rise into a steadier thrum as we lift higher, cutting through clouds and distance and whatever Underworld shadow still tries to cling to us.

The entire flight, she sleeps on my chest, and everything clicks into place with a clarity that sharpens my focus.

I'm on the Royal Council now.

The vow tasted like poison, but I'm going to use the seat as a weapon.

I'll have access to files, names, and histories of every order that anyone ever uttered. Masks won't protect any of them.

They thought branding her with a scarlet letter and dressing her in black would shame her. They thought dragging her through rituals would bend her into something smaller, quieter, easier to control.

They're wrong.

I look down at Valentina.

She sleeps, her mouth slightly parted against my chest, her curls spilling across my arm. She's not tainted. She's a woman who deserved better than the monsters who kept taking from her. And now, she's my wife.

I make a vow that has nothing to do with loyalty to the Underworld and everything to do with the woman in my arms.

It's to whoever decided to brand her, whoever decided she belonged in black, and whoever thought shaming her was a privilege they had earned.

I will find them.

And when I do, I will take them down piece by piece, with the same patience they used to try to erase her.

Valentina

Chapter

NINETEEN

*H*eavy, enveloping warmth presses against my back, wrapping around my waist, cocooning me like I'm something fragile. A heartbeat thumps against my spine, and a thumb circles my belly button.

I attempt to inhale, but my breath barely moves. My ribs ache like I've run a marathon with no training. My eyelids could be lead. My mouth's dry, my throat's rough, and my mind is as soggy as wet cotton.

Where am I?

My pulse spikes. I blink a few times, taking in the dark walls, floor-to-ceiling windows, expensive walnut furniture, and the faintest trace of cedar and firewood in the air.

Brax's penthouse.

And I'm in his bed.

Memories slam back in fragments. There's the jet cabin, Brax's body under mine, his arms locked around me, and the sense of floating, drifting, sinking. Then the ritual comes flying back. Chants haunt me. The lingering smoke in my hair turns thicker. The vision of Brax's body pressing mine into the mirror while he convulses against me makes my thighs clench.

I try to turn my head, but can't move very far.

He keeps me anchored against him. His breath ghosts down the back of my neck. His muscular leg hooks over mine as though I'm a flight risk.

Am I?

We got married.

Panic flickers, sharp and wrong. I try to move.

His arm tightens, and his gravelly, deep voice questions, "Where are you going, Minx?"

I freeze.

He lifts on his elbow and brushes my hair off my face. He cautiously asks, "You okay?"

I swallow, and there could be shards of glass in my throat. I wince, "I'm...awake."

"No shit."

I smile. "How did I get here?"

His expression darkens. "You don't remember walking in here?"

"No."

"That's because I carried you." He winks.

"Oh." I sit up.

He drags his hand over his face, sits next to me, and curses under his breath. "You scared the hell out of me, Valentina."

It knocks me off-balance. I snap, "I'm fine."

"You're not fine. At least you weren't." He stares at me as if he's waiting for me to crack.

I insist, "I'm fine. I was tired."

He gives a humorless laugh, "Tired? You were unresponsive."

My jaw clenches.

What did I say to him?

I sharply assert, "I'm awake now. You don't have to worry about me."

"Don't worry about you? Minx, you're my wife."

It lands like a punch. My chest tightens. Our vows come flying back to me. I blink, trying to ease the guilt.

He leans in and cups my jaw. "Don't do that again."

My voice goes tight. "Do what?"

"Disappear on me."

Heat flares across my cheeks.

What did I say?

I snap, "It wasn't intentional. And you hovering while I sleep is unnecessary."

His thumb strokes over my hip. "I'm not hovering. I'm making sure you're still breathing."

My breath hitches.

His fingers strum toward my inner thigh.

My core turns to fire. I bite out, "You're being dramatic."

His eyes narrow. "How's that?"

My stomach dips. I blurt out, "You didn't need to put me in your bed."

"I wasn't leaving you on a couch. You're my wife. Remember?" Arrogance flies across his expression.

My pulse pounds between my ears. I open my mouth, but nothing comes out.

"You're welcome," he fires back, turning angry.

We glare at each other. His breathing moves fast. Mine stays uneven.

We're too close. My stomach flutters and betrays me like an amateur. I toss the covers off and turn. "I was just tired."

He catches my wrist, demanding, "Look at me, Valentina."

I slowly meet his gaze.

Too many emotions flicker in his eyes. Relief mixes with confusion, and then his dangerous, hot, and all-consuming sarcastic ego takes over.

It rattles me all over. I yank my wrist back, sitting up straighter, declaring, "I'm fine."

He nods slowly, studying me like I'm a threat to myself.

"Don't look at me like that."

"Like what?"

"That!" I reply, pointing at him.

"Would you rather I look at you like this?" He crosses his eyes and sticks his tongue out.

I laugh. "Really?"

His face falls. "Glad you're back, Minx. You were out of it."

I arch my eyebrows.

He strokes my cheek. "I don't like to see you cry."

Silence detonates between us.

I cried?

My spine snaps straight. "I didn't cry."

"You did."

I look away.

He pulls my chin toward him so I can't escape his stare. "You kind of terrified me. And not in your usual badass way."

My stomach flips. I try to remember but can't.

He exhales hard, dragging a hand through his hair. "Just don't scare me like that again."

My chest tightens painfully. I look away and state, "I need water."

He offers, "I got it."

"I can do it myself," I declare, throwing the covers off and swinging my legs over the edge of the bed. I glare at him over my shoulder. "Stay put."

He grabs me and tugs me back into bed. "I have a glass here." He doesn't release me and hands me water.

"Are you going to keep me chained to the bed?" I mutter, then drink the water.

He retorts, "That's an idea. Should I buy some? You'd look hot in them."

I smirk. "Funny."

His lips curve, slow and wicked, and something molten slices down my spine. "I wasn't joking." He drags his fingertips over my breast.

"Brax..." I warn.

"Yeah?" he murmurs in my ear.

"You're crowding."

"I'm husbanding. There's a big difference."

I scoff. "What does that even mean?"

He nibbles on my ear, then lowers his mouth to my collarbone. Through kisses, he answers, "It means I'm going to revive you."

My breath stutters. "Revive me?"

His fingers trail down my thigh, deliberate and slow, like he's testing how fast he can melt my bones. "Minx, you scared ten years off my life last night. You weren't okay. So I'm starting husband duties now." He flicks his tongue, then sucks on my nipple.

I inhale sharply.

His voice drops lower. "You vowed to obey me. So you don't get to leave this bed until I say."

Heat sizzles between my legs. I declare, "I'm leaving now." I push his chest.

He presses my palm to his skin, locks his eyes on my mouth, and dares, "Try again to push me away."

My voice cracks. "You're taking obey the wrong way."

"Am I?" he asks, sliding his hand between my thighs. He continues, "I'm pretty sure you want to obey me right now."

My objection comes out weak. "No." I should get up, but I don't move.

His grin turns wicked. He grazes his thumb across my slit.

A tiny, traitorous gasp escapes me. My breath turns shallow.

His eyes darken in approval. "There she is."

"There who is?" I meekly fume.

"The version of you who stops pretending she doesn't want my hands exactly where they are."

I open my mouth, and he pins my wrists above my head. It steals the air from my lungs. My heart beats wildly.

His voice softens. He taunts, "I'll let you go and stop the second you stop lying to me."

"I don't lie."

"You lied five seconds ago." His grip tightens just enough to send heat pooling low in my belly. "Your breathing gave you away."

"I hate you." I glare at him.

His smirk turns to pure sin. "You sound breathless for someone who hates me."

"Because you're—" My voice cracks as his thigh slides between mine, nudging me open.

"I'm what, Minx?" He lowers his head and flicks his tongue on my nipple again.

"Annoying," catches in my throat.

He cages me with his body, pressing my wrists harder into the pillow. "Annoying? That's the adjective you're going with while you're dripping onto my leg?"

I scoff.

His grin turns obscene.

"Let me go," I repeat, weaker this time.

His lips brush the corner of mine, just barely. "Say it like you mean it."

"I—" His thigh presses up. My breath shatters. "Mean it."

"No, you don't." His voice is a dark caress. "Your hips are grinding."

"I'm adjusting."

"Mm-hmm." He kisses the edge of my jaw, slow and hot. "Adjust more."

"Brax," I hiss, fighting the tremble and slowly shifting an inch over his cock.

He drags his mouth down my throat and puts the tip of his erection next to my entrance. He puts his face over mine. His expression turns serious. "If I need to fuck your attitude back in you, I will, Valentina."

I hold my breath.

What the hell did I say last night?

"My wife isn't theirs. She's mine," he claims. He lowers his face to my neck.

I whimper when his teeth graze my pulse.

"Tell me you want me, Minx."

My heart punches hard. "I don't want you."

He suddenly stops.

His eyes search mine, sharp and unreadable. "Liar" sits between us like a third body. He grins and lowers his mouth to my ear. "Then why are your legs gripping me like you'll drown without me?"

I glance down and freeze. Then I curse under my breath, "Damn muscle memory, that's all."

He laughs a slow, low, deep, chuckle that only adds more heat. "Minx, I think your pussy wants to work its muscle memory, too."

I dig my nails into his shoulders, my lower body pulsing, trying to push him away, but I can't. My body won't allow it.

He keeps my wrists pinned and moves his mouth lower, over my torso and between my thighs. He flicks his tongue against my clit.

My back arches off the mattress.

His voice breaks, rough and hungry. "Fuck, you taste like you're mine." He flicks again.

"I'm not... Oh *Dio*."

He releases my hands, slides his fingers to a V, then slides a finger inside me and buries his mouth against my pussy.

My breath catches. My brain short-circuits. I reach for his hair and tug on it.

He chuckles against my body.

"We're not having sex," I pant, weak, furious at myself.

"No," he agrees easily, pushing my thigh into the air. "We're not."

He drags his knuckles up my inner leg and adds, "At least not at the moment. But you'll be begging me, Minx. Just wait."

"Try," I challenge, tugging at his locks harder.

A rumble vibrates against my pussy. He eats and fingers me like a predator, without mercy and unrelentingly.

It doesn't take long before I'm crying out in Italian, seeing stars, my veins flooding with adrenaline.

He keeps me high, then slides up my body, pinning his mouth to mine. His tongue devours me, full of my orgasm. He flicks my nipple and I break out into a helpless sound I've never made in front of anyone.

He swallows it, acknowledging, "You're shaking. Ready for my cock?"

"I'm cold," I lie.

He laughs into my neck. "You're burning for me."

His hand dips lower, slow, teasing, cruel in the best possible way. His two fingers brush through heat that has no business existing after the orgasm he just gave me.

"What do you want, Mrs. O'Malley?" he mumbles against my lips.

I kiss him harder, sliding my tongue deeper into his mouth.

He groans.

My spine bows off the bed.

He orders, "Say it, Minx."

"I—" His fingers tease again, and my breath strangles. "Hate you."

He slides his cock over my clit. "Try again."

I bite his shoulder to keep from moaning.

He shudders violently. "Looks like my Minx is showing up to play." His erection toys with my clit faster.

"No penetration," I manage.

"Yeah," he rasps, tugging on my tits, making my vision blur. "If that's what you want."

He moves his cock off my clit, and it lands on my thigh.

I press my hand on his hip to move him back.

"Tsk, tsk, tsk. You don't get it unless you ask for it," he taunts, then moves his fingers inside me.

I drag my nails down his back, then anchor them into his skin. "Brax—"

"I'm waiting," he says, then shoves his fingers in my mouth. He orders, "Suck. And I'm ready for you to drown me in your juice, Minx."

I suck my arousal off his fingers.

He pulls them out, teases my clit to the point I'm going to orgasm, then holds them next to my mouth. He rubs it on my lips and puts his cock over me. He orders, "Just say it." He dips the tip an inch inside me.

My world tilts. My hips jerk and breath breaks. My fingers dig into his shoulders, and I push.

He grins, not moving his cock. "You need to say you want me, Minx."

I cave, "I want you."

His cock glides so fast inside me, I lose my breath.

"Oh *Dio*. Oh *Dio*. Oh *Dio*!" I moan.

He watches every second of my expression with his eyes dark, jaw clenched, and breath heavy over mine. His hand reaches for my wrist, and he pins it above my head, slowly thrusting deep inside me.

My nails push harder into his shoulders. He groans, and I press his head closer until his lips are back on mine. Our tongues swirl together in a battle that no one wants to stop. Arousal fills the air, thick, hot, mixing with our sweat.

He murmurs between kisses, "Mine."

Every time he says it, my heart dances. I move a hand to his ass, so over-sensitized I'm already dizzy. I press him toward me, ordering, "Faster."

He doesn't argue, speeds up his thrusts, and my back arches. My cells explode with adrenaline, creating a euphoria so intense my sounds turn incoherent.

"Fuck, Minx," he grits out, his chest rumbling against mine. Then his erection swells, pushing me so high my eyes roll.

When I collapse back onto the sheets, shaking, he kisses my cheek, then my jaw, then my mouth. In a victorious tone, he taunts, "Still want to leave the bed?"

"Yes," I lie.

He smirks, resting his forehead against mine. "Good. I like when you lie."

I freeze. "Why?"

His expression darkens. "It means you're back."

I stay quiet.

He rolls off me and tugs me with him.

I don't fight. I lie on his chest, listening to his heart slow.

He rubs his hand over my hip and asks, "What's your plan?"

"My plan?"

"Now that you have your seat."

It catches me off guard. I don't answer for a moment, but finally say, "I'm not sure what you're asking me."

He turns me into him, pins his gaze on me, and asserts, "Let me know when you figure it out. I'm going to take a shower. Just remember, you and I are in this together now." He kisses me on the lips and gets off the bed.

I'm stunned, not sure what he means.

Brax stares back for a second too long before he steps away, like nothing between us just detonated. He gets to the door and spins. His voice is low. "Figure out what you want, Minx. If you don't, they'll figure it out for you."

"Is that a threat?" I ask.

He shakes his head. "No. Whatever path you choose next, I'm on it with you. But don't let them determine your fate." He disappears into the bathroom.

I stay frozen, pulse thundering, the sheets still warm with everything we just did.

All I ever wanted was to claim my seat. It was my only purpose, and Brax somehow just shifted the ground beneath me with one question.

I don't know how to answer it. I don't even know if I really under-stand what he's asking. And there's something else rattling me.

Together.

It's a word that's a warning and a temptation. I breathe it out slowly, steadying myself. I may not know what comes next, but one truth is undeniable.

Whatever this marriage was supposed to be, it's already becoming something far more dangerous. I'm only supposed to count on myself. I'm unsure how to even entertain the layers of complication that one word implies.

He threw two wildcards into the mix. When he's done showering, he comes out, tosses on a pair of gray sweatpants. He acts like he didn't just flip my entire world upside down and declares, "I'm hungry. Want some pancakes?"

Brax

Chapter
TWENTY

The smell of pancakes has never done unholy things to my blood pressure. But my wife's standing barefoot in my kitchen, wearing nothing but my T-shirt, watching me flip a hotcake with hawk eyes. Her hair is a mess of dark curls down her back, wild and sleep-rumpled, and her long, bare legs gave me another raging hard-on the minute she stepped into the kitchen.

She points at the dark edge. "You're burning them."

"No I'm not. That's called carmelization," I claim, but she's right. Her damn legs distracted me for too long.

She snorts, "You're stubborn."

"And you're bossy," I retort.

"It's called being correct." She grabs the flipper out of my hand and slides several pancakes onto plates with a flick of her wrist like she's on a cooking show.

I slather butter all over them and grab the syrup. I drown my pile in it.

She grabs the syrup. "Save some for me."

I stare at her, deadpan. "I will drown you in the bottle if you ever take my syrup away again."

Her lips twitch. "This is a better option anyway." She reaches for the whipped cream.

I order, "Put that down!"

"Why?" She shakes the can, the sound far too erotic for early morning. "You scared I won't leave any for you."

I wrinkle my nose. "Whipped cream doesn't belong on pancakes."

She gapes at me. "Take that back."

"I can't. It belongs on a few things," I claim.

She arches her eyebrow. "Which things?" She adds a heap on her pancakes.

I gesture down at the obvious tent in my sweats.

She slowly follows my gaze. Then she smirks. "What's that about, dear hubby?"

I lean closer, drag my knuckles down her arm, and grin. "It's about you doing whatever the hell you want and me dealing with the consequences."

She lifts the can of whipped cream and gives it a single shake. She threatens, "You really want to test me, O'Malley?"

"Be careful, Minx," I warn.

She beams with defiance. "I'm always careful." She presses the nozzle and leaves a cold strip of whipped cream across my forearm.

I blink at it.

She covers her mouth to hide a laugh and fails miserably.

"Really?" I ask.

"It looks good on you," she sings.

I close the space between us. She backs up a step, and I snatch the can from her hand.

She gasps. "Don't—"

I spray a perfect dollop onto the center of her collarbone.

She freezes, glances at it, then bursts out laughing.

I taunt, "Keep laughing, Minx. I haven't even started."

She lunges for the can. I hold it above her head. She jumps, and my shirt shifts up her hips.

"Give it back!" she demands, stretching on her toes.

"Try harder."

Her hands slide up my torso, and her body presses into mine. Her breath hits my throat.

Chuckling, I give in to a moment of weakness and relax an inch.

She snatches the can out of my hand like a thief. She shakes it.

I reach for her wrist, but she's quicker than I am. She sprays a line down the center of my chest.

"Shit, that's cold!" I blurt out.

Her laugh echoes in the kitchen. "Now *you* look ridiculous."

"Funny," I growl, stepping forward and grabbing the can.

She steps back, straight into the counter.

I cage her in and hold it over her head.

Her breathing quickens, but her smirk doesn't budge. "You wouldn't dare."

"I've been daring since the second you walked in here wearing my shirt."

Her voice drops. "Don't even think about—"

I swipe whipped cream off my chest and smear it on the tip of her nose.

She gasps. "Brax!"

"Valentina!"

Her eyes light up. She tugs my sweatpants toward her and, with her other hand, swipes the whipped cream down my torso and into my pants.

"Now you're in trouble," I warn.

She grabs the can, tilts her head, smiles, and sprays more in my pants. "Wouldn't want to be stingy."

I stare at her, unable to stop smiling.

She stares right back.

I grin. "Now's the point you get on your knees—"

The door shakes from a brutal knock.

We both whip our heads toward it.

Another round of pounds fills the air. "Brax! Open up!" Finn orders.

I mutter, "Perfect."

Valentina's eyes widen.

The pounding intensifies. "Brax! Don't make me tear this door down!"

"Shit." I rush to the door and yank it open. "Where's the fire?"

Finn storms past me without answering, shoving the door so hard it ricochets off the wall. "Don't give me your sarcasm. You've been missing for days. Scratch that. You've not been yourself for months."

"Sorry," I offer, feeling guilty like always.

He jabs a finger into my chest. "Don't give me sorry. You didn't show up for the meeting this morning. You've been blowing off training. You haven't answered a single goddamn call. Not from me, not from Liam, not even from Brenna."

I shut the door and state, "Shit. I forgot about the meeting."

"Forgot? What the hell has gotten into you? Liam's going nuts between your and Sean's disappearing acts."

My chest tightens. I never shirked my obligations before the Underworld sank its claws into me. I give a weak excuse. "It's been busy."

"Busy?" Finn steps so close that his breath hits my face. "Busy doing what? You've vanished off the grid more than once. You think you can disappear without consequences?"

My jaw ticks. "Finn—"

"No." He slices the air with his hand. "Don't 'Finn' me. I've been hunting your ass for forty-eight hours. We thought maybe you were dead in a ditch. Killian wants your head. Brenna's blowing up my phone asking if she should be planning a funeral."

I pinch the bridge of my nose. "Jesus Christ."

He adds, "You didn't show up to the gym. Again."

Finn paces with more fury rolling off him. He seethes, "You don't vanish unless shit's gone sideways. So enlighten me, Brax. What the hell is going on? Did someone come after you? Did someone threaten you? Are we at war? Because you sure as hell didn't—" His eyes snap toward the kitchen.

Shit.

Valentina stills in my T-shirt. Whipped cream is still on her nose and collarbone. Her hair is just as wild as before.

Finn's head tilts like a wolf catching movement in the dark. They stare at each other.

"Good morning," she says sweetly.

His eyes turn to slits. He spins back toward me and stares at my chest. His gaze lowers, and he looks at me as if he's just realizing I have whipped cream all over me.

"Listen, I'm sorry I missed the meeting. It won't happen again," I declare.

His gaze narrows further, and he peers at Valentina.

Tension explodes.

Her face turns red, and I slip between them.

No time like the present.

"Finn, this is Valentina."

"You have got to be fucking kidding me. You missed a meeting to get a piece of ass?" he says through gritted teeth.

Anger hits me. "No. She's not a piece of ass."

He turns toward Valentina. "Sorry, I didn't mean to insult you. I'm pissed at Brax. I'm sure you're a nice—" He freezes, then his face pales. His hand lifts, shaking. "What is that?"

"What?" I question.

He lunges toward Valetina, grabs her hand, and snarls, "That!"

Fuck!

I step between them, pushing him away from her. I warn, "Finn, calm down."

"Calm down?" His eyes blaze red. "You got engaged?"

I don't say anything.

He scowls, then pins his gaze past my shoulder and back on Valentina. A few seconds pass, then he pushes me aside. His voice comes out lethal. "You're Valentina Abruzzo. Aren't you?"

Her lip shakes. She nods and answers, "Yes."

I step between them again. "Back off, Finn."

"Back off?" Finn shouts. "Back off? You're half naked with an Abruzzo in your kitchen after ghosting your entire family. And you asked her to marry you? Are you insane? Are you cursed? Did you hit your head? Are you—"

"We're not engaged, we're married," I interject.

Finn staggers back like I stabbed him. His eyes widen.

My stomach twists. I quietly offer, "I'm sorry you're finding out this way."

He takes a deep breath, then slowly releases it. "You married an Abruzzo?"

I stand taller. "Yes. And once you get to know her, you'll see that she's not a threat—"

"Not a threat? Did that just come out of your mouth?" he shouts.

I cross my arms, scowling. My heart pounds so hard I think it'll explode.

Disappointment fills his expression. He softens his tone. "I thought I raised you to make smart decisions."

My jaw twitches. I hate hurting him. I knew eventually he'd find out; I just wanted it to be on my terms. I take a closer step. "Finn—"

"No, Brax." He holds his hands in the air and steps backward. He shakes his head. "Don't say anything else." He turns, opens the door, walks out, and slams it shut.

I stare after him, my insides quivering, my fists clenched at my sides.

Valentina steps next to me. She puts her hand on my arm and softly says, "I'm sorry."

I take several breaths, then glance down.

Her expression brings me as much pain as disappointing Finn. Guilt riddles it. Her eyes are glassy.

I tug her into me. "It's not your fault."

"It is," she states.

I shake my head. "No. It's not."

"I don't want your family to hate you."

"He just needs some time," I assert, though doubt knots in my chest.

Valentina keeps her hand on my arm, her thumb brushing once before she lets it drop. She glances toward the door as if Finn's anger might seep back in under the frame, and something in her shoulders shifts. It isn't fear. It's the kind of resignation people carry when they've been blamed for things long before any fault existed.

She states, "He looked like he wanted to tear my head off."

"He looks at everyone like that when he's pissed." I try for ease, but my voice doesn't lift the way I want it to.

She tilts her head.

I add, "You weren't the reason he came here swinging."

Her brow arches. "But I was the reason he stayed swinging."

I snort despite everything. "Okay. Maybe that part is your fault."

Her expression softens, and her lips curve.

"You should eat," I tell her, gesturing at the discarded plates on the counter.

"I'm not hungry anymore," she says.

"Me either," I affirm.

We quietly clean up the kitchen, then take turns showering. I slide into a pair of jeans, and my phone buzzes.

Sean's name flashes, followed by a screenshot that snaps the last thread of calm in my body.

Liam: *You two. My place. One hour. No excuses.*

I groan.

Valentina comes out of the bathroom in her robe and winces. "Bad?"

"It's Liam. Sean and I were just summoned."

Worry fills her expression. She looks away, and guilt claws at me. I step closer. "This isn't your fault."

She turns toward me and shrugs. "This was always going to happen, wasn't it?"

I sigh. "Probably."

Silence fills the space between us.

I add, "I'm taking you to Sean's. You can visit with Zara and the babies."

Her mouth curves into the faintest smile. "Okay."

I grab my keys and point toward the hallway. "Get dressed and get your shoes."

She bites her lip.

"What?"

"I think they're still in Pompei."

"Shit." I glance around, then grab her and toss her over my shoulder.

She shrieks. "Brax!"

I slap her ass. "I can carry you out!"

She laughs.

I swing her around my body.

She puts her arms around my shoulders. "We're going to look ridiculous."

I shrug. "I don't care."

Within minutes, we're in the parking garage. We get into my Mustang and I speed onto the street toward Sean's penthouse. I turn down four blocks, accelerate down two more streets, and pull up to the curb. I get out and open Valentina's door.

She wrinkles her nose. "This is embarrassing."

"You love it," I tease, then slide my arms under her and pick her up. I carry her through the building, nodding at security, and into the elevator. I press my hand on the screen, and it moves toward the penthouse.

Zara meets us in the foyer. Her hair's piled into a messy knot, River's strapped to her chest, and Willow's tucked into her arm.

I whistle. "Damn. You're talented."

She waves her hand in front of her face. "Nah. Piece of cake." She skims over us and states, "Well, this is a dramatic entrance."

Valentina snickers. "My clothes and shoes are in Pompei. You can put me down now," she says, looking at me.

"Can I?" I tease.

"You can."

I carefully put her down.

She reaches for Willow and coos, "Come here, my favorite girl." She kisses her on the cheek.

Willow's fingers curl around Valentina's hair. She cuddles against her.

Warmth spreads in my chest until my pulse changes its rhythm.

Zara offers, "Want to borrow some clothes?"

"That would be great. Thanks," Valentina replies.

Sean steps into the foyer. In a doomsday voice, he announces, "You're here. Can't wait for this one."

"Yeah. Finn busted through my door this morning." I admit.

"Shit," Sean mutters, and the room goes silent.

Zara cringes. "You two look like you're on your way to a sentencing."

"Pretty close," I mumble.

Zara clears her throat. She orders, "Go before Liam decides to show up here and demand explanations."

I give Valentina a quick kiss. "Stay here until I'm back, Minx."

"Okay."

Sean kisses Zara and the babies, and we leave. We drive to Liam's house in silence. When we enter, the entire front room is full of O'Malleys.

Killian's on the couch next to Nolan. Declan stands near the window, arms locked behind his back. Finn sits in the armchair, his scowl running deeper than before. And Liam stands in front of the mantle, his arms crossed tight across his chest.

"Sit," he snarls, pointing to the empty couch.

Sean and I take our seats.

Liam starts, "You two have chosen an interesting week to lose your goddamn minds."

We don't speak or move.

Liam rehashes the obvious. "You missed the morning meeting. Both of you. Again."

I clench my jaw, my pulse hammering in my head. Guilt flows freely, and I can't turn it off.

"Gee, don't both of you talk at once," Killian snarks.

Neither Sean nor I look at him. We keep our focus on Liam.

He turns his attention to me. "So it's true? You married Valentina Abruzzo?"

Heat slices through my chest. I lift my chin. "I did."

His voice rises. "Why in God's name would you do such a stupid thing?"

I continue to remain silent, unable to tell them the truth.

"Well, say something! Tell us you love her! Tell us you'd die if you couldn't marry her! Tell us something for Christ's sake!" Nolan roars.

My heart hammers harder. I finally say, "You wouldn't understand, so there's no point discussing it."

"No point discussing it!" Liam fumes.

I stare at the ceiling.

Sean interjects, "Fiona married Kirill, and everyone's okay with him, now. You'll see that Valentina is a good person, too."

"Don't you dare try to act like this is okay! You're in the doghouse as much as Brax!" Liam booms.

Sean breathes through his nose.

Liam's voice sharpens. "You both have vanished. And you don't get to vanish. Not when you hold responsibilities that affect this entire family."

Sean argues, "We weren't trying to disrespect anyone."

Liam lifts a hand. "Stop. I don't want a speech. I want the truth. What the fuck is going on? And don't give me your 'I can't tell you' story. I'm sick of hearing it. I know you're somehow wrapped up in whatever shit your father started. I want to know the truth and now!"

Sean closes his mouth.

I meet Liam's stare head-on. "We can't tell you anything. Not yet."

Liam's jaw ticks with quiet fury. "Not yet? You two don't get to decide what this family deserves to know. If you've stepped into something dangerous, the family should be prepared."

Sean carefully states, "We aren't dragging you into it. We're trying to protect you."

Liam snarls, "Protect us? By disappearing? By dodging calls?"

We stay quiet.

He turns toward me, adding, "By letting Finn believe you were dead in a ditch? By letting Brenna panic?"

More guilt eats me. I glance at Finn. He wears the same hardened expression as when I came in. It only makes me feel worse. I quietly say, "I'm sorry."

He doesn't flinch.

Liam steps closer and lowers his voice. "I've run this family for years. And I do not run it blind."

I try, "Liam, we're not betraying you."

"We would never," Sean reiterates.

His voice cuts sharp as glass. "Then show me. Because until you do, neither of you is stepping foot into O'Malley operations."

Sean stiffens. "What does that mean?"

"It means you're suspended."

"You can't do that," Sean argues.

Liam grunts. "I just did. No pay for six months. No privileges. No access to O'Malley resources. You will handle nothing related to family operations until I trust your judgment again."

Anger rises beneath my ribs, but I clamp it down. "You're cutting us off?"

He shakes his head. "No. I'm giving you consequences. You don't get to choose loyalty only when it's convenient."

"We aren't choosing convenience," Sean says quietly.

"I'll never be disloyal to the O'Malleys," I vow, feeling like my world's being stripped away from me.

Liam's stare doesn't waver. "Then you won't mind the next part. You're both on grave duty."

Nolan shifts in his seat. Declan smirks like he's already planning the rotation schedule. Killian cracks his knuckles. Finn just sits there, not moving.

Sean's jaw ticks. "Grave duty?"

"Yes." Liam nods toward Declan. "Report to him at dawn. Midnight watch, cleanup assignments, cemetery patrol. The jobs nobody wants and everyone needs if they plan to pledge their loyalty to the clan."

"We already did our rounds of grave duty. We've proven our loyalty over the years," Sean reminds him.

Liam's eyes narrow. He warns, "You're lucky you're still on grave duty."

My gut drops. I open my mouth.

"Don't," Liam warns.

I shut my mouth and look at the ceiling again.

Liam's voice turns final. "If you vanish again, if either of you misses a call, if you fail to show up to a shift, you're out. Permanently. I will not tolerate half-loyal men in our clan."

A long, heavy silence fills the room.

Liam studies us one by one before giving a single clipped motion toward the door. "Get your shit together. Now get out before I change my mind and mark you as traitors."

"We aren't traitors," Sean seethes.

I look at Finn, but he's not budging.

"Go!" Liam roars, pointing at the door.

Sean and I exchange a glance, then leave.

We get in my car before we speak.

Sean booms, "What the fuck."

I shake my head, speechless.

"This is..." Sean stares at me.

I start the engine, drive past the gates, then pull over. I turn, seething, "I never wanted to be part of your father's fucked-up, twisted cult."

His jaw twitches.

"If I get kicked out of the clan—"

"We won't! Just take a breath. We'll do our grave duty and be back in their good graces before we know it," he assures.

I clear my throat. "I don't think Finn is ever going to talk to me again."

Sean runs his hand through his hair. "He will. He needs a minute."

I tap the steering wheel, shaking my head.

"Brax—"

"How did you ever expect this to work long term, Sean? Tell me," I demand.

He goes silent.

I say the truth that neither of us knows how to change. "This doesn't work, and you know it."

He closes his eyes, takes a deep inhale, then pins them on me. "If I had a solution, I'd give it to you."

I stare at him for several minutes, then assert, "Well, we're going to need to figure one out." I veer onto the road and gun the Mustang, angry, guilty, and hating the predicament I'm in more than ever.

Valentina

Two Weeks Later

Chapter
TWENTY-ONE

Brax is barely a shadow in my life right now. Not because I want him to be but because the O'Malley graveyard shift has swallowed him whole. He sleeps in scraps of daylight, collapsing for an hour here or twenty minutes there, his body stealing whatever rest it can before the night pulls him back under.

When he told me about Liam's punishment, he wore his cocky shrug, lazy grin, and the exact kind of confidence that suggests even the Grim Reaper would need to take a number.

I knew it wasn't good.

He just tried to assure me, "It's temporary," then kissed my forehead like there was nothing to worry about.

But I know what temporary means in our world. Someone always has to bleed, break, or stop breathing. Only then does temporary end.

So the nights roll by with more space in my bed than I want to admit. The silence that used to steady me in my condo has shifted into something hollow and unnerving. And the brief moments I do spend with Brax stretch way too thin.

I stay in my place instead of his, even though he hates it.

"Your building isn't safe," he tells me again, standing in my kitchen with the collar of his jacket popped, his hair still damp from a cold night outside, the O'Malley tattoo on his chest peeking from his shirt.

"Safe enough," I counter.

He lifts one brow, unimpressed. "Security cameras in the hall. Two guards at the front. A steel door you don't even always lock."

I cross my arms. "Your place has a keypad you punch in with a smirk and a prayer."

He grunts.

I remind him, "It doesn't matter. If someone wants in, they'll get in."

Silence settles between us. It doesn't matter if we're on the Royal Council. The investigation into Kirill and Fiona's beheading is still active, and neither Brax nor I trust anyone outside of our circle.

We both know neither of us lives in a fortress, but safety is a myth served to children and tourists. If the Omni wants access to us, they'll have it, with or without permission.

So I default to my condo because it lets me breathe a fraction easier. I can see the lake from my windows and pretend the water can wash anything clean. My things are here, and being at Brax's only reminds me he's not there.

I hate that I miss him.

But I do.

"We need to get another place," he states.

"My place is fine and it's paid for," I declare.

His face darkens, and his jaw tics. "I have money, Minx."

"I didn't say you don't. But you also had your salary frozen for six months," I remind him gently.

His haunted expression deepens. He insists, "It's fine."

I don't say anything else. We've never discussed our finances. Brax insists on paying for everything whenever we do go out, but I don't know how deep his pockets go. Six months without pay is a long time. And Kirill put a freeze on all Omni payments until the investigation is over, so we're both living off savings.

"I know," I agree, giving him a soft smile, even though it scares me. I don't know how long the investigation will take, and living in Chicago isn't cheap.

He sighs, tugs me against him, then presses his mouth to the side of my throat. "Stop worrying, Minx."

"I'm not," I lie.

He murmurs, "Liar," then pulls back and gives me a quick kiss on the lips. His voice turns to annoyance. "I'm going to get some sleep for an hour before job two starts. See you later."

"Why don't you sleep here?" I ask.

"My computers are at my place, remember?"

"Oh. Yeah." Guilt eats me for not staying at his place.

He wiggles his eyebrows. "But I'm glad I got to see you for ten minutes."

A rush surges through my chest so abruptly it disrupts my breathing. It's traitorous and impossible to control. Every instinct I've honed to survive men who wield power with their shadows tells me to shut it down, to reinforce the walls I've spent years cementing. But his words slip past everything I've built, sinking into places I swore no one would ever reach.

But the truth is undeniable. Brax tilts my entire world with such little effort. And I hate how easily he steals the composure I pretend is unshakeable.

"Me too." I kiss him again.

This time, he doesn't pull back until I'm out of breath. He finally pats my ass and leaves. So the space between us grows. Not because the bond snapped but because schedules are weapons, too. And part of me wonders if Liam knew his punishment would also hurt me.

Brax isn't gone long before my phone lights up on the counter. I pick it up and read the text.

> Unknown Number: Royal Council masked meeting. Next Wednesday. 9 p.m. Attendance mandatory. No exceptions. Come to impress.

My stomach knots. It's the first meeting since Brax and I earned our seats, and it overlaps with the O'Malley graveyard shift.

My stomach flips.

I need to get Sean and Brax excused.

Are they intentionally setting a trap?

I grab my coat, leave my place, and get into the SUV. I text Kirill.

> Me: You home?

> Kirill: Yes.

> Me: Need to talk. I'm on my way over.

Vito eyes me in the rearview mirror.

I glare at him. "Need something, Vito?"

He asks, "How are things going, Ms. Abruzzo?"

"It's Mrs. O'Malley, remember?" I reprimand for at least the tenth time.

His eyes narrow. "Right. Mrs. O'Malley."

I don't answer, roll the divider window up, and add it to my list for Kirill.

The rest of the ride is quiet. I quickly get through Kirill's building and into his penthouse. He's standing by his window when I walk in, posture rigid, scar stark in the city glow. He turns slowly. "You look irritated."

"Why is Vito still my driver?" I fume.

"The request has been made. The Royal Council vote will take place at the next meeting. You will get a new driver," he assures.

"If I don't die in the meantime," I mutter.

Kirill's expression darkens. His scar flexes. He booms, "Did something happen?"

"Not yet. But every second I'm with him, I'm risking my life," I state.

"You're being dramatic."

"Would you keep a driver for Fiona who got head-locked by a passenger?"

Kirill doesn't answer.

I scoff, "Exactly."

"You'll get a new driver. You can use Fiona's for the next week until it's voted on," he offers.

"Fine. Thank you. Speaking of meetings, you have to change it to the daytime."

"I can't do that, Valentina."

"Why not? You're the king," I remind him.

He groans and scrubs his hand over his face. Then he pins his eyes on me, clenching his jaw.

"You are!"

He asserts, "You know there are boundaries of what I can do. Royal Council meetings are always at 9 p.m. while the moon is out."

I put my hand on my hip. "Then Brax and Sean need to be excused."

"It's a mandatory meeting. All meetings after new seats are taken are mandatory," he informs.

My voice quivers. "They have graveyard duty. They can't get out of it."

Kirill's breath comes out heavy.

I order, "Strike the right deal, Kirill. Remind them Brax is under your eye and Sean is the Chosen One. Remind them that if Brax and Sean lose O'Malley clan privileges, harmony will not exist in the Underworld."

He studies me, and his lips twitch.

"This isn't funny!" I seethe.

He chuckles. "You're thinking like someone at the table."

I take a few breaths to calm down, then I nod. "Then make it happen."

He nods. "I'll declare they must be excused for critical security measures."

Relief slices through me, quick and thin. "Thank you." I turn to go.

He calls out, "Valentina. There's one more thing."

I spin, lifting my eyebrows.

His face turns serious. "You know they can't stay on graveyard duty for six months. There won't always be exceptions granted."

My chest tightens. I admit, "I know."

"I'll call Fiona's driver for you."

"Thank you."

I don't linger. The ride home is quiet. I'm lost in thought, trying to figure out how to get the guys out of graveyard duty, when the elevator doors open. I step into the long, sleek corridor, barely noticing the gray tile, soft overhead lighting, and the faint hum of HVAC. I unlock my door, step inside, and my instincts flare.

It's a subtle flicker in my gut. Then I inhale a whiff of perfume that isn't mine.

I close the door quietly behind me, keys still in my fist, and reach into my pocket for my knife. I glance around, but don't see anyone.

Someone is in here.

My hallway mirror catches movement just beyond my peripheral vision. There's a blur of purple hair at the far end of the corridor.

That fucking girl!

I open my knife and call out, "I know it's you, Blue. Come out before I slit your throat!"

She steps out of the shadow like she's been waiting for applause. Her hair is loose, wild around her shoulders, and her eyes are glossy in a way that screams she's been crying or screaming or both.

Her red mouth twists. "Valentina."

"You don't belong here."

She takes a step closer. "You don't belong anywhere you've planted yourself lately."

My jaw locks. "Did you pick my lock or bribe security?"

She laughs, sharp and unstable. "Maybe they're tired of your family's poison dripping into Chicago."

I keep my voice level. "Get out."

She moves closer anyway, boots clicking on the tile, eyes darting over my body like she's searching for a weakness.

She spits, "You play them so well. Even I'll give you that."

"Them?"

Her nose wrinkles. "Brax. Sean. All of them. You Abruzzos always think you're clever."

I warn, "Careful. Your obsession is making you sloppy."

Her face crumples for a second, then hardens. "Obsession?" She presses a hand to her chest like I've stabbed her. "I have history with him."

The words are a blade slid right between my ribs. I step closer and state, "History doesn't mean ownership."

Her smile turns mean. "That's rich coming from you."

She has the nerve to come toward me, closing the distance between us. Her gaze drops to my hand, and a flicker of disgust crosses her face. "You're not fit for that ring."

The words land, and for a heartbeat, my lungs forget how to work.

Don't listen to her.

I tilt my chin. "Yet here I am wearing it. I'm the one he chose, not you. You're delusional, Blue. You need to get professional help."

She laughs so hard I stare at her, unsure what's so funny. She stops and her voice cracks. "I see how he looks at you. You're a weapon he's using until he decides how to use it."

My pulse jumps.

She leans in, her perfume heavy, invasive. "He used to look at me like that."

Jealousy is a weakness I don't often give in to. It's inefficient, loud, and distracting. But when Blue tilts her head and gives me an intimate stare, like she actually knows what's between Brax and me, the green-eyed monster I keep at bay bares its teeth.

I step back.

She follows, crowding my space like she owns it.

"You know what I remember about him? The way he—"

Steel slides into my voice. I snap, "Stop. You don't get to speak about my husband in my home."

Her eyes blaze. She scoffs, "Your husband? That's the point, Valentina. He's not yours. You think he is, but it's temporary."

There's that word again.

My heart clenches, and my teeth grind. "You're spiraling."

She jerks like I slapped her.

A brief flash of pity fills me. I soften my tone. "Blue, go home. Get help."

My sympathy disappears when she wedges her way another inch closer and lets her palm slide down my arm like we're sisters sharing secrets.

"Don't touch me," I warn quietly, gripping the knife tighter at my side.

She smirks. "He doesn't touch you much when he's only here a few minutes."

The jealousy in me claws upward. I step to the side, yank my door open, and stab my thumb toward my intercom button. I assert, "Security. I need someone escorted out of the building. Now."

Blue's face twists. "Are you serious?"

"Completely."

Her eyes go glassy again, fury and pain tangling. "You don't get to exile me. You don't get to keep him."

"You're trespassing. You can't be exiled when you were never meant to be here in the first place."

She clips the words with icy precision. "Tell him I came. Tell him I understand he's only using you."

My pulse skyrockets. I push her into the wall and put my knife to her throat. I keep my voice level. "Listen to me closely, little girl. The next time you come near me or my husband, or either of our properties, you won't leave breathing. Understand me?"

Two guards, Hugo and Rodriguez, appear.

Blue turns to me, eyes wet and wild. "You think you won. But you're still an Abruzzo. And he's still an O'Malley. Blood doesn't change because you want it to."

"Mrs. O'Malley, please lower your knife," Hugo requests in a worried tone.

I hesitate, then finally step back, keeping my gaze on her. "Leave before you embarrass yourself further."

The guards grab her arms before she can move. She tries to shake them off, but can't. "Get off of me."

"Are we pressing charges?" Hugo asks.

Blue lifts her chin.

I answer, "We'll discuss it with my husband when he returns."

Rage fills Blue's gaze.

"Very well. We'll get everything ready in case you decide to file charges, Mrs. O'Malley," Hugo assures.

They drag her away.

I step into the hallway, watching.

She gets to the elevator, then looks over her shoulder. She calls out, "He has other women. Lots of them. You're just another notch on his post!"

A claw grips my gut.

She's lying.

The doors swallow her. Silence crashes down. I lock my door, walk into my kitchen, pour a glass of water, and drink it like it's medicine.

Jealousy sits in my chest like a live coal. My mind replays the scene, making me feel ill.

I pick up my phone and text Brax.

> Me: Your little friend was in my condo when I got home.

> Brax: What are you talking about?

> Me: Just what I said. Security wants to know if we're pressing charges.

> Brax: Are you okay?

> Me: Of course I am. She almost got her throat slit open.

> Brax: I'm on my way over. Don't go anywhere.

I walk through my home, looking in every room, but everything seems to be in place. I pace for a bit, then go over to the window and stare at the waves crashing against the shoreline.

Brax flies through the door with worry and anger in his expression. But fatigue is also etched into the angles of his face.

It pisses me off further that she was in here.

He's working his ass off, burning the candle at both ends, and shouldn't have to deal with her.

His eyes sweep the room, then land on me. He stalks closer and asks, "Did she hurt you?"

"No. I already told you that."

His jaw clenches. "So she didn't touch you?"

"She grabbed my arm."

Brax's gaze darkens. "What did she want?"

I throw my hands up. "Who knows! She was unstable and ranting. I had her escorted out right before I took her out."

He exhales slowly. "She's really sick."

I cross my arms, trying to keep my voice neutral. "She implied she has a history with you."

His eyes flicker. A muscle jumps in his jaw. "Implied?"

The jealousy sparks again, and I hate that it does. I press. "So? What's the history?"

He lets out a low, humorless laugh. "You've got to be kidding me."

I glare at him, my insides shaking.

He points at me. "You're jealous."

"I'm not."

He steps closer, slow and decisive, until heat radiates off him and wraps around me. "You are."

"I don't get jealous."

His mouth tilts. "Everyone gets jealous. Just some people pretend they're too good for it."

I lift my chin. "Don't patronize me."

"Then don't lie to my face." His voice drops, rough and intimate.

I can't help myself. "Did you sleep with her?"

Anger fills his expression. "I've already gone over this with you."

"That's not an answer!"

"I don't answer ridiculous questions."

Heat flares in my chest. "She sounded entitled."

His gaze sharpens. "She is entitled. To her own delusions. Not to me."

"And the reason she's still circling you?"

He leans closer, too close, and his mouth brushes my ear as he says, "Because she doesn't know how to lose."

A shiver races down my spine. I step back to regain air. "You should have handled this."

His eyes drag over my mouth. "Agree. And I will. But I'm more interested in handling you right now."

My breath catches. Every nerve in my body lights.

His hand slides to my waist, fingers firm, grounding. "You're wound tight, Minx."

"Don't call me that when I'm trying to be angry."

He smirks. "I don't know any other way."

I glare at him. "You're barely around. I see you for an hour a day, if that."

His mouth softens. "I'm working."

"I know. I'm not stupid."

"No, you're not."

I stare at him, my heart racing.

His thumb strokes my hip once, slow enough to set my skin on fire. "You want me around more, Minx?"

The question knocks the air out of me. The space between us is starting to break things I don't want broken. But my jealousy still flares.

He dips his head, lips grazing the pulse in my neck. "Have I neglected my wife?"

Heat floods me, sharp and traitorous. My fingers curl into his shirt.

He orders, "Don't let her get to you."

"Blue didn't get to me," I snap and push away.

His eyes flash. "You sure about that?"

"One-hundred-percent sure!"

"Liar," he says softly, then grabs the back of my head and kisses me like he's rewriting my sentence.

A sound vibrates in his pocket. He freezes.

The shift is so abrupt I almost stumble.

He pulls back, breath coming hard, eyes still dark.

There's another buzz.

He curses, yanks out his phone, and the light from the screen splashes over his face. His jaw tightens like a steel trap. He mutters, "Fuck."

"What is it?" I ask, the hairs on my arms rising.

Brax meets my gaze, and the heat from a second ago is still there, tangled with something colder. "Adrian wants to talk to me. Now."

The room drops ten degrees.

He slides his phone back into his pocket, then cups my face. "I'll be back."

"When?"

His mouth curves, but it's tight. "Soon."

I try to stamp down the ache rising in my chest.

He leans in, presses a quick, hard kiss to my forehead this time, then steps away. He heads for the door.

"Brax."

He pauses, turning back.

I hold his gaze. "Be smart."

His eyes soften just a fraction. "Always." Then he's gone, and the door clicks shut behind him.

I stand in the middle of my living room with my breath still uneven, my lips swollen, and jealousy snarling somewhere in my rib cage alongside something worse.

Hope.

For a few minutes, his mouth made the world smaller. Nothing else existed except us.

More than ever, I wanted it that way.

Brax

Chapter

TWENTY-TWO

My pulse charges through me like it's trying to split my ribs apart. I slam the SUV door outside Adrian's building and stomp toward the entrance.

Adrian has no right to summon me like he's Liam, but there's no way I'm risking him showing up at Valentina's door. And our talk is long overdue.

I don't check in at security, and they don't attempt to stop me. I get into the elevator, press my palm on the screen, and it rises quickly to the penthouse. I step out into the lobby, past the open door, and come face-to-face with Adrian and Blue.

The air instantly sharpens. Adrian stands near the massive floor-to-ceiling windows, hands behind his back like he's preparing for a firing squad.

Blue sits on the couch, clutching her elbow, her face pale. A long red scratch trails up her forearm.

The hairs on my neck rise.

What the fuck is she up to now?

She catches my gaze, and a tiny smirk appears.

Adrian lunges toward me. His Russian accent is thicker than normal. He snarls, "We've got a problem, and you're lucky I'm letting you breathe right now!"

My self-control snaps. I seethe, "Oh, we definitely have a problem!"

Adrian moves toward me, and Blue jumps off the sofa. She slips between us. "Dad, don't do something stupid."

"Get out of my way," he warns her, his icy-blue eyes balls of rage.

She steps backward against me. "More violence doesn't solve anything!"

I take three steps to the left. I warn, "Don't touch me!"

She sucks in a wet, trembling breath and stumbles.

Adrian's scowl turns hotter. He grabs Blue and snarls, "Your wife slit my daughter's arm."

I jerk my head backward.

No way.

Maybe.

No. She would have told me.

I point at Blue. "She's lying."

Her voice turns to sweet victim-mode. "Brax, I didn't do anything, I swear. She—she saw me on the street and just lost it. She pulled out her pocket knife, and before I recognized who she was, she slit my arm!"

"Bullshit," I spit.

Blue flinches dramatically.

Adrian roars, "Look at the blood! She's going to have a scar!!" He holds her arm toward me.

I step forward, chest expanding with heat. "Valentina didn't touch her. But let me tell you what your daughter's been up to."

"What's that?" Adrian hisses.

"I've done nothing, Dad!" Blue claims.

I sarcastically chuckle.

Adrian booms, "You find this funny?"

I stop laughing. "Not at all. And what's really not funny is that your daughter's been stalking me for months. She's broken into my place several times, and today she had the nerve to break into Valentina's!"

Blue gasps, shoulders trembling. "You're lying." She turns toward Adrian. "He's lying, Dad. He's just covering for that...that Abruzzo wife of his!"

I point at her, snipping, "You need help, Blue. You're delusional."

"Watch your mouth," Adrian orders.

"Are you not hearing what I'm telling you? She's stalking us!" I say louder than I should.

His eyes narrow. He glances at Blue, then back at me.

I continue, "She's followed me to the gym. She lurks outside my place. She breaks into our homes. What more do you need to know to get her some help?"

"I don't need help, Brax! She's poisoning your mind!" Blue claims.

"More delusional crap," I declare.

Adrian's jaw clenches.

"H-how can you be so mean?" Blue asks, tears spilling over her eyes.

I step toward Adrian. "Think about it. How many years have you warned me to stay away from your daughter, and how many times have I told you I've never considered touching her and never will?"

He doesn't say anything.

"This sick crush she has on me isn't little anymore. She's got mental problems. You need to help her," I reiterate.

Blue puts her hand on my arm. "Brax! Don't say stuff like that."

I shrug out of it. "Don't touch me!"

Adrian barks, "Blue, leave. Now."

She gapes at him.

"I said now," he orders.

A wounded expression floods her face. She gives me a final look and sulks out of the room.

Adrian prowls closer, shoulders squared, anger radiating off him in controlled pulses. "What have you done with my daughter?"

I close my fists at my side. "Jesus Christ, Adrian. How many times do I have to go over this with you?"

Adrian thunders, "My daughter's arm is cut!"

"She obviously cut herself for this little stunt she planned in case Valentina and I decided to press charges!" I roar.

"Press charges," Adrian growls.

"That's what happens to adults who break into other people's homes," I point out.

His cheeks turn maroon. He grits through his teeth, "Traitor! You come into my home and threaten my daughter with the cops?"

I take several deep breaths and lower my tone. "No. You know I would never involve cops in anything."

"But that Abruzzo wife of yours would?" he says with disdain in his tone.

"Watch your mouth when you speak of my wife," I warn.

Tense silence fills the air.

I try again. "Adrian, Blue has serious issues going on. She crossed the line today by breaking into my wife's home. This has gone on way too long anyway."

"And why don't you fill me in a little more about what's gone on between you two?" he accuses.

I explode, "I haven't touched her. I've never laid a finger on her and never crossed a line. I've done everything I can to convince her to end this crush she has on me, which now is a full-blown obsession."

Adrian scoffs. "You expect me to believe that? When she looks at you with stars in her eyes?"

It's a punch straight to my spine. I declare, "That's not my fault."

"Isn't it?"

"No. It's not," I insist.

He growls, "You'd better get your wife in line. If she touches my daughter ever again—"

"Don't you dare threaten my wife! You keep your crazy daughter away from what's mine, and that includes my wife!" I shout.

"Her survival rate only goes up if she doesn't touch my family again!" he counters.

"That scratch was self-inflicted. Valentina didn't do that," I insist, but the back of my mind wonders if she left it out.

No. Blue is delusional and did it to herself.

Adrian circles me like he's ready to strike. "You're blind where she's concerned. And blindness creates catastrophe. If I must intervene to rectify this—"

I grab him by the shirt and push him against the wall. "Threaten my wife again, and you'll have a catastrophe on your hands."

He wraps his hand around my neck, squeezes, and pushes me backward.

I move my hands to his neck and do the same.

Skylar storms in, hair tied up, cheeks flushed, eyes blazing. "What is going on in here?"

Adrian and I don't take our glares off each other, both of us choking.

Skylar pushes her tiny body between us. "Enough!"

Blue shrieks, "Oh my God! Dad, let Brax go!" She shifts in front of Skylar and pushes her body against mine.

I release Adrian and pry his hands off my neck, then jump backward. I catch my breath and point at Blue. "Don't you dare touch me!"

"Adrian! What is going on?" Skylar demands again.

Adrian points at me. "His Abruzzo wife sliced Blue's arm!"

"What?" Skylar's eyes widen. She grabs Blue's arm, and the color drains from her face.

I insist, "Valentina did no such thing. Blue broke into her house and has been stalking us. She's broken into mine several times over the last few months."

Skylar gapes at me.

"It's true," I add.

She slowly looks at Blue.

"His wife is making things up. You know how Abruzzos are. Look at my arm." Her eyes fill with tears.

"Cut the act," I mutter.

"Don't you speak to my daughter," Adrian warns.

"Your daughter needs help," I repeat.

Skylar's eyes widen. "Help? What do you mean help?"

Adrian shoots me a death glare. "He's lying. Don't listen to such nonsense."

I bark a humorless laugh. "Skylar, please listen since your husband won't. Blue is stalking me and now my wife. She follows us, breaks into our homes, and blows up my phone even though I won't answer. I can show you the text messages."

Blue gasps.

Skylar looks at her in horror.

"He-he's lying," she weakly claims.

Adrian puts his stake deeper in the ground. "He is. If this were happening, he would have told us."

"I didn't want to embarrass her. Or you or Skylar. I thought it was just a stupid crush that would pass," I confess.

Skylar's hand flies to her mouth. Her eyes soften into worry. "Oh God."

Adrian's expression darkens further. "Printsessa, you're not buying this?"

Skylar looks between Blue and Adrian. Then she looks at me.

"I'm not lying," I softly repeat, begging her to believe me.

Adrian spits venom. "Your wife—"

"She's not the one sneaking around people's apartments."

"Valentina Abruzzo—"

"Enough!" Skylar turns toward Adrian.

Surprise fills his expression. He doesn't move.

Skylar's lips tremble. She orders, "Don't you dare say another word about his wife."

Adrian's eyes widen.

Her voice shakes. "Brax has never lied to us. If this is true, Blue needs a doctor."

"What? Mom!" Blue cries out.

Skylar spins on her. She grabs her arm. "How did you do this?"

Blue's mouth hangs open.

"Skylar!" Adrian scolds.

Her eyes well. She shakes her head at Adrian. Worry, fear, and sadness fill her voice. "These are serious accusations."

Adrian scoffs, "Yes. Accusations being the keyword."

I shake my head at him. "Why would I lie about this?"

"To cover for that snake of a wife you have!"

"Adrian! Stop it!" Skylar fires.

He breathes hard, staring at her.

"You are too blinded by pride," she softly states.

"Mom! Brax is lying!" Blue tries again.

I scoff. "Believe whatever you want, but I'm done dealing with it quietly. Keep your daughter away from me and from Valentina."

Skylar nods, earning a glare from her husband. Still, she says, "Brax, I'm so sorry."

My heart hurts. The Ivanovs have always been good friends with the O'Malleys, and Skylar has always been sweet to me. Adrian only started giving me shit once Blue got her crush on me.

I don't say anything. I nod.

Skylar puts her hand on my arm. "I'll walk you out."

I give Adrian one final look, ignore Blue, and move toward the exit. I press the elevator button.

Skylar quietly says, "I'm very sorry for what our daughter has done. Please tell your wife we are sorry as well."

I release an agitated breath. "Get her help, Skylar. Seriously. She's delusional. I tried everything to get her to stop on her own, but she won't leave me alone. Now she's going after Valentina. I won't have it."

A mother's heartbreak flickers in her gaze, mixing with fear.

I add, "Just like Adrian needs to protect his family, I need to protect mine."

She blinks hard and nods. "I understand. I'll handle it."

"Thank you." I step on the elevator and pull out my phone. I dial my wife.

She answers on the second ring, breathless. "Hey. You okay?"

"Did you scratch Blue?" I ask.

Silence sharpens.

My gut drops. "Did you?"

"What in God's name are you asking me?" she spouts.

"I'm asking you if you took your pocket knife and sliced her arm open." I close my eyes and lean against the wall.

Her tone stiffens. "No. Brax, what kind of question is that?"

"Just answer me straight."

Each word comes out clipped with restrained anger. "Are you serious right now?"

"I need to know."

"Of course I didn't. If you don't believe me, talk to security."

Relief fills me, but I still reconfirm. "You swear?"

She gasps, offended in a way that hits me straight in the chest. "I can't believe you're asking me this again. After everything I told you about her chasing me around? After every time I warned you? Wow."

"Valentina—"

"No. You got your answer. Talk to security since you don't believe me." Her voice cracks with fury. The line clicks dead.

The elevator keeps descending, but everything inside me sinks faster.

By the time the doors open, the entire situation haunts me. Adrian's accusations, Blue's lies, and the fact that Valentina hung up with ice in her voice instead of warmth, all give me a pounding headache.

I step out onto the sidewalk, shove a hand into my hair, and let the cold hit my face like punishment.

Everything is falling apart.

And I'm the idiot standing in the middle of the wreckage with no damn clue how to fix any of it.

Valentina

A Week Later

Chapter

TWENTY-THREE

Wednesdays specialize in trapping you with the thoughts you'd rather ignore. All week, I've been dodging mine with Olympic precision. Today, nothing is working.

Ever since Brax went to Adrian's penthouse and then called me to ask if I hurt Blue, we've been off. He told me he stuck up for me and assured them she was lying. Yet he still had to ask me and then question me again when I told him I didn't.

That girl gets to break into my home, throw shade at me, and then accuse me of cutting her, and I'm the villain?

I should have cut her.

I would have gone directly across her face.

The thought of Blue with a scar similar to Kirill's gives me a momentary surge of satisfaction.

Then it dies quickly.

Everything was good between us until Blue showed up. Now, I don't know where we stand. It's not a big enough rip to unmake the mess we created, but it's enough to wedge itself between every thought I have about him.

We've barely spoken in days. I'm not intentionally avoiding him, but he's been buried with the O'Malley fallout and his Underworld duties. I've been drowning in my own business endeavors, and they are the kind that demand precision and composure, which right now, I'm faking.

Secretly, I'm freaking out.

My pulse crawls raw under the surface. I snap at Zara every time she asks if I'm "okay." Then I have to apologize when she winces from my aggression.

It's surprising that she and Fiona even asked me to go to yoga with them. But they came over, demanded I go, and since I was only sitting around spiraling about Brax, I didn't argue.

So now I'm in the last stretch of class. Zara's on my left. Fiona's on my right. Both of them watch me like I'm a porcelain vase someone dropped once already.

"Your breathing is loud," Fiona whispers.

"That's the point," I mutter, sinking deeper into the stretch.

She counters, her lips twitching, "No. Yours sounds like you're trying to strangle the floor."

Zara snorts inelegantly. "She's stressed."

"I'm not stressed," I say sharply.

Zara raises an eyebrow. "You did a downward-dog during tree pose."

Fiona adds, "And we had to stop you from telling the instructor her voice 'lacked purpose.'"

I argue, "It does. She sounds like she does enlightenment on Decaf."

Zara presses her lips together to keep from laughing.

Fiona doesn't bother hiding hers.

The instructor looks our way and scolds, "Shh."

I roll my eyes and move into a child's pose.

The class soon ends, and I hug them both and head for the lobby.

I walk to the SUV. Fiona's driver stands at attention. I slide into the back with my mat strapped under my arm, every muscle in my body humming with frustration. And it's not the yoga kind. It's the Brax kind that I can't escape.

The drive to my condo is quick, and I'm rehashing the same crap I've been all week.

I rehearse what I'll say if he calls.

I rehearse what I'll say in text if he doesn't.

Then I rehearse the conversation I will absolutely never have with him because that would require us to actually see each other.

The SUV pulls up to the curb. I get out, step into my building, nod at the concierge, and ride the elevator up. I tell myself the same thing I've been repeating all week.

He's busy. You're busy. Space is normal.

Then the one thought that hurts me the most flares bright.

He's bored with me already.

My heart hurts, and I unlock the door, and my pulse betrays me. The faint scent of his cologne is unmistakable, and every part of me turns electric.

Then his voice ricochets through the condo. "Did you learn any new positions you want to try out, Minx?"

I freeze.

Brax sits on my sectional, leaning back like he owns the place. His gray T-shirt stretches across his chest. His thighs bulge against his jeans. His arrogant expression burns bright.

Flutters fill my stomach. I narrow my eyes. "Why are you here?"

He lifts a brow. "I'm not allowed to see my wife?"

"I don't know." I toss my yoga mat in the closet and spin toward him. "Are you?"

His jaw tics. "You tell me."

I unzip my hoodie, suddenly hot. "You've been ghosting me for days."

He stands abruptly. "I've been working."

"So have I."

"I know."

I can't help it. I cross my arms. "Interesting. It didn't seem like you remembered that when you asked if I cut Blue."

His mouth flattens. "I didn't ask. I wondered if you didn't tell me everything."

"That's worse."

He stalks toward me, each step slow and deliberate. I force myself not to step backward and keep breathing. He scowls. "How long are you going to stay pissed at me for asking you a question?"

"How long are you going to pretend you shouldn't have already known the answer?" I counter.

He snorts. "Because you've never cut anyone before, right?"

I shake my head. My voice rises. "No, Brax. Because I would have told you I cut your precious Blue!"

Anger flies across his expression. He warns, "Don't ever use those three words together like that again."

Our stares lock. The air pulls tight, charged with that dangerous thread we dance too close to. My pulse stutters, and his gaze flicks down my body before snapping back up.

He runs his tongue along the inside of his cheek, then shakes his head. "We're not doing this."

"We're already doing it."

He steps closer. "What do you want from me, Minx?"

I stay quiet.

He lowers his voice and slides his palm on my chin. "Want me to say I'm sorry I asked?"

My voice wavers. "You didn't just ask. You asked again after I told you no."

His face hardens. He inhales slowly, then exhales even slower. "Okay. I should have only asked once."

I shake my head. "No. You should have known I would have told you an important detail like that."

"You're right. I'm sorry, Minx."

The apology hits like a punch I wasn't ready for. My chest warms, then aches, then wants too much. I'm tongue-tied, unable to put any coherent thoughts together.

"So are we going to fix this little problem of ours or turn enemies?" he asks, running his thumb over my jaw.

I look away before my expression betrays me.

He exhales through his nose. "Can we forget about Blue and deal with an actual problem?"

I look back at him, fretting, "What problem?"

"Royal Council meeting is tonight."

I blink. "Yes. I'm aware."

"I don't like you going without me."

The words hit differently. My stomach knots in a way that isn't anger, or logic, or anything I want to inspect too closely. His protective instincts always hit me sideways, mostly because I'm used to surviving without anyone taking my safety personally.

"I'll be fine," I insist.

"You're going with Kirill and Fiona."

I freeze, arching my eyebrows.

"I set it up. They'll pick you up at nine."

Confusion, heat, and something else twist through me. "So you made arrangements behind my back."

"Yes," he challenges.

I should argue. I should snap something cruel or defensive. Instead, all that leaves my mouth is a quiet, "Thank you."

His eyes darken, and the tension between us shifts. His mouth curves. "You want your gift?"

"My what?"

He points toward the far side of the room. "Over there."

A black velvet box wrapped in a crimson bow sits on my entryway table.

How did I miss it?

My breath catches. "What is it?"

His lips twitch. "Open it."

Excitement fills me more than I want to acknowledge. I pick it up and look at him.

He grins, urging, "Go on."

I untie the bow, lift the lid, pull out a scarlet eye mask, and gape.

It's stunning, crafted in deep, lacquered red and onyx black. Sharp, sensual lines on the mask command attention while they seduce and threaten in equal measure. The ornate filigree crown along the top glitters with crimson gems that catch the light like drops of fresh blood. Roses in lush shades of scarlet and wine spiral along the edges, their petals so vivid they could be real. The darker leaves curve through them, layered with black pearls and onyx stones. The entire thing looks painted and alive. It's beauty shaped into armor.

A whisper escapes me. "Brax... It's beautiful."

His voice drops low. "You haven't looked at the best part." He steps closer, hooks a finger under the central crest, and tugs.

A narrow steel blade slides free.

"Holy shit," I mutter.

"I'm not letting my wife go anywhere unarmed again," he declares, pinning me with his heated stare.

My throat tightens unexpectedly. A sharp sting I can't swallow down builds behind my eyes. I blink fast, but it doesn't stop the warmth rising through me like a tide.

He watches me closely, expression shifting from smug to concerned. "Don't cry."

"I'm not crying."

"You are absolutely crying."

I swipe a tear quickly. "No, I'm not. Something got in my eye."

"Sure, Minx. Whatever you say."

I study the mask and the knife, then toss my arms around him. "Thank you."

He hugs me hard and mumbles, "No one's fucking around with my wife."

I softly laugh.

His hand slides to the back of my neck, fingers threading through my hair, and he lowers his forehead to mine. "One more thing."

"What?"

"I trust you. Even when I'm an idiot who forgets how to show it," he proclaims.

My breath catches.

He brushes his thumb across my cheek. "And I don't want distance between us anymore."

My voice barely rises. "Me either."

He kisses me, stealing my air and anger alike. His hands grip my waist, pulling me closer, and anchoring me in a way that unravels everything inside me.

I tighten my arms around him, kissing him with every ounce of affection I have.

When he finally pulls back, his mouth lingers on mine. "We're good?"

I nod against his lips. "We're good."

He kisses me again.

And just like that, the fracture between us seals. All my hours of worrying fade away.

Brax presses one more kiss to the corner of my mouth, slow and lingering, before pulling back to stare at me. His gaze sweeps over my flushed cheeks and damp lashes with an expression that makes my stomach tighten in a way I don't dare to examine yet.

Then his phone buzzes.

His jaw tightens. The muscle in his cheek jumps. He doesn't look away from me as he groans.

I step back, adjusting the mask box in my hands. "Liam?"

He checks the screen. "Yep. He's been calling all morning. I can't ignore him."

"I know. Go ahead and take it."

He swipes the phone, kisses my forehead, and answers, "Yes, sir." Within seconds, his face falls further. "On my way." He hangs up.

"Duty calls?" I say, trying to hide my disappointment.

"Yeah. But when I get back, we're starting where we just left off," he declares.

I softly laugh. "Deal."

He kisses me again, then murmurs against my lips, "This meeting makes me nervous. I'm sure the council members will be on edge because I'm not there. Stay safe, Minx."

"I will," I assure him.

He hesitates, then kisses me again and retreats. His eyes narrow playfully. "Kirill and Fiona will be your bodyguards."

I shoot back, "They're both cutthroat and married. That's more like babysitter energy."

He chuckles, but then his face turns serious. "Minx, stick close to Kirill. If anyone starts running their mouth, let him handle it."

"I'm capable of handling myself."

"You're capable of starting an international incident."

"Sometimes those are necessary," I tease.

He smiles, then adjusts my hair behind my shoulder. His fingers graze the nape of my neck. "Just humor me."

"Okay," I concede, rubbing a hand down his chest. "But if Kirill tries to drag me around by the elbow like I'm his rebellious cousin, I'm stabbing him with my new accessory."

Brax replies dryly, "That's partially why I gave it to you. In case you decide to enforce manners at the Royal Council."

I laugh.

His phone goes off again. "Jesus. I'd better go." He pecks me on the lips and disappears.

The moment he's gone, the condo quiets in a way that makes everything inside me reorder itself. The whirlwind of uncertainty that's been buzzing around my rib cage for days finally settles.

The rest of the day passes in a haze of Underworld projects, two long calls with Cassian, and one irritating email from my condo association about not giving my keys to people I don't trust. Then they have the audacity to tell me building security isn't for personal issues.

Fucking Blue.

By the time the sun starts sinking, my thoughts keep drifting back to the mask.

I take it out again and run my fingertips over the carved roses and dark leaves. The piece is lighter than it looks, sturdy and impossibly elegant. It's the kind of thing that promises beauty and danger in the same breath. When I lift the central crest again and glimpse the hidden steel, a small spark ignites deep inside me.

Brax made this for me.

It's important to him that I'm safe.

I smile and study it for over an hour.

By eight-thirty, I'm fully dressed in a black jumpsuit tailored through the waist and flaring at the legs. My hair's curled, pinned half-up, and I put the mask in my oversized bag.

My phone buzzes.

Fiona: We're here.

Me: Coming down now.

I exit my condo and the building, and their black SUV pulls up to the entrance. Kirill's driver gets out and opens the door.

Zara slides across the seat and tosses me a wide grin. "I'm being protected tonight, too."

I laugh.

Kirill and Fiona sit across from us. He teases, "Three beauties. I'm going to be the talk of the Royal Council."

We laugh, and conversation is easy as we weave our way through town.

I ask, "Are all the Royal Council meetings in Chicago?"

Fiona's face falls. She answers, "Until we find out who tried to overthrow us."

I nod, wishing we knew who all the traitors were.

Kirill's driver takes the next turn, and the city gives way to a stretch of anonymous concrete and steel that could be any corporate district if you didn't know what slept underneath it. The SUV glides into a private underground entrance tucked behind a wall of mirrored glass. There's no signage or visible cameras, but I know we're being recorded just like every other member who enters.

Two men in black stand so still they could be statues, palms resting on the hilts of their weapons. Kirill rolls down his window and says a single word in Russian. The guards step back, and a gate opens.

We descend into the belly of the building. The elevator doors open onto a corridor. Low, amber lighting casts everything in soft shadows.

The reinforced concrete walls etched with old symbols make my skin prickle.

Fiona leans toward me as we pass a black iron archway. "Did you bring your mask?"

"Of course." I push my fingers in my bag, tracing the flowers. My pulse stays steady, but the weight of the crest knife presses against my palm like a secret heartbeat.

We approach a black steel door. Kirill puts his mask on. The others follow, and I slide Brax's present over my head. A calm I've never felt floats over me, and I'm confident it's from the hidden blade that's now my insurance.

The antechamber is a circular room with a domed ceiling painted so dark it looks like a night sky without stars. Twelve family crests hang in a circle, each one representing a crime family bound to the Underworld. A single long table sits in the center.

Fiona adjusts her blue filigree mask, then checks mine with a small nod.

Kirill's black-and-silver mask is all hard edges and authority. He says, "Stay close."

"Brax already gave me the same order," I tell him.

"Then obey it twice," he answers, and I can't tell if he's joking.

We step through the final door into the council chamber.

The room is a cathedral built for criminals. A crescent-shaped platform raised six feet looms at the far end, backed by a black wall of carved volcanic glass. A table curves in a wide circle around it, each seat marked by a colored skull. Twelve chairs with black velvet seats surround it, but tonight, only ten are occupied.

The moment our feet cross the threshold, voices cut off. Heads turn. Masks hide faces, but not power.

A thin man with a gold mask leans forward, pointing at the empty seats. "Where are the O'Malleys?"

A woman in a white mask snaps, "Did you not get the exception memo?"

Kirill doesn't bother with pleasantries. He rises out of his seat, announcing, "As stated, Sean and Brax have been suspended from clan operations and are fulfilling those duties."

Murmurs ripple through the room like a disturbed pond.

The gold mask tilts. "Suspended? If the O'Malley line loses its roles, the balance fractures."

Kirill's voice is calm enough to be lethal. "Exactly. You should be praying their seats remain intact. The Underworld does not survive if one of its strongest pillars falls."

A broad-shouldered man wearing a purple mask scoffs. "Unless that pillar was already rotten."

Fiona moves a fraction forward, but Kirill lifts a hand and stops her. He scans the room slowly, letting the tension thicken until it's hard to breathe. Then he speaks again, and every word burns with anger. "We have traitors in our world. Who has information for me?" His gaze sweeps the tables.

The room turns cold.

"Someone funded it. Someone sanctioned the beheading of a royal bloodline. Someone believed my wife and I could be dragged onto a platform and butchered for their ambition," Kirill seethes.

Silence continues to mix with tension.

Kirill plants both hands on the table. "I want the names of everyone involved, from the hands that held the knives to the mouths that issued the command, to the money that funded it."

The woman in white shakes her head. "We investigated. The traitors were apprehended. The matter no longer exists."

Kirill lets out a laugh that has no warmth in it. "You think I believe that a coup stops with two pawns and a ritual stage?"

The purple mask leans back. "We have no additional evidence. No communications. No transfers. Nothing beyond what the O'Malleys already uncovered."

"Then you're lying, or you're incompetent. Which is it?" Kirill snarls.

Voices rise around the circle, full of excuses, deflections, and no answers. Each family rep insists they had no knowledge, no hand, no role in the attempted coup.

Kirill's restraint frays visibly. His fists clench. His shoulders go rigid. The frost in his tone turns to fire. "You either give me names, or I start taking them."

Another round of tension mounts.

Kirill finally slams the session closed. The air is thicker than when we walked in. We file out through the bunker the same way we entered, but his sharp, angry exterior never fades.

By the time we reach the elevator, I wonder why I wanted a seat so badly. Besides Kirill, Fiona, and Zara, there's no clear alliance. Everyone's an enemy. The Royal Council only represents more powerful people playing dangerous games.

And like always in the Underworld, the truth stays hidden in the dark, wrapped in masks and lies.

Brax

Chapter
TWENTY-FOUR

The cursor blinks on the last line of red code, the kind that eats through firewalls like acid and still leaves you with nothing but a dead screen and a warning you can't unsee. I stare at it anyway, knuckles tight around my mouse, jaw locked so hard my molars protest.

Access denied.

You shouldn't be here.

Leave now.

I brace for my computer to blow up again, but it stays lit.

Whoever built the Underworld's digital perimeter didn't just slam a door in my face. They stood on the other side and whispered my name through the keyhole.

I lean back in my chair and roll my neck once, twice, letting the ache slide down into my shoulders. I glance out the window.

The Chicago traffic hums below. I stare at it until the wall radiator roars like a bomb, then return to my project.

Six monitors glow in front of me, each one waiting for my next move.

I tap my fingers on the desk, then stop myself.

I open a new window and start running a trace back through the access denial, hunting for a breadcrumb I can yank into daylight. The minute I do, the same looping red warning flashes on a side screen. Not as text this time but as a pulsing block in the shape of a heartbeat.

Cute.

They're watching in real time.

I tilt my beer bottle to my mouth, swallow, then set it down with a soft thunk. The doorbell rings, and I freeze.

I'm not used to unannounced visitors who ring the bell. Sean normally knocks or uses the code for the keypad. Valentina has it as well.

The bell rings again, sharper, impatient.

I stand, cross the hallway, and check the peephole.

Brenna.

My chest tightens in a way I don't appreciate. I haven't seen or talked to her since I married Valentina and all hell broke loose. I cautiously open the door.

She stands in the corridor wearing black leggings, a loose sweatshirt, hair twisted up like she threw it there on the drive over. No makeup, no jewelry. Just Brenna, raw edges and all, eyes bright with the kind of hurt that makes you want to punch a wall on her behalf.

"Hey," I say, voice rougher than I intend.

She brushes past me. "I'm not here for small talk, Brax."

"Good. I'm not in a small-talk mood."

She turns in my living room, arms folded, gaze slicing me. In a pained voice, she says, "Did I do something to you?"

I shut the door and lean my shoulder into it. "What do you mean?"

Her laugh cracks out, humorless. "Don't do that. Not today."

I scrub a hand over my face. "Brenna—"

"You didn't tell me about Valentina. Then you get married and stop talking to me."

My instincts flare, the same ones that made me survive alleys and cages and rings. I keep my expression blank. "Finn's not talking to me."

"So I get punished, too?"

I sigh. "I'm sorry. I thought you would be mad, too."

Her eyes flash. "Oh, I'm mad all right. I'm pissed you got married, didn't invite me, and still haven't even introduced me to your wife."

"She's an Abruzzo. Or didn't you get the memo?" I tease, but it's in bad taste and comes out stale.

"That's bullshit, and you know it." She steps closer, voice shaking but sharp. "You walked into our lives as a kid with nothing but street dirt under your nails, and I treated you like blood before you even had the name. You slept under my roof. You ate at my table. You called me family. And now I hear through the grapevine that you got married and couldn't spare me one damn sentence?"

Guilt eats me. I open my mouth, then close it again. There's no clean answer. There's only truth, and it's messy.

She blinks hard.

I soften my tone. "I didn't mean to hurt you."

She lowers her voice. "Intent doesn't erase impact."

"That's a fair statement."

Silence forms.

"Come sit down," I offer, push off the door, and walk into the kitchen, needing movement so I don't say something stupid. I grab a water bottle from the fridge, twist it open, and take a long drink. I hand one to her and grab a barstool, admitting, "I thought you'd take Finn's side."

"Oh, I'm on his side. I'm livid you didn't bother to tell me anything about her or your nuptials," she declares.

My grip tightens on the plastic until it crinkles. "It wasn't a wedding you send out invites for."

She taps her water bottle. "That's not the point. The point is you made a choice that changes this family, and you left me out of it, then didn't even fill me in."

I set the bottle down, searching for the truth so I don't have to lie to her. "It all happened really fast."

"And you didn't think to slow down and invite your family to your wedding?"

I grunt. "I married an Abruzzo."

"So I've heard."

"You've seen how Finn's reacting," I offer.

She takes a sip of water, then replies, "Not an excuse, Brax." Her hurt flares again. She looks away.

My pulse tics. I put my hand on hers. "I'm sorry, Brenna. The last person I'd ever want to hurt is you."

She turns toward me. "What's she like?"

Warmth fills my chest. My lips twitch. I don't have to think. It all rolls out. "She's...she's beautiful. And smart. Way too smart for me. She's also infuriating, stubborn, complicated, and brave."

Her face softens. A tiny smile forms, but she asks, "Is she dangerous?"

I hold her gaze. "She can hold her own. But she would never try to hurt the people I love or me."

Brenna's eyes flicker with something I can't put my finger on. She blurts out, "Then you're to bring her to dinner tonight."

The sentence hits so fast my brain stalls. "What?"

She sits back in her chair. "I want to meet your wife, Brax."

"Brenna, that's not—" I search for a word that won't make this worse. "Expected."

"Well, I didn't exactly expect it when Finn brought you home fifteen years ago."

I stare at her, caught between gratitude and the old, brutal instinct to keep everyone I love away from incoming fire.

She keeps going, voice lower now, gentler. "You're family. If she's family too, then I need to know her. Not through rumors. Not through Finn's silence or anger. Through my own eyes."

Finn's silence.

I scrub my face in frustration. "What about Finn? He still won't talk to me. Every morning, I see him at the gym, and he ignores me. Pretty sure I'm not welcome in your house."

Brenna's gaze dips, then lifts again with a steadiness I recognize from the times she overrules Finn. "I talked to him."

My stomach knots. "He knows you're here?"

"Of course. And he knows I'm inviting you to dinner."

I blink. "He agreed?"

She scoffs. "He will be on his best behavior."

I stare at her in shock. Then I rub the back of my neck. "You realize what you're asking could put you in the middle of something ugly."

"You think this is the first time I've been in the middle of ugly?"

"Touché."

Her eyes sharpen. "Is Valentina a permanent fixture in your life?"

I study her, thrown by the sudden pivot.

"You married her," Brenna says quietly, like she's stripping away the excuses before I can reach for them. "Is she permanent, or is this something you did and regret?"

The question slides right under my ribs and hooks something tender I didn't know was there. Before I married Valentina, I told myself I was trapped. That this was a chess move, a leash, a play I'd break the moment I got a chance.

Permanent tastes like gunpowder and promise. But the moment I gave her that ring, I was already all in, so I don't lie. "Yes. She's permanent."

Brenna's breath catches. Then her shoulders loosen in a way I didn't expect, relief braided with something like hope. "Great. Dinner's at six. Don't be late."

I nod once, slow. "Okay."

She rises and holds her arms out. "Good. Give me a hug."

I chuckle, then hug her harder than I ever have, happy to see her and know she's still in my life.

She pulls back. "See you at six." She walks toward the door.

"Why are you okay with this?" I blurt out.

She freezes, then spins. She studies me for a moment while my pulse beats between my ears. She tilts her head, sadness fills her expression, and she answers, "Because my parents didn't accept

Finn. They thought he wasn't good enough and hated him. It changed the trajectory of our lives. So Finn and I are going to do better."

A cold chill runs down my spine. It's the first time I've ever heard of this. I know about Finn and Brenna's love story, but I spent a lot of time with her dad before he passed. I look at her in question.

"Some day, I'll tell you about it. Not today," she says.

I don't push. "Okay."

She smiles big. "Bring your wife to dinner. Let's fix things before they get worse."

Hope fills me. "I'd like that."

"Good. It's settled." She hugs me again, pulls back, and her voice turns sharp again. "One more thing?"

"Yeah."

"If she hurts you, Abruzzo or not, I will bury her myself."

I huff a laugh. "Noted. But she won't," I insist before I even realize I already believe it.

"Good." Brenna heads for the door, pauses with her hand on the knob, then looks over her shoulder. "You're not alone. You've not been since you entered our lives. That doesn't change because you do something Finn doesn't approve of."

The words land harder than she realizes. I choke up, so I just nod.

She leaves, door clicking shut behind her, and I stand in shock.

Underworld shadows still sit on my monitors. O'Malley punishments aren't over. Finn's silence hasn't broken.

But tonight, Brenna wants my wife at her table.

I grab my phone off the counter, thumb hovering over Valentina's contact, my pulse running too fast for a man who swears he doesn't get cornered.

"Permanent fixture," I mutter to myself, smiling. Then I hit the call button. It connects on the second ring.

Her voice barrels in, teasing, "What happened? Who died?"

My lips twitch. "Good afternoon to you, too, Minx."

She chirps, "You never call me in the middle of the day unless there's a crisis."

I say, leaning back in my chair. "There is. We're going to dinner."

Excitement hits her voice. "Dinner? As in food? In public? Together?"

"That is normally what the word means."

She sputters, then mutters something filthy in Italian under her breath. The language only makes my blood heat. She asks, "Where are we going?"

Anxiety leaps into my gut. I try to stay calm. "Finn and Brenna's."

Dead silence fills the line.

I check the phone to make sure the call hasn't dropped. "You still there?"

She answers in a low, tight voice, "Yes. You just shorted out my brain. Did you say Finn and Brenna's?"

My lips twitch. "Yep. Dinner at their place. Tonight at six, and we can't be late. Brenna wants to meet you."

"She what?"

I inform, "She came by my place. She isn't thrilled that she heard about our marriage from everyone except me."

Valentina cautiously asks, "So she's okay with me?"

My stomach flutters with nerves. I joke, "She ordered me to bring my wife to dinner so she could decide for herself whether to bury you or adopt you."

A strangled sound cracks down the line. "Those aren't comforting options."

I chuckle. "Minx, she wants you there. She wants to meet you."

Valentina blurts out, "What about Finn? Does he want me there?"

I collect my thoughts, then answer, "He'll deal with it."

"That sounds optimistic," she mutters, with hurt in her voice.

"Have I ever lied to you?"

"Yes."

I smirk. "Recently?"

A reluctant huff escapes her. "No."

"Then trust me again," I say, voice dropping. "I want you there, Valentina. I want you sitting at their table with me, not shunned from my family while everyone else decides who you are. And once they meet you, they'll love you as much as I do."

Tension explodes.

Did I just say I loved her?

It's just a phrase.

Do I?

I quickly add, "I'll be over after I finish working. See you then." I hang up before I get myself into more trouble.

Why did I say that?

I try to push it out of my mind and return to my office. I swivel my chair away from the monitors and stare at the city through the window. Traffic crawls. Clouds stack low. The apartment suddenly feels smaller than it did ten minutes ago.

"Fuck it," I mumble, get up, and go over to Valentina's, surprising her when I walk in unannounced.

She's in her closet, fretting over clothes. Her black satin robe's tied tight around her waist.

I ask, "What are you doing?"

She jumps, then spins like she's ready to assassinate me.

"Easy," I tease, holding up my hands.

"What are you doing here?"

I wiggle my eyebrows. "Missed my wife." I close the gap between us and kiss her long and hard. She whimpers against my mouth, clutching my shoulders, and then I retreat, repeating, "So what's going on in here?'"

She scrunches her face. "I don't know what to wear tonight."

"Something hot," I say with a grin.

She laughs and slaps my arm with the back of her hand. "I can't be too sexy."

"Minx, it doesn't matter what you wear. You're going to look sexy."

Her face heats.

I shuffle through her clothes, then pull out a red dress. It's not too fancy but still a showstopper. "Wear this. You look great in red."

"I do?"

"Duh."

She bites her lip.

My grin falls. "What's wrong?"

She doesn't respond for a second, then her tone softens. "What if they hate me?"

"They won't. They have to get to know you."

"You don't know that."

"I know Brenna. She'll be nervous and blunt and probably overshare, and by the end of the night, she'll probably hug you. But she understands you're mine, and I am not giving you up."

"That doesn't exactly fix the 'hate me' part."

"Yes, it does."

She exhales slowly, and something in my chest shifts with it. She glances at the garment. "Are you sure I should wear that dress?"

The question comes out smaller than her usual tone. I insist, "Wear it or pick something different. Whatever makes you walk into a room as if you could bulldoze it. But don't take your knife. We're aiming for approachable tonight."

"Says the man who gave me a weapon in my mask," she shoots back.

"That's for council business. Tonight is family. I'll carry the weapons."

She corrects, "Your family. Not mine."

I correct, "My family and yours. I'm not married to myself."

"You aren't?"

"Pretty sure."

Her eyes drift over me. She offers, "You clean up nicely, O'Malley." She smooths a hand over my chest. "Brenna will probably approve."

"I am not worried about Brenna's approval," I say, sliding my hands down to her hips. "I am worried about yours."

She arches a brow. "You think I would punish you for bringing me to dinner?"

"I think you might punish me later for how it goes," I answer, letting my thumbs trace slow circles against her dress. "So I think I need to collect interest in advance."

Her lips curve, eyes dropping to my mouth. "Interest?"

"Collateral," I amend, dipping my head.

I kiss her, not gently. There's no point pretending dinner is all that's on my mind. Her mouth opens under mine, the taste sharp and addictive. She steps in, closing the last of the distance, pressing fully against me. One of her hands goes to the back of my neck, the other slides under my shirt at the hem. She drags her nails along my bare skin.

Relentless heat slams through me. I walk her backward until her knees hit the mattress and she tumbles onto it with a small, startled sound that turns into a low laugh.

"We're going to be late if I don't shower and wash my hair," she warns, even as she hooks a finger in my belt loop and pulls me down over her.

"Fashionably late," I murmur against her throat, kissing down the column of it, tasting the hint of whatever lotion she used, reveling in the way her breath hitches.

"If we are late, Brenna will blame me," she protests weakly.

"We won't be. There's plenty of time for a quickie. Besides, if we're late, I'll tell her I couldn't keep my hands off my wife."

Her pupils blow wide, and her fingers tighten at my nape.

I kiss her neck, murmuring, "My wife is coming to dinner after I ruin her lipstick."

"Then you'll have to take a shower to hide the evidence."

"Great. I'll show you a good time there, too," I boast.

She laughs, low and genuine, and whatever anxiety she had about tonight drains out of the room, replaced by something hotter, stronger, more dangerous. It has nothing to do with clans and councils and everything to do with us.

For a few stolen minutes, I'm convinced that everything will be okay.

Valentina

Chapter

TWENTY-FIVE

Brax's mouth drags up my throat. He nibbles on my pulse until it's running so fast my vision blurs. His hands slide along my hips, anchoring me against him as if the entire world has narrowed to the inches between our bodies.

Every thought I had about Finn, Brenna, and dinner evaporates. There's nothing careful about the way he kisses me. There's no hesitation or conflict, just his intention to consume every part of my being.

I fist the collar of his shirt and yank him closer, swallowing the low sound he makes as I slide my leg against the inside of his. His thigh muscles tighten. His grip on my waist sharpens, pinning me to him.

I slide my hands under his boxers, stroking his shaft and rubbing the tip with my thumb.

"Slow down," he breathes against my mouth.

"Why? Thought this was a quickie?" I answer, biting his lower lip.

His breath stutters. "Doesn't mean I want to cum in two seconds."

I snicker, then flip out from under him. He turns on his back, and I stand over him. His eyes light up, and I unzip his pants. "These have to go." I grab the waistband and yank them off, displaying his hard erection.

Flames burn on his expression. He takes his finger and circles it in the air, ordering, "Take that robe off."

I slowly untie the belt, then slip it off. It falls to the floor. "Is this what you want, dear hubby?"

He scans my body, then mumbles, "Hotter than Wonder Woman." I glance at my chest, and he grabs me and tugs me over him.

I can't dwell on my branded mark. I shriek, laughing.

He smacks his palm into my ass and keeps it there. "I've missed you."

"I've missed you," I admit, my heart pitter-pattering.

He moves his hands to my thighs, then yanks my knees next to his hips. "Quickie now. Longer session after dinner."

I lean down, smile against his lips, and sink over him.

"Fucking hell, Minx," he groans.

My breath hitches into his. His palm hits my ass cheek again. The sting bounces to my core. His mouth claims me harder, his tongue moving deeper against mine.

I roll my hips, taking all of him in, then pulling away. He pushes me back as soon as there's only an inch of him inside me. I moan, breath shaking harder.

Heat pools low in my stomach, spreading through me in a slow, irresistible sweep. His shirt brushes my skin, and he drags a knuckle down my spine.

I tremble, whimpering louder, and rotating my hips faster.

His voice dips, quiet and heavy. "That's my wife."

Wife.

Every time he calls me that pride fills me. It's unexpected, not a feeling I ever allow. I realize it's because he sounds proud to claim me as his.

He kisses the corner of my mouth, mumbling, "I love watching you unravel."

Love.

It's the second time he's said it today.

Did he mean it on the phone when he said it?

I counter, "I don't unravel." My pussy throbs around him.

He smirks, dragging two fingers up the inside of my thigh. "You're unraveling right now." He pushes his thumb against my clit and circles.

I gasp.

His eyes darken in satisfaction, the shift so blatant it courses down my chest. He kisses me again. It's slow at first, then deeper, then with a hunger that threatens to set the entire room on fire. His hand grips my ass tighter.

I lift my hips, unapologetically inviting more adrenaline, and it rolls through my veins.

He circles his thumb faster and thrusts harder. "Valentina," he murmurs against my jaw, voice low and reverent. "God, you're—"

He doesn't finish. Words get lost when his mouth finds the spot under my ear that turns my pulse chaotic. My fingers thread through his hair, tugging gently, guiding him back to my lips.

His fingers draws slow arcs that send heat sparking across my skin, pulling me under in the best possible way.

I arch against him, and he lets out a muffled growl.

He lifts his head, forehead pressing to mine, our breaths mingling.

"You good?" he asks, voice rough from the way he's holding himself in check.

I drag my nails down his back, deliberate, slow enough to make his teeth clench. I pant, "Do I look unsure?"

His eyes flicker shut for a single heartbeat. He pins them on me and orders, "You have to come first."

"Then...make...me...oh *Dio!* Oh *Dio!* Oh *Dio!*" I blurt out as I fall over the cliff. Endorphins burst in my cells, and white light flashes.

"Fucking hell, Minx," he grits, thrusts a few more times, then a rumble drags from his throat. He grips me tighter and drops his face into the curve of my neck. His body convulses under mine.

The adrenaline heightens, then slowly falls again against his shudders. His hot breath beats into my neck. My vision returns to normal.

He circles his arms around me and holds me tight to him, stroking my back.

Dinner with his family.

"Brax."

"Mmm?"

"You're going to make us late."

He kisses the base of my throat. "I don't care."

I curl into his body for another minute, then moan. I push up off him. "I don't want to be late. That can't be my first impression."

His lips twitch. "Finn already met you."

I wince. "Don't remind me."

He chuckles. "I thought you looked hot with all the whipped cream on you."

My cheeks reheat. I groan, wincing. "And you had to remind me."

He chuckles, then nips lightly at my collarbone. "Maybe we should skip dinner and stay here all night."

I grip his jaw and force him to look at me. "Really?"

His face falls. "No. We need to go."

I nod, nervous. I've been since he called and gave me hope that Finn and Brenna will forgive him and give me a chance. And if that's possible, I want it. Not just for him but me too. I haven't had family since my parents died.

His hand slides into my hair, tugging just enough to pull a small gasp from me. He orders, "Get off me before I decide dinner doesn't happen."

"You started this," I remind him.

"I'll finish it when we get back."

Heat shoots through me so sharply my breath stumbles. He watches the reaction strike, and wicked satisfaction crosses his face. It makes me want to shove him back down and get a replay.

He kisses me once before easing me off his lap. "Let's get ready."

I stand with shaky legs.

He straightens his shirt, still breathing unsteadily, and looks at me like he wants to pull me back into the bed and forget the outside world exists. He warns, "We're not done here."

"I never said we were," I reply, shooting him a coy look and sauntering into the bathroom.

He whistles, and I laugh, then jump in the shower. I wash my hair, dry and curl it, then put on my makeup. I slip into the dress and heels and step out of the closet.

He mutters, "You're going to be the end of me, Minx."

My flutters erupt.

He grabs my hand and escorts me through the building to his Mustang. He holds open the door, and I slide in. He gets in next to me.

My anxiety flares the second Brax turns the key and the engine roars to life. The Mustang vibrates beneath us. It's steady, powerful, and impatient, mirroring the way my nerves climb up my gut. I keep my hands folded in my lap, fingers tight, then loose, then tight again as he pulls out of my parking garage and onto the street.

He glances at me, reading every twitch and micro-expression I don't have the energy to hide. "You okay, Minx?"

I watch the city blur past my window. "I'm thinking."

"About what?"

"About Finn possibly stabbing me with a fork during dinner."

His mouth curves. "Finn prefers the steak knife."

"That's reassuring."

He laughs under his breath. "He won't stab you. Not tonight."

"What a relief," I mumble.

"Take a deep breath. Everything will be fine," he confidently states.

I crush my fingers together again.

He reminds me, "Brenna invited us. You've already got another ally."

"Because she said she either wants to 'adopt me or bury me'?" I ask.

"It was a joke, Minx, relax," he orders. Then he reaches over and slides his palm across my thigh.

My breathing settles by a fraction.

He reassures, "We walk in together, and I'll stay beside you the entire time. If you want to leave early, we leave early. If Finn says something stupid, I shut it down. Sound good?"

I nod. "Yeah."

His hand doesn't leave my thigh for the rest of the drive. He veers into an older neighborhood.

Finn and Brenna's house sits on a quiet street lined with mature trees and soft lighting. Brax parks, kills the ignition, and turns to me before I can open the door. "You ready?"

"No."

"Good." He leans in to kiss me, his lips twitching, then says, "Let's go."

He gets out, opens my door, takes my hand, and leads me up the driveway.

I try not to think about Finn sharpening steak knives.

Brax knocks and tugs me into his waist. Within seconds, the door swings open.

Brenna greets us in fitted black jeans and a cream sweater. She offers me a cautious smile. Her voice is warm, but measured. "You must be Valentina."

I straighten, returning her same expression. "I am."

"I'm Brenna." She steps aside. "Come in. Dinner's almost ready."

Brax's hand finds the small of my back, guiding me forward.

Finn stands in the living room with his arms crossed over his chest, shoulders stiff, jaw clenched. His eyes track every inch of me in one sharp sweep. It's just as calculating, guarded, and suspicious as it was in Brax's apartment.

A chill runs down my spine.

He hates me.

"Finn," Brax greets.

"Brax." Finn nods once toward me. "Valentina."

"Nice to see you again, Finn," I respond, steady even though my stomach twists.

He doesn't smile or scowl. His eyes continue to watch me.

Brenna announces, "I'm ready for a drink. Valentina, do you drink wine?"

"Am I Italian?"

She laughs. "Red good?"

"Please."

"Good. If you didn't like red wine, I'd have to question everything."

I smile, appreciating the effort she's making. I add, "You have a lovely home."

Her eyes dart around the gray-colored walls. "Thanks. I've been thinking of giving it a facelift."

"Really? It's so nice," I genuinely state.

"It's been like this for a while. I kind of want a color change." She turns her attention to Finn.

He doesn't move.

"Finn, go pour some whiskey for you and Brax," she instructs.

He tears his stare off me for a moment.

She tosses him a warning look.

He caves and walks toward the bar.

She grabs a bottle of wine out of the fridge and opens it. She fills two glasses and hands me one.

Finn hands Brax a crystal tumbler of whiskey.

Brenna toasts, "Welcome to the family, Valentina." She holds her glass out, then nudges Finn.

He raises his glass and mumbles, "Welcome."

Brax tugs me closer.

My pulse ticks higher. I clear my throat. "Thank you. And for having us for dinner."

"Anytime," she states.

We click glasses, and the smooth, full-bodied, rich with berries and oak slides down my throat. I comment, "This is delicious."

"It's from a wine tour the girls and I took last year. Should we sit?" she asks.

"Yes," Brax replies and leads me to the couch. We settle in, and he puts his hand on my thigh.

Brenna takes a sip, then inquires, "So how did you two meet?"

My anxiety flares.

Brax answers, "Through friends."

"Oh? Who?" she asks.

It makes my nerves oscillate faster. I look at him, feeling ill.

He lies, "Kirill and Fiona."

Finn shifts on his seat.

"Ah. I see," she replies and takes another sip. Before any more interrogation can begin, she stands. "Okay, stay there. Finn, help me bring everything out."

He grunts something that might be an agreement. They disappear into the kitchen.

I exhale, leaning closer to Brax. "I'm going to combust."

"You're doing great."

"Finn looks like he wants to skin me alive."

"He doesn't do that to women," Brax deadpans.

My eyes widen.

He chuckles, then presses a kiss to my temple. "Relax. Brenna already likes you."

"How do you know that?"

"She didn't sling wine on you."

"She does that?"

He grins. "Only when it's warranted. Welcome to the O'Malleys."

Brenna returns carrying a large platter. The rich pomegranate glaze, savory lamb, and caramelized aromatics drift through the air.

Finn follows with the sides.

My mouth waters and stomach growls. I realize I haven't eaten today.

We move to the table. The lamb shoulder glistens under the light, its ruby glaze lacquered across tender meat that looks like it would fall apart at the slightest touch. Roasted garlic and herb couscous sit beside it, dotted with pine nuts. Charred broccolini drizzled with lemon-tahini adds a bright, earthy aroma.

Brenna takes her seat. "Let's dig in."

Finn cuts the lamb and I try not to focus on the knife, but I watch him carefully. He puts slabs on plates and hands me one first.

"Thank you."

He grunts again, then passes plates to the others.

I bring a piece to my mouth, and the second it hits my tongue, the world narrows to tender, bold, and savory flavor. There's the slightest sweetness from the pomegranate and warmth from cinnamon and pepper.

Brax groans. "This is so good, Brenna."

"Agree. It's incredible," I compliment and take a bite of couscous.

Brenna beams. "Thank you. I've been perfecting this one."

"It's one of my favorites," Brax adds.

Her expression softens even more. "You used to beg me to make this when you were younger."

Brax scoffs, "Beg? I don't beg. I requested."

"No. You begged," Brenna insists, smiling.

Finn grunts again, but his lips twitch.

The conversation threads itself more easily after that. It's not totally effortless, but smoother than I expected.

Brenna and I talk about yoga. She asks how I have such a beautiful Italian accent, and we end up exchanging Italian sayings. Before I know it, I'm relaxed and laughing.

Finn finally speaks. "Where in Italy did you grow up?"

I nervously answer him, and he slowly lets down his guard a bit.

Brax refuses to take his hand off me, sometimes teasing my inner thigh so my brain doesn't want to function.

Halfway through the meal, Brenna curls her fingers around her wine-glass. "Valentina, what about your family? Do they live in Chicago?"

The question drops like a stone into my chest. I straighten my fork on my plate. "I…don't have any family left."

Her expression shifts to sympathy. She lowers her voice. "None?"

"My parents died in a plane crash. There's no family left. Well, none I associate with," I add, thinking about how Luca won't ever accept me. And Zara's family, but I don't want to get into that conversation. It's best to keep it under wraps.

Plus, I can never tell the real truth.

My uncle Salvatore killed my parents in a ritual when I was sixteen. Then he told me I was to forgive him and let him raise me as his, or he'd put me in a brothel. I chose to play the game, vowing to get a seat at the table so I could be the one making decisions on rituals and not him. No one should lose their parents for no reason. Mine did nothing except fall in love. Salvatore only killed them because he didn't like my mother's blood, and that defies the purpose of the Underworld.

Now, he's dead. Sean killed him to save Zara.

Brax's hand clamps gently around my thigh under the table. It's protective, steady, and grounding.

Brenna's voice softens. "I'm so sorry."

I nod. "Thank you."

Finn says nothing, but his gaze flickers, sharp and assessing.

Brax clears his throat, almost defensive. "She has us now."

Brenna smiles faintly. "Yes, she does."

I blink hard, not expecting the emotions welling in my chest. Before I can stop myself, I blurt out, "I'm sorry. I just lied and you deserve better than that. Zara's my cousin. She and I have gotten really close. Luca used to love me but now…" I turn away and blink hard.

Brax slides his thumb over my thigh.

I look back at Brenna, adding, "Luca won't have anything to do with me anymore because of my father. It's complicated."

Silence electrifies the room.

Crap. Why did I just admit all that?

I don't dare look at Finn. I glance down at my plate.

Brenna says, "Luca's missing out. I'm sorry to hear that."

I meet her gaze.

She smiles then stands. She chirps, "Dessert time. I made a dark chocolate tart with cherry glaze. Valentina, want to help me?"

"Yes," I say instantly, grateful for the escape.

We carry plates into the kitchen. The moment we're alone, Brenna places a hand on my arm. "You're doing great."

I blink, unsure how to respond.

She adds, "Finn's protective. He's slow to trust, but when he does, it's permanent."

"Permanent in the good way?" I ask lightly.

Brenna laughs. "Yes, in the good way. And deep down, he wants to get things back to where they were with Brax. It's killing him, but he's so damn stubborn."

"I can see that," I comment.

She winces. "Sorry."

A genuine laugh escapes me. Tension drains from my shoulders.

She adds, "We should probably get back." She picks up the tart.

We return to the table, serve dessert, and finish the night with lighter conversation. It's nothing deep or sharp, just small bridges forming where cliffs once stood.

When we finally leave, Brax slides his hand along my back as we step onto the porch. The night is quiet and the air's cool.

He exhales when he gets to the car. "Thank you for going."

"That wasn't bad," I say.

"You mean Brenna wasn't."

I shrug, unable to hide my smile. "Finn didn't slice me to pieces. And she likes me. That's a start."

"Miracle one accomplished," he states in his sarcastic voice.

But it is. And I don't take it lightly.

If Brenna's going to allow me into the family with open arms, I'm going to dive headfirst.

Brax

Chapter

TWENTY-SIX

The city exhales under the noon sun, but my curtains black it all out. I sit alone in my office, the glow from my monitors the only thing keeping the room lit. My apartment is too quiet, and the silence stretches across the space, heavy with a tension I haven't been able to shake for weeks.

I miss my wife.

I've barely seen her. Liam has Sean and I doing the same shitty work newbies get assigned. I usually see Valentina for an hour or so, then get on my computers, trying to find out who was behind the attempted coup.

She came over a few times while I was working, but it always ended up with us in bed, so I got no work done. As much as I prefer to spend time with her, I know my job is important. If they come after Kirill and Fiona, they won't stop coming after Valentina. And I'm not going to allow that.

It's felt like forever since the Underworld has summoned me. There have been no surprise rituals, no messages, no emergencies to fix. Valentina hasn't had any either. And the lack of activity feels off.

Zara's adjusting to life with twins, with little help from Sean. Unfortunately, he's in the same boat I am.

Kirill's trying to act like ruling the most dangerous organization on the planet is something he can do with a straight posture and a steady jaw. But he's also over-the-moon excited about Fiona's pregnancy.

It's all normal life with a bomb waiting to explode. And time's running out to change whatever course the Omni have us on.

My focus drops to the screen again. A red square blinks in the corner. I peer closer to figure out if it's another security message or a leftover warning from one of the firewalls I pushed too hard. So I stare, watching the slow, steady pulse. It speeds up, then slows again. But it's not timed the same, so after counting out several rounds, I decide the heartbeat has to be a human, and heat tightens in the center of my chest. It's sharp, pulled taut by instinct and anger.

I move the cursor near the edge of the pulsing square, not touching it, just tracing the air above the glow. The second I get close, the beat speeds up and the lights get brighter.

My jaw tightens. It's not a firewall. It's a trace. Someone on the other side of this is watching me the same way a predator watches a twitch in the grass.

I tap the arrow key. Nothing happens. Then I lightly drag the mouse halfway across the edge of the square, barely grazing it.

The heartbeat erupts into a rapid pounding rhythm, and a line flashes across the screen.

INTERFERENCE WILL RESULT IN REMOVAL.

My shoulders push back slowly as the truth slides through me. They see me. They always do.

I let the cursor hover for a moment. Then I test it carefully, moving it a hair. The screen responds instantly. A new warning bursts across the top.

YOUR SEAT WILL BE EMPTY FOR OBSTRUCTION.

A chill prickles across my skin. I pick up my phone and send a text.

> Me: You seeing this?

> Sean: Loud and clear.

I exhale through my nose, gritting my teeth. My fingers hover above the keyboard. I don't know what's on the other side of this pulse, but I need to find out. If I access it, I'll discover the truth. Otherwise, they wouldn't be trying to scare me. So I tap another key, and the heartbeat jumps again, slamming into a frenzied pace.

Another line flashes.

STAY BACK. LAST WARNING.

Sure it is, motherfucker.

My phone vibrates.

> Sean: At the top of the minute, type this in. I'll do the same.

He sends a long line of code.

> Me: Got it.

I stare at the clock on my cell. It switches to the next minute, and I type fast.

My hard drive whirs. A second square appears beside the first, pulsing in sync with the heartbeat like a mirrored organ. Then a directory opens, but only for a fraction of a second.

Still, I catch a glimpse before the system slams shut again, locking everything behind a wall thick as steel. It's a handful of lines, but every one of them drives something hot and unforgiving through my spine.

SCARLET HOUR – SUPPLEMENT RECORD

SUBJECT: V.A. SCARLET HOUR — COMPLETE

CEREMONY OF EXPOSURE – SUPPLEMENT RECORD

FAILED: CEREMONY OF EXPOSURE

SUBJECT: S.O. — ONGOING

SUBJECT: Z.O. — ONGOING

SUBJECT: B.O. — ONGOING

SUBJECT: V.O. — ONGOING

SUBJECT: K.P. — ONGOING

SUBJECT: F.P. — ONGOING

My throat tightens, and my fists clench, but fear swirls into my anger. The same people who are behind the coup came after my wife when they branded her chest. And now, they have other plans.

The screen turns black, then the same warnings start scrolling. When **SUBJECT: V.O. — ONGOING** pops up, I click before it disappears.

Then my gut twists with bile.

DIRECTIVE 19: BREEDING CYCLE – CONFIDENTIAL

SUBJECT: V.A. — REQUIRED PARTICIPATION

STATUS: ENFORCEABLE

The last line blinks over and over. I swallow hard and click on it again.

Then there's a document stamped in bloodred ink. At the top sits the Underworld skull, followed by a title that punches the air out of my lungs.

THE SACRED LINE MUST BE ENFORCED - MONTHLY HARVEST UNTIL 40 THEN ELIMINATE.

A chart unfolds. It's clinical, organized with obsessive precision. Bloodlines. Fertility windows. Genetic compatibility matrices.

Valentina's name sits at the center of a grotesque diagram, branching into hundreds of projected offspring.

A series of bullet points scroll across the screen, making my gut flip faster.

MANDATE: OVUM EXTRACTION TO COMMENCE UPON NEXT FULL MOON.

TARGET OUTPUT: 6–12 VIABLE EMBRYOS PER CYCLE.

GESTATIONAL ASSIGNMENTS: VARIED (SEE ATTACHED PAIRING LIST).

My stomach knots into raw violence.

STRONGEST OFFSPRING WILL BE ALLOCATED TO FAMILIES DEEMED MOST FIT FOR THEIR UPBRINGING. WEAK SOLD TO HIGHEST BIDDER.

A video mock-up follows. There are metal tables, surgical restraints, torches with masked men and women, and my wife naked with only her eye mask on.

Another file appears.

FIRST ROUND — SURROGATES

I click on it and only grow sicker. Faces of a dozen younger women appear. Some don't even look eighteen. Then their voices startle me, one at a time, all saying the same thing.

"The lineage belongs to the table, not the woman."

The page vanishes, leaving a photo of Valentina, bare, with her red V bright across her chest.

I hold my breath, my insides shaking, fists clenched.

They don't want her allegiance. They want her for a breeding program that steals her DNA and children. And then they decide who they think is worthy and sell the undesirables to the black market.

My phone buzzes. I glance at it.

Sean: Jesus Christ. I know you saw that.

My insides shake with rage. I stare at the blinking red square for a moment. Determined to find out more, I plug in more code, trying to find out who's behind this disgusting plan.

Sean: I'm putting more code in.

I don't reply, my fingers already working at lightning speed. It takes a few minutes, then there's a series of four beeps, and images pop up. Some faces I've seen; others I haven't.

Sean: It's the entire Omni and Royal Council. Everyone but the six of us.

Another file begins to run. Our faces appear with ELIMINATE stamped across them. Valentina's is the last. It flashes, disappears, and my computer fans whir harder before the screen turns dark.

"Fuck, not again," I bark, hitting the on switch, but I already know I'm dead. It's the fifth time it's happened.

Sean: You burned, too?

Me: Yep.

Sean: I'll order another set. We need to know what they're planning for the rest of us.

I shove away from the desk and let out a bitter breath.

Valentina's not safe.

The hairs on my neck rise. I leave the office, grab my jacket, and lock up my apartment. More anger rips through me the second the elevator doors shut. I text her.

> Me: Where are you?

> Valentina: At Fiona's.

> Me: Stay put.

> Valentina: Why?

> Me: I'll come get you. Don't go anywhere, Minx.

> Valentina: Brax, what's wrong?

> Me: Not over the phone. Just promise me you won't go anywhere.

> Valentina: Okay.

Valentina should be safe. She's done nothing but give her loyalty to this twisted cult. And the image of her face with ELIMINATE across it won't stop hammering inside my skull.

I hit the parking garage, climb into my Mustang, and take the fastest route to Sean's penthouse.

Traffic is light. The city glints with glass, metal, money, and all the rot hidden between the cracks. I grip the wheel harder. Every street I turn down reminds me that Chicago operates under invisible rules the public will never see, rules dictated by an organization so powerful it has its own traditions, rites, and punishments.

They plan to steal my wife's eggs then kill her.

A rage so deep fills me. I can barely see. I park on the street, get through Sean's building, and into his penthouse.

The soft murmur of hushed baby noises drifts from down the hall, heightening my anger. Zara stands in the doorway, her hair in a loose knot, two swaddled bundles pressed against her chest. She rocks side to side with the ease of someone who's memorized their children's breathing patterns. She smiles in surprise, whispering, "Hey. They just drifted off. Walk quietly."

My throat tightens at the sight of the twins' tiny fists peeking from their blankets. They're pure innocence with zero knowledge of the kingdom their grandfather built.

I lower my voice. "Hey, Zara."

Her hushed voice warns, "If you wake them, I'm making you stay until two a.m. to rock them back to sleep."

"Noted. Sean in the office?"

She nods. "He's in one of his moods. You're officially warned."

"He tell you why?" I murmur.

Worry fills her expression. "Not yet."

I give the babies a final look and brush past her. I don't knock and open the door.

Sean stands behind his oversized desk, rolling his shoulders like he's minutes away from punching the wall. The second he sees me, he drags both hands through his hair. His voice is low but threaded with something sharp. "You saw everything I saw?"

I seethe, "That was a map of the future. And if we don't intercept, we're all dead."

He stays silent.

I bark, "They aren't getting to my wife's eggs, Sean!"

His jaw clenches. His eyes cut toward the window as though he can physically see the Underworld moving through the streets. He finally pins a frustrated expression on me. "They're all involved."

"No shit."

"It's too large. We're fucked."

"Those are all semantics. The system is rotted beyond repair. It needs to be destroyed," I point out.

Sean leans against the wall. "You don't take down an empire, Brax. You maneuver around it. You cut off the pieces, try to devour it, and leave the structure intact. That's how you stay alive."

"No. You burn it to the ground."

He shoots me a warning glare. "You're talking about a death wish."

"Maybe. But it's the only thing that guarantees my wife won't end up on a slab having her eggs pulled out of her body every month until she's forty and they decide she's too old to breed."

Sean's color drains from his face.

I sarcastically grit, "I thought I was the only one feeling ill."

Sean's stare turns more lethal. "Of course not. And we don't know what's in the other files, either. You think I want Zara in danger? Or our twins?"

"That's why we have to take them out," I insist.

"You think I don't wake up every night wondering if the next message from the Underworld will demand one of them as tribute?" he snaps.

"Then you know I'm right."

His voice drops; a growl brews underneath. "It's impossible to slash the throat of a beast. We find the traitors and take them out one by one."

I step closer, fire rising inside me. "And the next traitors? And the next? And then the ones after that?"

He doesn't speak.

I point out, "You know how this works. Every time you fix one thing, three more erupt. You can't repair a house built on burial grounds. You have to destroy it all."

"You think blowing it up won't kill innocent people?"

"I think leaving it alive guarantees that it will."

He rubs his temples. "You're not listening."

"I'm listening. And the next full moon my wife is on the fertility black market!" I hurl.

He sighs, scrubbing his hand over his face.

I point at him. "Accept the truth. Your father built this thing, hoping to create order. He dreamed of unity. He died before he understood what his actions created."

His expression fractures, the sadness and anger cracking just enough to reveal something raw underneath.

I lower my voice, asking, "Do you really think your father wanted all this?"

It detonates the space between us. He pushes off the wall, pacing so hard the floor nearly shakes. He snaps, "For all I know, he did want this fucked-up world. Maybe he wanted masks, rituals, and punishments. Maybe he wanted power above everything."

"What's going on?" a soft voice says behind us.

We both turn.

Zara stands in the doorway. Her eyes rim with worry. "Loop me in. What are you arguing about?"

Sean tenses, and I step forward.

"The entire system is broken. Utopia doesn't exist now and never will. It's rotten to the marrow. They plan to harvest Valentina's eggs every month until she's 40 then kill her. We have no idea what they're planning for the rest of us. We didn't get into those files yet. But they're trying to orchestrate all of our executions. And it won't stop at the six of us. It'll eventually include the twins."

Zara's color drains down her face. She puts a hand on her stomach. She swallows hard and pins her gaze on her husband. "Sean?"

He stares at her with an equally pale expression, grinding his molars.

I step closer. "We saw our faces on an execution directive. Yours. Sean's. Kirill's. Fiona's. Valentina's. Mine."

Her eyes go glassy with a quiet terror that hits me harder than any threat on a screen. She accuses, "You kept this from me?"

Sean closes the distance between them in two strides and wraps an arm around her waist. "I'm sorry. I just learned about it and didn't want you to worry."

She presses her palm harder against her stomach, like she's anchoring herself. "Didn't want me to worry? Sean, you'd better tell me everything right now."

I speak before he can, rattling off every warning the Underworld shoved in our faces, along with the inconsistencies that prove these aren't just rogue factions. They're part of the backbone of the entire operation.

She listens without interrupting. By the time I finish, she looks between the two of us with steady, haunted clarity. She states, "So you want to destroy it?"

"Yes."

"How?"

"Zara! This is a slippery slope! We could all end up dead, including the babies!" Sean frets.

"We're dying if we don't!" I argue.

Zara glances between us, then lifts her chin toward Sean. "You think you can fix it from the inside?"

"Yes."

"How?" She arches her eyebrows.

Tense silence forms.

"You can't. You know you can't. You'll always be hunting and dodging. We all will," I insist.

He pins his green eyes on me. "I don't know any other way."

Zara softly asks, "Do you think this is what your father envisioned?"

He casts a pained expression on her. Defeat fills his voice. "No. Unless he was a sick bastard instead of who I knew him to be."

Silence stretches through the room.

Zara's voice softens even further. "Then why are you still trying to save something that doesn't deserve to exist?"

"I'm not trying to save it. I'm trying to keep us alive."

"There's only one way. Brax is right," she affirms.

Sean's jaw flexes, like he's chewing through twenty years of inherited duty.

She adds, "Let's talk to Kirill. He's the only one who knew your father well enough to speak on his intentions."

He swallows hard. "What if this is what my father wanted?"

A chill runs down my spine.

Zara steps forward and puts her hand on his cheek. "Is this what you want for our children?"

He shakes his head. "No."

"Then you have your answer."

He inhales deeply, then slowly nods.

She pins her gaze on me. "We need to speak to Kirill, Fiona, and Valentina. If we're going to do this, the six of us all need to be on the same page."

"Zara—"

"What, Sean?" She spins, eyes narrowing.

He drags a hand down his face. "This could backfire. The chances of it blowing up in our faces are higher than success."

Zara crosses her arms. "There's no other option."

My pulse bangs between my ears.

He finally agrees. "Okay. But if we do this, there's no going back. And we don't know what Fiona and Kirill will say."

"They almost got beheaded," I remind him.

He drops a bomb. "What about your wife?"

"What about her?" I defensively ask.

"Is she going to agree to this? She's obsessed with her seat," he points out.

My gut flips. I assert, "Was obsessed."

"So she's not loyal to the Underworld anymore?" he challenges.

Tension mounts.

I affirm, "She'll be on board. They're trying to take her out too. Plus, once she finds out about their sick baby operation, she isn't going to have any loyalty left."

"Are you sure about that?"

"Yes," I say through gritted teeth.

Zara interjects, "Brax is right. There's no way Valentina is going to agree to being a baby machine. I'll call Fiona. We can meet tonight."

I stand straighter, with the truth hardening inside me like tempered steel.

I didn't crack open the Underworld's system to steal their secrets.

I cracked it open so I can burn it to the ground. And now there's no choice but to do it.

"There's one more issue we have to address," I say and pick up the phone. I dial Liam.

Sean and Zara stare at me in question.

It rings twice. He answers, "Brax."

"I need you to come to Sean's penthouse. Immediately."

Sean's head jerks back.

"I'm busy and you don't give me orders," Liam snarls.

"This isn't a request. It's the most important thing you'll ever do," I insist.

The line turns quiet.

I add, "Bring your guns with you if you don't trust me. But get here soon." I hang up before he can ask any further questions.

"What are you doing?" Sean demands.

"We can't do this if we're on grave duty. And the only place that's safe for us to talk to him is here," I claim, knowing that the previous month, Sean built walls around his office that won't allow any spy devices to work. It's a safety net, and Kirill did the same to his entire penthouse.

"I'm going to check on the babies," Zara mumbles and leaves the room.

Sean and I both pace for a half hour until Liam finally shows up.

"This better be good," he booms, entering the room.

"Shut the door," Sean orders.

He slams it and steps forward. He points at us. "You two better start talking."

"We can't stay on graveyard duty," I start.

Liam's green eyes flare hot. He sneers, "This is what you called me here for?"

"Just listen," Sean says.

Liam's gaze narrows. He crosses his arms. His jaw twitches.

I step closer and lower my voice, even though the room is safe. "We are involved in something."

"No shit," he barks.

"We can't tell you everything right now."

"Jesus Christ, you two! I'm getting sick of this dog and pony show!" he roars.

I hold up my hand. "Just shut up a minute so you can understand what's happening!"

"You'd better watch your mouth," he warns.

I take a deep breath.

Sean interjects in a calmer tone. "Liam, please sit down."

He turns his scowl on him.

Sean points to his seat. "Sit here." Then he takes the chair across the desk and taps the one next to him. "Sit, Brax."

I obey, and Liam reluctantly does too. His glare intensifies.

I start, "What we're about to tell you can't leave this room. Not now, maybe ever. Understand?"

He leans closer. "Keep talking."

Sean informs, "The world my dad created is bigger than anything you'd ever imagined, and has representation from every crime family. Governments know about it and royalty bows to it."

Liam doesn't move.

I put my elbows on the desk. "We're taking it down. All we can tell you right now is we can't be on the graveyard shift. Relieve us of all duties, and when this is over, we'll take whatever punishment you want to give us. But if we don't do this, everything is at risk, including the clan."

He breathes through his nose.

Sean adds, "You have to trust us."

He scoffs. "I'm supposed to trust you right now?"

"Yeah. We're O'Malleys. If you didn't, deep down, still know that we wouldn't be sitting here. We'd already be in our graves," I claim.

A moment passes, then he asserts, "I need to know more."

"Sorry. This is all we can say right now," Sean reiterates.

Liam grinds his molars.

Sean rises. He goes to a picture, moves it, and a safe appears. "I'm going to write down the code. Memorize it. If anything happens to us, everything you want to know will be inside."

Liam's chest lifts high. He releases it and rises. "Fine. Give me the code."

Sean goes to his desk and writes it. He hands it to him.

Liam studies it.

"Have it memorized?" Sean asks.

"Yes."

Sean grabs the paper, goes to his fireplace, and lights it on fire. The edges curl and incinerate. Then he hits buttons on the safe. He directs Liam, "Put your palm on it."

Liam walks over and presses his hand on the screen.

It beeps several times, flashes red, then green, then blue. It pops open.

Before Liam can see anything, Sean shuts it. He reiterates, "Only if they take us out. Promise me?"

Liam nods. "Okay. I'll give you some leeway. You have my word." He spins, and his eyes dart between us. He finally orders, "Make sure you do whatever it is you need to do. I don't want to have to open this." He gives us a final look and then walks out.

Valentina

Chapter
TWENTY-SEVEN

$\mathcal{F}$iona drags the back of her wrist across her forehead, smearing flour in a streak that would irritate her on any normal day. Today, she doesn't care. She stands in front of the mixer, watching the dough hook turn inside the gleaming bowl, its thick weight slapping against the metal.

She woke up wanting three different kinds of cookies, a lasagna big enough to feed an army, homemade pasta, and the lemon-ricotta cake my mother used to make for every occasion. Zara, who never misses an opportunity to brag about anyone she loves, told Fiona, "I'm a 'little Italian kitchen witch' who can cook anything without measuring." So Fiona called me this morning and asked me to come over.

The invitation was welcome. Being bored has a strange way of making my thoughts turn heavy. Every time things get quiet, an odd, crawling uneasiness settles into my bones. It's been weeks without an Underworld message. And the same routine of my exhausted husband coming home in the early morning hours, only to shut himself in his office with a determination to find out the truth behind Kirill and Fiona's attempted assassination seems to never end. So, I nearly leapt out the door when she called me.

Now we're two hours into alternating between laughing, kneading dough, scolding each other for forgetting ingredients, and making an ungodly mess of her oversized gourmet chef's kitchen.

But then Brax texted, and the atmosphere turned heavy.

My stomach keeps dipping as though it's tracking a storm I can't see. The wooden spoon in my hand drags slowly through the bowl of creamy ricotta and sugar, creating smooth, pale swirls. I glance at the clock again.

Fiona notices. "You've looked at that clock nine times in the last ten minutes."

Heat creeps up my neck. "Sorry."

"Don't apologize." She turns off the mixer and leans a hip against the counter. "Is everything okay?"

"I don't know." I stir the bowl with more force than necessary. "Brax has something going on. He told me he's coming over and I can't leave without him."

Her eyebrows lift. "That's all he said?"

I nod. "He didn't want to talk about it over the phone."

She takes a deep breath and slowly releases it.

I ramble, "He's burning the candle at both ends. He barely sleeps, and when he does, he jolts awake like his brain refuses to let him rest."

Fiona narrows her eyes slightly. "Sounds familiar. Kirill does the same thing. That man would rather swallow a bullet than admit something's wrong to me."

"Same as Brax," I murmur.

She pushes off the counter, wipes her palms on a towel, and gestures at the ricotta. "That looks yummy."

"It is," I assure, then lose myself in the quiet rhythm, continuing to stir, yet my chest tightens. Brax found something, and it's so bad that he doesn't want me outside Kirill's protection.

What did he find?

My mind races. I finish making the dessert, and there's a buzz.

Fiona announces, "I bet that's Brax."

I wipe my hands on my apron, fingers trembling. I barely step past the kitchen when Brax barrels into the family room. Sean and Zara appear next, both carrying the twins.

Kirill enters the room, teasing, "Are we having a dinner party?"

Brax crosses the space between us. He tugs me into him as if he's been suffocating for hours, and I'm the only thing holding him to the earth. His arms band around me, tight, almost punishing, but not for me. It's against whatever shadow he's been wrestling.

"What's going on?" I mumble into his chest.

His jaw presses against my temple as he murmurs, "Don't worry. We're going to fill you in. I'm just glad you're safe." He hugs me again, stronger this time, then kisses the top of my head with a rawness that shoots through me like a current.

Safe.

My stomach twists.

A sharp, disgruntled cry pierces the space.

Zara bounces slightly, adjusting one of the swaddled babies. "Aw. I think River wants you, Valentina."

My chest warms instantly. I retreat from Brax's embrace.

River stretches his tiny hands in my direction, his fingers curling and uncurling in soft, desperate attempts to reach me.

"Hey, sweetie. It's okay," I coo, and take him from Zara.

He grips my hair and tugs.

"Whoa! Easy now," I laugh.

"River," Zara lightly scolds, removing his death grip from my hair. She moves my locks behind my shoulders.

"It's okay," I say, offering my pinky.

He grips it just as hard.

Kirill asks, "So? Are we having a dinner party?"

Brax announces, "We're going to burn the Underworld."

The room freezes.

Sean groans. "Jesus, you could have eased them into it."

Kirill's gaze turns sharp enough to cut through bone. "What did you just say?"

Brax repeats, "Every Omni. Every Royal Council member. Every one of them needs to get taken out. They're all involved in something so twisted it makes every ritual up until now look like kindergarten crafts."

Zara shifts her weight, her voice trembling with controlled anger. "They're going to kill all of us."

River lets out a small sigh, unaware of the storm brewing. He leans against my chest.

My heart slams against my rib cage. I kiss the top of his head. "What are you talking about?"

Fiona steps closer to Kirill. He slides his arm around her waist, as if to protect her.

Sean inhales deeply. "We got into one of their hidden databases. There are files documenting plans for the six of us. Execution directives. It's all been approved, and every Omni and Royal Council member has full knowledge."

The air thins around me. My mouth goes dry, but I stay silent as my brain scrambles to put the pieces together.

Then Brax's voice drops into something rough and lethal. "And that's not the worst of it."

Zara squeezes Sean's arm as if anchoring herself.

Brax's eyes meet mine, and I don't like what I see. There's anger mixed with fear.

I demand, "What is it?"

He steps closer. "It involves you."

My insides twist, then tremble. I barely get out, "How?"

"They plan on turning you into a breeding machine."

"Excuse me?" I blurt out.

Sean clears his throat. "It's true. They plan on extracting your eggs every month until you're 40. The strongest babies go to Underworld members of their choice. The weakest get sold on the black market."

Blood drains from my face to my toes. I gape at them, horrified. Then a cold rush drenches my limbs, crawling up my spine with icy fingers. I force words out. "No."

Brax adds, "They mapped out your cycles. They projected how many embryos they can pull per round. Their goal is six to twelve per cycle."

I open my mouth and shake my head, holding River tighter to me.

Fiona's hand flies to her mouth.

Kirill's expression detonates into something monstrous.

Sean continues, "They created pairing lists. Gestational assignments with surrogates. They plan to distribute your children like cattle."

A sharp ringing fills my ears. The world narrows. My knees go weak for a split second, but Brax's arm curls around my waist instantly, steadying me before I sway.

Brax finishes quietly. "At 40, they eliminate you. And that's why we're taking the Underworld out."

The ringing intensifies. My lungs struggle to expand, as if invisible hands are tightening around my ribs.

I stare at my husband, who would burn the entire secret society for me. And guilt eats me raw.

He fought for my seat with me. He watched me bleed for it. He married me for it. And now that same seat has turned into a cage designed to drain me until I'm no longer useful.

A wave of revulsion slams into me, hollow and electric, running through every nerve. "After everything I sacrificed, they want to use my body like I'm an incubator? They want my children? They want—" My words splinter. A sharp cracking sensation opens in my chest and spreads fast.

Brax tugs me closer, pressing his forehead to mine, voice frayed at the edges. "It's not happening. Do you hear me? Not a single hand is going to touch you."

River shifts against our chests. I hold him tighter, grounding myself through his small warmth.

Fiona blurts out, "This is sick. Why Valentina?"

Zara answers, "I assume they want a bloodline they can control and weaponize. She's pure Italian. Her DNA has Marino and Abruzzo in it."

"They're deranged," Kirill says, his jaw clenched so tightly his muscles twitch. "They've lost their humanity."

Zara asks, "Did they ever have humanity?"

The question hangs in the air, fueling my shock and horror.

The conversation erupts into a chaotic volley of questions and curses, strategy and disbelief.

Kirill demands, "Who authorized these files?"

Sean relays, "Every council member. Every Omni."

"So they're all involved?" Fiona asks in shock.

Brax affirms, "Yes. Everyone is on board with their plans."

Kirill growls, "I'll kill every one of them."

Sean warns, "There's more layers of security we haven't cracked. We don't know their plans for the rest of us. We just know we're all on the execution list when they get from us what they want."

Deafening silence fills the room.

Fiona asserts, "We're not letting them near Valentina."

Brax keeps one arm locked around me, as if he can shield me from shadows, pixels, and ghosts.

My entire life flashes before me. It's all been a lie, built on the belief that gaining my seat in the Underworld would give me power. I thought it would allow me to step into a position to work with the Omni to ensure the evil my uncle Salvatore inflicted upon my parents and other members never happened again.

How wrong could I have been?

River shifts again. His tiny fingers fist the fabric of my shirt.

They will never have my children.

I draw a steadying breath and lift my chin. "Tell me what the plan is."

Brax's eyes darken with a vow. "We burn the Underworld to ash."

"How?" I question.

We all stare at each other.

Sean rubs his face, pacing in front of the windows. Zara holds Willow, rocking gently, her expression a storm barely held together.

Fiona presses closer to Kirill. "This isn't like busting into a ritual."

Zara nods. "We need a plan that dismantles every pillar at once. Otherwise, they regroup and retaliate."

A knot tightens deep in my chest.

Sean slows his pacing and levels a grim stare. "The Underworld has too many secrets. They all need to go."

Fiona squeezes Kirill's fingers, but her voice is steady. "There are thousands of people in the membership. They're parents. They don't know what the Omni planned. They hide their fear behind masks."

"That doesn't make them innocent," Sean counters.

"It doesn't make them targets either," I snap, unable to stop the sharp edge in my tone. "If the Omni and the Royal Council engineered all of this, then go after them. But the membership doesn't have the power. They don't all deserve to die and leave their children orphans."

"We can't trust any of them," Sean insists.

Kirill interjects, low and cold. "Fiona and Valentina are right. You scorch from the top down."

My stomach twists, but I stay quiet.

Fiona asks, "What about all their backups? Their shadows? Their enforcers? If we kill leadership, the middle tier will scramble for power."

Kirill's expression darkens. "There will be mass chaos. Every branch will start eating its own. Then we will see who we take out next."

Brax's jaw ticks. "That will take years."

Kirill lifts an eyebrow. "But it's the right thing to do."

Sean crosses his arms. "We have to hit the infrastructure at the same time with simultaneous detonations at every point where the leadership or membership can meet. Nothing stays. Not the arena, chambers, or ritual spots. The fortress wing Kirill found beneath the archives goes with it. Every secret space gets buried."

The room drops cooler.

Kirill grinds his molars, then says, "That requires timing and precision. We'd need a demolition team that's willing to die for us."

Brax glances at Sean.

Sean meets his eye, nods once, then looks at Kirill. "We know exactly who can do it."

Fiona stiffens, suspicious. "Who?"

Brax finally declares, "The O'Connors."

The room jolts into stunned silence.

Fiona blinks. "What do you need our uncles for?"

Brax doesn't answer. He looks to Sean again.

Kirill interjects, "Because no one knows bombs better than them."

A chill races through me.

Sean grunts, then his lips twist. "That's right. Uncle Brody built explosives for fun when he was twelve."

Zara mutters, "They also built a smoke grenade that blinded a SWAT team for eighteen minutes."

Sean lifts a finger. "Allegedly."

Kirill grunts. "Allegedly, my ass."

Brax lifts his chin. "We need them."

I burst out before I can rein it in. "No. You can't blow up the membership. There are innocent people inside those walls. People with families."

Zara's voice softens. "She's right."

River shifts uneasily in my arms.

"I didn't say we'd blow it up with them inside. I just said it has to go off at the same time as when we take the Omni out," Sean states.

Kirill adds, "If there's nowhere to convene, it silences everything."

My blood thickens.

Brax insists, "They'll still come after us. If we're the only ones still standing, it's inevitable. The ones who believe the Omni protects them from the outside world will demand our blood."

The silence that follows is suffocating.

Fiona shakes her head. "They won't. Not if we show them what they wanted to do to Valentina."

The hairs on my neck rise again.

Zara adds, "Then we control the narrative. Kirill, those who want peace will look to you for answers. You can send communication electronically and tell them to stand down. Only those who are evil will try to rise up against us."

"Then we take them out," Brax says.

My throat tightens. Fear hits me. "What if something goes wrong? What if the arena collapses too early? What if the wrong surveillance catches your uncles, and that assumes they'll agree to this?"

Brax tugs me into him. "We won't allow for any mistakes."

Sean declares, "My uncles will need everything. Layouts. Entry points. Security spots. Air ducts. Tunnel maps."

Kirill answers, "I have everything."

Zara encourages, "Then we can do this."

Brax's grip on my waist tightens. He orders, "Sean, call Brody."

Brax

Several Days Later

Chapter
TWENTY-EIGHT

Steam curls through the bathroom doorway, drifting across the hardwood floor. Valentina stands in front of the mirror, head tilted, towel wrapped around the ends of her dark hair as she rubs gently, trying not to tangle it. The morning light spills across her bare shoulders, softening the sharp edges of her exhaustion and illuminating the bruise of worry under her eyes.

Several days have passed since we discovered what the Omni wanted to do to her. Those images of her on the operating slab still claw at the back of my mind in the quiet moments. I haven't slept more than two hours at a time since that night, but I hide my fear from her.

She drops the towel and reaches for the blow dryer. When she catches my reflection in the mirror, her lips curve gently. She murmurs, "You're watching me again."

I step behind her. My lips brush her neck. "Can't help it. You're the best thing in this fucked-up penthouse."

Her lips twitch. "This is a fucked-up penthouse?"

"You know what I mean, Minx," I offer, feeling like the walls are closing in on me. Ever since Kirill ordered none of us to leave, I've felt like a caged animal. I'm not used to not being able to come and go freely. And all the threats surrounding us aren't helping.

Sean had new computers arrive the day after we got here. After ensuring they weren't bugged, we set up shop in Kirill's office, the two of us spending most of our hours online, but not getting any further than before.

"Hopefully we can go home soon," she says, but neither of us knows how long this is going to last.

I slide my hands around her waist and kiss her cheek. "I'm going to go wait for the O'Connors."

She smiles. "Okay."

I give her another peck, then step back.

She turns on the hair dryer, tugging a wet brush through her long strands.

I give her a final glance before I change my mind and drag her into bed instead. I leave the bedroom, heading toward Kirill's office. The corridor stretches long and silent, every step echoing the tension of the last few days.

Sean is already inside, pacing like a caged wolf. Kirill stands near the windows, arms crossed, jaw tight, staring at the skyline as if mentally mapping out where he wants to watch the Underworld burn from.

"You ready?" I ask.

Kirill doesn't look away from the glass. "Yep."

A knock pounds against the door hard enough to rattle the hinges.

Four large Irishmen fill the threshold, broad-shouldered, thick-armed, unmistakably O'Connor. Brody steps inside first. A scar drags along his cheekbone, disappearing into the scruff of his jaw. His accent hits the air like a fist.

"Well, lads," he announces, sweeping the room with an assessing glare. "Which one of ya wants to tell us why ya dragged us out here? And the reason had better be worth the bloody airfare."

Behind him, Aidan flicks a lighter open, holds the flame too long, then snaps it shut with a smirk. Devin and Tynan step inside last, both watching everything with expressions that say they're just as curious and annoyed that they don't have any information on why they got summoned halfway across the world.

Kirill closes the door and gestures toward the seats. "Please. Sit."

Aidan flicks the lighter again. "Fecking hell, this better be serious."

"It is," Sean states.

The atmosphere shifts.

Brody's gaze snaps to Sean. "Start talking." He drops into the leather chair closest to the desk like he owns the place. Aidan leans against the wall, still playing with his lighter. Devin and Tynan stand shoulder to shoulder near the table, arms crossed.

Sean looks at me.

Brody fixes us with a stare. "Right. Let's hear it. What mess did ya soft-handed Chicago boys fall into now?"

Sean's jaw clenches. "You want the short version or the full one?"

"The one that gets my blood goin' fastest," Brody says with a grin.

I take a step forward before Sean answers. "We need your help blowing something up."

Brody's grin widens. "Now you're speaking my language."

Aidan flicks the lighter open again. The flame dances under his eyes. "What needs turning into ash?"

Devin's gaze narrows. "Who are we killing?"

Kirill steps forward and commands their attention instantly. "The leaders of the Underworld."

The four brothers straighten. Even Aidan stops clicking the lighter.

Brody's expression darkens. He pins his gaze on Sean and lowers his voice. "This better not be what I think it is."

Kirill interjects. "Sean's father built a system to create peace between rival families. A place where they could negotiate and avoid bloodshed. But everything he intended has been corrupted. The Omni and the Royal Council turned it into a breeding ground for torture, manipulation, and power grabs."

Brody snorts. "No shit. It's not possible to have a world like that. You can't build a throne without everyone wanting the crown. You build a temple, someone turns it into a slaughterhouse. Sean knew this, too."

Tynan points between Sean and me. "You two should've known better than to get involved in anything that isn't clan business."

Sean's stare hardens. "We didn't have a choice."

"Everything is a choice," Tynan asserts.

Sean's expression hardens.

I shift on my feet.

Kirill lifts his chin, reclaiming the room. "They're planning to kill us and our wives. They already drafted the orders. If we don't stop them, they'll harvest Valentina's eggs for a breeding program. They'll control future generations and eliminate anyone not loyal to their wishes."

The O'Connors freeze.

Brody wrinkles his forehead. "What did you just say?"

I bark, "They want to steal my wife's eggs on a monthly basis until she's 40, then kill her off. Her strongest will go to who they choose, and the weakest they'll sell on the black market."

"Bloody hell," Devin mutters.

Aidan's lighter clicks open again, flame flaring brighter. "They're takin' lassies' bodies now? Jesus Christ."

Tynan's stare sharpens. "And you want us to end them?"

I step forward again. "We need you to help us blow the entire thing up."

The room goes still. Not a breath moves.

Brody leans back slowly, a dangerous grin tugging at one corner of his mouth. "Alright, boys. Now this is getting interesting. What exactly are we blowing up?"

"There are thirteen targets across the world. They all need to get blown up simultaneously," Kirill deadpans.

There are a few seconds of silence, then Tynan chuckles.

"What's so funny?" I ask.

"This is a joke, right?"

"Are we laughing?" I demand.

His face falls.

Kirill strides to the large table in the center of the room. He presses a concealed switch. Cabinets slide open along the wall, revealing massive rolls of thick blueprint paper. He pulls them out one by one and drops them across the table.

Brody whistles. "Now that's foreplay."

Kirill ignores him and spreads the first roll across the table. The blueprint unfurls to reveal the complete structure of the arena, exposing every column, tunnel, trap door, ventilation shaft, and hidden chamber.

The O'Connors move around the table.

Kirill states, "Every Omni gathering passes through this arena. It's in an ancient ground in Pompei, and security is tighter than your assholes, just like every target."

Aidan studies the tunnels, continuing to flick his lighter. He comments, "Looks like this place was built by a lunatic."

"Takes one to know one," Sean offers.

Aidan smirks. "Aye."

Kirill unrolls the second blueprint. A sprawling underground facility emerges with corridors spiraling like a spider's web. "This is the fortress wing beneath the archives and the Royal Council's private refuge. No other members can access it. It's the most dangerous location on the map and has a blast-resistant chamber."

Brody taps a square etched in red. "And you want it gone?"

Kirill nods. "Yes. While they're in it."

Devin drags the blueprint closer and leans in. "We'll need charges on the support beams. The tunnels are the weakness. Bring those down, and the rest follows."

"So you'll do it?" Sean asks.

Brody studies him, then me.

I offer, "We'll owe you one."

He snickers. "One? No. You'll owe me thirteen."

My gut flips. I nod. "That's fair."

Tynan traces a long corridor. "This one here has opportunity. The ventilation shaft connects to the central chamber. If we send a blast through the shaft, it'll compress and multiply. Could take out three rooms in one go."

Aidan's eyes gleam. "We'll need shaped charges. They hit exactly where we want to cause maximum structural damage."

Brody crosses his arms. "What else are we hitting?"

Kirill rolls out additional blueprints, revealing the séance chambers, ritual halls, and the original council meeting place with pillars made of imported stone.

Tynan whistles low. "How did you get all these places?"

Kirill answers, "Sean's father obtained all of them."

The O'Connors jerk their heads backward, then glance at each other.

Brody looks at Sean. "So you want to destroy your father's warped legacy?"

"It's not what Sean Sr. wanted," Kirill insists.

Brody doesn't tear his gaze off Sean. "Is that right?"

Sean lifts his head, his green eyes full of conflicting emotions. "It's not. But if it is, then it needs to go."

"It's not what he wanted," Kirill repeats.

Devin asks, "So you want to kill everyone?"

I interject. "No. Just the Royal Council and Omni."

"And then what? You take over whatever this fucked-up group is?" Devin pushes.

Kirill shakes his head. "No. We allow the innocent to survive and take out any threats as they arise."

Brody points between Sean and me. "We warned you to stay out of whatever this fucked-up shit was that Sean created."

"There wasn't a choice. People would have died," I insist.

Brody's eyes turn to slits.

Anger fills me. "Are you going to help us, or do we need to find someone else?"

Tynan breaks the tension. "How much time do ya want from detonation to collapse?"

"As fast as possible. We can't risk anyone escaping," Kirill replies.

"And ya want all of this to happen at once?" Brody asks, looking across all the open plans.

"Yes."

"That's going to take several large teams on our part."

"Yes. I realize we're asking a lot," Kirill affirms.

"And they really want to steal your wife's eggs?" Aidan asks.

I nod, feeling ill.

Aidan mutters, "Feck me."

Brody studies me for a long moment, eyes narrowing like he's measuring how far my fury stretches. Then he nods once. "We're in."

Tynan cracks his knuckles. "Aye."

Devin smirks. "About damn time someone asked us to do something fun."

Aidan snaps his lighter closed with a soft click. "When can we get access?"

Kirill pulls a small device from his pocket. It's a tablet with encrypted files. "This has all the building schematics, like structural weak points and tunnel depths. Security rotations, cameras, and login details, along with the alternate exits they don't think anyone knows about, are all on here."

Brody grins like a wolf. "Now you're speaking my language."

"Sean and I can override the security—"

"No. If we do this, we're the only ones involved," Brody cuts me off.

"We won't fuck it up," Sean assures.

"No. It's our job, and we do it all, or we don't do it," Brody demands.

Another round of tension passes.

"Your call," Kirill answers.

Brody nods. "Run us through the security setups."

We spend the next hour dissecting every inch of structure, arguing over pressure waves and blast echoes, gesturing wildly as they map out the order of detonation. The office fills with their thick Irish voices, their violent enthusiasm, their absolute comfort discussing destruction like it's an art form.

Watching them work is the first time in days I've felt even a trace of relief. These men don't hesitate, flinch, or moralize. They level threats like skyscrapers with no apologies before or after.

It's exactly what we need.

By the time the O'Connors gather their notes and start toward the door, the plan screams terrifying and brilliant.

Brody points at me as he leaves. "Be ready. Once we start, there's no stopping it."

"That's what we want," I assure him.

They leave, and Kirill folds the last blueprint, his expression carved from stone. "This is happening."

"Yes," I say.

Sean drags a hand through his hair. "No turning back."

"There never was," I reply.

They leave the office, and I stay behind for a moment, staring at the rolled blueprints, and the evidence of a future we're about to rewrite in fire. My chest tightens, part fury, part determination, part something heavier and more human.

Valentina.

I leave the office and walk down the hallway, past the photographs Fiona hung to make the penthouse feel like a home, not a fortress. The closer I get to the family room, the more something in me settles.

Valentina is on the floor with the twins, Willow babbling in her lap while River kicks his feet against a cushion. Her hair falls over her shoulder in soft waves, her cheeks flushed, her eyes searching the babies' faces with a tenderness that shouldn't exist in a world like ours.

When she notices me, her gaze lifts, and immediate worry shadows her expression. "Well?"

I lower myself to the floor beside her, then pick up Willow and hold her in front of my face. She squeals and reaches for my jaw, her tiny fingers latching onto my stubble. I coo, "We're going to take them down, aren't we, Willow?"

She giggles, oblivious to everything. It's innocent and pure, the only kind of future worth protecting.

Valentina watches me with a question trembling in her eyes.

And everything in my body confirms it. This is the beginning of the end. Not just for the Omni or Royal Council. It's the obliteration of every sadistic tradition, masked ruler, and ritual soaked in blood.

The Underworld thinks it's going to steal my wife and her babies.

They have another thing coming.

I lean over and kiss my wife, retreat, and order, "Stop worrying. The only babies you're having are mine."

Surprise fills her expression.

Warmth fills my chest as I realize what I just said. More heat hits when I realize it's true. If anyone's having babies with Valentina, it's going to be me. And no one's taking our kids. Not now, or ever.

I turn back to Willow and grin, teasing, "What? You want a cousin? Should we go get busy now?"

Valentina laughs, playfully slapping the back of my arm. "Brax! Don't talk to Willow like that."

"Why?"

"She's a baby."

"So?" I shrug, then lift Willow up and down in the air, asking her, "Girl or boy?"

She giggles, and I avoid looking at Valentina, wondering how long she needs to be off her birth control before I can put my baby in her belly.

Valentina

Two Weeks Later

Chapter
TWENTY-NINE

Two weeks pass inside Kirill's penthouse like we've been swallowed whole by the walls. I used to joke about how massive this place was, how it stretched across two floors with enough space to fit every secret Kirill has ever hidden. Now it's a luxurious prison wrapped in anxiety and forced patience.

No one leaves for anything. The only fresh air we get is on his rooftop, but even that is in small increments. Whenever I look down at the city, it's the slightest reminder that the world outside still lives on.

The only visitor is Liam. He delivers us groceries, still pissed no one is telling him anything. But Kirill said it was better if he didn't know the details. Not until everything is burned to the ground.

Each day, the walls press further inward. The morning starts the same. The six of us wake in different patterns of exhaustion, then find new ways to share space without imploding. The babies coo or cry, depending on which one needs what. Someone brews coffee that tastes progressively more desperate. Someone else scrolls through channels with the same energy as a hostage mapping escape routes with their eyes.

The men spend hours in Kirill's private gym. The sounds drift into the hallway of fists hitting heavy bags, the sharp breaths of sparring, and the occasional curse when someone gets clipped harder than they expected. Two days ago, all three of them came out of the gym soaked in blood. Sean had a fat, bloody lip. Brax had a swollen, bruised eye. And Kirill's scar swelled across his face.

All of them were grinning, the happiest we'd seen any of them in months.

When they aren't beating each other's bodies, they're crawling on the floor with the twins. Sometimes they argue over how to handle the strategy with the membership, whiteboarding their contingencies like they're planning for Armageddon.

Despite all the suffocating tension, we're holding it together. It's not easy with six adults, two babies, and zero certainty about whether we'll all be alive in a week.

And yet I haven't once woken up dreading being trapped with them.

Even the arguments burn out fast, soothed by exhaustion or the weight of the bigger threat pressing down on all of us.

The best part is that Brax can't keep his hands off me. Being trapped like this has lit something under both of us, turning every inch of space we share into something charged. He touches my back when he walks past. His arms wrap around me during conversations that have nothing to do with danger. He'll pull me into shadowed corners like the desire might suffocate him if he waits another second.

Some days, we barely make it through breakfast before he drags me to a guest room, locks the door, and reminds me how fast his blood runs when he's near me. Other days, it's late at night, whispers against my throat, his mouth staking territory across my skin as if the danger outside has carved out a new, hungrier version of him.

I'm not complaining, but the obsession threads with something darker. It's a residue of fear neither of us addresses out loud. It's as if our world is about to collapse, so he wants to claim every part of me before he no longer can.

Today, the babies finally nap at the same time, which is a rare miracle. So Zara, Fiona, and I sit at the table in the family room with a Scrabble board between us. We all try to forget that we're waiting to see if the men who promised to destroy half the world's criminal infrastructure can pull it off without dying, thus saving us from our own fate.

Zara lays down five tiles and grins. "Siphon. Triple word score."

Fiona drops her head back with a groan. "I swear you're cheating."

"I swear I'm just smarter," Zara fires back.

I look at my tiles and try not to laugh. "Smarts and cheating aren't mutually exclusive, you know."

Zara flips her hair like she's accepting an award. "Bless you, Valentina, for acknowledging my gifts."

Fiona snorts. "Gift is a strong word."

Zara grumbles into her mug. "Your attitude could use an exorcism. Plus, I never cheat."

I hold my tiles close and search the board. None of my letters wants to cooperate. I groan, "I hate all of these."

"Same," Fiona says.

"It's because your vocabulary keeps shrinking," Zara teases.

Fiona argues, "That's because I haven't left this place in two weeks. I'm losing brain cells."

Zara presses a hand to her belly. "You're growing a baby. You're literally making brain cells."

Fiona shoots her a glare. "Not mine."

I laugh under my breath. It's been so long since anything felt normal that even pointless bickering over board games offers relief.

Across the room, the men are in the kitchen, clustered around the stove, attempting to cook. But they're just as antsy.

Sean groans dramatically. "Kirill, for the love of God, those are chopped, not sliced."

Kirill stares at the cutting board as if Sean has personally insulted his ancestry. "Your instructions were vague."

Brax's laugh drifts across the island. "He's right. You said 'cut them.'"

Sean points at him. "You stay out of this."

Brax grunts, absolutely unbothered. "No. I won the card tournament. You lost. You cook, I supervise. That was the bet."

Kirill's eye twitches. "Still think you stacked the deck."

"No need for me to do that. I have pure skills," Brax boasts, then takes another swig of beer. He glances over his shoulder at me, and the warm flicker in his eyes transforms the air in my lungs. It's the same dangerous expression that says he's counting down the hours, or maybe minutes, until he pulls me into a dark corner again.

I rise, thinking I'll excuse myself to the bedroom, when Kirill's phone buzzes, stopping me dead in my tracks.

But it's not just me.

Sean stops moving. Brax's jaw goes rigid. Zara's mug halts midair. Fiona freezes with a tile in her hand.

Kirill pulls his phone from his pocket and glances at the screen. His eyes dart across it, then he lifts his head. "The last council member's flight arrived. I'm sending the time out."

A stillness rolls across the space so heavy it presses down on my ribs.

Even the walls seem to exhale, recognizing the threshold we've just crossed.

Three days ago, Kirill sent instructions that every Omni and Royal Council member was to attend a mandatory meeting tonight. He stated that the time would be announced an hour before.

Brax pins his gaze on mine.

My heart races.

Silence fills every corner of the penthouse. No one moves at first. Even the air stops shifting. Tension sharpens into something solid, something that digs its claws into the atmosphere and refuses to let go. My chest tightens under it.

"We've got sixty minutes until showtime. Anyone want a fresh drink?" Brax asks.

"I'll take a glass of wine," I reply.

"Me too," Zara says.

"Water for me," Fiona states.

Brax hands the guys a beer, pours two glasses of wine, and gives Fiona a bottle of water.

The next hour drags like a slow suffocation. We gather in the kitchen, watching Sean and Kirill make beef stir fry. When it's done, we take the plates into Kirill's office and turn on the 13 screens on the table.

The babies wake from their nap, their cries slicing through the quiet. I go with Zara to get them. I lift Willow into my arms and bring her into the office. She cups my face with her tiny hand, oblivious to the war circling around her. I rock her gently, humming without thinking, my voice uneven.

Brax passes behind me, brushing a hand across my back like he's checking that I'm still breathing.

Zara bounces River, murmuring nonsense to him softly. Fiona plays with her broccoli, pushing it with her fork. Kirill presses buttons on hidden panels around the penthouse, double-checking every lock. Sean paces, stops, rubs his forehead, then resumes pacing.

The clock in his office ticks loudly. The tension mounts higher, and we all sit on the edge of our seats. The first SUV arrives, and a Royal Council member enters what will soon be their coffin.

The moon pulls itself up over the water outside, heavy and bright, casting a pale glow across the lake. Brax takes a seat with me and tickles Willow.

She giggles.

I smile at him, thinking about what a good dad he'd make.

"It's time," Kirill says finally.

Those two words hit harder than any ritual announcement I've ever heard.

The live feed shows all the different locations across the world. And at every site, the O'Connors planted death.

Please work.

Brax rises, stands behind me, and puts his hands on my shoulders.

I look up.

He winks, then leans down and kisses me softly on the lips.

Kirill slides the list of every Omni and Royal Council name to me. One by one, figures begin entering the buildings on different screens. All the highest-ranking bastards who thought they'd own my babies and me.

I cross out names as they appear.

~~Tiberio Marino.~~

~~Alessandrina Rossi.~~

~~Paddy O'Malley.~~

~~Lucien Ivanov.~~

~~Svetlana Petrov.~~

~~Kaitlyn Bailey~~

~~Franco Abruzzo~~

Names I once respected. Names I once believed held enough power to change the world.

Brax leans down and murmurs, "Want me to do it?"

I realize my hand is trembling. I force it to stop and shake my head. "No. I have this."

Something about checking off the name of the person who thought they'd steal my eggs gives me satisfaction.

When the last person arrives on the screen, I put the check mark next to their name. My voice barely comes out. "They're all inside."

Brax straightens slowly. His face hardens, transforming into something lethal. "Kirill. Give the orders."

Kirill types three commands on his phone.

In under thirty seconds, screen after screen erupts in flames. Explosions bloom like expanding suns, walls collapse inward, ancient structures implode as if the earth itself refuses to hold them anymore.

One by one, the feeds cut out with static.

Sean lunges toward the TV mounted on the wall and switches it to a news channel.

The broadcast is immediate with all the major headlines about simultaneous explosions across multiple continents.

Every channel says the same thing. Each reporter speaks with a mix of terror, bewilderment, and urgent speculation.

No one understands what happened except for the six of us and the O'Connors.

We sit in silence, our eyes glued to the screen, waiting for signs of life or a monster so powerful that they survive and walk out of the rubble.

The smoke only thickens. The news drones on, and nothing moves.

Sean's phone rings. He answers it on speakerphone. "Liam."

"Assuming that was you?"

"Yep."

"Is it over?" Liam questions.

"It's over enough," Sean replies.

A moment of silence fills the line then Liam says, "I want a full report tomorrow."

Sean glances at Brax and states, "We'll see you at ten." He hangs up.

Brax sits and pulls me closer, his expression a mix of vicious triumph and sarcasm. He murmurs, "Told you, Minx. No one's turning you into their baby factory."

A laugh bursts out of me, full of nerves and relief. It's not funny. They could have accomplished everything they wanted had he not cracked into the files. Yet all I can do is laugh. Then my eyes water and my lips shake.

"Hey. It's alright. No one is coming near you," Brax assures, tugging me into his chest.

My emotions win, and I sob against his shirt, unable to stop the onslaught of tears.

Zara's voice turns raw. "Is it really over?"

I take a deep breath and turn toward the others.

The question lingers in the middle of the room like a ghost, with everyone staring at Kirill.

He steps forward, points at the computer, and orders sharply, "Brax. Turn on the chatter."

Brax immediately types on the keyboard. Lines of encrypted text flood the screen as the membership's private channels ignite.

Thousands of messages pop up on the screen.

What just happened?

Who attacked us?

Are we at war?

The membership panics with the instant confusion we anticipated.

Kirill takes over the keyboard. The room holds its breath as his fingers fly across the keys. Then a message from Kirill's secured identity flashes across every screen.

All members check in immediately. Stay where you are until I can assess what happened. Do not travel or continue communication after you check in. This is an order.

He opens another chat box.

Within seconds, responses pour in with members obeying his order. For thirty minutes, it comes in fast and furious, then slows to a trickle. Ten minutes pass with nothing.

Brax pushes away from the desk and rises. He reaches down and pulls me up. "Show's over. Time to go to bed, Minx. We should sleep well tonight."

And for the first time since the Underworld branded my chest, he might be right.

Brax

Chapter
THIRTY

A month has passed. Life inside Valentina's condo is nothing like what I imagined the aftermath of blowing up the Underworld would be. I expected celebration, chaos, maybe some twisted version of liberation where people walked around in disbelief, realizing the board of monsters dictating their lives had turned to smoke. Instead, the Underworld membership is in a suspended rhythm, quiet and watchful. Barely anyone has spoken, with most following Kirill's order of silence. And those who haven't obeyed were considered threats and taken out by the O'Malleys.

Valentina's old driver, Vito, and her assistant, Cassian, were the first to speak out. Those were the only ones I personally handled. The rest I've left to the clan.

Sometimes, the silence is louder than the bombs that detonated every piece of infrastructure. It's been especially hard on Valentina. She spent years planning, strategizing, and manipulating an entire corrupt infrastructure. She constantly tried to survive so she wouldn't end up trapped in some sick ritual with no control over her fate. Now that the enemy is gone, she doesn't know what to do with her time.

Her movements are starting to lose the sharpness she carried when we were drowning in danger. They are being replaced with something adrift, but still something she can't identify. She doesn't say it out loud, but I see it in every slow breath she releases and every long stare she gives the windows as if waiting for orders she no longer wants but doesn't know how to live without.

I lace my shoelaces, and she enters the bedroom.

She smooths her hand along her thigh, distracted, still shoeless.

"We're going to be late," I point out.

Her expression stays neutral. "We aren't going anymore."

I arch my eyebrows. "What are you talking about? You miss those kids more than air. Zara said Willow started focusing her eyes during tummy time, and you acted as if someone told you Santa Claus was real. You're dying to get over there."

"That was before." She grabs her gold earrings off the dresser and fumbles with the clasp. She mutters under her breath and tries again.

Disappointment fills me. We promised we'd see the twins today. After weeks spent trapped in Kirill's penthouse with them, seeing them once a week doesn't cut it. I'm not ashamed to admit I miss the tiny sounds they make, their plump little fists reaching for whoever walks by, and the way Willow scrunches her nose when she's concentrating like she's solving taxes and not trying to hold her head up.

But Valentina misses them in a way that guts her. Zara's babies became an anchor for her when everything else in the world was smoke and mirrors. She needs them today.

So whatever stopped her from walking out this door is something I need to solve, fast.

I step closer. "Before what?"

She hesitates one heartbeat too long. "Before Zara called."

I tense. "What did she say?"

"We can't go." She steps out of the bedroom.

I follow her. "What's going on, Minx?"

The muscles in her shoulders tighten, then sink as she releases a slow exhale that carries more defeat than she ever willingly shows me. She repeats, "We're not going. Just leave it at that."

I move closer. "Not happening."

She picks up her purse, sets it back down, presses her palm to the counter, and stares at nothing.

I spin her into me. "What did Zara say?"

A flicker of pain crosses Valentina's face. "Her father showed up."

My chest tightens. "Luca?"

She nods.

"So why can't we go?" I ask.

Valentina's face hardens. "You know why."

"It's time he got over his issues. It's all bull shit anyway," I declare.

"He's not going to," Valentina quietly asserts.

"So Zara uninvited us?" I seethe.

"Pretty sure you can still go."

I narrow my eyes.

She argues, "It's not Zara's fault. She shouldn't have to worry about managing the situation. She should focus on her babies."

"That doesn't mean we cancel," I counter.

"I'm not going over there and making the situation worse."

"You wouldn't."

"I would," she insists.

"It'll get sorted out," I maintain.

"It won't." She turns, and for a heartbeat, the old, painful wound splits open. It's the one she normally hides. Yet today, she can't seem to.

"Valentina—"

"It's fine," she adds sharply, as if the word can force the truth back into its box. "We're not going."

"It isn't fine. And you know it."

A flicker of frustration crosses her expression. "I don't want to talk about this anymore."

I step in front of her, blocking her path to retreat. "That's not how this works."

Her jaw tightens. "You can't force me to go."

"I'm not trying to force anything. I'm trying to understand why you're letting someone else make decisions for you again," I point out.

Her eyes flash with anger. "This isn't someone else making decisions. It's me refusing to walk into a house where I'll watch Zara tense, the twins sense it, and Luca get so angry he might have a heart attack."

I remind her, "You spent years surviving people who wanted to own you. Don't hand your power to someone who didn't bother to stay."

Her eyes dart away. "I'm not."

I reach for my keys.

She notices. "Where are you going?"

"Out."

Her voice sharpens. "That's not an answer!"

"I'll be back."

She hurls, "You're being shady. I don't like shady."

"You love shady," I say, but my tone doesn't carry humor. I can't soften this. Not when she's unraveling right in front of me, and the root of it is a man who has lived in the shadows of her life for far too long.

Her brows pull together. "Don't go over there, Brax."

"I'm not. I'll be back later," I lie.

"This isn't your problem," she declares.

I sarcastically laugh. "That became a false statement the day you decided you wanted to marry me."

He freezes. Her lip trembles.

"What?" I question.

"There it is. I've been waiting for it to come out," she says.

The hairs on my neck rise. "For what to come out?"

She turns her head, scrunching her face.

I step closer, lowering my voice. "What's going on now?"

She tries to reel in her emotions, but she can't. She's two seconds from falling apart and blurts out, "You don't have to stay married to me anymore."

Every cell in my body goes still. I bite out, "You want to run that by me again?"

A few tense moments pass.

"I'm waiting," I state, crossing my arms.

Her voice cracks. "You're allowed to go. No one is threatening to parade me into a ceremony and turn me into some breeding machine. You're not trapped in a marriage designed to save my life. You don't have to carry me anymore."

My chest tightens with something violent. "You think I'm here because I *have* to be?"

She doesn't look at me. "Let's not sugarcoat it. I forced you to marry me. Now you can be free."

That sentence cuts deeper than anything she could've thrown at me. She says it calmly, like she believes and accepts it, which makes my blood run hotter. I bark, "You really think that's what I want?"

"Isn't it?" she challenges.

"Is that what you want?" I retort.

Her breath shakes. "It's not about what I want."

"Last time I looked, there were two of us in this marriage," I argue.

She sputters, "You deserve someone uncomplicated."

I scoff, "Uncomplicated? I would last ten minutes with uncomplicated before I chewed my arm off."

She doesn't laugh. Doesn't smile. Her gaze stays glued to the floor like she's bracing for impact. She murmurs, "You're allowed to want a clean start."

My breath leaves in a slow, controlled exhale. I order, "Valentina. Look at me."

She resists at first, but eventually her chin lifts, and her raw, guarded, too-familiar-with-abandonment eyes lock on mine.

I inform her, "I didn't marry you because the Underworld forced me to. I chose to marry you. And I stay because the thought of losing you makes the ground open up from under me. I wanted you when bullets were flying, and I want you even more now that the world isn't trying to kill us."

She blinks hard, but a tear falls. She chokes out, "You don't have to say that."

I take her face in my hands. In a firm tone, I demand, "Listen to me closely, Minx. I'm not saying it because I have to. I choose you. Not as a shield. Not as a duty. Not as a consequence of war. I choose you because you're mine and I love you."

Her breath catches, tears gathering again. She blinks rapidly, trying to force them away.

I continue, "And since we're clearing the air, let's tackle something else."

Her brows pull tight. She sniffles, "What?"

"It's time we make our own babies," I declare, my pulse ticking up.

Her entire body goes still.

I don't look away and add, "I want a life with you. A real one. One that isn't built on trauma, strategy, or survival. One that's just ours...well, and our babies." I wiggle my eyebrows, grinning.

A tearful laugh escapes her. She shakes her head slightly, questioning, "You think we're ready for babies?"

I grin wider. "Nope. I'm sure we'll fuck up a lot of shit. But is any parent ever ready?"

She bites her lip and shrugs her shoulders. "I-I don't know."

"I'm sure they aren't. But we're smart. We'll figure it out," I assure her, then pull her against me, my arms locking around her. I state, "You aren't some burden I've been dragging across the finish line."

She softly cries against my chest.

I pull back and wipe the tears from her cheek. "Okay. You can tell me."

"Tell you what?" she asks, with confusion all over her expression.

My heart thuds against my chest. I answer, "That you love me."

Time seems to stand still.

My gut flips.

Maybe she doesn't, and I've been wrong?

She finally declares, "I love you."

"Jesus Christ, you scared me for a minute," I tease, but it's the truth.

She laughs.

I press a kiss to the crown of her head, then tilt her chin up again. "We survived hell. We ended an empire. Now we get to build something else. Something that has our name on it and is our choice."

Tears spill freely down her cheeks now. "You really want that?"

"With you? Yes. With anyone else? Never."

Her breath stutters, and she smiles.

I kiss her slowly, sealing a new understanding between us. Then I retreat, adding, "You're not getting rid of me, Minx. Not now. Not ever. And definitely not before we make a whole brood of little terrors that drive everyone else insane."

She laughs harder, and for the first time in weeks, the world around us stops feeling lost. It starts feeling like a beginning.

I give her another kiss, then step back. "I need to go."

"Go?" she asks.

"I'll be back soon." I step toward the door.

"Brax, where are you going?" she questions.

"Toss your birth control out. When I get home, we're going to start making babies," I proclaim, and exit the front door.

I get through the building, into my Mustang, and floor it.

The drive to Zara and Sean's is quick, but by the time I pull up to their building, my pulse is a drum.

I nod at security, get in the elevator, and press my hand on the screen. It shoots to the penthouse, and the doors open, showcasing the magnificent red cherry blossom tree.

The moment I open the main door, Luca's voice booms, "Look at how big you've gotten!" He holds River in the air.

"Brax. What are you doing here?" Zara asks, with worry on her expression. She looks past me.

"Don't worry. She's not here," I state.

Guilt floods Zara's face. She opens her mouth, but nothing comes out.

"I need to talk to you, Luca," I demand.

His eyes narrow. "I'm with my grandbabies."

"Now," I order, and brush past him, telling Sean, "Need to use your office."

He nods, eyes wide.

I storm down the hall, trying to manage my anger. I step into the office and wait, leaning against the window, my arms folded.

Luca finally steps inside, closes the door, and points at me. "You'd better get rid of your disrespectful tone."

I point at the chair. "Sit down."

He stays put. "You don't give me orders."

"Sit," I seethe.

He doesn't flinch. Neither of us moves for what feels like forever until he finally sits, clasps his hands in a triangle, and keeps his scowl on me. "Well? Why are you interrupting my time with my grandchildren?"

"You owe my wife an apology."

His head jerks backward. A flinch of guilt crosses his face, lined with age and choices he won't say out loud. He recovers. "You're treading on thin ice, Brax."

I grab the chair and sit, realizing I can't fight fire with fire. Not with Luca. And this is too important not to get the result Valentina deserves. I take a deep breath and calm my voice. "Zara and Sean told you about the Underworld?"

His face fills with disapproval. He affirms, "Yes."

"Then you know Valentina doesn't deserve for you to abandon her anymore."

His jaw twitches. He doesn't blink, but his eyes darken.

I add, "Salvatore killed her parents in a ritual. Then he took her to live with him and forced her to abide by his rules. If she didn't, she would have been sold."

The twitch expands to his cheek. He seethes, "Salvatore was the devil."

"Yes. And your sister's daughter—the niece you once loved and cared for—was left with the monster. You cast her aside like trash," I accuse.

"Watch your mouth!" he warns.

"What do you call it?" I ask.

His eyes turn to slits.

"She was a child. She had no one to turn to, and all she did was fight to survive. And they tortured her. One ritual after another, they brutalized her and persecuted her. You're her blood, and you did nothing!" I say louder than I anticipated.

He slams his hand on the desk. "I didn't know! Her father took my sister and her to Italy and disappeared. I didn't even know she was still alive until she was older. I assumed she died with them. Then I learned Salvatore raised her, and she was doing all the things that Abruzzos do!"

"Because she had to in order to survive!" I roar.

Silence fills the room, hot with growing tension.

I lean closer, my voice dropping to a deadly calm. "They branded her. And not just with the skull."

The words stop him cold. His lips part, but no sound comes out.

"They took a heated iron as big as her torso and burned a V into her chest. Then they turned it scarlet to shame her for the world to see," I announce.

His face drains of color.

I don't give him time to recover. "She blamed herself for not understanding why you never came for her. She'd never speak of it, but I know. I see it in her. And you're partly to blame."

His hand grips the armrest so tightly his knuckles turn white. His voice finally cracks. "I had no idea—"

"No, you didn't want to know."

He flinches.

"You left and never checked the debris left behind. You didn't look for the niece you once loved."

He swallows hard, throat bobbing unevenly, eyes turning wet.

"She's finally free. The council is gone. The monsters are ash because she took down the demons who killed her family...the same ones who wanted to kill your daughter and grandbabies. She survived the impossible. No. She did the impossible. Yet one phone call from Zara and she folds in like she's the bad person."

Luca presses a hand to his forehead. He admits, "I never wanted to hurt her."

"But you did. You still are."

He looks at me, glassy-eyed, voice unsteady. "What do you want from me?"

I take a deep breath. "Responsibility. Not excuses. Not the noble self-sacrifice you've fed yourself for decades. I want you to understand the destruction you didn't bother to try and stop."

"I can't fix the past."

My chest curls. I control my voice, insisting, "She spent her entire life suffering consequences from decisions you had a hand in. Directly or not."

His jaw tics. "I don't know what she told you—"

"She didn't tell me anything. She never gives herself that much permission. I learned by digging," I snap.

His eyes widen a fraction.

I pound my finger into the wood. "She's my wife. And your blood."

He turns his face and grinds his molars.

"You're going to make this right, Luca," I firmly assert.

He slowly turns back toward me, but the hardness is gone. Regret, guilt, and sadness fill his expression.

I continue, "From this point forward, she's done hiding. She's as much of a part of this family as anyone. So if you're here, she's allowed here. No one is keeping my wife hidden, including you."

He looks at his hands, his face scrunched.

I wait for him to speak.

He finally looks at me, a shell of the man he entered the room as, and asks, "Why would she even want to be in a room with me?"

"You're her blood, Luca. She remembers you, the uncle who used to love and care for her," I softly tell him.

He closes his eyes, taking deep breaths.

"You get one chance to do this right," I tell him.

He opens his red-rimmed eyes.

I warn, "Make it right, Luca. My wife is mine. She's like a sister to Zara. And she's not going anywhere." I get up and walk out, ignoring the others, and returning to the woman that somehow, in the middle of total chaos, I learned to love.

Valentina

Chapter

THIRTY-ONE

My new reality still shocks me in the morning. There's no distant gunfire, echo of ritual chants, or alarms from my phone followed by orders. Only soft daylight pushes against the curtains.

For once, the silence doesn't threaten to swallow me. It just wraps around me, heavy and oddly tender, like a thick blanket still carrying Brax's scent from last night.

Last night.

Heat creeps up my neck as memories surge in an unsteady reel. Brax pinning my wrists above my head and growling against my throat that he wants my belly swollen with his babies. His body taking mine again and again until I lost track of how many times I whispered his name into the dark. The way his voice dropped when he said, "This is our life now."

Ours.

I shift on the mattress and wince. Every muscle between my thighs protests, sore and overused in the best possible way. My legs brush against the cool sheets, and a tired little laugh slips past my lips. My husband was on a mission.

My husband.

He didn't want to get divorced.

I smile bigger and turn my head toward the nightstand. The digital clock blinks an accusation. It's almost noon.

I jerk upright, then sway as my body reminds me how little sleep I got. Normally, I'm up hours earlier with my brain wired for threats even when there are none. Today, my limbs carry a pleasant heaviness that says my husband did exactly what he announced he would do and then some.

My gaze lands on a folded piece of paper resting against the lamp base. Brax's messy handwriting stares back at me in dark ink.

> Minx,
> Went to the gym before I climb on top of you again,
> and we never leave this bed.
> Pancakes for breakfast?
> Love you.
> B

My lips twitch. My idea of a morning used to be coffee and plotting the downfall of monsters, not domestic sugar bombs. Now, if someone casually mentions pancakes, my stomach turns into a needy traitor.

I trace the word love without touching the page, as if contact might smear the ink. The fact that he wrote it, that he says it now without hesitation or drama, sends a strange warmth radiating through my chest. Yesterday, I still assumed one misstep would send him sprinting in the opposite direction. Somehow, he's proved that assumption wrong.

I swing my legs off the bed and test my weight. My thighs protest again. I smirk toward the door as if he can see it through the wall. "You are ridiculous," I murmur under my breath, my voice hoarse from sleep and all the ways he stole it.

I rise and scoop my hair up, twisting it into a messy bun on top of my head. A few strands escape, and I tuck them behind my ear.

The floor is cool beneath my bare feet as I cross to the en suite bathroom. Steam fills the glass shower stall within minutes, swirling around me once I step under the spray. Warm water courses over my skin, washing away dried sweat and the faint ghost of Brax's cologne that clings to me. Images from last night flash again, disjointed but vivid. His mouth on my throat, his hand splayed low over my stomach, his voice raw when he said he wanted to put a baby there.

My throat tightens, and not from the steam.

For so many years, my body belonged to the council. So did my blood, my signature, my compliance, my pain. Even my future children were weaponized against me. Now, the idea of a baby isn't rooted in evil, but in a desire from the man who chose me when he had the chance to leave.

I press my forehead against the tile for a moment and let the water cascade down my back. The spray drowns out everything except my own heartbeat. Maybe another woman would be terrified at how quickly life has shifted, but terror has been my constant companion for too long. More than anything, I want to break up with it and never see it again.

I shut off the water and reach for a towel. Droplets slide down my arms as I wrap the thick cotton around my body. I glance at the mirror. My cheeks hold a faint pink flush that has nothing to do with the heat.

"Get it together," I mutter, grabbing my toothbrush. My reflection arches an eyebrow back at me, as if to say, *You spent an entire night trapped under an overprotective hacker who wants to breed you into oblivion. You're allowed to be a little dazed.*

I smirk more and brush my teeth. I do the bare minimum with skincare, ditch the towel, and pull on a pair of soft black shorts and an oversized gray T-shirt that dips off one shoulder.

I step out of the bedroom, mumbling, "From obeying orders to flipping pancakes. Who would have thought..." I walk down the short hallway toward the kitchen.

Sunlight pours through the floor-to-ceiling windows, turning the living room into a bright, open space that seems bigger than it used to be. Maybe it's because no more Underworld messengers are threatening to summon me, and no more rituals loom like storms over my calendar. The condo holds only my furniture, my things, my husband's scattered gadgets, and the faint echo of moans I'll never admit out loud we made.

I move into the kitchen and head straight for the pantry. My stomach gives an impatient twist. Apparently, my body has decided to remember I'm human and require sustenance. I pull out the container of flour, sugar, baking powder, and salt, setting them in a line on the counter. I grab a bowl from the cabinet and open the fridge for milk and eggs.

The cool air rushes against my bare legs. For a second, my gaze lands on the shelf where my birth control used to sit before I shoved the remainder of the pack into the bathroom trash last night while Brax watched with his dangerous, reverent expression.

A shiver works its way down my spine. I shut the fridge door harder than necessary.

I crack the first egg into the bowl, then the second. The yolks spread in glossy islands of yellow. I measure flour and pour it in, watching the white powder devour the color. When the baking powder hits the surface, some of it dusts my fingers. It anchors me in the strangest way. It's a simple domestic motion with no blood, no signatures, no surveillance. It's just breakfast.

I whisk through the ingredients, bringing them together in a thick swirl, and for a moment, my mind wanders to what Brax might be doing at the gym.

He's probably intimidating everyone within a ten-foot radius while lifting unholy amounts of weight and thinking again about getting me pregnant.

I roll my eyes at nothing, a smile tugging at my lips despite the absurdity of that thought.

A sharp sound cuts through the quiet, making me jump. I realize it's the doorbell, and the whisk freezes mid-stir. Batter drips slowly back into the bowl.

My head snaps toward the front entryway. No one is supposed to be here. Zara would call. Fiona would text. Kirill would never drop in without twenty layers of security protocols. Sean doesn't casually swing by, and the council is gone.

My blood runs cold.

Shake it off. It's fine.

Is it?

I set the whisk down, and the metal clinks against the rim. A thick hush settles over the condo.

Ding-dong.

The second chime ricochets along my spine. I wipe my batter-dusted fingers on a dish towel, then move toward the hallway with reluctant steps. My heart rate climbs higher with each one. Old training kicks in before I can stop it.

My eyes sweep the space, and my ears tune for any sound beyond the door. I reach the entryway and pause with my hand inches from the handle. I lean in close and peer through the peephole.

The world narrows to a fish-eye circle. I blink once.

It can't be.

My lungs forget how to work.

Luca stands alone in the hallway. His broad shoulders fill part of the frame, suit jacket open over a crisp shirt. His dark hair has more gray than I remember, and deep lines bracket his mouth. He stares at the door with an expression I don't recognize.

My stomach drops. Heat surges through my chest, up my throat, and behind my eyes. I step back as if I've been shoved.

For a second, I consider the possibility that I'm hallucinating. The lack of sleep mixed with too many orgasms and too much unresolved history has broken something in my head.

A loud thud slams against the door.

My brain splinters into a dozen disjointed thoughts.

Why is he here?

A younger version of me roars to the surface. I'm the little girl who stood at the windows in an unfamiliar house and wondered why her uncle never came. It's the same girl who convinced herself he didn't exist, because that explanation held less sting than the alternative.

But he did. He chose distance and to hate me.

My legs threaten to give out. I grip the handle to keep myself upright.

"Valentina." His voice carries through the wood in a low rumble. It holds a deeper rasp than I remember.

My throat closes.

I stand frozen in the small entryway, bare legs, messy bun, shirt slipping off my shoulder, pancake batter drying on my fingers.

"Please," he adds, the single word threaded with something raw. "I'd like to talk to you."

My lungs pull in a sharp breath. It scrapes against my ribs. I stare at the handle as if it might shift my entire reality. The girl from the past wants to run, barricade herself in the bedroom, and wait for Brax to return and make this choice for me.

Except my husband made me make a promise to him. I swore I wouldn't let other people decide my fate ever again.

My hand turns the dead bolt before I fully process the action and open the door. It creaks just a fraction, then swings wide enough to reveal my estranged uncle standing a few feet away.

He straightens when he sees me, his sharp Marino eyes sweeping over my face in one swift, assessing pass that can make men twice his size flinch.

I expected to see contempt. Yet they seem to hold something shattered and uncertain.

For a heartbeat, no one speaks. We just stare at each other.

He looks older. The realization hits me like a slap. There's more silver at his temples, more lines at the corners of his eyes, deeper grooves in his forehead. This isn't the man I last saw. This is a grandfather of two babies I love.

"Valentina," he says quietly.

Seeing him after all these years cracks something in my chest. A sharp, stinging pressure rises behind my eyes. I stare at his mouth, as if the shape of it might morph into the man who used to bring me sweets behind my mother's back.

My tongue sticks to the roof of my mouth. No words emerge.

His Adam's apple bobs as he swallows. He glances past me, taking in the condo over my shoulder. Then his gaze returns to mine. "May I come in?"

My brain screams every argument at once. This is Luca, my uncle, who vanished when I needed him most. It's the same man whose absence branded me nearly as deep as the iron.

My body answers before my brain does. I step back and to the side.

He crosses the threshold slowly, as if he expects the floor to open and swallow him whole. His nostalgic cologne wraps around me, tangled up with ghosts.

I shut the door behind him and press my back to it for a second, one hand still on the knob.

The silence between us stretches again, thick and charged.

He moves into the entryway, then stops, turning to face me fully. His gaze drags over my messy bun, my bare legs, and the batter smudge on my right hand. Something in his expression softens and tightens at the same time. Then he blurts out, "I'm sorry."

The words hang in the air.

For a second, I question whether I heard him correctly. Sorry isn't something I ever expected him to say to me.

I push off the door slowly, my hand dropping to my side. "You are..." My voice comes out raspier than I intend. I swallow and try again. "You're what?"

"Sorry," he repeats. The word sounds rough, scraped from somewhere deep. "I didn't know."

My heart slams so hard against my ribs that my vision blurs at the edges. My fingers curl into my palms, nails biting into my skin.

He takes a step closer, then appears to reconsider and stops again. "I did not know, Finzia." His voice cracks slightly on the term he used when I was small enough to sit on his knee.

Finzia.

Another emotion lodges in my chest. No one's called me that in years. Not since my parents moved me to Italy to hide. A strangled noise claws its way up my throat before I can stop it. It emerges as a half laugh, half sob. My tone comes out sharper than glass. "You didn't know I existed?"

He flinches as if I struck him. "That is not what I said."

"No?" My hands shake. I fight the urge to wrap my arms around myself like armor.

He closes his eyes briefly, as if bracing against an impact. When they open again, they're damp. "Your parents took you and disappeared before I had any chance to stop it. When news came that they had died in the accident, I buried my sister. They said you died with her."

Rage at Salvatore burns through my veins anew, hot and familiar. At the same time, a jagged shard of something else slices through my chest. I grit out, "They lied."

"Yes." He scrubs a hand over his jaw. "I didn't learn you lived until years later, and by then, you were in Salvatore's house, and part of his world."

My vision blurs. Hot moisture gathers, then spills over before I can stop it. I drag the back of my hand across my face, but more follow.

A confession rips from someplace so raw it nearly knocks me backward. "I waited for you. When I was younger, I used to stand at the window and invent stories about why you hadn't come. Every birthday, I pictured you walking in and twirling me in the air." A sob pushes through the words, jagged and humiliating.

His face crumples. Deep lines rearrange, turning his features into something devastated. "I failed you and your mother. I chose what I thought was the safe path and left you with wolves. I should have turned the world upside down to find out what happened inside that house. I should have dragged you out if I had to crawl through their blood to do it. I did none of that. I stayed away. I told myself you chose the Abruzzos, but I was wrong."

"Chose?" I scoff.

"I'm sorry," he repeats.

The tears come harder, and my chest spasms. I press a hand there, trying to hold everything in as it cracks wider. Part of me wants to rage, to throw every memory at him like knives. Another part hears the wreckage in his voice and recognizes the agony there, different from mine but real. Yet all I can do is silently sob.

He moves before I can step away. One second, I'm standing rigid and shaking in the entryway. Next, his arms wrap around me in a rough, desperate hold. His broad chest anchors solid under my cheek. The scent of expensive soap and regret swirl around us.

For one suspended moment, my body locks. Then something inside me snaps. A sharp sob bursts free, followed by another and another. I clutch the front of his jacket, fingers twisting in the fabric as years of abandoned hope spill out of me. My shoulders shake. I press my face against him, hating that he still makes me feel safe and protected, just like when I was a little girl.

He lowers his chin to the top of my head, one hand cradling the back of my skull. His other arm bands around my back, holding me as if I might disappear. He murmurs, "I'm so sorry, Finzia. I was wrong."

My knees threaten to buckle. His hold tightens, supporting my weight. Tears soak into his suit.

"I hate you," I gasp, the words torn from somewhere deep as another wave of grief crashes through me.

He holds me tighter and says softly, "I know. You have every right."

"And I missed you," I add, the admission ripping my throat raw. "I missed you every single day."

His body jolts as if I stabbed him. His breath shudders against my hair, and I realize he's crying too.

We stand there for what could be seconds or hours. My sobs slowly quiet, turning into softer cries. His hand moves in slow, careful strokes over my back, just like when I was a little girl, and he was my entire world.

Finally, when my throat aches and my head throbs, I pull back.

He lets me go immediately, as if he is afraid any prolonged contact might overstep some boundary. His eyes are red, the whites streaked with veins. A damp stain spreads across the front of his shirt where my face pressed.

I swipe at my cheeks with shaky fingers.

His words come out hoarse. "If there is even the smallest chance that one day you might allow me back into your life in some capacity, I will do whatever it takes to earn it. But I will not demand it. I have no right to demand anything of you. I hope you can forgive me one day."

He looks older than ever, standing there, shoulders bowed under the weight of his choices in a way I've never seen. It's not the Luca who rules rooms with a single glance. It's a man stripped of titles and pretense, asking for mercy.

The strange pressure in my chest swells until it aches.

Forgiveness.

If anyone else asked, it would sound saintly and ridiculous. Forgiveness is not a currency in my world. It is a luxury for people who did not grow up in blood-soaked halls.

Except I know exactly how much it cost me every time the Omni chose vengeance and I had to be their administrator. And I don't want to be shackled to ghosts.

So I stare at Luca, taking in the regret carved into every line of his face, the way his hands shake, the wetness in his eyes. I think about little me at the window and Zara holding her babies. Then I think about the life Brax and I are trying to build, and it's not anchored to old wounds.

The answer rises in me without hesitation. "Okay."

His brows crease with confusion. "Okay?"

"Okay. I forgive you," I declare.

He staggers back a half step, as if the words physically struck him. His mouth opens, but nothing comes out. Moisture spills over his lower lashes, drawing fresh tracks down his cheeks. "You forgive me?"

"Yes. Holding onto the past doesn't make either of us winners. We both lose, and I've already lost enough," I state.

A short, broken sound escapes him. He lifts a hand as if he might reach for me again, then drops it. "I don't deserve that grace."

"No one in our world deserves much of anything," I reply, a wry edge slipping in.

Emotion flickers through his gaze, too complicated to name. He finally swallows hard. "Thank you. I..." He takes a deep breath.

The door opens, and Brax steps inside. He protectively steps next to me. "Luca. What's going on here?" He cautiously glances between us.

Luca rises taller. "I was apologizing to Valentina. And I must leave now, or I'll miss my meeting."

Disappointment hits me, along with surprise. He just got here, but what should I have expected?

Luca steps closer to me. He asks, "May I?"

For a split second, I consider telling him no out of sheer spite. Then I nod. He draws me into a second hug, gentler than the first but no less sincere. His lips press briefly to the top of my head, just like they did when I was small.

He murmurs, "I will not disappear again. If you ever want to talk, shout, throw things, or just sit in silence, I am a phone call away."

I swallow hard. "We will see how brave you are when I throw things."

His mouth tilts in the shadow of a smile. Amusement fills his tone, and he replies, "You always had a good arm."

I softly laugh at a flashback of when I was a little girl and had a temper tantrum. I got mad at him and threw his candy back, only to beg for it again an hour later.

He lets me go and turns to Brax.

The two men regard each other for a long beat. The air between them hums with unspoken things, but there's a shared protectiveness over me.

Luca extends his hand. "Thank you."

Brax takes his offered hand, gripping it firmly. "You're welcome."

Luca nods, releases his hand, then steps toward the door. He spins. "Tomorrow night, the family is getting together for dinner. I would love it if you could come?"

My heart takes off in a sprint. I don't hesitate. "Sure. We'll be there."

Brax glances at me, then nods in agreement. "Count us in."

Luca's shoulders drop another notch, as though I just lifted a weight he has carried alone. "Good. I'll send you the details."

He gives us a final, loaded look, then steps toward the door. He opens it and pauses in the frame, turning back for one last glance. "Finzia, your mother would be proud of you. So would your father."

The words punch straight through my chest. My throat closes too tightly around any response. More tears fill my vision.

He dips his head, then steps into the hall and closes the door behind him.

The condo falls into silence once more. Only this time, it is not heavy with absence. It hums with something new.

I stare at the closed door, swaying slightly as adrenaline drains from my system. My knees wobble. The wall tilts an inch.

Brax's hands find my waist, steady and warm, anchoring me back in place. He searches my face. "Minx? You okay?"

I let out a shaky breath that is half laugh, half leftover sob. "I think so. I'm not entirely sure what just happened."

He brushes his thumb along my hip, then slides one hand up to my cheek, his palm cupping it gently. His grin slides over his face. "Sounds to me like you just got your family back. Or at least the stubborn, guilt-ridden, expensive-suit-wearing part of it."

I burst out laughing.

He glances behind me, then asks, "Did you get hot and bothered with the batter without me?"

I laugh harder.

He leans into my ear, murmuring, "I think it's time we get out the whipped cream."

Brax

Four Months Later

Chapter

THIRTY-TWO

Four months ago, my life shifted so sharply it might as well have snapped into a new spine. One day, I had a wife who woke up braced for ambushes and rituals, and the next, I had a woman who slept through mornings because she finally trusted the world not to devour her in her sleep.

Now, it's summer in Chicago. Humid air presses through open windows, sunlight flashes off high-rises, and Valentina moves through our new penthouse with a softness that still knocks the breath out of my chest.

Everything is different.

My name carries weight again with the O'Malleys. Luca and Valentina talk almost daily. Sometimes it's short, and often it's longer. At times, they get emotional, in arguments, or cry with laughter.

Finn's gruff exterior has thawed to the point he introduced her to someone as "my daughter-in-law," then muttered about not making a scene when she squeezed him so tight he coughed.

And tonight, every thread of our stitched-together family is coming together under one roof for one reason.

I asked them to.

But that's not the biggest thing on tonight's agenda.

I adjust my suit collar in the mirror and glance toward the bedroom doorway. "Minx? You ready?"

Her voice floats back, tart and amused. "If you rush me, I'm changing into sweatpants."

I laugh and lean a shoulder against the wall. "You look hot in sweats."

"You would say that if I wore a trash bag."

"You'd make it couture."

She mutters something in Italian I can't fully hear, then steps into the doorway.

My pulse jumps.

Her red sundress has thin straps, daintily placed over her shoulders, a fitted bodice, and a soft, loose skirt brushing her thighs. Her hair hangs in waves, her glossed lips match her dress, and her expression radiates steady confidence and happiness.

There were days I wondered if I'd ever see her this way.

I straighten, wiggling my eyebrows. "Wonder Woman better look out."

She lifts a brow. "It's a dress, Brax."

"It's criminal."

She snorts and reaches for her clutch. "Let's go before you start trouble we don't have time to finish."

I chuckle and offer my arm. She slips her hand into the crook of my elbow, and together, we take the elevator down and step into the warm summer evening.

Our driver pulls up. I open the door for her. She pauses before climbing in, her gaze sliding over me in a slow inspection. She says, "You're being suspiciously calm."

"Just enjoying my wife."

She narrows her eyes. "Hmm. I smell danger."

I laugh and pat her ass. "Get in, Minx."

She settles into the backseat, I slide in beside her, and the city moves past the windows as we head toward the restaurant.

We arrive within minutes and go directly to the rooftop, reserved for our party. My fingers graze the box in my pocket. My stomach tightens, not from nerves but from raw anticipation.

Valentina leans against me, shoulder to shoulder. The doors open, and everyone is already here. She tilts her head up at me. "You didn't tell me what this dinner is actually for."

"You'll see."

"That's vague."

"It's specific."

She side-eyes me. "Suspicious."

I grin. "Always." I place my hand on the small of her back. "Come on."

She steps into the open air, and the city stretches in every direction under a deep-gold sunset. Hanging lights zigzag overhead, glinting off wineglasses and polished cutlery. Cocktail tables line up near the edge of the roof. Long tables covered in satin gold linen, floral arrangements, and place cards fill the rest of the space.

Zara has the twins on her hip. Kirill holds a very pregnant Fiona close to his side. Sean gives a chin lift. Finn wears a crisp navy suit, and Luca's in a charcoal one with a cautious smile.

I scan the Marinos and O'Malleys. Everyone who's anyone to us is here.

Hugs and cheek kisses start. Zara squeezes her until she squeaks. Luca holds her a beat too long, quiet but steady. Finn kisses her on the cheek and teases her.

My wife's overwhelmed but glowing, and she's never looked so happy or beautiful.

When the greetings settle, I slide my hand into hers. "Come with me."

Her steps falter. "Where?"

"To the front."

"Okay..."

I lead her forward. We reach the head of the rooftop, where the skyline frames us, and I lift both hands in the air and shout, "Time to be quiet!"

A ripple of laughter moves through the crowd, and conversations taper off. The twins babble loudly for another second before Zara and Sean shush them.

Valentina looks at me, eyes narrowed, head tilted. "What's going on?"

I lower my hands, take hers, and turn to face everyone. I announce, "Thank you all for being here."

The group quiets, leaning in.

I swallow hard, not from fear but from the weight of how much this woman matters to me. Then I turn to her.

"You popped into my life in a way I never saw coming. And you're the greatest thing that has ever happened to me."

She holds her breath, blinking hard.

I continue, "Every day since, you teach me how to be stronger and a better human being."

Her eyes glisten.

My pulse ticks hotter. I add to the crowd, "It's true. She's made me a better man than I ever planned to be."

"He's not lying," Sean calls out.

The crowd laughs.

I reach into my pocket. "I think it's time we do this right."

Her eyes widen.

I drop to one knee.

Gasps rise.

Zara, Fiona, and Brenna squeal. Finn mutters a curse that sounds suspiciously emotional. Luca stands straighter, blinking hard.

I open the box, revealing a platinum band with several rows of diamonds. It's classy, elegant, and going to look amazing with her engagement ring.

My voice thickens. "Minx, you're the love of my life. You stole the air from my lungs and the sleep from my nights from the moment we met. And since we didn't get a real wedding the first time, I want one now, with rings and vows we choose and all of our family to celebrate with us."

She presses a hand to her mouth.

I grin. "Well, Minx, you want to marry me again?"

Her mouth opens…then shuts.

It happens several times, and my heart slams.

Why isn't she saying anything?

I arch my eyebrows. "Minx?"

She swallows hard. "I…um…yes, but—"

"But?" My stomach twists. "But what?"

"I have something for you."

The crowd murmurs.

I blink. "What?"

She opens her clutch and pulls out an envelope. She hands it to me. "Open it."

My chest tightens as I pull out a thin sheet of paper.

There's a black-and-white, grainy image. My vision narrows to a pinpoint. I gape at it, my heart racing, then look up at her. "Is this what I think it is?"

She nods, smiling.

Static rushes across my skin. I look from the picture to her, to the picture again. "You're pregnant?"

She nods again, slower this time, lips trembling as tears gather. "Seven weeks."

Happiness detonates inside me, along with a pinch of fear, but I'm sure it's what every father feels.

She adds, "I found out this morning and was trying to figure out how to tell you."

"Minx." My voice breaks. I stand so fast she startles. I cup her cheeks. "You're pregnant."

A tear slips down her face. "Yes."

Cheers fill the rooftop.

A stunned laugh shoves out of my chest. Then another. Then I kiss her hard, with echoes of clapping and hollers surrounding us.

Finn lifts his glass and mutters something about grandchildren, bloodlines, and finally, something being "done the right way."

I pull back, brushing her hair behind her ears. "You're carrying our baby."

Her mouth curves. "Yes."

"I'm marrying you again," I say, thick with conviction. "Not because of this." I hold up the tiny photo. "But because I want every version of the world where you're mine. So tell me you want to marry me again."

She nods, crying. "Of course, I'll marry you again."

The cheer that breaks out around us is deafening.

I slide the ring onto her finger as the city lights flicker across her skin. She stares at the band, then at me, eyes shimmering with something deep and raw.

For a few long seconds, I hold her while the people we love surround us in applause and shouts and toasts.

After the crowd settles and everyone moves in to embrace us, Luca steps forward. He rests a hand on my shoulder. "You'll be a wonderful father."

"Thank you," I answer quietly.

Finn pats my back so hard I nearly lurch forward. "Congratulations, kid."

Brenna pulls me tight to her. "I get to be a grandma!"

Zara cries into Valentina's neck. "You're going to be an incredible mom."

Kirill leans toward me and murmurs, "I knew you two would create chaos."

I grin. "Chaos is our brand."

Dinner becomes a blur of champagne, speeches, laughter, and stolen touches. Valentina rests a hand over her abdomen more than once, each time sending a shock wave through my chest.

When dessert arrives, she sits close beside me at the head table. Her fingers graze my thigh under the linen. She whispers, "You okay?"

"Not remotely. I need to get my shit together for this kid we're having."

Her eyes widen. "Me too."

"Nah. You'll be a pro," I assure her.

The rooftop quiets again as conversations slow. The moon hangs above the city like a gold coin. Soft music drifts from speakers.

I take her hand and guide her to the far side of the rooftop, where the lights dim slightly, and the city hum softens into a gentle pulse.

She steps into my arms without hesitation. I sway with her, one hand at her lower back, the other laced with hers against my chest.

She glances up. "What are you thinking?"

"That I didn't know I had a missing piece until I met you."

Her breath catches.

"You changed everything I understood about loyalty, courage, and devotion."

"You're killing me tonight, Brax," she says, tearing up again.

I grunt. "I can't wait to marry you again, raise our babies with you, and build a life no one can tear apart."

Her forehead presses to my chest. My heartbeat hammers against her cheek. I lower my chin to her hair and close my eyes.

The world narrows to the woman in my arms.

After a long moment, she murmurs, "You're going to be such a good dad."

Emotion punches through my ribs. I swallow hard. "Only because our kid gets half of you."

She huffs a quiet laugh.

I tilt her chin up and kiss her slowly, sealing everything we've survived and everything we'll build. When I pull back, all I see is the mother of my children and the love of my life.

Her voice catches. "We're really doing this?"

I grin. "Yep. But we've already done it. Now we get to enjoy it."

With the city below us, our families behind us, and our future kicking off inside her, I kiss her again. Love swells between us, but it's only the beginning of the future I plan to guard with my last breath.

Brax

Four Months Later

Epilogue

Aurora shrieks with laughter, her chubby legs pumping as she toddles across the rooftop backyard like she's training for a marathon she has every intention of finishing. Sunlight bounces off her dark curls, and the tiny red bow clipped into them wobbles with every excited step.

"She's getting faster," Brax mutters beside me, narrowing his eyes like our daughter's a fugitive he's tracking. "She wasn't that fast yesterday."

"She turned two today. Maybe she's embracing her power," I tease, adjusting the floral sash on my dress.

He grumbles, "She already embraces her power. She tells me no fifty times a day with confidence."

"And you pretend you hate it."

He slides me a dark, narrowed stare that vibrates through my chest. "I never said I hated it."

I bite back a smile and rest a hand over my rounded stomach.

Our son, Finn, kicks in response, as if chiming in to say he's part of this circus, too.

"Is the little guy beating you up again?" Brax asks, with pride in his voice.

"Yep," I chirp.

Aurora swings around and spots us again. Her face splits into a giant grin, reminding me of my mother, who she's named after. She squeals, "Ma-ma! Da-da!"

Brax instinctively moves toward her.

She launches into a tiny jump over absolutely nothing, lands on her bottom with an oof, and freezes. She looks at Brax.

He gives her a funny face.

She laughs.

I relax, glad she's not crying.

Brax drags a hand down his face. "She's going to give me a heart condition."

"She's two."

"She's reckless."

"She's your daughter," I shoot back.

He throws me a lethal, amused glare. "And your clone. Double the danger."

He's not wrong.

Our home is full today. Balloons, streamers, and signs decorate the rooftop. A table's piled high with cupcakes and our family's everywhere. Zara rocks her newborn daughter, Sloane, in a soft wrap, while the twins sit on Sean's lap, shoving blueberries into their mouths with alarming enthusiasm. Fiona's chasing her toddler son, Zavier, who's inherited his father's impossible speed and grin. Kirill's egging him on to run faster.

Uncle Luca and Finn stand next to the grill, flipping burgers. Three years ago, I couldn't have imagined either of them here, smiling freely, wearing matching aprons that say WORLD'S BEST GRANDPA in bold print.

They're both here almost every week, dropping off pastries, reading Aurora bedtime stories, and making sure we never forget we have family.

Everything is better than anything I imagined was possible. I watch my daughter wobble back to her feet, brushing grass off her sundress. It's the one with tiny red flowers that Brax insisted she needed so "she matches her mama."

She gets halfway upright before beelining straight toward me. Her cheeks are pink, her curls wild, her arms outstretched. She shrieks, "Mamaaaa!"

I crouch, or attempt to, because my stomach is far too present to allow anything graceful. She crashes into my legs with the full force of a two-year-old missile. I laugh and scoop her up, kissing her forehead. "There you are, birthday girl."

She pats my cheeks with cake-sticky hands. "Boom."

I laugh, repeating, "Boom," which is her newest word.

Brax reaches us, plucks Aurora out of my arms, swings her once, then settles her against his hip. He asks her, "You running the neighborhood yet, princess?"

She nods solemnly, curls bobbing. "Yes!"

He kisses my cheek, lingering longer than necessary and with zero shame. "You good?"

"You ask me that every twenty minutes," I tease.

He huffs. "You're eight months pregnant and stubborn. Can't be too careful."

"I'm fine."

He slides a hand over my belly, thumb brushing the curve of it. "Finn's kicking like he's trying to escape."

I smirk, "He gets that from you."

"Kid's probably already planning an empire," Brax states.

"Don't give him ideas," I warn.

Aurora wiggles in Brax's arms, pointing wildly. "Cupcake."

I groan. "We shouldn't have given her one before lunch."

"After presents," Brax reminds her.

Her eyes widen, then she shouts at full volume, "Presents!"

Half our guests jump.

Sean groans, clutching his chest. "Why does she scream like that?"

"Genetics," Zara sings, rocking her baby.

Brax smirks. "Must be the Marino in her."

I elbow him. "Excuse you?"

"You heard me."

I shoot him a warning look but can't stop my smile.

He steals a kiss before Aurora shrieks "Boom!" then laughs.

"We need a dark corner," Brax murmurs in my ear.

My cheeks flush. No matter how much time goes by, my husband's desire for me doesn't fade. Nor does mine for him.

Throughout the party, Brax sends me looks, and a few times mouths, "dark corner." It only makes my hormones grow wilder.

Once the presents have been torn open, the meltdown over a missing toy is narrowly avoided, and the cake has been devoured by children and aggressively taste-tested by adults, Brax wraps his arms around my waist and guides me to the edge of the roof.

The sun dips lower, bathing the artificial grass in gold.

Aurora is in the middle of the lawn, spinning in circles until she collapses in giggles. Luca and Sean cheer her on like she's competing.

Brax murmurs against my ear, "Three damn years, Minx."

I rest a hand over his. "You're getting sentimental."

"I blame you." His voice drops, warm and rough, the sound that always sinks into my spine. "I never imagined life like this."

"Neither did I."

"Do you miss it?" he asks.

"What?"

"The Underworld," he answers.

It's a bomb. We haven't mentioned it in over a year. I consider the question. The old world is still there, but it's silent and dormant, a true ghost without claws. Membership only exists now. There are no rituals, punishments, or meetings in shadowed chambers. There're only names on lists that Kirill keeps locked away.

I shake my head. "Not in the least."

He presses his lips to my temple. "Good."

"Don't tell me you suddenly developed a love for them?" I tease.

He scoffs, "The only thing I miss is hacking their systems for fun."

"You still hack their systems."

He grins. "Only to make sure they're not stupid enough to rise again."

"And if they do?" I fret, and old worries wake up inside my gut.

His arms tighten around me. "They won't. Kirill sends out too many reminders to stay quiet until it's safe to reconvene."

But it's not temporary. We all know it, but they don't. The Underworld can't resurrect itself. And none of us will allow it to even try.

So for now, they obey, unaware they're submitting to extinction.

Brax shifts. His hand slides up to cradle my jaw. "You happy, Minx?"

I don't hesitate. "More than I ever thought I could be."

His arrogant grin floods his expression. "Good. Because I'm not done with you."

I arch a brow. "You never are."

He smirks. "And I never will be."

A shriek cuts through the yard. "Da-da!"

Aurora barrels toward us at top speed, half toddler, half demolition crew. Brax turns just in time to scoop her up before she slams into me.

She launches her tiny arms around his neck. "Da-da, I fall down!"

He kisses her cheek. "Did the ground survive?"

She nods, then beams. "I win." She puts her arms in the air.

He chuckles. "Yes, you did."

She gasps suddenly, eyes swelling wide. She reaches for my stomach. "Finn!"

I laugh softly. Finn's foot presses so hard against my stomach you can see it. I say, "He's saying hi."

She presses both hands to my belly, awe on her face. "Hi, Finn. I wuv you."

Brax's arm slides around my shoulders as our daughter whispers secrets to her unborn brother. Sunlight glows across her curls. The breeze carries the sound of Luca laughing, Zara humming to her baby, Fiona telling Kirill to stop trying to inseminate her with his stare, and River and Willow bouncing around from too much sugar.

For the first time in my life, my world isn't divided between loyalty and survival.

It's whole, warm, and full of light.

Brax kisses the top of my head. He murmurs, "Happy birthday to our girl."

"And happy everything to us," I answer.

Aurora presses her cheek to my belly. "We fam'ly."

I stroke her curls. "Yes, baby. We're family."

Not the one I was born into. The one I built. The one who chose me. The one I choose every day.

Brax leans in, his voice a low promise meant for only me. "I'm still going to find a dark corner."

I inhale. "You're impossible."

"You love it."

I look at him coyly. "You know I do."

His grin turns wicked.

Aurora wiggles again. "Cake more?"

Brax sighs, defeated by a two-year-old. "No, princess. No more cake today."

"Yes!"

"No."

She wriggles out of his arms and sprints toward the cake table.

He groans. "I said no, Aurora!" He chases after her, grabbing her before she gets to the table.

Our daughter shrieks with joy and our son kicks harder against my belly. As Brax hauls Aurora back, muttering threats he'll never enforce, I realize this is exactly the kind of chaos meant to be ours.

* * *

A note from Maggie Cole

Thank you so much for reading Bride By Ritual! I've been holding my breath for you to experience Valentina and Brax's explosive love story. I hope you loved the The Underworld series as much as I adored writing it.

And because my alpha reader team couldn't get enough of Blue Ivanov and begged me to write her story, up next is Resisting Blue.

Enter the alluring, taboo world of Blue and Dr. Red Mercer, where a therapist's ethical boundaries blur under the weight of a patient he can't resist. Prepare for stalking, revelations, temptations, and power plays that push every forbidden line.

You don't want to miss this if you love:
Forbidden Therapist Romance
Psychological Slow Burn
Caretaker / Touch-Starved FMC
Emotionally Dark Romance
She Falls First (Stalker & Emotionally) / He Falls Harder
Straight-and-Narrow morphing into a Morally Gray MMC
Unhinged FMC (Sympathetic)

Coming April 1, 2026!

Read Resisting Blue, book one of the Beautiful Delusions Duet. Grab it at your favorite retailer or for exclusive collector's editions, autographed books, discounted paperback and audio visit Maggie's bookstore at www.maggiecolebookstore.com

RESISTING BLUE

BEAUTIFUL DELUSIONS DUET BOOK #1

From International bestselling author Maggie Cole comes a morally gray psychological romance where boundaries are temptation, ethics are foreplay, and a dangerously perceptive woman sets her stalker sights on her therapist.

My parents made me see a therapist for stalking.
They thought Dr. Red Mercer would cure me. They assumed he would teach me restraint, discipline, and distance. What they didn't count on was the way his gaze lingers too long, like he's undressing

the truth instead of treating it. Or how his voice tightens every time I say exactly what I'm thinking.

He says *boundaries*. I hear an invitation.

He says *ethics*. I see a man begging not to want me.

I'm not spiraling. I'm precise. I know where he draws the line and exactly how to leap over it.

Red calls my fixation a disorder.

I call it fate already in motion.

This is my version of the sessions.

And no matter how hard he fights it, I'll strip away his control until Dr. Red Mercer admits what we both know.

He was never meant to resist me.

* * *

Read Resisting Blue, book one of the Beautiful Delusions Duet. Grab it at your favorite retailer or for exclusive collector's editions, autographed books, discounted paperback and audio visit Maggie's bookstore at www.maggiecolebookstore.com

RESISTING BLUE PROLOGUE

A PSYCHOLOGICAL STALKER AND HER THERAPIST ROMANCE

***This has not been edited so excuse any errors as it's still in writing process**

lue Ivanov

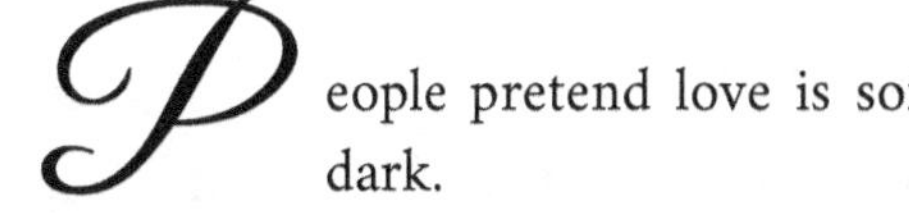

eople pretend love is soft. Gentle. A warm hand in the dark.

They lie.

Love is the sharpest blade in the drawer. It cuts before it comforts. And I learned that moment when I realized the difference between a crush and a true obsession.

That's what devotion is, not just some flaky feeling. It's a hunger that crawls under your skin and refuses to leave until it owns every inch of you. The gravity's so heavy it drags your bones toward one person until you forget how to stand anywhere else.

Most people call that unhealthy.

I call it my center.

Real love isn't balanced. It isn't sweet. It doesn't share space with doubt.

It consumes, devours, and rewrites the shape of your world so completely that the object of your affection becomes the only bright thing in a universe full of static.

That's what Brax O'Malley was supposed to be. My bright thing, full of certainty and overflowing with hunger.

But obsession is a jealous creature. It doesn't vanish just because someone disappoints you. It mutates and sharpens. It finds something new to cling to.

And if the universe wants to throw another man in my path, a man who sees beneath skin and excuses, whose eyes feel like they're peeling me open, well, that's not obsession misbehaving.

It's obsession evolving.

So no, love isn't a feeling. It is a choice. A commitment so fixated it refuses to die, even if everyone's throwing flames on it.

Once my heart settles on someone and they actually see me, it never lets go.

Not ever.

No matter how wrong or dangerous it becomes.

* * *

Read Resisting Blue, book one of the Beautiful Delusions Duet. Grab it at your favorite retailer or for exclusive collector's editions, autographed books, discounted paperback and audio visit Maggie's bookstore at www.maggiecolebookstore.com

He's a Ruthless Stranger. One I can't see, only feel, thanks to my friends who make a deal with him on my behalf.

No names. No personal details. No face to etch into my mind.

Just him, me, and an expensive silk tie.

What happens in Vegas is supposed to stay in Vegas.

He warns me he's full of danger.

I never see that side of him. All I experience is his Russian accent, delicious scent, and touch that lights me on fire.

One incredible night turns into two. Then we go our separate ways.

But fate doesn't keep us apart. When I run into my stranger back in Chicago, I know it's him, even if I've never seen his icy blue eyes before.

Our craving is hotter than Vegas. But he never lied.

He's a ruthless man...

* * *

Download Ruthless Stranger at your favorite retailer or for exclusive collector's editions and discounted paperback and audio visit Maggie's bookstore at www.maggiecolebookstore.com

MORE BY MAGGIE COLE

For exclusive collector's editions, autographed books, and discounted paperback and audio visit Maggie's bookstore at www.maggiecolebookstore.com

Beautiful Delusions Duet - Blue Ivanov and Dr. Red Mercer's Forbidden Therapist Romance

Resisting Blue-April 1, 2025

Chasing Red - TBD

The Underworld

Bride By Initiation (Sean Jr. and Zara)

Bride By Coronation (Fiona and Kirill)

Bride By Ritual (Brax and Valentina)

Mafia Wars - The Ivanovs & O'Malleys

Ruthless Stranger (Maksim's Story) - Book One

Broken Fighter (Boris's Story) - Book Two

Cruel Enforcer (Sergey's Story) - Book Three

Vicious Protector (Adrian's Story) - Book Four

Savage Tracker (Obrecht's Story) - Book Five

Unchosen Ruler (Liam's Story) - Book Six

Perfect Sinner (Nolan's Story) - Book Seven

Brutal Defender (Killian's Story) - Book Eight

Deviant Hacker (Declan's Story) - Book Nine

Relentless Hunter (Finn's Story) - Book Ten

*** If you're looking for Dmitri and Anna's love story, the book that created the Ivanov and O'Malley families, then grab book six of It's complicated: Secret Mafia Billionaire - Book Six

Mafia Wars New York - The Marinos

Toxic (Dante's Story) - Book One

Immoral (Gianni's Story) - Book Two

Crazed (Massimo's Story) - Book Three

Carnal (Tristano's Story) - Book Four

Flawed (Luca's Story) - Book Five

Mafia Wars Ireland - The O'Connors

Illicit King (Brody)-Book One

Illicit Captor (Aidan)-Book Two

Illicit Heir (Devin)-Book Three

Illicit Monster (Tynan)-Book Four

Club Indulgence Duet (A Dark Billionaire Romance)

The Auction (Book One)

The Vow (Book Two)

Wilted Kingdom Duet- (A Dark Bully Romance)

Seeds of Malice-Book One

Thorns of Malice-Book Two

It's Complicated Series (Chicago Billionaires)

My Boss the Billionaire- Book One

Forgotten by the Billionaire - Book Two

My Friend the Billionaire - Book Three

Forbidden Billionaire - Book Four

The Groomsman Billionaire - Book Five

Secret Mafia Billionaire - Book Six

Behind Closed Doors (Former Military Now International Rescue)

Depths of Destruction - Book One

Marks of Rebellion - Book Two

Haze of Obedience - Book Three

Cavern of Silence - Book Four

Stains of Desire - Book Five

Risks of Temptation - Book Six

Brooks Family Saga

Kiss of Redemption- Book One

Sins of Justice - Book Two

Acts of Manipulation - Book Three

Web of Betrayal - Book Four

Masks of Devotion - Book Five

Roots of Vengeance - Book Six

ALL IN BILLIONAIRES

The Rule - Book One

The Secret - Book Two

The Crime - Book Three

The Lie - Book Four

The Trap - Book Five

The Gamble - Book Six

The Cartwright Family - Holiday Billionaire Novels

Holiday Hoax - A Fake Marriage Billionaire Romance

Holiday Hire - A Billionaire Single Dad Nanny Romance

Holiday Rider - Coming November 1, 2025

STAND ALONE NOVELLA

JUDGE ME NOT - A Billionaire Single Mom Christmas Novella

ABOUT THE AUTHOR

Amazon Bestselling Author

Maggie Cole is committed to bringing her readers alphalicious book boyfriends and fiercely strong heroines.

She's been called the literary master of steamy romance. Her books are full of raw emotion, suspense, and will always keep you wanting more. She is a masterful storyteller of contemporary romance and loves writing about broken people who rise above the ashes. Her books can often be found hanging out in the top 100, even years after publication.

Maggie lives in Florida with her son. She loves tennis, yoga, paddleboarding, boating, other water activities, and everything naughty.

Her current series were written in the order below:

- All In (Stand Alone Billionaire Novels with Entwined Characters)
- It's Complicated (Stand Alone Billionaire Novels with Entwined Characters)
- Brooks Family Saga- A Dark Family Saga – Read In Order (Each book has different couples)
- Behind Closed Doors-A Dark Military Protector Romance – Read in Order (Each book has different couples))
- Mafia Wars (Stand Alone Novels with Interconnecting Plot and Entwined Characters)
- Mafia Wars New York (Stand Alone Novels with Interconnecting Plot and Entwined Characters)
- Mafia Wars Ireland (Stand Alone Novels with Interconnecting Plot and Entwined Characters)
- Club Indulgence Duet A Dark Billionaire Duet – Read in Order (Same Couple)
- Wilted Kingdom Duet-A Dark Bully Billionaire Duet - Read in Order (Same Couple)
- Interconnecting Plot and Entwined Characters)
- The Cartwright Family - Holiday Billionaire - Stand Alone w/ Same Family
- The Underworld (Next Generation Mafia Wars Secret Society with Stand Alone Novels with Interconnecting Characters)
- Beautiful Delusions Duet - Read in Order (Same Couple)

Maggie Cole's Newsletter
Sign up here!

Maggie Cole's Website
authormaggiecole.com

***Get your copies of Maggie Cole
signed paperbacks!***

www.maggiecolebookstore.com

Pickup your Maggie Cole Merch!
Click here!

Hang Out with Maggie in Her
Romance Addicts Reader Group
Maggie Cole's Romance Addicts

Follow for Giveaways
Facebook Maggie Cole

Instagram
@maggiecoleauthor

TikTok
https://www.tiktok.com/@maggiecole.author

Complete Works on Amazon
Follow Maggie's Amazon Author Page

Book Trailers
Follow Maggie on YouTube

Feedback or suggestions?
Email: authormaggiecole@gmail.com